CW00552860

the unBALANCED Equation

H. L. MACFARLANE

Copyright

Content Warnings

THE UNBALANCED EQUATION CONTAINS:
SWEARING
SEXUAL CONTENT
CANCER-RELATED PARENTAL DEATH PRIOR TO THE EVENTS OF
THE BOOK

FOR JAKE, WHO IS MY TOM

YOU CAN SAY WHAT YOU WANT
BUT IT WON'T CHANGE MY MIND
I'LL FEEL THE SAME ABOUT YOU

SAY WHAT YOU WANT (TEXAS: 1997)

Before

FOUR YEARS AGO

TOM

IT IS A UNIVERSAL CERTAINTY THAT, every October, a new PhD student who likes anime joins the biology department. Sometimes it's a single otaku amongst the first year cohort – as was the case eleven years ago when that otaku was me – whilst other times several of them pop up at once. This year was no different.

The only difference between now and any other year was that, for the first time in my life, I found one of these students distractingly attractive.

It was a typically rainy evening in Glasgow. A staff-student mixer was in full swing with the aim of introducing the first year PhD students to their peers and colleagues. I was in reluctant attendance. Already I was two terrible institute-funded mimosas down with a third currently in my hand; like hell was I suffering through the mixer sober when I was missing a rerun of *Red Dwarf* season one just to be here.

Although the attractive anime fan seemed well on her way to

making the mixer worth attending.

She was cornered against a wall by a trio of very enthusiastic young men – I didn't recognise them which meant they were probably first years – whose gazes kept sliding from her eyes to her chest.

Classy.

"I just think the TV shows no longer serve the older audience they've garnered throughout the years," the woman explained to her captive audience. Or was *she* the captive? Either way, they hung onto her every word with an expression I was familiar with seeing upon the faces of impatient students: a look that told me they were itching to interrupt her. "And the new shows completely ignore the anti-war message the original anime was all about. The films, on the other hand—"

"Oh come off it!" one of her suitors interrupted, right on time. I almost laughed; the woman had managed to get in all of two points before she'd been cut off. That was a record in my books. "Have you seen the *Gundam* models coming out of the newer shows? They're amazing!"

"But—"

"And we all know the franchise was only saved because of the merch," guy number two added. "Why waste time on the characters just standing around talking instead of having a well-animated fight sequence? *Hathaway* totally dropped the ball with that one!"

"No—"

"Yeah, they made Hathaway seem so weak," said student number three. "And we're supposed to believe he's the rebel leader? Give me a break!"

"That's—"

As each of the three young men continued spouting their opinions the woman grew ever more impatient to get a word in edgewise. But they were talking *at* her, not to her, and every time she managed to vocalise a single syllable she was drowned out by their tirade.

I wasn't normally one to save a maiden from a fire-breathing dragon, but when there were *three* of them? I gulped down the awful mimosa in my hand and manoeuvred through the crowd towards them without a second thought.

"Tell me, gentlemen," I said, raising my voice when I reached the group so there could be no doubt they'd hear me, "what are your opinions on the pacing of *The Two Towers* and *The Return of the King*?"

The first student stared at me as if he couldn't believe I'd interrupted him. "Frodo and Sam slow the narrative, of course!" he said. His friends nodded in agreement. "Every time Jackson builds the momentum with the rest of the Fellowship their part of the story totally drags it back."

"*Ah.*" I very deliberately put myself between the three dragons and the maiden I was rescuing, revelling in their splutters of indignation. "I'm afraid there's no point arguing with them. They are completely and utterly wrong about anything that matters."

A bemused smile crossed the young woman's lips. They were painted a perfect shade of apricot that, lord help me, made me think of kissing her.

"Glad I'm not the only one who thinks so," she said. Her voice was even better than her lips; low and coy and aching with the promise of dry, acerbic wit.

I leaned in closer.

"Are you part of the first year cohort?" I asked, though I already knew the answer.

She nodded. "I also did my genetics undergrad here."

"You did? I haven't seen you around before." Given that I'd been finagled into teaching three of the final year DNA lectures last December I *should* have recognised her.

"Um..." she laughed, sheepishly running a hand through her

hair. "I may have missed a few lectures in favour of sleeping in."

She wasn't the first student I'd met who'd skipped out on the DNA block; she certainly wouldn't be the last. I shook my head in mock dismay. "How disappointing, Miss...?"

"Elizabeth Maclean. Liz to my friends; Lizzie to my family."

"Tom Henderson. Thomas to my mother."

When I held out my hand Liz shook it. Her cheeks dimpled when she returned my smile. "Doctor Henderson. Good to put a face to a name. You work in the small Molecular Genetics lab, right?"

"I do indeed." I was impressed she knew that about me. "Where's your project based?"

"In the big Molecular Genetics lab."

Ah, that explained it.

"Would you like to join me in drinking terrible mimosas whilst discussing why *Hathaway* is a masterpiece?" I asked Liz, holding my arm out just wide enough to give her an escape route away from the young men still standing behind me. They were yet to take the hint that they were being ignored.

Liz's brown eyes twinkled at my request. I didn't know eyes could do that. "I think I'd like that very much. The buzz from the three I've had already seems to be wearing off."

"Being told *Gundam* is all about shiny mecha toys will do that to you."

As we wound through the crowded room towards a table laden with plastic cups – full of cheap prosecco mixed with even cheaper orange juice – I couldn't stop myself from sneaking glances at Liz.

Her hair was a deep, dark brown, falling in controlled waves just past her shoulders. There were perhaps seven or eight inches between us in height which, given I was rather tall, wasn't surprising.

Even wearing a massive cardigan draped over a simple, Vnecked white top and plain black leggings I could tell she had a good figure. Add on the appeal of her being an anime fan and I was certain Liz was likely popular with the opposite sex... although that was a very specific personal preference, I supposed.

Mine, to be exact.

She caught me staring. Of course she caught me staring.

"What is it?" Liz asked, a small frown creasing her brow. There were no freckles on her cheeks or other unique features to her face, like a scar or a piercing, only a well-defined jaw and eyes that were marginally lighter than her hair. And those dimples when she smiled. I wanted her to smile again.

"I was trying to work out if I'd definitely never seen you before," I lied. Liz didn't look convinced.

"I emailed you back in third year about doing a summer project, actually," she said, which was not at all the answer I was expecting, "but you never replied."

"Then consider this a very overdue apology for never replying." I had the sense to look ashamed as I handed her a mimosa. After a moment I added, in an undertone, "Though it was probably a good thing I didn't."

Liz's frown turned into a raised eyebrow. "What was that?"

"Oh, nothing. Here's to working on the same floor."

I held up my plastic cup. Liz knocked hers against mine, then in unison we drank the contents in one go. She grinned mischievously when she realised we'd done the same, juvenile thing, apricot lips gleaming from the remains of the dangerous alcoholic concoction she'd just consumed. "How many mimosas do you think we could get away with before the rest of the room realises only two people are drinking up the institute's alcohol budget for the night?"

"A woman after my own heart. I guess it wouldn't hurt to find out."

It most definitely wouldn't hurt to find out.

Two more mimosas later and we'd finished the prerequisite small talk about the research we were working on – truly a topic for another day – and had circled back to the subject of anime.

"So you're a *Gundam* fan, Dr Henderson?" Liz asked, her cheeks rosy from alcohol. I knew mine were, too, given the heat currently creeping across them.

"Call me Tom," I insisted. "I'd just turned eighteen when *Wing* finally aired in the UK. After that I scoured the internet to get hold of the main timeline series."

"I didn't actually like *Wing* much. Looked nice, though."

"Ah, a woman after my own heart."

A flash of amusement crossed Liz's face. It was the second time I'd said that. I didn't care. "How old does that make you? Thirty-something?"

"Thirty-four."

"Positively ancient!"

She laughed at the appalled look on my face. "I'll have you know that I was the youngest teacher in the Institute of Molecular, Cell and Systems Biology," I complained, "until all the *genuinely* ancient members of staff retired this summer. Then the university panic-hired a load of researchers who are even younger than I am."

"I guess it's all about perspective."

From *my* perspective it looked like being at least a decade older than Liz was not a problem for her. "And you?" I ventured.

"And me what?"

"How old are *you*? If you're straight out of your undergrad... twenty-two?"

"Twenty-three." Liz smiled brightly. "I was one of those incredibly irritating gap year students."

Eleven years, then. Jenna Daniels from the Plant Molecular Genetics lab was fifteen years older than her husband. Mark the technician was fourteen years older than his wife. Eleven years wasn't too bad at all.

I tilted my head slightly, feeling my smile growing wider when Liz blushed under my gaze. "Oh?" I said, keeping my voice low. "Where'd you go on your gap year?"

"A-all over the place." I thoroughly enjoyed the stutter my undivided attention had produced. "First I went to – *ah, watch out!*"

Liz's warning was too little, too late for the person coming towards us carrying a tray laden with jugs of orange juice. They tripped over a projector cable on the floor – not the first person to have done so that evening – and, in the process, spilled the entire contents of the tray.

Over me and Liz.

Silence filled the room as everyone stared at us, waiting for our reactions. Then: "Oh my god I'm *so* sorry!" cried the timid-looking woman who'd tripped. She wrung her hands rather uselessly. "Please let me help you clean up. I'll—"

"There's no need," I cut in, smiling through the orange juice dripping down my face. I didn't dare look at what the stuff had done to my clothes. "It'll be easier for us to go upstairs and dry off. Right, Miss Maclean?"

Mutely Liz nodded. She was clearly in shock; going by the way she averted her gaze from the crowd she was understandably mortified by what had just transpired.

We were quick to vacate the room. Much to my relief the lift was already on our floor, so I wasted no time in pressing the button to open the door before gesturing for Liz to get in first.

A beat of awkwardness passed between us. Two. Three. I listened to the sound of the lift ascending to the fifth floor and the drip, drip, drip of orange juice sloughing off our clothes. I kept my eyes firmly – respectably – on my shoes.

But there was nothing respectable about the way I was imagining Liz in soaking wet clothes, regardless of them also being stained orange. Her top was white, after all.

"That was...karma for hogging all the mimosas?" Liz eventually said, breaking the awkwardness between us in one fell swoop.

I chuckled. "Serves us right, I guess. Heaven forbid we actually drink the terrible things."

I shifted my gaze from my shoes to Liz's eyes just as she did the same thing to me. She let out a feeble cough. "Um, I don't actually – I don't have a change of clothes. I'm not sure how I'm ever gonna get my clothes dry using the hand-dryer in the toilet."

"Oh." Well, that was a useless response. Then my brain finally began working properly. "I have a few spare shirts in my office. You never know when you're going to spill TEMED or ethidium bromide on your clothes."

"Shouldn't you be using a fume hood if you're working with them?"

I could only laugh. "That's true. Maybe they're bad examples. In any case" – the lift doors pinged open, and the two of us filtered out into the dark corridor – "I have a spare shirt if you don't mind borrowing it."

Liz's eyes lit up. "If you don't mind lending it."

"Not at all. Just follow me through to the lab."

I left Liz by the sink in the small Molecular Genetics lab then swiftly headed into my office to shrug off my shirt and jumper. I had no spare trousers which left me no choice but to leave my current ones on. At least they were black; nobody would be able to see how deeply uncomfortable the wet material was against my legs. In any case it wasn't as if I planned on going back to the mixer. I could suffer through the stickiness until I got home.

Hidden in a drawer in my office were two shirts, one blue

linen and one green flannel. The flannel was for winter, of course, whilst the linen was for summer. I was nothing if not always prepared.

"Flannel for Liz," I murmured, buttoning on the linen shirt before leaving my office. With a flash of my key card and a shove of my shoulder I opened the door to the lab, wondering how to continue my conversation with Liz when I knew I needed to head home and change sooner rather than later. Could I ask Liz for her number?

I hoped so.

"I take it you don't mind—"

Whatever I was about to say was immediately forgotten in the face of what was awaiting me in the lab.

Liz had stripped off both her cardigan and top and unceremoniously dumped them in the sink. She stood there, right in front of me, shaking her dripping phone dry whilst wearing nothing but her leggings and a white bra stained fluorescent orange.

When Liz caught me unabashedly staring her cheeks flushed an intense shade of crimson, though she made no move to cover herself up. I took that as permission to *keep* staring.

The cardigan Liz had been wearing truly had obscured all of the irresistible curves of her body, confirming my initial suspicions that she was an absolute knock-out.

Had anyone ever been successful asking someone out in a situation like this before? If not, I was only too eager to be the first to try.

"Ah, for you," I said, holding out the flannel shirt and finally looking away for all the good it would do: I had the image of Liz half-undressed seared onto my eyes forever.

After a pause Liz took the shirt from me. "...thanks." There was an unmistakeable smile in her voice.

I waited a few seconds before looking at her again – giving

Liz plenty of time to pull my shirt on – only to bear witness to her wriggling out of her bra beneath said shirt and flinging it into the sink with the rest of her clothes.

She shrugged when she caught the incredulous look on my face. "The flannel's thick enough to go without it. Can you imagine wearing an underwired bra soaked in orange juice beneath a clean shirt?"

She had me there. "I guess not. Do you—"

"Oh, one minute," Liz interrupted, for her phone had begun buzzing in earnest. She frowned at the screen. "That's my friend Chloë. She's downstairs at the mixer. I won't be long!"

And with that Liz ran off to the lift, disappearing from my sight as if she had been a mere figment of my perverse imagination. I waited a very long minute for her to return, which turned into five, which slowly but surely turned into ten.

After fifteen minutes came and went I could only conclude that Liz had become distracted by whatever her friend needed her for. I glanced at her clothes in the sink. She probably didn't have anything to put them in so I fished out a plastic autoclave bag from the storage cupboard and placed the juice-stained garments inside. Then I headed down to the mixer to hand them back over.

As the fates would have it, Liz was nowhere to be found.

"Are you kidding me?" I grumbled, tossing back a final terrible mimosa in my anxiousness to find her and return her clothes. I hadn't even asked Liz for her number yet. How had everything so rapidly gone downhill?

After far too long I had to admit that fruitlessly searching for a woman who had clearly left the building was a waste of my time – not to mention the fact my trousers were beginning to dry in a disgusting, tacky fashion against my legs. Deciding to return home and find Liz the following day I finally called a taxi, which to my relief arrived within minutes.

When I got home I threw my own clothes as well as Liz's into the washing machine with an overly generous quantity of stain remover. I couldn't help it; letting her clothes marinate in orange juice all night was unfathomable to me.

By the time I reached my bedroom I was naked, sticky, tipsy and tired...a dangerous combination when thoughts of Liz in her bra kept flooding my brain. Considering how self-conscious she'd been at the mixer when everyone had seen her covered in orange juice, her lack of shame as she stood there in front of me, and only me, was an incredible turn-on.

She wanted me to look at her. She wanted to look at *me* whilst I was looking at her.

God, I had to ask her out. I hadn't been this excited about a woman in years. Plus, if I asked Liz out, I didn't have to feel like a lecherous creep about the raging hard-on I was currently fostering at the mere thought of her.

I jerked off before I fell asleep. Of course I did. I was mimosa-horny. It happened to the best of us.

I'd be sure we drank something decidedly free of orange juice on our first date.

"...we didn't expect him to be retiring so soon. I know you're already assessing two students but at least this is only *one* extra student, Tom."

No. This wasn't happening. Not today. Not about her.

"Can't someone else be her assessor?" I complained, running a hand over my face at the mess I'd just walked into. "There must be someone more senior—"

"Not someone who'll actually understand her work," the Postgraduate Convenor, Gill, interrupted. "And what with all of the staff retiring this year...I'll be honest, we simply don't have enough people to cover the workload yet. But going by her supervisor's comments Miss Maclean should be an easy student to assess. I'm sure it won't be difficult for you."

I didn't know what to say. What *could* I say? I somehow doubted *I'm sorry, I was kept up half the night thinking about Miss Maclean in a very compromising state of undress* was going to go down well. I'd only just been promoted, after all. Turning down the work without a valid reason was going to be terrible for my career.

And that's what it came down to. My career. I couldn't afford to jeopardise it for a stupid crush. Because that's what it was, and I knew it: a schoolboy crush. There would be other women. Ones I *didn't* have to assess in a professional setting for four years.

I sighed my surrender to a delighted Gill. "Fine. I'll be her assessor."

Elizabeth Maclean's clothes were currently sitting, washed, dried and folded in a bag, back on my kitchen counter-top. I'd forgotten to bring them in. Maybe she'd *also* forget – or would be too embarrassed – to ask for them back. That would be the best outcome for us both.

Avoid each other. Don't look at each other. Don't speak a single word outside of the required biannual assessor meetings.

But one thing was universally certain: in order to keep Elizabeth Maclean out of my reach and out of my head I was going to have to be a complete and utter bastard to her.

So much for getting her number.

Chapter One

PRESENT DAY

LIZ

I**T WAS ELEVEN O'CLOCK ON A** Friday night and I couldn't wait for my shift to end. My *final* shift in service work. Ever.

I'd thought the day would never come.

"Lass from table two asked me to bring over some water – could you handle it, Liz?" my soon-to-be ex-manager asked. I nodded my assent, all too cheerfully providing table two with their requested water.

Throughout my undergrad I'd worked countless bar jobs to help me pay my rent. Thankfully I'd avoided such work during my PhD by being careful with the frugal stipend my research afforded me, but when that stipend dried up and I still had my thesis left to write I had no choice but to find a job to make ends meet. Just until I found a postdoc position, of course.

I only wish it hadn't been a bar job.

It was soulless work. Thankless work. I was desperate to get back into a lab. If Mum had still been around I knew she'd have told me to suck it up and do what I had to do, so that's exactly what I did. Of course that's what I did.

But finally – after a year of late night shifts, my PhD graduation and almost fifty research applications – a laboratory right here in Glasgow decided I was the best fit for their open postdoc position. And though it might have been at the same university as my PhD lab it was, blessedly, in a completely different building to my PhD lab.

More specifically: it was in a completely different building to my PhD *assessor*. If I never saw him again for as long as I lived it would be too soon.

Maybe it was because I had accidentally allowed my thoughts of lab research to be plagued by him, or maybe it was because this was my last shift, but suddenly The Whisky Barrel didn't seem so bad. The bar was classy. It had good music, even better cocktails and low, atmospheric lighting. I liked the people I worked with and I was paid above minimum wage. The tips were great.

But, at the end of the day, I was still a woman in her twenties and The Whisky Barrel was still a bar. I could cope no longer with the lecherous gazes, sexist comments and *I-swear-I-didn't-mean-it* grabs of my arse that had plagued my employment over the last twelve months.

Monday, and the beginning of my career in the Functional Genomics lab – run by my long-time favourite undergrad lecturer Daichi Ito – could not come soon enough.

"Grab me something at the bar while you're at it!" hollered a man from the other side of the room. He was part of a group of no fewer than twelve guys – a stag do, I suspected – who had waltzed in a mere ten minutes ago and commandeered the largest of our private, circular booths as if they owned the place. Normally I wouldn't have to bother with them, since Holly was on table service, but if they insisted on coming straight up to the bar I'd have no choice but to interact with them.

Well, at least this was the final stag do I'd ever have to serve.

I plastered on my best, most luminous smile as I finished polishing the pint glass in my hand and prepared to turn around and greet the man whose footsteps I could hear approaching the bar.

"Could I have a gin and tonic when you're ready?" the man asked, his voice low and good-natured and...familiar? The smile slipped from my face. "Oh, and two – make that three – pints of house lager. Please."

I didn't want to turn around. Oh, for all that was good and holy I desperately did not want to turn around. Anything to stop the interaction I now knew was inevitable. As I gripped onto the pint glass in my hands almost hard enough to shatter it I considered simply walking out of The Whisky Barrel without serving the man. After all, what was my manager going to do – fire me? I had all of one hour left of my final shift ever.

But the man would see me. He would see me running off, and that would be worse.

I turned around.

"Is that everything for you?" I asked, ensuring my work-ready megawatt smile was firmly back in place.

"Yes, that's – that's – Elizabeth Maclean?"

I gave Thomas Henderson the smallest of nods. "It would appear so. G and T and three pints of house lager?"

Mutely he nodded. I hoped to god my former PhD assessor would *stay* mute. But that would have been too kind of the universe to bestow upon me.

"What are you doing working in a bar?" Tom asked, the moment I turned from him to grab the gin. I gave him the only answer that mattered.

"To pay my rent."

"You aren't staying in research?"

"Who said anything about leaving research?"

"You—"

I slammed a glass full of ice and gin onto the polished wooden bar top, then poured in the tonic as slowly as I dared. "I start a postdoc this month," I said, careful to keep my eyes trained solely on the despicable man standing in front of me. Tom's dark blonde hair was longer that it had been a year ago, swept out of his face and naturally curling around the back of his ears. It looked fucking excellent like that. Damn him. "Jobs don't line up perfectly all the time. What does that matter to you?"

A pause. Once again I hoped Tom would remain silent even though I knew he wouldn't. "I didn't want to see a promising researcher go to waste behind a bar," he said. His voice sounded so genuinely concerned I'd have applauded his acting skills...if my mood hadn't been simmering far too close to furious at his judgement of my life choices. I was allowed to complain about my current line of work because I had *experienced* it. I doubted Tom had ever seen the other side of a bar in his life, which meant he wasn't allowed to comment.

"I wasn't aware you thought so highly of me," I drawled, pulling the three pints he'd ordered with slow deliberation. "And bar work isn't demeaning."

It was somewhat vindicating to witness Tom run a hand through his hair and awkwardly turn away from my chilly gaze; during my PhD assessments *I'd* been the one who'd faltered under his unsmiling, hyper-critical appraisal of my work. Repeatedly I'd had to beg and grovel for Tom to understand why I did X instead of Y or Z even when I'd been sure the answer was obvious.

Now I was very clearly not putting up with a single word he said.

"I—"

"That'll be £27.50," I cut in before Tom could utter whatever lame apology he had on his tongue, setting the perfectly poured pints of lager down in front of him with a serene smile on my face.

Tom looked as if he could scarcely believe it. His eyes – which I knew from annoying experience were somewhere between green and grey – fixed back on mine and widened almost comically at the figure I'd announced. If I didn't hate him I'd have sympathised. "For three pints and a gin?"

"Go to a student bar if you want cheaper prices."

"Miss M—"

"Doctor."

"Of course. Doctor Maclean. I didn't mean to offend you."

"I'm sure, Doctor Henderson."

His lips quirked into the infuriating ghost of a smile. "It's Professor now."

"I know. I meant to offend you."

Even though Tom's almost-smile remained firmly in place, it was clear from the slight frown colouring his expression that he knew our conversation was over – and that I really *had* meant to offend him. We stared at each other for far too long. It reminded me of every shounen anime ever where the camera zooms in first on the hero's face and then the rival's without either of them blinking for a full minute.

Then, just as my lips began to twitch with the beginning of another not-quite-veiled insult, Tom broke eye contact and picked up his gin and one of the pints of lager.

"Well, then," he murmured, "best of luck with the postdoc, Dr Maclean." One of his friends came up to help him carry the remaining pints, and with that Tom skulked back to the stag do or whatever it was he was part of.

Just the barest twinge of guilt twisted my stomach as I turned my back on him to continue polishing glasses. I'd never particularly enjoyed being mean for no reason, and it felt entirely wrong to do so whilst at work. But Thomas Henderson was Thomas Henderson.

There was always an exception.

Once upon a time I'd thought Tom was actually a nice guy. Funny, charming, hot as high hell and a huge nerd to boot. Okay, I worked in science. Most of us were nerds. But Tom was my favourite kind of nerd: an anime one. After the pain I'd been left in after my two-year relationship ended on the day of undergrad graduation, Tom seemed like the *right* guy for me to push forward with.

After the staff-student mixer I'd been sure he was going to ask me out.

He didn't.

Then I got the email saying he'd been assigned as my biannual PhD assessor, and the next time I saw him he'd turned into a cold-hearted monster.

Of course I'd thought about complaining to the postgrad convenor about Tom. He was cruel to me from the get-go. Mercilessly so. The problem was that *nobody else* seemed to think Tom was a complete and utter rat bastard. The other students Tom assessed always insisted that he was fair, approachable and incredibly helpful.

If Tom was what other people deemed fair, approachable and helpful, then had I been overreacting? It was true that Tom's eviscerations of my work always contained a kernel of truth. Whenever I sat down and properly thought through his remarks my research came out better at the other end.

But that didn't excuse the way he *said* anything. Especially not after the way we met. I knew it was stupid to expect preferential treatment from him. I never wanted that, anyway. But maybe, just maybe, I'd wanted Thomas Henderson to smile at me again.

God, why hadn't he asked me out when I thought he would?

A familiar wave of anger and shame prickled my skin. I'd long since stopped thinking about Tom in such a stupid way. But it had been hard during my PhD to *not* think about him in one way or another when his lab was on the same floor as mine, even though we resolutely avoided acknowledging the other existed. Except during my hellish panel assessments, of course.

"You're the only one left unattached, Tom my man!" one of the members of the stag do announced far too loudly, slapping a hand on Tom's back as I peered at the group out of the corner of my eye. I couldn't help it; they were the brashest group in the bar and impossible to ignore. "It's high time you settled down. We're all fed up with our wives flirting with you!"

God. Of course Tom was a womaniser. Given how shamelessly he'd flirted with me the day we met I shouldn't have been surprised.

Tom laughed easily, then reclined against the leather booth as if he were a king and the booth his throne. I made no attempt to stop watching him even though I knew I absolutely should. "You know I don't want that. I've never wanted that."

"Come off it! Everyone says that until they meet the right person; you just haven't met them yet. But once you do...trust me, Tom, before you know it all you'll be thinking about is putting a ring on their finger, having kids, and going on family holidays to Tenerife."

Huh. Just what the hell was wrong with not wanting to get married or have kids? The mere idea of a family holiday in Tenerife with a couple of toddlers was nightmare fuel to me. Besides, it wasn't as if you needed marriage and kids to find the right person to settle down with in the first place.

The only problem was *finding* that person. And they were rare, rare, rare. I should know; I'd been trying and failing to find them ever since Eli broke up with me.

I pushed thoughts of Elliot from my head. I'd been doing so well not thinking about him for the last couple of years, and now memories of him had flitted through my head twice in one evening. Even listening to Tom's idiot married friends was better than dwelling on the past.

"And I'm sure your trust fund means you'll find the right person in under five minutes if you actually started looking," another man – the groom, I could only assume from his centre position in the booth – said. "How many millions did your grand-daddy leave you again?"

Tom waved a dismissive hand. "You all know I earn more than enough to pay my own way."

"I'm sure the massive fortune in your account doesn't hurt you!"

At this I forced myself to stop watching (and listening) to the group. I already knew Tom was rich going by his clothes and the car he often drove to work. Not to mention Rachael – a PhD student from his lab and ever a wannabe detective – found out Tom lived in a huge town house in Park Circus that I couldn't imagine anyone human actually being able to afford.

But hearing Tom acknowledge this so dismissively made me want to hit something. Preferably him. He was wealthy, handsome, smart and unattached. He was the epitome of white male privilege. Thomas Henderson could do whatever he wanted without consequence.

Well, me hating him was a consequence of him doing what he wanted, but I doubted Tom cared about that.

When my phone buzzed in my pocket I ignored it. I was still working, after all. But then I glanced at the time on the wrought-iron clock behind the bar and realised my shift ended two minutes ago, so I pulled out my phone to see who was contacting me at midnight. Currently I had all my dating apps deactivated for the third time this year; I wasn't used to getting a message so late.

A barely-smothered gasp was my response to what Chloë, my best friend and notoriously late-night researcher, had sent me. I darted my eyes to Tom then back to my phone again. Going by his woefully ignorant, easygoing attitude he had no idea what was currently happening. Part of me filled with glee at this dramatic turn of events – I had the upper hand! – but a much larger part of me knew it was wrong to feel happy about something so potentially dangerous.

I had to tell Tom. Of course I did.

I walked over to the group of revelling men before giving myself the opportunity to think about what I actually needed to say. Thank fuck this was my final shift because most of them – groom included – cast their gazes up and down my figure with approval. All except Tom, who caught the unsettled expression upon my face immediately. He sidled out of the booth just as I numbly held up my phone so he could see Chloë's message.

"Professor Henderson," I said, emphasising the *professor* part even though now was absolutely not the time nor the place for barbed comments, but I couldn't help it. This was Tom, after all, and I was me. "I think your lab might be on fire."

Chapter Two

TOM

BY THE TIME I ARRIVED AT THE university all the gin I'd been drinking at Henry's stag do was threatening to rise back up my throat. The building I'd worked in for ten years was largely obscured by billowing, choking smoke, the shattered windows on the top floor licked by orange tongues of flame.

The windows of *my* lab.

Two fire engines were busy shooting lethally powerful jets of water to extinguish the flames but I already knew it was too late. The damage had been done.

I couldn't believe what all my senses were telling me was happening. I'd taken over the lab barely a month ago. I'd been a professor for all of five weeks. So why was my lab on *fire?*

"Tom!" Mark, the technician for the building, cried out the moment he saw me. Going by the pyjamas he was wearing beneath a fluorescent yellow anorak – the trouser legs hastily tucked into a pair of wellington boots – Mark had jumped straight out of bed to get here.

"What happened?" I asked his red, puffy face.

"It seems an undergrad completely ignored the rule that they're not supposed to be in the lab after hours," Mark said, shaking his head. My heart dropped to my stomach. "They accidentally left a Bunsen burner on. I'm sure they've learned their lesson now but the lab's going to be in a sorry state once they've put the fire out. Never thought I'd be so glad Jerry set fire to the plant lab in '02, otherwise things could have been a whole lot worse."

Mark was speaking the truth, though given the circumstances the truth didn't exactly cheer me up. After Jerry Riddle set the second floor ablaze the building had been closed for renovations for almost two years. Every floor had been relaid in concrete, thus ensuring that if a fire ever broke out in one of the labs again it wouldn't reach the other floors.

All I could think about was the fact I'd left work early to attend Henry's stag do. Lee, the first of my two undergrads and by far the more efficient student, had completed his work by lunch, which left Carly. Mia, my third year PhD student, had assured me she could watch over her until she finished her transformations. I'd completely forgotten to tell her not to leave Carly on her own – or let her stay past five – but I'd thought it had been obvious.

Clearly I was wrong.

Well, there was nothing I could do about it now other than sober up and wait for the fire to be quelled. Then the university would assess the damage...to my lab *and* to my career.

All I could hope for was that neither was irrevocably destroyed from this debacle.

"Three *months?*"

"I'm afraid so. Maybe more. It definitely won't be ready until the new year, at least."

"And my students?" I took off my glasses to pinch the bridge of my nose against an impending headache.

Gill smiled sympathetically. "The course heads for Genetics and Molecular Biology will redistribute your undergrads to new projects; they'd only been in your lab a week, anyway. As for your PhD students, isn't one of them already writing up?"

I nodded. "But Mia still has five months left of lab research."

"Michael Sorrel can oversee her. A final year PhD student will hardly be much trouble for him!"

Okay, that made me feel better. Mike ran the larger Molecular Genetics lab and he always took on far too many students, but he was great with them. Now all that was left to solve was the matter of my new postdoctoral researcher. "James Freeman from Cambridge is meant to start a postdoc next week. What will happen with that?"

"You'll have to discuss that with your postdoc. I'd recommend delaying his start date to January if he agrees to it."

It was the answer I was expecting but not the answer I wanted. I was relying on James to work on a set of experiments I'd designed to bolster the lab's new funding application. Without him to help I'd have to do all the research myself alongside writing the grant. Well, at least I had no more undergrads to look after, so that was something. But now I had to find a lab who'd take *me* in to work on my research.

Everything truly was going to shit.

"Thanks for the update, Gill," I told the Postgrad Convenor, inclining my head politely before stalking away towards the building's staff room. The strong need for a gin coursed through my brain but, given that it was a Monday afternoon and I was at work, coffee would have to do.

The thought of alcohol momentarily dragged my mind away from my awful lab situation to Henry's stag do. The last thing I'd expected that night was to run into Elizabeth Maclean.

Naturally I'd spent the entire weekend thinking about her and her icy demeanour when I wasn't anxiously waiting for an update about the fire.

Was everything that was currently happening somehow karma for how I'd treated her during her PhD? It hardly seemed like an appropriate relative punishment for my sins. Not that I believed in karma, anyway. But it was situations such as this one that gave me reason to understand why people *did*.

I'd deserved Liz's ire. Of course I had. That hadn't stopped it from stinging, though. But what was I supposed to have said? It was far too late now to explain why I'd been such an arse to her – not least because the reason was shameful. It was better for the both of us for me to accept what I'd done and move on. It was hardly as if I was likely to run into her *again*.

Where did she say she was undertaking her postdoc?

"She never said..." I grumbled, sullenly filling the kettle in the staff room because it had been left pitifully empty. Considering Mike hadn't said anything about Liz staying on in his lab it was highly unlikely she'd be going back to work there. For all I knew Liz's postdoc wasn't even in Glasgow; it could be in London or Barcelona or Texas for all I knew.

Except she was still living in Glasgow, and of the three universities within the city the University of Glasgow was the far superior one for genetic research. Given those variables, it was reasonable to assume Liz would be joining a lab either in this building or one of the other two research buildings on the west side of campus.

I'd probably run into her again.

Well, we'd managed to ignore each other outside of her assessment panel meetings during her PhD. We could simply continue to do so.

Potentially for years and years and years.

So what if the mere sight of Elizabeth Maclean still made my heart race? So what if my supposed schoolboy crush had not waned in the slightest after four years? So what if I'd wondered again and again whether Liz ever thought about the day we met the same way I did, or why she never asked for her clothes back? So what if they were still folded away at the back of a drawer in my bedroom just in case she *did* want them back?

"You did this to yourself, Tom," I muttered through the noise of the kettle reaching boiling point.

"And just what was that, pray tell?"

I flinched when a hand grabbed the kettle from my hand before I could use it, then relaxed when I realised I recognised the voice. "Daichi," I said, knocking shoulders with my best friend of over ten years. "What are you doing here? Has your entire building run out of coffee?"

Daichi stabbed my arm with a ballpoint pen. "You weren't picking up the phone so I came over to find you. So what did you do to yourself?"

"It doesn't matter."

"I think it does. Coffee?" Daichi poured water into a mug when I held it out for him.

I didn't much like instant coffee – who did, really? – but I wasn't in the mood to traipse through the rain to pick up a latte from my favourite café to replace it. The steam from the mug filled my nostrils, the scent dark and too bitter for my tastes, so I riffled through the cutlery drawer for a spoon and ladled sugar into it. Then I grabbed the last of the milk from the fridge to help make my poor excuse for a coffee more palatable.

With a wince I saw Daichi drink the awful stuff unsweetened and undiluted. "What did you want to see me for, anyway?" I asked him, ignoring his previous comment about what exactly I did to myself. After gulping down several mouthfuls of barely tolerable coffee, I added, "I thought I was meeting you for lunch tomorrow."

Daichi's sharp gaze told me he knew perfectly well that I was deflecting, but that he would allow it...for now. "I heard your lab will be out of action until January. Sucks to be you."

"Thanks for the words of support."

He gave me the finger. "Lucky for you I *do* come bearing words of support. You need somewhere to work until then, right? Does Michael have space for you?"

"He's already taking Mia," I said, shaking my head, "and he had to take on four undergrads this year. *Four!* I don't know how he does it. In any case there's no space for me – I need actual lab space to finish some experiments for my grant proposal."

"Want to work in my lab, then? I have half a bench available. You can share my office, too."

My hands stilled around my coffee. "What's in it for you?" With Daichi no good deed went unpaid for.

But the man merely laughed. "What kind of friend would I be if I didn't help you right now? You lab was literally on fire. I'd feel terrible if you never got your funding because you couldn't finish your experiments."

"Do you even have the equipment I–"

"Are you suddenly planning on changing the model organism you've worked with your entire life?"

"No?"

"Good. Then I have everything you need for your silly *E.coli.*"

"Silly, indeed," I tutted. At this point mine and Daichi's bacteria versus fruit fly rivalry had long since passed childish. "Are you sure you can offer me the space?"

In all honesty his offer was better than any other I could hope to have land in my lap. Daichi was my best friend, an easygoing lab leader and an excellent researcher. *And* he was offering me (almost) private office space.

There really had to be a catch.

Daichi looked offended by my continued suspicion. "Would I be offering if I wasn't? It isn't as if you have many options, anyway."

He had me there. "Point taken."

"Then do you want to come back with me to the lab now and meet everyone?"

I didn't particularly want to, all things considered, but if I was going to be working in Daichi's lab for the next three to four months I was as well making a good impression with the rest of his researchers. I knew most of them already but the newest grant for the Functional Genomics lab had allowed Daichi to take on a few people recently whom I was yet to meet.

With a sigh I poured the rest of my terrible coffee down the sink. "Lead the way."

It wasn't a long walk to the building which housed my friend's lab, but the rain had gotten heavier since I'd arrived at work. By the time we bolstered through the front doors my glasses had steamed up – I'd been too tired that morning to put in contacts, which I now thoroughly regretted – and my hair was dripping rainwater onto my shoulders.

"I hope you brought a change of clothes for meeting Jenny later," Daichi said, shaking himself dry as he led the way to his lab.

I raised an eyebrow. "How in the world do you know I'm going for dinner with my mum tonight?"

A wicked grin. "She told me to remind you about it in case you forgot."

"I forget *one time*—"

Daichi's cackle broke through my complaint, and he swiped his key card to gain entry to his lab. "You'll be sharing a bench with my new postdoc, by the way. Similar background to you so if you need any help with your research I don't mind her helping you – just give her credit when you publish it, of course."

I froze in the doorway. "A new postdoc? Who started today?"

"You don't have a problem with that, do you? It's hardly like I'm pairing you with an undergrad." With a jerk he tugged me out of the doorway and into the lab proper, an unconvincingly innocent expression on his face. "Come on, I'll introduce the two of you."

No, no, no. This was *not* happening. It couldn't be. Now I knew why Daichi had so easily offered me lab space: he knew all about my crush. Of course he did. All it had taken was one foolishly drunk night and I'd spilled everything to him.

He was setting me up.

"Tom," Daichi said, sweeping a hand towards a woman currently setting the volume on a Gilson Pipette, her dark hair tied back in a perfect braid, "this is my new postdoc, Elizabeth Maclean. Liz, this is Thomas Henderson. He'll be working on your bench for a few months whilst his lab gets repaired – it was the one set on fire last Friday."

Elizabeth clattered out of her seat as if she'd been electrocuted, staring first at my traitorous friend and then at me. Unmistakeable horror coloured her expression, eyes wide with disbelief and – yes, that was definitely anger.

I awkwardly waved my hand before I could stop myself. What else could I do, after all? I'd been completely and utterly screwed over and could do nothing now but accept my fate.

"It seems we meet again, Dr Maclean."

Chapter Three

LIZ

It was clear even through the shoddily put-together veneer he'd created for the sake of an audience that Tom was thinking the exact same thing I was: you have got to be fucking kidding me.

Seriously. *You have got to be fucking kidding me.*

Just how on earth had I ended up with Thomas Henderson working on the same bench as me on my very first day of my brand new postdoc? I was supposed to never have to see or interact with the man again. So why was this my new reality?

I'd died and gone to hell. That was the only logical reason I could come up with for why this was happening to me. Not that I believed in hell, though I supposed that actually gave further weight to it being the only *logical* conclusion I could reach.

"I'm sure he won't be much of a bother to you," Professor Ito continued when I didn't respond to Tom's greeting, cheerily ignorant to the tense atmosphere surrounding us. "He'll be spending half his time holed up in my office working on a grant proposal!"

A crooked half-smile crept up Tom's face which looked

even more awkward than the hand he still held up in a wave of greeting. It was then I realised that I was supposed to *say* something – otherwise my new boss was never going to leave and Tom was likely to continue standing there, looking at me expectantly, until the day I died.

"Um, hello," I eventually managed, seething at how ineffectual my greeting was. I wanted to say something bold and witty and clever; with Professor Ito around I could do nothing but respond to Tom's awkwardness with more awkwardness. Somewhat clumsily I sat back down on the tall stool in front of my lab bench, turned my attention back to the pipette I'd been working with, then added, "Hopefully we won't get in the way of each other too much."

I didn't have to look at Thomas Henderson to know he was well aware that he was already in my way far more than could ever possibly be warranted.

If Professor Ito sensed the tension between myself and Tom, he didn't show it. Bouncing on the balls of his feet, he said, "Tom, I have to take a call but I'll introduce you to everyone you don't know in the lab once it's over. Oh, and you, too, Liz! How convenient."

"How convenient, indeed," Tom muttered darkly right before Professor Ito· left us dangerously alone. My shoulders tensed at his words. Just what kind of a comment was that to make towards a fellow researcher doing him a favour? Were he and Professor Ito good friends? It was the only conclusion that made sense. And if that were true, it meant that even if I somehow made it through the next few months of my ex-PhD assessor being my bench partner I was going to have to put up with him showing up regularly to see his friend, my new boss.

I really couldn't catch a break.

For an achingly long moment it seemed as if Tom might simply walk away. But then, just as I thought he was going to chase after Professor Ito to protest where he'd been placed in the lab, Tom hunkered down on the adjacent stool in front of my bench.

"So your new position was with Daichi, then," he murmured, which seemed a fairly redundant thing to say given the circumstances.

I didn't bother looking at Tom. After how I'd spoken to him in The Whisky Barrel on Friday night there was zero point in me pretending to be civil. "Clearly."

"This is a great lab. I'm happy you—"

"Why aren't you spending *all* your time holed away in an office?" I cut in, taking my hostility up a notch. Just because I had to work beside the guy for a few months didn't mean I wanted him talking to me. I had to ensure Tom realised this, pronto. "You run your lab now, right? Shouldn't you have, like, given up actual research in favour of a mountain of paperwork?"

Tom coughed softly before answering. "Given that a fire just burned the place down I had to delay the start date for my new postdoc. One of my PhD students is currently writing up whilst the other has an endless list of experiments to repeat for her thesis, and now my undergrad students have been given new projects in different labs."

"That's a whole lot of words that didn't answer my question."

"My point – if you would have let me finish," Tom replied, an edge to his voice that made my heart thump in a painfully familiar way, as if he were about to reprimand me in a PhD assessment, "was that said grant proposal Daichi mentioned requires a bank of experimental data from which to base the entire proposal. Without anyone else working on the experiments that leaves it all to me."

A heavy silence fell between us. I realised, in that moment, that I was being unfair. I could be hyper-critical and thorny to Tom about literally any other subject than this; whatever I thought personally of the man he didn't deserve to have his lab destroyed. He'd only just taken it over.

Steeling my nerves I forced myself to look at Tom. Really, properly look at him, as opposed to when Professor Ito introduced him to me and I'd gone numb in horror. He was wearing large-lensed, green tortoiseshell glasses, which was odd because I'd never seen Tom wear glasses before. It annoyed me more than it rightfully should have that he looked bloody great wearing them. He'd gotten caught in the rain I could hear currently pummelling the roof, his wavy hair plastered to his head. But beneath his glasses and general wet state I could see Tom was very, very tired. Dark shadows under his eyes and a tautness to the set of his mouth implied he was likely close to losing his shit entirely.

My instincts told me to give him a break...just this once.

"I'm sorry about that," I mumbled, forcing myself to hold Tom's gaze even though I desperately wanted to look away.

He leaned on the lab bench, an eyebrow raised in quizzical confusion. "About what?"

"Your lab burning down, obviously."

"*Are* you?"

"Why wouldn't I be?" I fired back, immediately defensive and regretting feeling even a little bit sorry for the damn bastard.

"Your attitude doesn't exactly lend itself to sympathy right now." It was true, but it rankled me to hear Tom say it considering his attitude to *me* throughout my PhD. So I decided to call him out on it: after all, what did I have to lose by doing so?

"And yours doesn't, either," I said, giving Tom my best withering glare, "so consider yourself lucky I sympathise at all."

Silence. Had I really managed to get the final scathing word in before I stopped having to interact with Thomas Henderson forever? Not wishing to jinx it by giving him an opening to begin conversation once more, I swivelled my stool to face away from Tom, then pulled out my phone to text my dad.

Me: You'll never guess who I have to work besides until

January!

A mere twenty seconds of delay. Then:

Dad: Who?

Me: Only the PhD assessor from hell. I'll tell you more at dinner.

I expected Dad to respond with immediate rage on my behalf. Instead, after a few minutes of impatient waiting, he replied:

Dad: See you at dinner. Talk then. Love you x

Me: Love you, too xoxo

"You shouldn't be using your phone when you're wearing gloves," Tom said from behind me. "You shouldn't be using your phone at all when you're in the lab." My face darkened; was he really going to pull me up over something *everyone* did?

"I know," I bit back, hoping against hope that Tom would leave the issue alone.

He didn't.

"So why are you?"

"It was important."

"Then text in the staff room."

"I'll be sure to do that next time," I said, slipping my phone back into the pocket of my lab coat and returning to the restriction enzyme digest I'd been preparing. The sample I'd been waiting to thaw out had long since defrosted. Damn Tom, wasting all my time.

I'd barely finished preparing my digests, carefully placing them in the water bath to work their magic for an hour, when I noticed Tom was watching every move I made with hawk-like precision.

He inhaled deeply when he noticed me noticing him, which is how I knew he was going to offer me unsolicited advice before he uttered a single word. "You should—"

"Look, are you going to comment on every little thing I do every time I do it?" I interrupted, determined to set a line in the sand before Tom well and truly crossed it for good. "You aren't my assessor anymore. You aren't my supervisor or my boss, either. So can you just stop it?"

For a moment it looked as if Tom might argue. Then he ran a hand through his damp hair and sagged on the stool, all the fight driven out of him. To his credit he looked genuinely apologetic. "...noted. I'm sorry."

"Are you?" I asked, echoing his earlier sentiment.

"Yes. I'm being awkward. I don't mean anything I've said. Well, I do, it's all standard lab protocol, but—"

"That's got to be the worst apology I've ever heard." I crossed my arms over my chest, the scowl on my face making my thoughts as obvious to Tom as I could physically make them. "Can't you leave me to silence? Is that too much to ask for?"

Just as Tom was about to reply – I already had a rebuttal prepared on the tip of my tongue – Professor Ito seemingly materialised out of thin air to introduce us to the rest of the lab.

"Glad to see the two of you getting on," he said, as cheery as a spaniel. "I could see you chatting away from my office!"

Tom and I quickly glanced at each other in unison. I fought the mad urge to laugh when I saw his lips quirk with the impulse to do the same. But then I counted to three in my head, forced myself to relax and adopted a perfect smile to address my new boss.

"Professor Henderson was my PhD assessor," I said, "so we're already familiar with each other."

"Oh!" Professor Ito exclaimed. "Is that so? I had no idea!"

"Nice acting, Daichi," Tom muttered, but the man ignored him.

"Come now, let's go into the computer room and meet

everyone. I think I just heard Peter get in."

I perked up at the sound of my friend's name. Chloë and I met Peter in the second year of our PhDs; we'd quickly become a sickeningly close trio who did everything together. It was because of Peter I'd had the heads-up to apply for the postdoc in the Functional Genomics lab, for which I was eternally grateful. I'd always wanted to work in Ito's lab.

Although Thomas Henderson was currently testing just how *much* I wanted to work here.

"Sounds good, Professor Ito," I said, following him towards said computer room.

He waved a dismissive hand. "Daichi. Call me Daichi. No need for formalities around here!"

"Daichi, then," I replied, testing the name on my tongue. Him potentially being friends with Tom be damned, I really liked my new boss so far.

I wasn't going to let Tom ruin all of this for me.

Tom quickly overtook me with long strides to walk besides Daichi, then muttered something which sounded suspiciously like a string of curse words into his ear. Daichi merely laughed.

Okay, definitely very good friends.

The computer room was more akin to a small, communal staff room which just-so-happened to have three computers in it. I had it on good authority from Peter that they used to be ancient Macs but had been upgraded to desktops running Windows over summer. Apparently Daichi was still complaining about the change.

Peter was sitting in front of one of the computers, checking his emails whilst riffling through his bag for a bottle of water. Daichi tapped him on the head to catch his attention. "I have a couple of people to introduce to you, Peter," he said, when Peter straightened his posture and swivelled his chair around to see what was needed of him.

He grinned when he saw me; I eagerly returned it. "I know Peter already," I told Daichi. "We met three years ago."

Daichi chuckled good-naturedly. "Do you secretly know absolutely everyone, Liz? Seems as if it's impossible to introduce you to anyone new!"

"It does seem that way, doesn't it?"

"So does that mean you already knew Liz was our new postdoc?" Daichi asked Peter. "Of course that means you know. Well, that makes my job easier! Do you know Professor Henderson?"

"Only by name," Peter said, standing up to shake Tom's hand; Tom dutifully complied. "It's nice to meet you."

"And you. How long have you been working in Daichi's lab?" Tom asked.

"Only a few months."

"Peter came over from Nigeria for his PhD," Daichi said. "Clearly something about Glasgow's awful rain was worth sticking around for instead of going home!"

"What can I say?" Peter shrugged his shoulders, a small smile on his face. "I hate the heat." The comment garnered a laugh from everyone, as it always did whenever Peter said it.

"You definitely came to the right place, then, if you wanted to escape the sun," Daichi said. He indicated towards Tom. "This idiot will be working with us for the next few months until his lab is repaired."

"Speaking of which," Tom said, "we need to speak about that. Now."

It was clear Daichi knew he was in trouble but didn't care. With an exaggerated sigh he directed Tom towards his office. "The rest of the introductions can wait!" he shouted back over to me. "Peter, please show Liz where the coffee room is."

The moment Tom and Daichi disappeared I dumped myself in the seat beside Peter. "This is an actual nightmare," I cried, leaning against Peter's side in despair.

He patted my head as if I were a dog. "That wasn't *Tom* Tom, was it?"

"In the flesh."

"Sucks to be you. Want to complain?"

"I better not when he might be within earshot. Knowing my luck Henderson has superhuman hearing."

Peter stroked my hair absent-mindedly for a few seconds. He appeared to be deep in thought, though knowing him he was probably working out what to eat for breakfast. Both he and Chloë were huge night owls where I was an early riser; though it was almost five I knew Peter had barely been up three hours.

"Are you doing anything after work tonight?" Peter asked. "I don't have much lab work to do today. I could finish up around seven to pour some heavily alcoholic drinks down our throats."

"I have dinner plans with my dad," I said, shaking my head at Peter's offer.

"Ah shit, yeah. I forgot. Say hi to him for me?"

"Will do." I stretched my arms above my head and stood up. "On that note, I better finish up my work so I can clean myself up."

"You look plenty lovely to me already," Peter said, which warmed my frozen heart a little. He was always ready to dish out compliments – even when they weren't deserved.

Tom blessedly did not return to our shared lab bench, so I managed to complete my work in silence. When the clock on the wall read six o'clock I headed to the bathroom to touch up my make-up, sort out my hair and change clothes for dinner. Seeing my dad really couldn't have come at a better time, though a now-familiar pain twinged inside me at the reason for us having dinner on this specific Monday.

Two years had been and gone since Mum passed away.

"Don't think about it, Liz," I told my reflection, eyes

burning through the threat of tears. The last thing I wanted was for my mascara to run when Tom might be lurking around to bear witness to such weakness. Like hell was he going to see me in any state of upset.

After I undid my braid and carefully ran my fingers through the waves it had set in my hair I headed back to the lab to grab my bag and jacket. Tom was still nowhere to be found, and I exhaled in relief. I didn't have the time – or the patience – to deal with him before seeing my dad.

Which meant, of course, that I ran into him just as I reached the exit to the building.

Tom had dried his hair and changed his clothes, looking for all the world like he was going on a date in a slate grey turtleneck, cream-coloured trousers and brown leather shoes, paired with perhaps the most disgustingly perfect grey woollen trench coat I'd ever seen in my entire life. Withholding the urge to make any kind of comment I merely nodded at him before opening the door and walking away as quickly as I could. At least it had finally stopped raining.

I'd barely taken ten steps from the door when I realised Tom was, in fact, walking *with* me. I wanted to scream or hit something; was nothing sacred anymore? Was Tom determined to haunt my free time as well as my work hours?

"Why are you following me?" I threw at him.

Tom's expression was mild in a way that seemed painstakingly practised. "I'm not."

I pointed over to my right. "You live *that* way."

"And how do you know that?"

"Everyone knows you live in some mansion on Park Circus."

Tom rolled his eyes, easily keeping pace with me when I not-at-all-subtly increased my walking speed. "It isn't a mansion. It's a townhouse."

"Same thing to me."

"Why are you being so rude to me?"

It felt like the question came out of nowhere when, in truth, part of me had been waiting for Tom to call me out on it all afternoon. I abruptly stopped walking, rounding on Tom so quickly he almost walked into me.

"I'm sorry," I said, "but have you ever given me cause to like you?"

It took Tom far too long to answer the question. Something I couldn't quite figure out coloured his expression, though it caused my stomach to twist not entirely unpleasantly. But then his features returned to their usual, easy neutrality.

"...regardless," Tom murmured, choosing not to answer my question, "I'm not following you. I have dinner reservations at Brel."

"Oh for fuck's sake!" I cried out, no longer able to control my temper. This was *not* happening. I threw my hands in the air. "Fine, whatever. That's where I'm going, too."

"Does that mean I have permission to walk beside you or are you going to make me give you a head start so you can avoid me?"

I was tempted to take him up on his sarcastic second option; instead I reverted to silence and stormed towards Ashton Lane. I couldn't stop him walking beside me but I certainly didn't have to be good company.

Luckily, Brel was but a scant five minute walk away, and I breathed a sigh of relief when the restaurant came into sight. I fired a glare at Tom when he opened the door for me.

"Thank you, Tom," Tom said when I remained quiet, which only sharpened my glare as I walked past him.

"You're such a dick," I murmured under my breath, reaching the front-of-house staff before I could work out if Tom had heard me or not. I didn't care either way.

"Table for Maclean," I told the waiter. "I think my dad is

here already."

The man smiled brightly as he led me into the restaurant. "Right this way," he said, just as a waitress asked Tom for his name.

"I'm sorry, there isn't a booking under Henderson," I heard the waitress say. I smothered a laugh at this small inconvenience wrought against Tom.

"There must be some mistake," he said, confusion evident in his tone.

"Over here, Thomas!" a feminine voice shouted from the direction I was being taken in. Clearly that was the end of Tom's inconvenience for the night; I was annoyed it hadn't lasted longer. But then I noticed the woman who had shouted – an effortlessly elegant older woman with shoulder-length, platinum blonde hair – and the familiar man sitting beside her.

My dad.

"Surprise," he said, an awkward smile on his face at what was clearly a *what-the-fuck* expression on mine.

"Mum, just what on earth is going on?" Tom said, suddenly right behind me. I jumped in fright, then hated myself for doing so.

The unfamiliar woman beside my dad who was clearly Thomas Henderson's mother beckoned for us to sit down. Neither of us did. Then she took Dad's hand in her own, and for a moment I saw nothing but black.

"Please sit down, Liz," Dad said. "We have a lot to talk to you about."

We, plural. My dad and Tom's mum, holding hands, together.

Oh, no. Oh, fuck no.

Chapter four

TOM

"WHAT IS ALL THIS?" I ASKED, frozen in place behind Liz. She wasn't moving – had gone completely stock still – and I couldn't blame her. Given the day we'd both had I imagined the last thing she wanted to deal with was a man I could only assume was her father holding hands with my mother.

It's the last thing *I* wanted to deal with.

Mum waved impatiently at the table. "Sit down, sit down!" she insisted. "Have some wine. You aren't driving, are you, Thomas? White or red?"

My response was pure instinct. "Red," I muttered, gently side-stepping Liz in order to sit down. She stood for what felt like the longest five seconds I had ever experienced, patting down non-existent creases in the lovely teal dress she'd changed into after work whilst she clearly weighed up the pros and cons of simply running out of the restaurant. When eventually Liz took the remaining seat – her father on her right, me on her left – her expression very much suggested that she *would* have run away had she not been outnumbered three to one.

As my mum called over a waiter and ordered a bottle of

Merlot (a nod from Liz being taken as approval of the wine choice) I used the awkward silence that followed to take stock of Mr Maclean. The facial resemblance between father and daughter was striking. They shared the same wavy brown hair, though the man's temples were greying. They shared the same pale brown eyes, though Mr Maclean's were lined and far more tired that his daughter's. They even had the same frown of concentration when they both stared at the menu, resolutely determined not to be the first person to break the horrific quiet that had taken over the group.

"Why are you wearing your glasses, Thomas?" my mother said, finally cleaving the silence in two. "You have such lovely eyes – don't hide them!" She fussed with my glasses, removing them from my face even as I protested against it.

"I didn't have time to put lenses in this morning. Give those back, Mum. I can't see without them."

"If only you'd put just a little bit of effort into seeing your poor mum. And on such an occasion, too!"

"I wasn't aware that the mere presence of glasses detracted from my overall well-dressed appearance," I countered, gesturing towards my clothes.

Mum laughed easily. She didn't seem phased by the tension at the table in the slightest. "Oh, so full of yourself, son. Your father would be—"

"Just *what*," Liz interrupted, so quietly that in any other circumstance I wouldn't have heard her speaking. But in this specific situation her voice cut through my mother's teasing like a hot knife through butter. "What is going on here?"

The waiter took this exact moment to bring over the bottle of Merlot, filled everyone's glasses and then asked if we were ready to order.

"Yes, we are!" Mum exclaimed. "Can we have the saffron and chorizo risotto, the prawn linguine, the mac 'n' cheese with bacon and brie, and the sweet potato salad?" She rolled off everyone's order in a way that had clearly been memorised beforehand – not surprising for me, given that we often ate here so she knew what I would have wanted, and likely not surprising for Mr Maclean because they'd had a chance to look over the menu whilst they were waiting for us. But on Liz's behalf? I could only assume she must have told her father what she wanted in advance given that she didn't protest what Mum ordered for her.

No, all Liz did was down half her glass of wine in a matter of seconds. I quickly followed suit. Something told me this dinner wasn't going to be a sober affair.

After the waiter left Mum finally handed me back my glasses in order to squeeze Mr Maclean's hand. "I'm sorry, dear," she said, aiming the conversation at Liz. "I get carried away sometimes. I'm so pleased to finally meet you! It's Elizabeth, right? Do you prefer Liz? Lizzie? I'm Imogen, this useless boy's Mum. Please call me Jenny. Thomas, this is James Maclean."

"Jim," the man said, in a gruff manner I took to be the result of shyness rather than rudeness. He held a hand out for me to shake, surprising me when his grip tightened slightly too much for the gesture to be entirely polite.

Perhaps he *was* being rude.

I glanced at Liz, who was resolutely staring at her father with a stunned expression on her face. It was clear she had no idea what to think about what was going on...whatever it actually was that was *going on*. "I'm assuming you know I'm already acquainted with Elizabeth," I said, choosing my words carefully. The way Jim's eyes darkened for just a moment told me that, yes, the man definitely knew who I was and, yes, his manner towards me was probably due to him being rude rather than shy.

I had a fairly decent idea of what kind of things his daughter had said about me.

"Yes, I know who you are," Jim said, slowly. Then all of the tension in his frame dissipated in a moment when he turned his attention first to my mother, then to Liz. "Lizzie, I know you must be confused about what's going on right now."

"That depends on what's going on," she murmured, echoing my thoughts completely before downing the rest of her wine. "Why isn't this dinner just the two of us? This was supposed to be for Mum." My mother topped up Liz's glass, then my own, then flagged down a waitress to order another bottle; clearly whatever news she and Jim had required more alcohol.

"It's still about her, sort of," Liz's father said, eyes growing soft and sad as he spoke. "Jenny and I met a year ago. You know I wasn't doing well in those months after your mum died. You suggested I go to a support group, right?"

Liz crossed her arms over her chest, indignant. "But you said no."

"Well, maybe. But then I thought about it, and I knew I couldn't only lean on you for help. I wanted to go back to work but just...couldn't." The man sighed, his shoulders sagging with the weight of his confession. But then he brightened once more. "Something had to change, so I took your advice and went to the group you recommended. And there was Jenny, who was following the same advice that I was. And then...well, you know how these things go."

Ah.

Now I understood.

Looking at Liz I could tell she had come to the same conclusion as I had. There was a too-bright sheen to her eyes that I reasoned was to do with the mention of her mother. Given that the support group *I'd* recommended Mum go to was for those who'd lost someone to cancer – my dad, specifically – it wasn't difficult for me to work out how Liz had lost her mother.

My heart shattered at how hard Liz was obviously working to stop herself from crying in front of everyone; it was a feeling I had grown achingly familiar with over the last couple of years. Beneath the table I could just barely discern her hands shaking in her lap.

Then something else entirely clicked. Going by what was being said, Elizabeth Maclean's mother had died during the final year of her PhD. The year in which I'd made her assessments particularly awful because I was going through hell due to my father's rapid decline and eventual death from pancreatic cancer. Because I was suffering I'd taken it out on her, when the whole time Liz had been going through the exact same thing.

I was the worst person on the planet.

Part of me wanted to know why she'd never told the university about it or asked for time off, but then again...I hadn't asked for time off, either. And I hadn't told anyone about Dad's cancer other than Daichi. I'd wanted to stay busy. I'd wanted nothing about my work life to change.

At the end of the day, none of that made a difference to how terrible I'd been. *Worst person on the planet* couldn't even come close to describing me.

"Why don't we leave it at that for the evening?" I suggested, just as two waiters brought out our food – either blissfully ignorant to the tense atmosphere at our table or expertly ignoring it. At this point I wanted nothing more than to save Liz from whatever it was our parents were about to admit to out loud. And me, too, if I was being honest.

But Liz fired a warning glare at me the moment the waiters vacated the table. "I'm *fine*." She turned to my mother, who had a warm smile on her face and an excitable buzz to her manner which I knew very well she weaponised against nerves. "So you're...going out, then?" Liz ventured, squeezing her hands beneath the table to stop them from shaking. She made no effort to touch her food.

It was her father who answered. "Actually Lizzie, we're... we're getting married."

"*What?*"

I didn't know I was the one who'd spoken until all three of them stared at me. My mouth was hanging wide open in disbelief. I couldn't close it. My mother was getting *married*?

To *Elizabeth Maclean's* father?

"I know it seems sudden," my mum said, and I could tell a nervous ramble was imminent. "But, really, what's the point in waiting? Your dad's been gone two years, Thomas, and life's too short to keep grieving him all by myself. I can still miss him – still love him – but also meet someone new to spend my twilight years with. God, twilight years. That sounds awful. I'm not dead yet!" An anxious laugh. "In any case, before I knew it I was head-over-heels for Jim here, and how lucky I was that he felt the same about me! So why wait? We're getting married at Christmas!"

"You're – you're what—"

"Getting married," Mum continued, steam-rolling through the announcement faster than either myself or Liz could process what was being said. "At Christmas. In the country estate! It's getting remodelled right now especially for the event – you know your dad never wanted a flashy affair so I didn't get a big, beautiful wedding back when I was young. Luckily Jim was only too happy to let me have my way."

They threw huge fawn eyes at each other, oblivious to mine and Liz's stunned silence, and I knew in that moment that their love was genuine.

"We'll need to stay with you for a couple of months, Thomas," Mum said, so casually I almost missed it. "Lord knows the townhouse is too big for you, anyway."

I almost choked on a mouthful of linguine, unsure when I had actually begun eating in the first place. It wasn't as if I could taste anything right now. "What do you mean, *we*?"

"Why, me and Jim, of course!"

"Ah, I suppose that should have been obvious," I said, although at this point precisely nothing was obvious to me anymore. Mum was getting married to a man she'd never mentioned before, and that man had a daughter I wasn't allowed to have a four-year-long thing for.

"Oh, and you too, Lizzie!" Mum continued, much to my horror. Just what on earth was she saying now? "You don't mind if I call you Lizzie, do you?"

It was as if Liz's brain had shut down and was busy restarting. That familiar frown creasing her brow was back. "Wait, what about me?" she asked, clearly in no position to process more information that she'd already been bombarded with.

My mother ploughed on regardless of the poor woman's stilted reaction. "Your father was telling me all about how hard you've been working just to pay your rent. How are you supposed to save for a deposit that way? Come stay in the townhouse for a few months and spend some time with us."

The mere notion of having Elizabeth Maclean living in the same space as me, considering the way I still felt about her, was a very specific kind of torture that only Pinhead from *Hellraiser* could have come up with.

It wasn't going to happen. Of course Liz would say no. She had to.

Thankfully, Liz believed the idea was equally as torturous as I did – though for quite different reasons, I was sure. "Um, no, I...I couldn't possibly intrude." The sideways glance she gave me informed me that the idea of *intruding* on my house was the last thing she could imagine ever doing. That stung, somehow, though I knew I didn't have the right to such a feeling of disappointment.

"You wouldn't be intruding, not at all!" Mum protested, as if that was enough to ease Liz's reservations. "I'd so love to get to know you better." A conspirational glance in my direction, and I knew I wouldn't like what she said next. My mum was a Class A meddler. "And, truth be told," she continued, "I heard from Jim that you're not all too fond of my idiot son. I'd really like it if you gave Thomas the chance to prove to you he's not a terrible person. It would make all our lives so much easier going forward!"

God, I did not deserve that chance. Not in a hundred million years did I have the right to prove my decent character to Elizabeth Maclean, especially when I wasn't entirely sure I actually possessed one.

To my absolute surprise, instead of baulking at the request – or rightfully screaming that she'd rather die before doing something so stupid like giving me a second chance – Liz laughed at my mother's comments. It was then I noticed that, over the course of the last few minutes, Liz had successfully managed to completely and utterly compose herself. She had up a perfect, professional veneer, one which I knew well from her PhD assessments.

It was her armour. She was protecting herself. The entire night was too much for her, and now she was running on the only program she knew would get her through this nightmare.

"I think Dad might have exaggerated my dislike of Professor Henderson," she said, firing a disarmingly lovely smile in my direction. I looked away shamefully. "We simply had a difference of opinion on a few things, that's all. That's natural in science."

I knew what she was doing. She was easing my mother's conscience about the whole thing, but at the same time ensuring there would be no further meddling to make Liz *have* to spend more time with me. Jim glanced at his daughter curiously, then at me, then gently *huffed* as he reached a conclusion I, unfortunately, could not work out.

My mother was naturally pleased that Liz did not at least *seem* to hate me. She beamed at the young woman. "Well if that's the case, all the more reason to come and stay with–"

"Mum," I interrupted, in a tone that very much told her to drop the subject, "let me get the bill." We'd barely finished our main course; Liz hadn't touched her food at all.

Mum pouted at my suggestion. "Oh, but dessert! You always

order dessert, Thomas."

"I'm too full for one." I stood up to head for the bar before she could protest further.

"He has *such* a sweet tooth," I heard her babble to Liz and her father as I walked away. "I'm surprised his teeth are so good, considering all the sugar he ate as a child!" Of course she'd she'd moved onto embarrassing childhood tales already.

I paid for the bill without bothering to look at it. At least I never had to worry about money – I didn't think I could handle another hurdle in my life right now. Providing I didn't somehow get roped into a cryptocurrency scam or fall under the sway of a foreign prince in dire need of my bank account details I was reasonably certain I'd be financially secure long after the day I died.

When I returned to the table I saw, to my dismay, that Liz had already left. I'd wanted to speak to her privately about everything – about us working in the same lab, about our parents getting married, about her mother passing away. Not that I'd known *what* I was going to say, but still. I had to say something at the very least.

"Poor soul wasn't feeling well," Mum said, patting Jim's arm sympathetically. "She insisted on getting a taxi as quickly as possible. Is she okay, Jim? This was all too much for her, wasn't it? I was too much for her. I should—"

"Just leave her be, Jenny," the man soothed. "Trust me. Lizzie's a bit overwhelmed but she'll be fine. I already told you that she'd love you. Give her a couple days to sleep on it." Jim turned his immediately sharpened gaze on me. "You. Don't bother her at work, you hear me?"

"Loud and clear," I said, holding my hands up in surrender. "I'd never dream of interfering with her job."

"Sure thing."

"I swear it."

A pause. Jim regarded me critically; I didn't like it one bit.

Then he turned back to my mother, who watched our interaction with the nervous disposition of a mouse caught by a cat.

"Fine," he said, clearly not wanting to upset my mother, for which I was supremely grateful. "We're staying behind for another bottle of wine. I'm sure we'll have plenty of time to find out *exactly* how much you have or haven't interfered with my daughter's career from tomorrow onwards."

Fuck, fuck, fuck. If the ground could swallow me up and transport me to some fantasy anime world that didn't contain Jim Maclean, now would be a great time for it to happen. I'd never much liked the isekai genre but its appeal was very much baring its fangs at me right now.

All things considered, my life couldn't possibly get worse than this.

Chapter five

LIZ

"So I'm going to need you to move out as soon as possible. By Friday, ideally."

I couldn't believe it. I was *not* hearing that I had to move out after everything the last few days had thrown at me. What possible reason could there be for me to have to deal with all of this? I was a scientist – I wasn't supposed to believe in fate. Yet how could I deny it when the last few days had so thoroughly punched me in the face?

I was still in shock from what I'd learned (and run away from) the night before. Now my landlord was calling me at quarter to nine in the morning – I was going to be late, damn it – to tell me I had to *move out by Friday*? It was Tuesday. How was I supposed to find somewhere to live in three days? Never mind that my brain was overloaded with my new job, new lab bench partner and new bloody *step-family*?

I was cursed. Sometime, somehow, somewhere, a wicked witch in the darkest depths of the woods had cast upon me a nefarious curse. Had I stepped on the tail of her cat once upon a time? Run over a frog with my bike? Or was life really just this cruel?

"Earth to Liz? Elizabeth? You okay?"

I blinked, stunned to discover I was outside the door to the Functional Genomics lab, both Peter and Chloë standing there watching me stare at the door with glassy eyes.

"What are you doing here?" I asked Chloë, knowing my question sounded rude but unable to do anything about it.

Luckily, my best friend was more than used to my response to traumatic events. We'd made it through many a tight deadline together, after all. "Thought you might need a coffee," she said, holding out a reusable coffee cup covered in colourful drawings of dinosaurs. The contents smelled amazing. Damn, she knew me too well.

"You thought correct," I said, taking the cup from her and gratefully holding it beneath my nostrils to inhale its addictive scent properly.

"Jeez, when Peter told me Henderson was your new bench partner I couldn't believe it," Chloë said, wasting no time in getting right down to her favourite topic of conversation: gossip. "Why didn't you tell me about it yourself? You ghosted all my messages last night asking how your first day went."

"I told you she was at dinner with Jim," Peter said, gently careening me away from the lab door so a technician I was fairly certain was called Trevor could exit the place, pushing a trolley heavy with the weight of two liquid nitrogen drums.

"Aye, but that couldn't have taken up the entire night. So what—"

"Dad's getting married," I cut in, knowing that saying the words aloud would make them true. "Obviously you're both invited to the wedding." In all honesty, now that I'd had time to think it over, I was okay with it. I wasn't the kind of daughter who wanted her dad to never move on from a dead spouse. I wanted him to be happy. And Jenny seemed genuinely lovely, if a little scatterbrained and over-the-top. Chatty where my dad was quiet. Excitable where he was reserved. But I had seen the way they looked at each other; there was no denying their feelings were genuine.

But why, oh why, did he have to get married to *Thomas Henderson's* mother?

My brain couldn't compute this fact.

"Your dad's a-what now?" Chloë gasped. Peter's shocked expression echoed her sentiment. "Married? Did you even know he was, you know, going out with anyone? Who on earth is it?"

I didn't want to tell them. As with the fact Dad was getting married, if I spoke the words then that would bring them to life. But they *had* to know. Otherwise, how could I complain about the awful circumstances that had befallen me?

"You're not going to believe me," I said, building anticipation for my answer. I was as well milking the drama for all it was worth for the benefit of my friends. Their lives were remarkably drama-free, after all. Chloë had long-since lived vicariously through my haphazard dating exploits and hatred of Thomas Henderson.

Tom.

I wanted to ram my head against a wall at the mere thought of him.

"Well don't just keep us standing here in silence!" Peter exclaimed, uncharacteristically impatient. I must have zoned out again.

"Professor Henderson's mum," I said, flat tone of voice belying the literal words I had just uttered aloud for the first time. This was it; I'd told them. There was no turning back now.

"Oh fuck off." Chloë made no attempt to hide her glee at this turn of events, though there wasn't any malice behind it. She simply revelled in gossip.

"I am being deathly serious. I went to dinner and she was sitting there with my dad, waiting to meet me and...Tom. Yeah, they told us at the same time."

"Jesus, Liz," Peter murmured, gazing at me with big, brown, sympathetic eyes, "you just can't catch a break, can you?"

"It gets worse."

"*How* could it possibly get worse?" Chloë demanded.

"My landlord told me I need to move out by Friday." I put on my best pleading face for her. "I don't suppose I could stay with you for a few days? With my stuff? Just until I can find a new place?"

But Chloë shook her head. "I wish I could but you know Harriet just moved in. There's no way we could fit all your stuff in my tiny one-bed flat, anyway!"

I knew that was going to be her answer. My place was unfurnished; I needed somewhere that could house a hell of a lot of crap. Not feeling especially lucky, I turned to Peter. "Any chance...?"

Peter very much looked like he wanted to say yes but, tragically, he shook his head just as Chloë had done. "Ray would freak out. You know what he's like." Ray was Peter's very anxious, very neurotic flat mate. He loved parties and other extravagant social events but, when it came to his day-to-day life, didn't like anyone existing in his private space. I couldn't blame him. "Do you need help finding a place? I could ask around."

"Thanks," I said, though I knew I didn't sound it. "Maybe I could move my stuff to my dad's for a while."

"Doesn't he live in Balloch? That's a bit far for you to commute!"

"I don't really have a choice, do I?"

It was then I remembered that my dad was going to be staying with his new fiancée. In Tom's house. *I need to ask him what's happening to the house,* I realised, tipping the scalding coffee Chloë had given me down my throat in feckless disregard for any damage it might cause. I doubted Dad would continue paying rent if he wasn't living there. If Jenny Henderson had a literal country estate why on earth would Dad keep the lease on his tiny house?

"I need to call my dad," I told my friends. "I'll give you an update when I have one."

"You better!" Chloë said.

I held open the lab door so Peter could walk in first, but he didn't move. He gave me a sheepish grin. "I actually just finished. I'm going to bed."

"You worked *through the night*?"

"You know what I'm like. Chloë did it, too."

"You're both mental, that's what you're like," I said, giving them the finger when Chloë told me to fuck off.

I dealt with the experiments I needed to set up before calling my dad but he never picked up. Figuring he was busy, I fired over a message asking about the house in Balloch.

A few minutes later he replied:

> Dad: Sorry, nursing a hangover with Jen. Didn't renew the lease on the house – no point, is there? Are you OK? Do you want to meet up later and talk? I know yesterday was a shock.

I wasn't ready for that – not yet – but I didn't want my dad to worry, either. I replied to his message as nicely as I could muster.

> Me: No, I'm okay. Really happy for you. Honestly. Jenny is great. Just shocked about who her son is! Did she have him when she was really young or is she a cradle-snatcher out to get my poor dad?

> Dad: Ha ha. You're such a comedian. She's only 4 years older than me. Had the bane of your existence when she was 22. You sure you're OK with this? I delayed telling you because of him.

Me: I'm sure I'll be fine. Just so long as you don't expect us to become best friends or anything.

Dad: Only step-siblings!

Me: Call us that again and I'll revoke my blessing of your marriage.

With that I bid good-bye to my dad and began scrolling through vacant flat listings in earnest. Thank god Tom wasn't in yet – or, at least, he was in Daichi's office. I couldn't be bothered with his reprimands regarding the use of my phone in the lab. But more than that: I had no idea what to say to him. What *could* I say? I'd made my opinion of him perfectly clear the moment I was out of my PhD and therefore free to do so. That had already come back to bite me in the form of him working beside me for the next few months, but now...

Now his mum was marrying my dad, which made us—

No. I couldn't even think the word. It was unthinkable on so, so many levels. Wrong. Absurd. I was fairly certain it should be illegal to become related to someone you once – even in the far distant past – desperately wanted to see naked. Amongst other things.

I shook the notion of a naked Thomas Henderson from my head. The forbidden gutter was not where I wanted to be right now. Or ever.

So why had I ended up there half a dozen times ever since he waltzed into The Whisky Barrel and back into my life?

"Dr Maclean."

"Jesus Christ!" I cursed, banging my knee on the bench in fright. I rubbed at it to force away the pain. It was going to bruise and I knew it. "Did you float through the ether or something? I didn't hear you!"

Tom was trying to resist laughing at my response, I could tell. His brow twitched with the effort it took to keep his expression neutral. "I walked over here just like any other mere mortal. You were too lost in your phone to hear me."

God, I hated him. The first thing out of his mouth was a criticism. Hadn't Tom said *only yesterday* that he would stop? That he'd leave me alone? Clearly he'd been lying.

Seeing what I'd concluded plain as day on my face, the hint of laughter on Tom's lips disappeared. He ran a hand through his hair. He seemed to do that a lot when he was put on the spot. "That wasn't a dig, I swear. What were you so focused on, if you don't mind me asking?"

"You don't have anything to say about last night?"

"What do you want me to say? Going by the speed with which you ran off I assumed the last thing you wanted to do was talk to me."

Through a scowl I tried to work out if Tom was making fun of me. But he looked, for all the world, entirely genuine, and I was too tired to argue. "It was a shock," I admitted.

"You and me both. Mum never told me she was seeing anyone. But she's been much happier lately – and not so insistent on seeing me every weekend – so I guess I had a notion something was up."

"I didn't have you pegged as a mummy's boy," I said before I could stop myself.

Tom laughed softly. "I'm an only child. Her only son. Of course I am. Seems like something similar could be said about you and your dad."

I could only shrug. He wasn't wrong. "...your mum seems nice," I said, begrudgingly – not because I didn't mean it but because it felt like giving Tom himself a compliment. "It's clear Dad really likes her."

"Your dad's scary as hell."

"Are we talking about the same man here?"

To my surprise and suspicion, Tom averted his eyes and ran his hand through his hair again. I wished he'd stop doing it – I couldn't tear my gaze away from the simple motion of his arm moving and the way it pulled the sleeve of his lab coat away from his wrist. It felt as scandalous as a Victorian gentleman spying the bare ankle of an unmarried lady.

Ugh. Fuck off, forbidden gutter.

"I certainly felt intimidated by him," Tom said, fiddling with a box of pipette tips as he spoke. "Although...I imagine he didn't know very much about me that was pleasant."

"Oh, so you *know* you're a dick, then? That's refreshing."

Silence. Slowly, Tom put down the box of tips and returned my stare with a very careful, put-together expression on his face. "Yes," he said, confirming my suspicions once and for all. "There's no point in dwelling on it, I assure you."

It was in this way that Tom minimised every ounce of pain and suffering he'd caused me during my PhD with but a single sentence.

The guy was a bastard.

When I didn't reply Tom indicated towards my phone. "What are you looking at, anyway?"

If he didn't hear from me he'd no doubt end up hearing from his mum via my dad. No matter how hard I wished otherwise Tom wasn't going to stop being in my life; I was as well being straight with him.

"My landlord's kicking me out on Friday. I'm looking at flats."

"So you waited until *now* to find a new place?" Tom spluttered, incredulous.

"Just how incompetent do I look to you?!" I exclaimed. Then, realising other members of the lab were beginning to pay attention to us due to my raised voice, forced my temper back down. "She only told me today. I got the flat through Gumtree and never signed a proper lease."

"Why on earth would you do that?"

"Because it was cheap. Not that you'd know anything about

being poor."

To his credit Tom didn't retaliate. Instead, he leaned over my shoulder - into my *personal space* - and began scrolling through the flats I'd bookmarked on my phone with the index finger of his left hand. I was so startled by his sudden closeness I could do nothing but accept this change in circumstance.

"Hmm," Tom murmured, a slight frown creasing his brow. He was wearing contacts like usual; I could see the edge of them circling his grey-green eyes. "With your postdoc salary you could go for much nicer places than this...in much safer areas."

"I'm trying to save up to buy a place. I don't mind living in some minuscule one-bed flat in a shitty tenement building for another couple years. And besides, I can't afford to be picky. I need a place by *Friday.*"

Tom's expression screamed *that's impossible.* Which, of course, I knew, but I had to at least try.

"You know," Tom finally said, (dis)satisfied with everything he'd seen on my phone, "you *do* already have an offer of somewhere to stay."

"Say what now?"

"My mum was serious when she invited you to stay at the townhouse," he said, which was the last thing on earth I'd ever expected Tom to say. He chuckled softly against my ear, reminding me that he was far too close. Entirely against my will my heart began beating so furiously I thought I was in danger of dropping dead to the floor. "Not that she conferred with me first, of course - not something she's ever done, to be fair - but I don't mind. If it'll makes things easier for you whilst you find somewhere more suitable then I'm happy to help."

"I...have an entire flat's worth of furniture," I said, too stunned to properly respond and my heart beating too quickly for me to do anything but steal millisecond-long glances of Tom out of the corner of my eye. Was he really saying what I thought he was saying?

No fucking way.

Tom pursed his lips for a moment, calculating something in his head. Then he moved away from my shoulder and straightened up, allowing me to finally breathe properly. "As you so astutely pointed out yesterday evening, I live in a mansion."

"And you refuted this."

"My point is that there's plenty of space for you to store your stuff. It isn't as if you need to stay for longer than a few weeks, anyway. We can store your furniture in the basement."

"You're serious, aren't you?" I spun my stool around to face Tom with such abruptness he took a step back. Thank god. I could still smell his damn lovely aftershave upon the air, he'd been so close to me.

Too close.

"What leads you to believe I wouldn't be?" Tom asked. He had the gall to look insulted by my lack of faith in his seriousness. "My mum will be delighted. I'm sure your dad will be, too."

He had a point there. Dad would be over the moon. But of all the things I'd expected Tom to do, the very last thing I could have expected was for him to suggest we spend more time in each other's company than we absolutely had to. Had he gone insane? Was he a sadist currently revelling in the idea of criticising not just my lab work but my personal life, too?

But then that very thought gave me an idea. There was no reason I couldn't use this to *my* advantage and make Tom's life a living misery. He was the one offering me a place to stay; it was on *him* to deal with whatever I dished out.

Which could easily be utter hell on a plate.

"I take it that's a yes," Tom said, perceiving the smile that curled my lips as confirmation of my approval. Why did he have to look so *happy* about it? Was he the kind of guy who drew satisfaction from helping a damsel in distress?

Given how we met, I reasoned this was true.

"I guess so," I said, not entirely sure if I was managing to keep my smile from looking absolutely evil. "It would really help me out. But I'll be out of there as soon as I can, I swear."

"Take all the time you need." Tom just barely brushed his hand against my shoulder as he sat down on his stool beside me, then signified that the matter was closed by pulling out his lab book to check over some results. I wasn't sure if the touch had been intentional or not but it coloured my cheeks brick red all the same. I wasted no time in spinning around to face the window.

Okay, maybe I still thought Thomas Henderson was hot. Maybe I was still very physically attracted to him. But I could easily keep that under wraps in favour of making his life a bloody nightmare.

Whatever else I could say about my life right now, I certainly couldn't call it boring.

Chapter Six

TOM

"Get in."

"Do I have to?"

"You could walk to mine through the rain whilst I drive there, nice and warm and dry, if you'd prefer."

Liz made a face as if she was about to tell me to stick it where the sun doesn't shine, but the insistent pattering of raindrops on her head ultimately made the decision for her. With a furtive glance around the car park as if we were doing something sordid and secret, Liz bolted around to the passenger door of my car and slid in as quickly as possible.

"What are you, a spy?" I asked, incredulous at her shifty, nervous demeanour.

"People are watching us," she scowled, pulling down the passenger visor to use the mirror to fix her hair. The rain had caused it to curl wildly around her face, giving Liz the distinct appearance of a Regency-era heroine from a romance novel.

Rain looked far too good on her.

"What does it matter if Frank and Anita from the cell

signalling lab and Joe from the chemistry department and a gaggle of final year genetics undergrads are watching us?" I said, knowing the fact I'd observed each and every one of them observing *us* was going to piss Liz off.

She reacted exactly as expected, covering her face with her hands as if that would make her any less noticeable to passers-by. She shook her head in dismay. "It's even worse that you know them all!"

"But *why?*"

"Because they'll all be wondering what's going on!"

I smothered a laugh. So Elizabeth Maclean could be a neurotic mess just like the rest of us, after all. I quirked an eyebrow when she slammed the visor shut and rounded on me, clearly expecting an answer as to why I was laughing. "And what *is* going on?" I asked, feigning ignorance. "As far as I can tell, a man is giving his co-worker a lift home because it's raining."

"You know fine well what I mean."

"Do I?" I was discovering very quickly that it was fun to wind Liz up, and as I turned on the engine and reversed out of the car park I couldn't help pushing her buttons further. "Perhaps you're the one who thinks something lurid is going on, Dr Maclean."

"Don't *Doctor Maclean* me."

"I thought that's what you wanted me to call you? You certainly made that clear back in that bar you worked in. Although I think our parents might find it odd if I call you that at home."

"Why did I agree to this?" Liz decried, already at her wits' end. "This was a huge mistake."

"Too late to back out now. Your dad's taken all your stuff over to mine already." I turned out of the car park and began the short drive to Park Circus. I felt lazy taking my car to work when it was only a fifteen minute walk from my front door to my lab, but whenever it was raining I always found myself falling prey to wealthy privilege and driving. What use was a dedicated parking space if I didn't use it, after all?

After a beat of silence – during which time I caught Liz watching me through the reflection in the windscreen – I asked, "So what will it be: Doctor Maclean, Elizabeth, or Liz?"

"...Liz," she said, slowly, as if I had forcibly pulled the word out of her with a fish hook.

"I thought only your friends called you that?"

I realised my mistake the moment I said it. I'd promised myself I would never refer back to the day we met directly to Liz; I wasn't meant to remember anything she said on that ill-fated night four years ago, let alone *everything*. I was supposed to be her heartless PhD assessor, graciously offering her a place to stay whilst she found a new flat in order to make our new-found family situation a little better.

Well, that's what I told myself I was doing when I surprised even myself by telling Liz she could move in, but I knew fine well why I'd *really* suggested such a thing. I wish I could just cut my dick off. Or block the blood supply to it for a while, at least. It was going to be the death of me – sooner rather than later.

Liz caught on to my mistake. Of course she did. She was one of the most detail-oriented people I knew; it had been hellish trying to find fault with her research by the final year of her PhD.

"I didn't know you remembered that, Professor Henderson," she said.

"Tom," I insisted, taking a left onto Argyle Street. Someone was walking a sodden, sullen poodle down the street and into Kelvingrove Park for a compulsory after-work walk. "Call me Tom."

"Not Thomas, like your mother?"

I smiled before I could stop myself. This all felt very much like an echo of our first meeting, and I found myself unable to lie that I possessed no memory of it. "Tom is fine. And of course I remember. You made quite an impression on me."

"Hmm." Liz focused on the rain-splattered windscreen, arms crossed over her chest as she considered what I'd said. In truth I had no idea what I was *allowed* to say or not. I knew for certain I could never tell Liz how much I'd liked her four years ago, and that I'd turned into her own personal tyrant in order to protect my career. I now knew how stupid that had been – completely and utterly idiotic. Daichi had reprimanded me for it on numerous occasions after I'd drunkenly admitted my folly to him.

But it was too late to change that now, and admitting it to Liz would do more harm than good. And though it was clear we'd started this new stage of our relationship on very bad footing, the union of my mum and her dad really did look like the opportunity I needed to mend things with her.

Maybe. Possibly.

Hopefully.

A not *entirely* awkward silence fell between the two of us as I drove to Park Circus. Liz let out a low whistle when we finally broke through the Friday evening traffic, turned left onto my street and eventually slowed to a stop on the gravelled driveway beside my house. "Wow, you actually have a driveway? In the West End? Impressive."

"If such a small thing impresses you then you're in for a lot of Owen Wilson moments."

A frown. "A lot of what?"

"Wow," I mouthed, putting on my best impression of the actor.

Liz burst out laughing. Before she could remember that she disliked me, before she could remember to put on a cool mask of disapproval, she laughed.

I felt far too victorious than I was reasonably allowed to be.

"That's such a dad joke, you know that?" Liz said, getting

out of the car and holding her rucksack over her head to protect herself from the rain.

"You could be a dad at fourteen," I replied when I followed suit, locking my car before directing Liz to the varnished forest green front door of the townhouse. "Do fourteen-year-olds make dad jokes?"

She rolled her eyes. "You know what I mean."

"I do indeed. My point still stands."

Liz was about to toss a rebuttal my way, I was sure, when a flurry of movement and noise interrupted us the moment I unlocked the door.

"Lizzie!" my mother cried excitedly, pulling a nonplussed Liz into her arms for a hug. To Liz's credit it took her all of half a second to return the gesture, and she didn't even look uncomfortable about it. When Mum pulled away she held Liz out at arm's length. "I'm so happy you decided to rethink my offer. We're so happy to have you here. Aren't we, Thomas?"

"Yes, Mum," I said, painfully resigned. She hadn't stopped going on about it all week.

"Your dad's just popped out for some wine but he'll be back soon. You really are so pretty, Lizzie. Don't you think, Thomas?"

Oh for fuck's sake. We'd barely even made it through the door and this was already turning out to be my own personal circle of hell. "That's not something I can comment on," I said, just as Liz turned her attention to me to see what I would say. "We're colleagues."

Mum waved a dismissive hand. "Ridiculous. You can still *objectively* know someone is beautiful even if you work with them. What a shame that you're unattached! Your dad's been telling me all about how unlucky in love you are."

At this Liz closed her eyes for a brief moment, clearly willing for the ground to swallow her up. It was a feeling I was most familiar with. "It's good to see Dad's found someone to gossip with about me. But I'm not 'unlucky in love'. I'm just single. Happily so."

Oh.

If I'd known that, by the end of her PhD, Elizabeth Maclean was still going to be unattached, then I could well have been nicer to her, however despicable that made me. I could have found a way to delay asking her out until my professional responsibilities had ended. But that's the thing about hindsight: nobody has it when they actually need it.

Besides, if I hadn't been such an arse to Liz I *wouldn't* have been able to hold back from doing something inappropriate such as ask her out. I knew that for a fact, no hindsight required.

I had to give up on this stupid crush. In all honesty it was quite startling that I still had it four years later. I was a grown man, after all; why on earth was I pining for a woman eleven years my junior? Well, ten and a half – I discovered that her birthday was the thirteenth of January when her lab celebrated it every year during her PhD. Not that half a year mattered.

And now we were going to be step-siblings. We were going to be living and working in close quarters, even if it was only for a few months.

Something told me that living and working together was going to make it *especially* hard to stop thinking about her.

"Hmm," Mum said, mirroring the unconvinced way Liz had said the exact same thing back in my car. When she frowned at me I knew exactly what she was going to say next.

"*Don't say it*, Mum," I warned.

Mum said it anyway. "My Thomas is still single, Liz." Liz was torn between amusement and confusion at where the conversation was going, if the expression on her face was anything to go by. "At his age!" Mum continued. "I keep trying to introduce him to some truly wonderful women, but he always turns them down. Why do you do that, Thomas? You're almost forty—"

"Thirty-eight."

"With no wife or children—"

"I don't want them."

"Well you could at least bring home a lovely woman that I can call my daughter-in-law, marriage or not!" she huffed, and I despaired.

Liz, unsurprisingly, had landed on finding the entire conversation hilarious. "His friends all said the same thing about him," she chimed in entirely unhelpfully. "They came into the bar I worked in before my postdoc for a stag do. Professor Henderson here insisted he preferred the womanising life of a bachelor."

"*Doctor Maclean* is fabricating nonsense to give you more gossip to chew on," I said, moving past the two of them to hang my jacket up on the copper coat rack in the hallway and remove my boots.

My mother clapped her hands in delight. "Look at the two of you, arguing like you're siblings already!"

"Don't call us that," both Liz and I said in unison, which of course only added fuel to Mum's fiery delight. I turned my scowl from her to Liz. "Do you want a tour, or do you want to further encourage this kind of behaviour?"

"The former," she said, following my lead in removing her jacket and shoes. I was gratified to discover she had good house manners from the get-go. When we walked down the hallway my mother made for the stairs.

"I'll be in the lounge," she chirped. "I have a cup of tea waiting for me!"

The quiet that followed Mum's tornado of interference was deafening. I wanted to be angry at her but in truth this was the liveliest I'd seen her since before Dad died. Who was I to bring her mood down?

"This is the living room," I told Liz, when I opened the

double doors on the right of the hallway into the space.

Confusion flashed across her face. "I thought your mum—"

"The lounge is her own private space on the first floor," I explained. "Or, rather, the entire first floor is hers when she stays over. Apparently I'm not allowed to use it. In any case" – I turned on the lights in the living room, allowing Liz an actual view of the space – "I rather like it down here, so I don't mind that Mum hogs the first floor to herself."

'Rather like' was an understatement; I spent most of my time at home within the living room and its adjoining kitchen. A gigantic bay window took up the south-facing wall of the room; when it wasn't dark and grey and raining it lit up the entire room with copious amounts of sunshine. Because it currently *was* dark and grey and raining, the windows were obscured by plush, thick curtains the colour of pine needles.

In the corner closest to the bay window stood my late grandfather's favourite reading chair made of well-worn, wine-coloured leather and a tall bookshelf containing all manner of books, as well as several potted cacti and a tiny model steam train. The room was then split in half by the most obnoxiously large, brown leather corner sofa I could find to take up the space when I moved in five years ago – although its size was lost against the massive scope of the room. It sat upon two Persian rugs, each one easily the size of Daichi's office back in the lab. A tiled fireplace ensured at least the sofa area remained warm in the depths of winter.

On the northern wall, beside the door leading into the kitchen, was a one-hundred-inch OLED television which I'd bought to celebrate my promotion to professor. The eastern wall was largely taken up by a huge mirror and far too many framed photos of the Henderson family through the ages. I wanted to take the newer ones down – the ones containing me as a child – but every time I tried to Mum guilted me into keeping them up.

"This is..." Liz murmured, stepping onto the first of the

Persian rugs as carefully as if she were in a museum. She turned on the spot to take in everything, her sharp eyes zoning in on the photos before turning on me. "This is a rich person's living room."

"That it would be," I said, not really knowing what else to say. I swept a hand towards the door into the kitchen. "Do you cook much?"

"Yeah, but Dad's much better at it than I am."

Given that I'd had his cooking the night before – and it was great – that didn't really give me an idea of how good or terrible Liz might be. In any case she murmured in approval when I led her into the well-lit kitchen. It connected to both the living room and the hallway through two separate doors, with a third door made almost entirely of glass leading out onto the small front garden. This was still the middle of Glasgow, after all; even the wealthy folk of Park Circus didn't get a huge, private outdoor space.

Liz eyed me suspiciously. "Why do you have such a huge cooker? You're only one person."

"My grand-dad put it in before he died," I explained, smoothing a hand over the stainless steel of the gargantuan eight-pot gas cooker. It had two ovens beneath the hob, which was precisely one-and-a-half more ovens than I needed on a daily basis. "He came from a era where hosting fifty people for business parties within your own home was a regular occurrence."

Liz almost laughed at my comment but her curiosity over her new surroundings got the better of her, choosing instead to scrutinise every new object that fell into her line of sight. The kitchen was huge, all polished work surfaces, thick wooden chopping boards and white-painted unit doors. The tiles between the wall-mounted cupboards and the work surfaces were terracotta, which I noted Liz seemed to approve of.

Just as I was beginning to wonder if she was going to riffle through every drawer and cupboard in the kitchen, Liz headed for the door which led out to the hallway.

"Lead on," she said, with a glance back at the kitchen which heavily implied she *would* search through every drawer and cupboard when I wasn't around.

After the kitchen there was the downstairs bathroom, which contained a clawfoot bath that was far more decorative than it was functional, and a grand dining room that my father used to hold private business functions in many years ago. During my childhood I remembered it being used for extended family Christmas parties. For the last five years, however, barely a soul had gone inside the room for any other reason than cleaning purposes.

When we passed the heavy wooden door to the basement I held out a hand to stop Liz from opening it and descending the stairs.

She raised a quizzical eyebrow. "What's down there, dead bodies?"

"Just your furniture, an extra pantry and absolutely Baltic, draughty air," I said. "Better to not let it up here. Heating is expensive, you know?"

I made the joke for Liz's benefit and it was clear she knew it. Resisting the urge to smile she headed back down the hallway to the ascending staircase. "Up it is, then?"

"Up it is."

The first floor landing contained a storage room and a small room my grandfather used to use as a study but now sat as a relic of his past. It contained a dark, varnished mahogany armoire, bookshelves filled with rows and rows of dusty books, and several glass-encased shelves housing model trains.

"Your grand-dad would have gotten on well with my dad," Liz mused, a contemplative expression on her face. My heart softened at the observation.

"Does that mean there's hope for me getting on with Mr Maclean, too?" I asked. "I got on better with my grandfather than I did my dad."

"Has he been awful to you the last couple days?"

"He's been mostly quiet but he glares at me a lot."

"Then maybe you aren't *all* bad, after all."

My stomach flipped.

"Um," I coughed, suddenly self-conscious, "the first floor proper is where my mum and your dad are staying. There are two bedrooms – your dad has most of his stuff filling one of them – as well as a bathroom and a lounge. Mum said your dad –"

"Just call him Jim. It's weird that you keep saying *your dad.*"

"...Jim. He's at the shops, and then we'll probably all be in the lounge, so I'll show you the second floor first."

The flipping of my stomach only grew more acrobatic in nature as I led Liz up to where I slept, worked, showered and – well, did just about everything else. "This is my office," I said, feeling far too much like an awkward teenager. "I don't imagine you'll have need to be in here much."

"No, I don't imagine so," Liz mused, poking her head through the door to take in my perfunctory corner desk, desktop computer and filing cabinet.

"And...this is the bathroom," I said, when we moved on from the office. It was ridiculously large, with a deep-set jet bath, a glass-encased shower big enough for four people, and a small steam room to boot. It was the only room in the house aside from my own bedroom I'd specifically upgraded when I moved in. "Recently fitted with the world's best shower. That's a peer-reviewed fact."

I winked at her, then wanted to kill myself for doing so.

To Liz's credit she seemed entirely unfazed by this apparent lapse in my sanity. "I'll have to review it myself to be certain, of course," she said, walking over to the shower with an expression that suggested she wanted to jump in and try it that very moment. She threw a glance my way. "Then the peer-reviewed process can consist of two people, not one."

Well, fuck. I'm sure she hadn't meant it as anything but a perfect response to my joke but I took the comment to entirely filthy places.

"This is – this is your room," I was quick to say, moving past Liz when she exited the bathroom to open the door directly on its left. "You'll get all the evening sun. Well, what's left of it now it's autumn. I hope you'll like it."

Liz didn't step into her new bedroom, instead eyeing the door opposite hers. The only one left unexplored. My room.

"I suppose that's yours, then?" she asked, stating the obvious.

"Yup." *Yup?*

"Can't I sleep downstairs?" Liz asked, and for a moment I thought she was being dreadfully serious. I was fully prepared to move all of her dad's stuff from the spare room one-by-one in order to fulfil her request. But then she smiled. "I'm kidding. Unless you snore like a monster and this place isn't soundproof."

"You'd hope, at the very least, a house as expensive as this would be soundproof."

"Ah, so you *do* snore?"

"Very clever. No, I don't."

"But how do you know? If you're as *unattached* as your mum says?"

"Do you really think someone that looks like this could possibly snore?" I wanted to punch myself for being so arrogant, but I couldn't stop myself. A flirt is a flirt to the end.

Liz was torn between laughing in my face and...something else. I didn't dare read too much into it. "It would be only fair," she said, cocking her head to the side as she regarded me. "After all, men like you need to have at least a few flaws, right?"

"I certainly have a few."

"Oh, I know." A stoniness coloured her expression, which told me Liz had starkly remembered who she was talking with. Flirting with, almost. It crumbled my heart to pieces. "Is it all right if I settle into my room for now? Before Dad gets back."

"Of course," I said. "Be my guest. Or, rather, my flatmate. Or housemate, or—"

"I get it," Liz said, heading into her bedroom and closing the door in my face.

Standing there alone, looking at the door, I was faced with an inevitable conclusion that had been chasing me for four years. I was stupidly crazy about this woman. It wasn't simply a crush.

There was no point in denying it. The next couple of weeks were going to be torture. No, they *already* were. And then Liz would find a new place to live, and though we'd still be working together for a few months – and our parents would get married after that – I doubted I'd have as good an opportunity as I did now to bring her around to the idea that I was still the guy she met on that rainy October evening four years ago. But how could I make her stay longer?

Then it hit me: Liz needed to find a flat. All I had to do was sabotage her flat-hunt. I mean, it was far less awful than being a bastard to her during her PhD assessments. She had a place to stay already, and her father was here, too. She wouldn't have to pay any rent. She could save up her money staying with me far quicker than she could otherwise. I was doing her a favour, really.

Well, whatever got me to sleep at night. I knew it was a dick move. It wouldn't be fair to go behind Liz's back like this just to force her to spend time with me.

I was going to do it, anyway.

But first, it was time to go for a run to release the ball of pent-up energy currently pulsing inside of me. Usually I found it harder to go out running when the days got shorter and colder, but something told me that, with Liz around, my dedication to jogging was about to skyrocket.

Chapter Seven

LIZ

Okay, so Thomas Henderson didn't live in a *mansion* but it was a pretty fucking gorgeous house. The kind I'd only witnessed once or twice before, except this time I actually got to touch everything and, you know, live in it.

The bedroom I'd been allocated was nothing short of beautiful in its simplicity. The walls were painted a pale jade, with a long, tiled-frame mirror taking up the wall opposite a huge west-facing bay window. A king-size bed made of solid hardwood and adorned in cream bedding – with a forest green throw across the foot of the bed – was set against the north wall, whilst the southern wall was made up of pristinely white built-in wardrobes.

But for the first five minutes of my being inside the room all I did was stare out of the bay window at absolutely nothing. My heart was pounding so hard I could feel it in my mouth.

I knew Tom had been flirting with me. I knew I'd flirted back.

I knew it shouldn't have happened.

Not for the first time I wondered if Tom had simply been

amusing himself with me at the mixer four years ago because he'd been bored. I'm sure Tom had taken great pride in rescuing me: the silly little first-year student trapped in a conversation with three guys who wouldn't listen to her. We'd barely touched the surface of what I was researching, after all. He hadn't been interested in what I planned to do with my life, and threw off all my own questions about his work. He'd wanted someone to flirt with, and that was all.

But at the time I'd thought everything had been mutual between us. The smiles, the subtle touches, the horny-tipsy glances. We'd been having fun, hadn't we?

God, why had I stripped off my *clothes* in front of him? Damn mimosas.

The memory would haunt me to my grave.

Clearly Tom had wanted nothing more to do with the drunken mess of a woman that I'd been after I ran off and completely forgot about my juice-stained clothes. I wondered, for the thousandth time in four years, what had become of them. I'd been too ashamed to ask for them back when it became clear Tom wasn't going to find me first and ask for my number.

He'd probably thrown them out. That's what I would have done. Okay, that was a bare-faced lie, because I still had his flannel shirt. But that's only because it was stupidly expensive and disgustingly soft against my skin. I wore it to bed as a secret *fuck you* to Tom for messing with my head.

"Oh damn, the shirt!" I gasped, making to run out of my new bedroom to find the bin bags I stuffed full of hastily-packed clothes the night before. But then I realised someone had brought them up to my room already, neatly placing them in front of the white wardrobes. I ripped into them immediately, tossing aside skirts and dresses and tops until I found the offending article of clothing.

A furtive glance at the door. Tom wouldn't just barge in, would he? He wouldn't come in unannounced and be met with the sight of me clutching *his* shirt to my chest, right? In any case there was no way I could wear the lovely green flannel shirt to bed anymore. What if I was wearing it when I ventured next door to the bathroom at two in the morning, and Tom just-so-happened to be doing the same thing?

"Surely he won't remember a shirt he had four years ago..." I mumbled, thumbs drawing circles against the fabric in my hands. I didn't want to give it up; I'd grown far too attached to it. I hardly ever slept in anything else nowadays. This, of course, had absolutely no deeper meaning to it whatsoever; the scent of Tom's aftershave had long since dissipated from the material.

So why could I smell it right now? Neroli and pine and sandalwood. It was such a basic bitch combination but I couldn't get enough of it – when it was coming off Tom, at least.

I sniffed at my dress and then my hair. Ah, that was it. It was on *me*, probably from sitting in his car. I reasoned this was why my heart was beating so fast, and why I'd flirted with Tom in the first place. It reminded me of the night we met and a primal part of my brain had completely forgotten about the four years between then and now.

Well, it was time for some exposure therapy, and quick. Whatever stupid crush I still harboured for Tom needed to disappear, especially since it seemed that he was prepared to act like a halfway decent person now he was no longer my PhD assessor.

Still holding his shirt, I moved over to the bay window to sit on the long, low bench built beneath it. It was adorned in jade pillows and had two latches on its side which suggested the bench opened up; looking inside I found a stack of well-folded towels and blankets, all coordinated by colour. *He's like a granny,* I mused, giggling despite myself, *or my mum.* A familiar dagger to the heart met this thought with the accuracy of an assassin. It was better not to think of Mum right now.

A flash of movement through the bay window caught my

attention, so I closed the bench and sat upon it to better peer at what was going on in the rapidly-darkening September evening. The street lights were turning on one by one. Old-fashioned, ornate ones made of blackened wrought iron, like the ones that lined Kelvin Way outside the park. Said park could be seen through the window, too, from the top of the hill all the way down to the University of Glasgow and Kelvingrove Museum.

So this was how the wealthy elite of Glasgow lived, with fancy street lights and benches full of clean towels.

I took a photo of the gorgeous view and sent it to Chloë, who immediately responded asking to see the rest of the house. I hadn't told Peter I was living with Professor Henderson yet, and had sworn Chloë to secrecy: he hated Tom almost as much as I did (on my behalf, of course) and since we were in the same lab now I didn't want anyone else who worked with us to find out and gossip, either.

Thank god Chloë was good at keeping secrets. Well, sometimes. I had to hope this was one of those times.

Beneath the street lights and heading down the hill towards Kelvingrove Park, despite the rain, a singular person caught my attention. Peering at their lithe figure as they began jogging I realised it was none other than Tom himself.

"What are you doing, you bastard?" I wondered aloud.

Tom was dressed in dark activewear that stuck to him like a second skin. I was grateful, then, for the fact my view was from afar; I doubted my stupid crush would disappear if I caught him in such clothes, soaking wet, up close.

If he hadn't been so fucking awful as my assessor...

But then what? If he'd been nice to me he'd have still been my assessor. That probably meant we couldn't have dated, even if Tom had, in fact, been interested in me. Whether he'd been the loveliest guy on the planet or the worst reprobate I'd ever had the displeasure of meeting ultimately made no difference to my current situation.

Except that it did, somehow.

I was here to make his life miserable without letting on what I was doing to my dad or Tom's mum – and also find a new flat. That's what I had to do. Not ogle Tom through the window. It was important I remembered that.

I stuffed his shirt beneath one of the hotel-quality pillows on my new king-size bed the moment I heard the vague sound of a door opening from down below. Figuring it was my dad returning from the shops, I gave him a few minutes to sort himself out before eventually making my way down to the first floor of the townhouse. I spied Dad and Jenny through the only open door on the floor, glasses of white wine in hand as they settled onto a handsome, forest green leather couch beside a roaring fire. God, there was a lot of green in the house. Was it Tom's favourite colour?

Dad's eyes lit up when he saw me enter the room. "Lizzie!"

I took a seat on a matching green recliner on the other side of the fire, grinning foolishly at him when he handed me a pre-emptively poured glass of wine. "You didn't have to move my stuff over before I finished work," I said. "I'd have helped you if you waited."

"Don't be daft. What good am I if I can't surprise you like this now and then?"

Jenny patted his arm affectionately. "You're so sweet, Jim. And it worked out for the best this way – Thomas gave her a lift after work so she could avoid the rain."

"Where is the son of a – where *is* Tom?" Dad said, catching himself just in the nick of time. I snickered into my hand, watching as he did the same thing out of the corner of my eye.

But Imogen Henderson was clearly far more shrewd than I'd given her credit for. "So what is this animosity the two of you have for my one and only son? I don't think I can handle the tension from Monday night's dinner all over again, every day, until Christmas!"

"Oh, please don't worry, Jenny!" I reassured her. "It won't be like that, I swear. That was just...I was so shocked."

"What did my son do that was so awful you disliked him before you even met him, Jim?" she directed at my dad, who absolutely hated being put on the spot.

He waved rather uselessly at me. "He was her PhD assessor."

"And?"

"And he was a real dick about it."

"I'm sure he wasn't *that* bad," Jenny murmured, evidently unconvinced by this statement. "He's always been so well-liked by his peers, his teachers, his students – right from when he was wee! I don't think he could ever stand to be disliked. It's part of his work ethic, you see. And since he doesn't seem to think having a wife or children is important then that means all he *has* is his work ethic, so you'd hope it was—"

"Please, stop, it's okay," I begged, cutting off Jenny's worried rant before it could escalate further than it already had. "He was just a bit hard on me. I'm sure he had...good intentions. And everything he said must have been great advice, because I got the prize for best thesis in my cohort."

At this Jenny's face glowed with pride and understanding, which was the reaction I'd expected to elicit with my warped-reality comment. "See, Jim! That must be what Thomas was trying to do with your lovely Lizzie: get the best out of her. So stop glaring daggers into him whenever you see him, please?"

"Yeah, Dad," I concurred, trying my best to sound genuine. I think I *almost* made it work. "Maybe it's time to give him another chance."

He huffed softly into his wine. "Last and only," he said, looking at my face for a hint that I was lying. When he didn't find one, his gruff exterior broke into a smile. "Fine, fine. If we're all living here and going to be a family then who am I to ruin it?"

Jenny clapped her hands together, delighted. "I knew I

could work through this with you. Oh, this wine isn't going to last long," she said, taking in my glass and my dad's – unknown to us both, we'd simultaneously downed our glasses. "Thomas showed you where the kitchen was, didn't he, Lizzie?" I nodded. "Then could I bother you to grab another bottle from the kitchen?"

Something told me she wanted a few minutes alone with my dad to discuss something I wasn't supposed to hear, but I was only too happy to oblige. I wanted to have a nosey at the rest of the house unsupervised and check out the basement to make sure Dad had moved my furniture without ruining it, anyway. Not that it was expensive, but it was all I had.

The lights were low in the hallway as I descended the stairs, first to the landing and then to the ground floor. The house seemed to be made for such lighting: atmospheric, shadowy, rich and almost Gothic. I could easily imagine a Victorian-era romance novel heroine crying on the stairs, heartbroken over the engagement of her childhood sweetheart to another woman.

Okay, maybe I had to start dating again. Or redownload Tinder and Bumble, at least.

Just as I reached the bottom of the stairs the heavy oak front door opened, letting in a burst of rain and wind before the even heavier storm door behind it was slammed shut.

"Jesus Christ," a thoroughly disgruntled Tom muttered as he came back into the warmth and safety of his house, reminding me in that moment that it was indeed *his* house and –

And I was now faced with him standing two feet away from me, dripping wet in clothes that clung to every stupidly defined muscle of his stupidly attractive body.

Tom's eyes widened when I remembered to look at his face, not his abs. What did a geneticist even need abs like his for?

"Oh," he said, surprised by my presence the very moment he walked through the door. "Um, hello."

"Wine," I barked, pointing at the kitchen. "Wine. Your

mum asked for more wine."

Slowly, very slowly, Tom processed this information, and his face relaxed into an easy smile. "Sounds about right. Did you get settled into your bedroom?"

"Not – not really. I went down to say hi to my dad pretty much straight after you went running." Damn it, now he knew I'd been watching him out the window.

But Tom didn't seem to catch onto this fact. Perhaps the rain had frozen his mental faculties; he was usually far sharper than this. "Leave the wine to me," he said. "You can go and check all your stuff's in the basement if you want – you were clearly itching to earlier. Just remember not to keep the door open for too long, else you'll let all the heat out."

Numbly I nodded and followed his suggestion, all too eager to escape the sight of Tom, well, looking like Tom. In soaking wet, skin-tight clothes.

The basement was indeed freezing, and it didn't take long to sort through my stuff, so I quickly escaped to warmer temperatures and the (relative) safety of my new bedroom. I could hear the shower going in the bathroom, which meant Tom was in there.

I was very much toiling in the forbidden gutter once more.

Chucking my laptop out of my rucksack and onto the bed, I put on an episode of *Gundam* for background noise – sitting and chatting with Dad, Jenny and, invariably, Tom, could wait thirty minutes or an hour or forever at this rate – then whipped out my phone.

It was *definitely* time to redownload my dating apps.

Chapter Eight

TOM

"I'm just waiting for more Nru1," Mia said, finishing her run-down of what she planned to do that week. "Apparently one of Michael's undergrads used it all and never told the technician to order more."

I let out an exaggerated sigh. "Ah, undergrads. Using all of the restriction enzymes, leaving Bunsen burners on to raze laboratories to the ground..."

Mia looked unsure as to whether she was allowed to laugh at this or not. She glanced towards the exit of the big Molecular Genetics lab – to the entrance of my own, completely eviscerated lab. "Have you been inside yet? To see...well, anything?"

"I'm not allowed," I replied. "The fire department still has to clear it as safe first before the refurb can officially begin. Hopefully by the end of the week we can have a look at the destruction Carly wrought on the place."

At this Mia's face crumpled. "I'm so sorry, Tom, I really didn't mean to leave her on her own. I thought she'd left already, so I went home! But she was still looking at a gel on the computer. You know how easy it is to forget anyone is in the UV room."

She spoke the truth. Since the room had to be kept in complete darkness to look at anything properly with UV, the most respectful thing to do whenever you *didn't* need to use the room was to leave it well alone. Everyone was supposed to open the door when they were done to let the rest of the lab know it was vacant...but nobody ever remembered to do this.

"It's all right, Mia," I soothed. I felt terrible that my own student thought *my* burden of responsibility was hers to bear. "It's my fault, not yours. At least Mike had space for you in his lab."

"To be reunited with me!" came a familiar voice. Rachael MacKay, my old PhD student who'd moved over to Mike's lab for a postdoc back in January. She and Mia were close friends; when they'd both worked in my lab it had been impossible to get them to be quiet for longer than five minutes.

Mia grinned at her. "Having you here definitely helps me wrap up these repeat experiments. Did you remember that ethylene glycol protocol I asked you about?"

Rachael whipped out a sheet of paper like it was a prized treasure map. "It took some major searching of my hard-drive but I found it. Is it true your mum is marrying Liz's dad, Tom?"

The question almost gave me whiplash. I rubbed the back of my neck and resisted the urge to awkwardly look away. "That would be correct. How'd you find out?"

"Oh, everyone knows. You know how it is around here."

Now that news of our parents getting married had somehow become the hot new topic of gossip throughout the Institute, if Rachael was to be believed, I knew I had to talk to Liz pronto about what we did and didn't tell our colleagues in response to this. I had to wonder if someone I knew had been in Brel when the announcement was made, and delightedly told everyone *they* knew.

To be fair, it may well have been Daichi. It was probably Daichi.

I could only hope our new living arrangements wouldn't become common knowledge; at least my best friend knew better than to betray my confidence over *that* not-at-all-insignificant matter.

A conversation behind me, Mia and Rachael caught my attention. "...flatmate's moving in with their girlfriend so I have to find a new place. Do you know any places going vacant?"

"Nah, sorry, looking at flats just makes me depressed. Everything is so expensive."

"Tom, where are you—" Mia began, when I moved from her side to join the undergrads currently complaining about their living situations. Taking out my phone I found the listings I remembered Liz looking at, which I'd bookmarked in order to keep track of what she was looking for.

To sabotage them all.

"I have a few places you might want to look at," I told the – startled – undergrad, handing them my phone and barely suppressing a laugh at the thought that Liz would no doubt complain about my double standards regarding using phones in the lab. In truth I had absolutely no problem with folk using their phone in the lab (so long as they weren't wearing gloves); I'd simply been reinforcing my absolute bastard persona at the time, even though I'd immediately regretted it.

The undergrad took my phone with dubious uncertainty, though his face lit up when he read the flat listings. Over his shoulder his companion also took stock of the places, and promptly took out her own phone to find them online.

"Thank you, Professor Henderson!" the first undergrad cried, clearly not believing his luck. "These are perfect. Just where did you find them?"

"Ah, a friend of mine was looking for a flat so I was helping her search, but she's found one now."

Calling Liz a 'friend' when I was currently sabotaging her for my own selfish desires felt perversely wrong, but I was hardly about to call her my step-sister. That sounded infinitely worse.

Once the undergrads had noted down the details of the flats I took back my phone, said my good-byes to Mia and Rachael, then left the lab. When I found myself in front of the door to my *own* lab it took all the strength I had in me not to check out how much damage the fire had caused. But I knew it would only serve to sour my mood, so I left the building entirely to buy myself and Daichi some decent coffee from my favourite café.

It was a sunny day – a welcome change from the rain that had plagued Glasgow all weekend – and the queue for coffee was short. I wanted it to be longer simply to delay my return to the Functional Genomics lab...and Liz. She'd barely come out of her room since Friday night, which meant she was almost certainly avoiding me. I felt so awkward about our encounter after my rain-soaked jog that I honestly couldn't blame her for not wanting to see me.

We'd been flirting before and after my jog, I knew that for certain. I also knew for sure that Liz didn't like how easy it had been to fall into step with me. A sick feeling twisted my stomach; had I really destroyed any chance I might have had at reconnecting with her because of my attitude over the past four years? Was my plan to keep her living in my house until our parents' wedding so we could bridge the distance between us all in vain?

If I kept avoiding her, too, then I'd never find out. I had to buck up and make the first move each and every time – otherwise Liz was certain to happily ignore me.

"For me?" Daichi asked, taking one of the coffees from my hand when I reached his office. Liz was engrossed in her lab work, too busy to have noticed my appearance, though her friend Peter regarded me with an expression far too close to dislike when I walked past him. I could only conclude that this meant Liz's dad wasn't the only one she'd complained to about me. I supposed I deserved it.

No, I *knew* I deserved it.

"Yes, for you," I told Daichi, "though if you've been gossiping about a certain wedding then I'm going to chuck it over your head."

Daichi shook his head when I made to close his office door. "Leave the door. I try to keep open hours for the students after lunchtime, and they're way more likely to bother me if the door's, you know, actually open."

There was a reason my best friend was one of the favourite teachers within the Institute, and his open door policy only served to solidify that. So I left the door open and leaned against the edge of his desk just as Daichi reclined in his chair, sighing happily into the steam of his double shot Americano.

"I didn't tell anyone about the wedding, I swear," he said, though he seemed thoroughly amused by the notion that everyone knew. "Jenna Daniels – you know, the new head of the plant lab—"

"I know Jenna." She'd been my PhD assessor way back when I was in my early twenties, and was happily married to a man fifteen years her junior.

"Well, she and her toyboy husband were at Brel the same time you were. She heard everything. And you know the plant scientists are the *real* gossips in the Institute."

"Well, damn."

"Was there a reason you didn't want anyone to know?"

"Not really. I guess I don't want people to know *more* than that."

"What, like how my brand new postdoc is currently liv—"

"Open door, Daichi," I warned, waving towards it.

He chuckled. "Right. Are we still on for drinks this Friday, by the way? May is working a double in the ER so I'll be very lonely if you say no."

Daichi's wife always worked on a Friday night so his blackmail was nothing new. "Of course," I said, sipping my coffee now that it was a drinkable temperature. "Considering everything that's happened over the last few days I'm in dire need of a drink."

"Excellent," he said, satisfied that I wasn't flaking on him – not that I ever did. Then Daichi coughed as if to clear his throat, and I realised he was about to ask me for a favour. A cough *always* preceded a favour. "Well, I was going to discuss it then but may as well bring it up now. There's a conference in London in November I'm supposed to be going to but it looks like May will actually get her time off approved, for once. I want to surprise her by taking her on holiday; you know how much she deserves it. Can you go, instead? I just need you to spy on what everyone's researching for me."

"Is this one of those requests where I'm not allowed to say no?" I asked, though I already knew the answer.

"Considering I've magnanimously given you office *and* lab space, I'd say the answer to your question is yes."

At this I spared the quickest of glances at Liz through the open door. She'd paused in her work to remove her phone from her pocket – gloves off, like a well-behaved researcher – and her face lit up with an excited smile when she read the screen.

"You didn't hire her just to mess with me, did you?" I asked Daichi in an undertone, because I hadn't been able to stop thinking about it all weekend. "Because if you—"

"Are you really going to diminish Dr Maclean's wonderful reputation as a researcher by finishing that sentence, Tom?" Daichi cut in, voice uncharacteristically flinty. "I thought you were better than that."

Shame rightfully washed over me, and I sighed. I had to stop making everything that happened to Liz somehow revolve around *me*. "You're right. You're right. I'm an awful person."

"No, I merely invited you to work in my lab when yours

burned to the ground *after* I realised my new postdoc was the woman you've been pining after for four years." A shit-eating grin. I could have punched him.

"You're a dick," I muttered, glowering at my best friend over the rim of my coffee cup.

"Better than being an awful person. Come on," Daichi said, standing up. "Come help me do a round of the lab."

"We're still drinking coffee."

"And? Live a little."

I could only laugh at Daichi's flagrant disregard for protocol as we made our way into the lab to see if anyone needed help. But of course I couldn't concentrate on anything except what currently had Liz so excited. Clearly I wasn't the only one; Peter had sidled over to her bench.

"What's with the grin?" he asked her, just as Liz finished typing something on her phone.

"I have a date," she said, eyes widening when she noticed I was within earshot. She resolutely zoned in on Peter with laser focus, though since I was deliberately eavesdropping I could still hear her, anyway. "On Friday."

Was it just me or did Peter's face fall at this announcement? No, it wasn't just me – the disappointment he felt upon hearing of Liz's date was painfully visible. His shoulders sagged, and he shoved his hands into the pockets of his lab coat to hide the fact they'd half-curled into fists.

Liz, however, was oblivious to Peter's reaction. I wondered how long he'd held a flame for her, fleetingly feeling bad for the man before remembering that he was my competition. Well, if he ever told Liz how he felt. And if she ever forgave me enough to consider me a romantic prospect, of course.

"I need to think of somewhere to go," Liz continued, blissfully dense to how much Peter did not want to be part of their conversation. "Somewhere cool. Do you know anywhere?"

"If I know anywhere then you know it, too," Peter said, not quite managing to cover the sullen tone of his voice. "We go everywhere together."

Liz ignored his jibe. "Hmm, maybe Harriet will know somewhere. I shouldn't suggest anywhere for food – that's too formal for a Tinder date, isn't it? Just drinks will do, right?"

"I thought you'd deleted Tinder. And Bumble. And all the other ones."

"I had...recent cause to download them again," Liz said, and I could have sworn she looked at me for the barest of moments.

Just what did *that* mean, exactly?

"How about Blue Dog?" I suggested before I could stop myself. Daichi stiffened beside me, giving me a look before turning his attention towards Liz.

"It's a jazz and cocktail bar on West George Street," he said, elaborating on my suggestion. "Very cool."

Liz frowned suspiciously at me, but Daichi's approval of the place seemed to assuage her. "Is it expensive?"

Of course Liz would ask that. She hadn't received her first month's pay from her postdoc yet. "Mid-price," I said, though it was clear she wanted Daichi to respond. "Good for a few drinks. Maybe if you're lucky your date will pay for them, anyway."

Both Peter and Daichi were shocked at my jibe, though Liz infuriatingly ignored it. "Blue Dog," she murmured, taking note of it. "I'll suggest it. Thanks, Profe—Daichi."

"Don't mention it," Daichi said, before gently tapping me on the back and walking towards his office. This time he closed the door behind us.

"Any reason you suggested our favourite bar as the location for Liz's date on Friday? The very evening we're going out for drinks, no less?"

"Absolutely no reason at all," I replied, unable to meet his gaze. We both knew fine well what I was doing. I'd already sabotaged Liz's flat hunt; at this point interfering with her dating life was well within my wheelhouse.

God, I was going to hell.

Chapter Nine

LIZ

"Oh, Lizzie, you look wonderful! Where are you going?"

"I have a date," I told Jenny, smiling at her in the reflection of the gargantuan living room mirror as I made some final adjustments to my hair. I'd gone for classy-but-flirty for said date: low-backed, knee-length, sleeveless black dress and bare legs paired with nude heels I'd been dying to wear for months now. An artfully messy French twist, a delicate gold chain necklace, earth-toned eyeshadow and my favourite apricot lipstick finished off the ensemble.

I looked good. I knew I did. If I messed up tonight it would lie entirely with the words that came out of my mouth, not my appearance.

The older woman clasped her hands together at the mention of a date. I'd learned over the course of a week that Jenny did that a lot when she was excited, and she got excited over, well, almost everything. "Did you hear that, Jim?" she called through to the kitchen. "Your daughter has a date!"

"With who?" Dad coughed back, the distinctive smell of onions sizzling in butter filling my nose when he swung the kitchen door wide open to interrogate me. He crossed his arms over his chest as if to intimidate me, though with Jenny's pink-chequered apron on and flour dusted across his face he was failing miserably.

I smeared some coconut butter over my lips from a tiny pot I kept in my handbag before answering, "Just a guy I met on a dating app. His name is Alan."

"Alan? What a stupid name. I don't like him. Cancel and help me make calzones – I know you love them."

I could only laugh. "Tempting as that is" – it was; in recent years, inspired by *Masterchef,* Dad had really gotten into cooking and was now great at it – "I think I ought to give him a chance, at least. Don't you think?"

Dad caught Jenny's eye and something passed between them that I couldn't quite understand. "A chance, aye?" he muttered. "Giving lots of these bastards chances lately, aren't I?"

I didn't ask him to explain.

"Look, I better head off or I'll be late," I said, grabbing my coat from where I'd tossed it over the back of the couch before waltzing over to my dad to kiss the bare inch of his right cheek that wasn't covered in flour.

He kissed me back with some reluctance. If it were up to him I'd remain single forever. "Don't be out late, you hear me? Get back before that son of hers comes home." Dad indicated towards Jenny.

I rolled my eyes. "I'm twenty-seven, Dad. I'll come back whenever I want to. Where *is* Tom, anyway?" I asked Jenny, curiosity getting the better of me even though I didn't want it to. I'd felt something infuriatingly close to disappointment when I finished in the lab at five only to discover that Tom was nowhere to be seen.

"Ah, on Fridays he tends to spend time with Daichi. Wonderful man. Wicked sense of humour. And his wife! Oh, she's just beautiful, Lizzie. You'll see what I mean when you meet her."

"And I'd have cause to meet her when...?"

"Why, at the wedding, of course!"

Oh. That should have been obvious, I supposed, though truthfully I couldn't have possibly known Imogen Henderson was on invited-to-her-wedding-with-a-plus-one terms with her son's best friend.

A honk from outside told me my taxi was impatiently waiting for me. "I better go," I said, double-checking my bag to make sure I hadn't forgotten anything, then leaving the house to step into the chilly September air. A week ago the mid-afternoon sun still held onto the last vestiges of summer; now all of that was gone, leaving only the pointed chill of autumn and, close on its heels, a dark and typically miserable Glasgow winter.

My stomach roiled with nerves as the taxi drove me to Blue Dog. I couldn't believe I'd actually used Tom's suggestion. Of all people! But when I looked the place up it turned out that he'd been right to recommend it: it looked perfect for a first, essentially blind, date. Okay, I knew what Alan looked like from his photos, but seeing someone in person for the first time was totally different to seeing a photo.

When my phone buzzed I pulled it out and saw Alan had messaged me. My heart skipped a beat, my stomach fluttering once more with typical pre-date jitters. So what if I'd rushed into organising said date to get Tom out of my head? Alan seemed funny, and he was handsome, and I hadn't gone on a date in months. For all I knew I was about to meet the man I could settle down into happily unmarried life with.

The message Alan sent told me he'd gotten us a booth table directly opposite the bar. God, I loved a man who actually told you exactly where he was. It made it so much easier for me to get out of the taxi, run my hands over the top of my hair to check for flyaways, then enter the bar and sit down as quickly as possible. I barely even took account of my surroundings.

"Hi," I said, sliding into the booth facing my date before wondering if I should have sat beside him. But sitting opposite him was for talking; sitting *beside* him was for snogging his face off. And I didn't want to do that...yet.

"Hi," Alan said back, his polite smile turning wider as he appraised my appearance. I flushed under his attention. Alan was – as was the case with so many men – more handsome in person than in his photos. What was it with guys and not being photogenic? His black hair was shaved at the sides but kept long enough on top to sweep over his brows, with brown eyes and freckles across his face. In truth he reminded me of Eli, which was never a good thing, but all I had to do was remind myself that Alan *wasn't* my ex-boyfriend and everything was golden.

"Your photos don't do you justice," I told him honestly. It was the kind of comment I knew would go down well, and as expected Alan reacted like a purring cat.

"You aren't too bad yourself," he said, adjusting the collar of his green flannel shirt as he spoke. Unbidden I thought that it wasn't nearly as nice as Tom's shirt before mentally telling myself to shut up. "You're quite gorgeous, actually."

"Do you think we can get through the entire date on compliments alone," I joked, "or should we get some drinks first?"

Alan laughed. Of course he laughed; we were already on track to a wonderful first date. Tom and his flannel shirt and impossible abs and curly-around-his-ears hair could get to fuck.

Three gin and tonics later and Alan and I had covered all the necessary small talk facts that we definitely already knew about each other by virtue of internet stalking: where we were from (Alan from Edinburgh, me from Stirling); how old we were (Alan would turn twenty-eight on the sixth of January – a week before I would); where we worked (he was a software engineer); if we had any pets (he had a cat, I wanted an entire zoo once I finally bought a house), and so on and so on.

As someone began playing soft jazz on the piano, and after I took a quick bathroom break to make sure I had on enough coconut butter to make my lips gleam in the low light of the bar, our conversation invariably turned to relationships.

This was always the make or break for me with dates. If they were looking for someone to start a serious relationship with – to marry, to have kids, to go on multiple holidays to Tenerife – then the date was likely to end early. If they just wanted to hook up...well, that's what usually ended up happening. Except that, too often, those hook-ups began to get serious after a month or two, and the guy would start talking about settling down with marriage and kids and that damn holiday in Tenerife firmly in the pipeline.

They never outright *said* it, of course. They were all far too 'cool' for that. But my staunch opinions about marriage and children were always met by far too many protests of 'you can't possibly know for sure!' and "you're young – it'll be different in five years!' and 'you'll change your mind!' for any of them to be content with simply being with me, no strings attached.

With all of that circling my mind, I dived into battle.

"I was with a guy for two years during my undergrad," I explained to Alan. "He got a PhD offer in the States and wanted me to go with him. I already had my offer here, so I refused."

It was the short-on-details, definitely-*not*-the-full-picture story, but it was the easiest version of events for me to give.

"I suppose that's good for me that he was crazy enough to leave you for the US," Alan said, a sly, boyish grin on his face that I thoroughly enjoyed. "Anyone else after that? That must have been a few years ago now, yeah?"

"Five years. I've only had casual relationships here and there since. You?"

"I was with this girl, Danielle, for three years," Alan said. "Honestly I thought we were going to get married, have kids, the works. Then she just...broke up with me. That was two years ago. Since then I guess I've not wanted to get serious until I could be sure I'm completely over her."

"Which would be...?"

"Now." Alan's grin widened. I didn't think it was possible – he had no room left on his face for it to get any bigger.

I pawed at his hand, showing I was game for his over-the-top flirtations. "Let's not jump straight to serious," I said, reflexively, before realising almost immediately it was the wrong thing to say.

Alan's Cheshire Cat grin slipped from his face. "Why not? Didn't your profile say you weren't looking for a hook-up? Don't you *want* to find someone you can have a serious relationship with?"

"Well, yes," I said, taking a large gulp of my fourth gin and tonic to stop myself from swearing at, well, myself. "But I don't want the whole marriage and kids thing. So I'm careful about getting to know someone – really, truly know someone – before committing to getting serious with them."

"Aw, you can't say that," Alan protested. I almost sighed. *Here we go again.* "You're still so young. Hey, I thought I was ready to marry Danielle but looking back on it I was way too young to settle down. I've learned from that, though, and I know I should enjoy the rest of my twenties before thinking about kids. That's still two years away. That's ages."

"It's not *that* long," I said, knowing I sounded sullen and hating myself for it. I was going to ruin this date with a perfectly lovely, handsome, funny guy (with a good job and a cat) all because of my stupid principles.

Alan didn't seem sure what to say in response. Going by his face alone I could tell he was re-examining our entire night, and the future – or lack thereof – of our potential relationship. "I need to use the bathroom," he said, which was the kinder way to say 'I need to call a friend and find a way to end this date early'.

I tried to give him my brightest smile. "Sure thing. Should I order another round?"

He hesitated. "Just wait until I get back. Maybe we can look at the cocktail menu and order something fancier?"

That was a resounding 'no', then.

The moment Alan left my sight I buried my head in my arms and gnashed my teeth. Another date ruined. Why couldn't I have left the serious chat for another night? Another date, several weeks or months down the line when, just maybe, the guy would like me enough to consider compromising with me?

Except there *was* no compromise between marriage and no marriage, and kids and no kids.

Feeling resigned but not nearly tipsy enough to go home yet I ordered another gin and tonic. After all, there was no point in staying sober only to witness in aching clarity the exact moment Alan blew me off.

I was going home alone tonight, and it was nobody's fault but mine.

Chapter Ten

TOM

I COULDN'T QUITE BELIEVE LIZ HADN'T yet noticed me in the bar. I was sitting in a corner booth with Daichi barely four metres away, but still she hadn't noticed my presence.

Was her date really so enthralling she hadn't taken note of her surroundings even once? And if that were the case...

God, I had to stop what I was doing. Liz was more than entitled to enjoy dating whomever she wanted, no interference from me required. The magnitude of my selfishness and sheer audacity was hitting me at a rate directly proportional to the gin and tonics I was knocking back.

"It's pretty clear what you're thinking about but I'll bite," Daichi said, amusement plain as day on his face. "What's got you looking so self-reflective?"

"The fact I need to stop acting like a fucking child," I sighed, glancing back at Liz even though it only made me feel worse. She looked amazing, wearing a backless dress that made me want to run my fingers down her spine, and curly wisps of hair framing her face that made me want to tuck them behind her ear, and that apricot lipstick that drove me absolutely mental with the urge to kiss her. Clearly she'd pulled out all the stops to impress her date.

"You could always, you know, talk to her like you're interested in her. That's usually what people do when they want someone to know they're attracted to them."

"Yeah, well, that would have been much easier if Liz hadn't gone and found a date immediately after moving into my house. What do I do if he's *the one* or whatever?"

At this Daichi spluttered out a laugh into his red wine. "Since when did you believe in any of that crap? Have you been reading too many of your mum's magazines?"

"You know what I mean. What if this completely average guy—"

"Average is a bit cruel, Tom. He's objectively good-looking. And he's making Liz laugh, and is engaging in what appears to be a very interesting conversation...if the fact Liz is yet to notice you spying on her is anything to go by."

"Just whose side are you on, exactly?"

"I'm on the side that hopes tonight gives you the kick up the arse you need to either step up or give up."

Daichi had me there. The problem was that – going by how well Liz's date was proceeding – I likely had to do the latter, and I didn't want to.

I was the biggest sham of an adult to have ever walked the earth.

"Let's just finish these drinks and leave, Dai," I finally decided, turning my attention away from Liz and her date. "It was wrong to have her come here just to spy on her."

To my surprise, however, Daichi shook his head. "We come here every Friday, and May doesn't finish work until midnight. I'm not leaving just because you decided to be an idiot."

"But—"

"And besides," Daichi continued, subtly pointing towards the door, "if we leave now then Liz will *definitely* recognise us, and then she'll know you suggested Blue Dog so you could spy on her. Which I have reason to believe wouldn't be a good thing."

He had me there.

Hoping Liz and her date wouldn't spend the entire night in my favourite bar – though if they left early I didn't imagine I'd like the reason why – I forced myself to while away the evening talking to Daichi about the repairs required for my lab. The damage report wasn't quite finalised, but the rough idea was that the entire lab needed redone. The repair work would take at *least* four months. It was the end of September now; that took me all the way to February or even March, well past my mother's wedding.

In four months just what would my relationship with Liz look like? If I gave up on pursuing her romantically, could I tolerate being friends? Was it something I could handle?

Right now the answer felt like a resounding *no*.

When Liz's date got up and headed to the toilets I followed suit before my brain could quite catch up with what my body had decided to do. The younger man had taken a cubicle; a moment or two later I heard him say hello to a friend. Updating them on his evening thus far, I could only assume. This was certainly one way of knowing just how well Liz's date was going – whether I wanted to hear it or not.

"She totally lied about looking for a relationship," her date said. "She's just like that girl I saw last week! Probably said she wanted something serious on her profile because she's gone through all the guys looking for one night stands."

I frowned at my reflection in the mirror as I washed my hands. That didn't sound like Liz at all. She struck me as the kind of person who wanted someone to simply be with and, given that she hadn't told me I'd change my mind after discovering I didn't want marriage or kids, I was inclined to believe she might also be veering in that direction. That didn't mean she *wasn't* looking for something serious, only that she knew precisely what her version of serious looked like.

Her date huffed indignantly after a few moments. "Exactly! It's so hard to find someone who isn't a slut these days. Think I'll just blow her off...don't want to risk catching anything. Such a fucking shame, though – she's hot."

And too good for you, you reprobate, I seethed, wishing to knock down the cubicle door to punch Liz's insolent date in the face on her behalf. Instead, I pulled myself together as best I could and headed back to Daichi.

"Liz doesn't look too good," he said the moment I sat down, having dutifully kept watch over her whilst I was away even though I'd never asked him to.

"Going by what her date was saying on the phone, I'd say that's a good thing."

"What do you – oh, hang on, that's May," Daichi said, when his phone buzzed and his screen lit up with his wife's name. I turned from him to give him some privacy for the call, which meant I saw when Liz's despicable date sat back down opposite her and began giving her whatever pathetic excuse he'd concocted to fob her off.

Once again my body moved before my brain knew what it was doing. I stormed towards their table with absolutely no plan in mind other than to make Liz look completely and utterly out of the bastard's league.

"It *is* you, Elizabeth," I announced loudly the moment I reached their booth. Liz's glum expression changed to one of incredulity – and then suspicion – when she turned her attention to who had interrupted her date and realised it was me.

"Tom? The hell are you doing here?"

"Blowing off some steam after you rejected me, clearly." I looked down my nose at her date, who was currently sizing me up and discovering that he was, in fact, inferior to me in almost every visible capacity. My arrogance played off sometimes. I waved a hand at the guy. "You turned me down for *this*? Seriously?"

Liz, to her credit, worked out what I was doing in the space of a second, though the raised eyebrow she threw at me told me she fully expected an explanation as to *why* I was doing this later on. "He isn't a dick," she said, "and he doesn't think having *millions* in the bank means he can automatically buy a date with me. I told you already I'm not interested, Tom. Just leave me alone."

"Fine then, be a bitch. Have fun with your beta boyfriend. I'm sure he'll fucking suck in bed."

"Not as much as you would have, I'm sure."

I had never called a woman a 'bitch' once in my entire life, but it sold the character. Liz's date looked from her, to me, then back again, his expression turned appraising now he saw Liz in a different light. There was nothing like seeing someone interested in the person you're pursuing to ramp up that interest. Obviously I hoped Liz would now turn him down, but that was up to her to decide and I knew it.

This would be the last time I interfered in her life. For her sake, as well as mine, it *had* to be.

When I returned to my table Daichi had thrown on his jacket and was getting ready to leave. "I thought you wanted to stay?" I asked, crestfallen. I'd gotten into the mindset to get well and truly wasted tonight after what I'd just done.

Daichi shook his head apologetically, though he was grinning like a mad man. "May got off early."

"She *never* gets off early."

"Exactly. Sorry, Tom, but a Friday night in with the wife trumps drinking with your grumpy, tortured self."

"I should be offended."

"And yet."

"And yet. Go have fun, you arsehole. Say hi to May for me."

"Will do," Daichi said, wasting no time in rushing out of the bar with the barest of waves. " I'll make up for it next week."

"No need!" I called after my best friend, slumping in my seat and taking a large gulp of gin and tonic in the process. I didn't want Daichi treating me like someone who *needed* to see their best friend every Friday night in order to assuage their crippling fear of being alone. I'd never much minded not being in a serious relationship before, though admittedly in recent years I'd found myself becoming envious of what Daichi had with his wife.

Did that make me lonely? Did that mean I wanted a meaningful relationship?

I watched Liz pick up her belongings, bid good-bye to her date and rush for the toilet, and a score of butterflies filled my stomach to mix uncomfortably with the gin.

Okay, I guess it did.

I didn't really want to go home. Likewise I knew that sitting in a bar alone at my age was bordering on pathetic. But I'd just about gotten a decent buzz on, and I wasn't interested in sitting with Mum and Jim as they watched *Eight out of Ten Cats* or whatever film would currently be showing on Channel Five.

"Is he gone?" a low, feminine voice murmured into my ear, causing me to just barely avoid spilling the rest of my drink down my shirt. It was Liz, hiding in the booth right behind my back to make sure her date had left the bar. She sighed in relief when it became clear the man had gone.

It was useless to try and stop the thumping of my heart from heating the entirety of my face at Liz's new-found proximity. I turned around to address her directly, thankful for the gin that could explain the flush across my cheeks. "Might I ask why you're hiding from him?"

"Might I ask why you interrupted my date?" she countered,

rightfully suspicious. This close to me I could smell her hair. It smelled like my shampoo. *My* shampoo. Coconuts and lime. It was amazing. "Or why you're here in the first place? I thought I just saw Professor It—Daichi leave."

I wondered how to explain my presence. It would be easy to tell Liz that Daichi and I came here every Friday, and I'd recommended the bar because we liked it. Then I could tell her I was going home, and she was free to come with me or not.

Except, now that she was sitting here beside me, the last thing I wanted to do was leave.

I offered Liz a smile. "Might I ask if you want a drink?" I offered in lieu of answering her question. "I'm buying. May as well use all those *millions* I have for something."

Slowly, conspirationally, Liz returned my smile. She squeezed my shoulder – fuck, her touch sent jolts of electricity straight through me – then stood up to head to the bar.

"I might be inclined to say yes. See, I just had a shitty date, and I *might* want to get wasted."

Oh, this was a terrible idea. It was the night we met all over again.

I pulled out my wallet. "No mimosas."

"Definitely not. I was thinking gin."

"A woman after my own heart."

There was a pause just before Liz replied, and I thought I'd royally fucked up once more. But then I saw a blush creep up her neck, just behind her ears, and Liz tucked an errant strand of hair across the heat of her skin. "...best make mine a double."

Chapter Eleven

LIZ

How was it that I'd gone from having a date with a guy I'd thought was great to getting trashed with my least-favourite-person-turned-house-mate-turned-future-step-brother?

"So why are you here?" I asked Tom, after we'd spent a few minutes talking about the state of his burned-down lab. It had seemed an appropriate – polite – topic of conversation to start with, all things considered.

But now it was time to ask the real questions.

"Oh, Daichi and I come here every Friday," Tom said, waving a dismissive hand as if this were hardly important in the least. "We're regulars; the staff always keep this booth free for us. Best seats in the bar." Looking around I realised he was correct – it was far enough from the piano that any live music wouldn't play directly in your ears but close enough to the bar that you hardly had to travel far to order a drink.

It also had an unobstructed view of every other table and booth in the room, whilst staying conveniently hidden from view itself by the bar.

I narrowed my eyes. "So you recommended I come here on

my date knowing full well you'd be here?" Tom nodded. "Why?"

"I was curious," he freely admitted, which in truth was not what I had expected Tom to say at all. But then again, what had I actually expected he say? I realised, then, that I hardly knew anything about Thomas Henderson. He was a geneticist, and he liked anime, and he was the strictest PhD assessor anybody on earth could ever have the misfortune of having if they happened to be named Elizabeth Maclean.

Other than that? Nothing. I knew nothing about this man.

Tom stretched his long-limbed arms above his head; the line of his muscles beneath the clearly very soft material of his maroon shirt distracted me to no end. When his shoulder audibly popped he sighed in relief. "That's been bothering me for hours."

"Are you going to elaborate on why you were curious or am I supposed to somehow deduce the answer?" I pressed, determined not to let Tom change the subject...or distract me with his physical presence.

"Given our recent, shared series of unexpected events I guess I wanted to know what kind of person you'd agree to going on a blind date with," he said, ruffling his hair back before taking a sip of his gin, not once taking his eyes off mine.

"But *why?*"

"Because I want to know more about who you are outside of being Dr Maclean. Aren't you curious about who I am outside of work?"

The sincerity of Tom's statement stunned me to silence, especially considering I'd only just been thinking how little I knew about him. But how could Tom say such a thing out loud so easily? Especially after, well, everything? Did it simply not register in his brain that him being awful to me in my assessments might incline me towards hating him rather than wanting to get to know him?

But that wasn't right. Tom knew he was hard on me, and he knew full well I hated him. He'd already admitted to that. So then...was his change of heart purely to do with the fact our parents were getting married, so he'd concluded he had to put some effort in? Was that all it was?

Why was that answer so disappointing to me?

"Elizabeth?" Tom murmured, voice barely audible over the din of the bar. He waved a hand in front of my face. "Are you there?"

I batted his hand away, knowing I should be irritated by the patronising action but feeling flustered instead.

I wanted *Tom* to be flustered by our unexpected evening together, not me.

"Say I *am* curious about you," I said, choosing my words very carefully, "will you enlighten me on what makes the great Professor Thomas Henderson the arrogantly sunny arsehole I so far know him to be?"

Tom laughed at my remark. Of course he did. Nothing ever seemed to faze him for longer than a second. "I guess that depends on what you want to know...and how set you are on hating me no matter what."

"Answer my questions and I guess we'll find out."

"Then answer mine, too, and perhaps the evening can end up being a success for both of us."

It would have been easy to say no. To say I'd rather go home – *Tom's* home – and wallow in bed about Alan and his dramatic change in attitude. But it was a Friday night and everything had been absolutely mental lately. So what if my drinking partner was Tom? I'd grill him about his life and work out what made him tick, then use that to my advantage going forward. Good, old-fashioned research was my speciality, after all.

Too bad it was also Tom's.

I knocked my glass against his, offering Tom a conspirational grin that felt annoyingly close to genuine. "Deal," I said, feeling as if I was signing my soul away to the devil who sat beside me. "Where did you grow up?"

"Balloch, then Glasgow. You?"

"Stirling, then Glasgow."

"Ah, I knew there was a reason I find your accent so lovely."

"Have you always been a massive flirt or did you grow into that?"

Tom chuckled good-naturedly, then reclined against the back of the booth in a way that could only be described as *elegant*. He looked so completely at ease I almost wanted to slap him just to see if it would bother him. But I wasn't choosing violence today.

"I suppose I've always been a flirt," Tom said, surprising me by actually answering the question. "Mum likes to embarrass me with tales of her friends all smothering me with love and attention when I was young. Clearly I got used to it."

"Hmm. Explains a lot."

"Well, what about you?" Tom countered, casting a sidelong glance at me that sent shivers down my spine, damnably exposed by virtue of me wearing a low-backed dress.

"What about me what?" I asked, frowning at the question. Just what was he getting at? "I'm not a flirt."

"Ah, so you're oblivious to it. Now *that* explains a lot."

"And what is that supposed to mean?!"

"It means that I imagine there's a fairly lengthy string of men who have been left unknowingly heartbroken by your hands throughout the years."

Just when had Tom drawn this conclusion about me? Who had he been watching me talk to in order to draw it? "Hey, I can't be held responsible for how someone feels if they never make said feelings about me known," I said, hoping that might needle Tom into elaborating who exactly he meant.

"Of course," Tom agreed, not taking my bait. "That doesn't change the facts, though." A pause. Another sip of gin. Another flick of Tom's gaze from my head to my toes. Another shiver down my spine. "So why did you turn down your date at the end there?"

I considered not telling him why. It was humiliating, really, that Alan had only shown interest in me again after Tom *feigned* interest in me. "We wanted different things," I eventually said, which was at least half-true.

Something that looked like understanding crossed with sympathy flitted across Tom's face. "That age-old problem. Something tells me you've been burned by that before."

"And what makes you think that?"

"You want to settle down but don't want marriage or kids," he said. All I could do was stare at him. I'd never told Tom that, had I? When his mum asked about me being unattached I'd said I was happily single and left it at that. "I made that observation on my own but feel free to correct me if I'm wrong," Tom added on quickly, in response to my complete and utter confusion.

"It's...not wrong," I admitted, swallowing a lump in my throat that felt awfully like a physical manifestation of *the fear of being known*. Tom had said he wanted to learn more about me so how was it that he'd found out so much already? Surely there had to be a limit to how observant a person was.

"That's still a tough pill for a lot of people to swallow," Tom said, when I didn't offer him any further details. "Despite the fact more and more folk are choosing to go down that route. What with the planet being fucked and all."

I sniggered before I could stop myself at the off-hand way he mentioned our inevitable demise. And then I remembered: Tom himself didn't want to get married or have kids. Was that why he'd guessed that I didn't, too? Had he sensed a kindred spirit of sorts in me, somehow? And if that were the case, was *he* happily single or did he, too, want to settle down?

"Your mum seems intent on you settling down," I said, testing my theory. "Do you not want to?"

Tom ruffled a hand through his hair again then downed his drink. Checking to see that mine was empty, too, he signalled to the bartender who promptly began preparing two more gin and tonics. Being a regular clearly had its perks.

"I suppose I never thought about it before," Tom said. And then, a little hesitantly, "Though lately it's been on my mind."

"Only lately?"

He nodded. "I've always been busy with work or friends or travel. Or I'm helping Mum pick out new curtains for her house." He laughed softly, but it sounded sad, which is how I knew he was going to talk about his father. "Before Dad was diagnosed I thought I had all the time in the world to decide whether I wanted a family or a partner. But then he got sick so fast, and then he was gone. I was seeing someone at the time who I'd sort-of thought might be the woman I'd settle down with, but after Dad's death I realised our relationship was pretty empty. So I broke it off with her."

It would have been easy for the two of us to wallow in companionable sadness, then. For the night to devolve into the exchanging of stories about our respective deceased parents, and with every gin we drank we'd get ever closer to tears. But it was clear from the way Tom held himself, and the way he shook his head as if that alone was enough to rid himself of negative thoughts, that he didn't want the evening to go down that route.

I didn't, either.

I kept my tone light and asked, "And you've been happily unattached every since?"

"Not necessarily happily, but yes." After a few seconds of quiet between us punctuated only by the sound of the piano playing a particularly erratic melody, the atmosphere between me and Tom headed back into easy and – if I had the balls to admit it – flirtatious territory. "So what about you?" Tom pressed, continuing our conversation. "Any long-term partners before?"

My stomach twisted uncomfortably as it always did when Elliot was brought up in one way or another. But Tom had been honest with me so far. For tonight, at least, I was determined to do the same. "I had a boyfriend during the final two years of my undergrad. He wanted me to move to California with him when he was offered a PhD over there; I wanted him to stay so I could study *here*. You can work out what happened."

Tom considered this for a moment. He sidled closer to me by a few inches, close enough for our shoulders to brush against each other. I didn't move away.   "When we met," he murmured, "would that have been just after you broke it off with him?"

"Ah, no," I laughed nervously. God, Tom was so close. Too close. "Eli broke up with *me*, not the other way around. On the day we graduated, actually, so four months before I...met you. I was willing to try long-distance but he said that wouldn't work if we were going to seriously consider our future together."

"Let me guess, complete with marriage and kids?"

"And a holiday in Tenerife."

When Tom laughed the sound seemed to vibrate right through me, sending a wave of heat down my neck. The only thought in my stupid brain was that if I turned my head to the right it would be the easiest thing in the world to kiss him. God, this entire night was fodder for the forbidden gutter.

"I didn't realise you eavesdropped literally the entire time I was out for Henry's stag-do," Tom said, thoroughly amused by the prospect. When the bartender dropped off our new drinks Tom shifted away from me slightly so he could use his left hand to pick up his drink. It was then that I realised Tom was left-handed, though I'd seen him write before without taking in that piece of information. It was a pointless thing to observe, all things considered, but in our current situation something about learning which of Tom's hands was dominant felt entirely dirty.

"It was hard not to overhear your friends," I said, finding it very difficult to concentrate on our conversation now every nerve in my body was attuned to Tom's physical presence beside me. "They were incredibly loud. And obnoxiously married."

Tom waved a dismissive hand. "They're not that bad. Most of the time."

"They were also *all* eyeing me up – even groom-to-be Henry."

Something dark flashed across Tom's expression, and with a seamless slide across the seat he closed the distance between us once more. He rested his arm on the top of the leather booth, behind my head, and leaned in towards my ear. His next words were a bare, whispered vibration against my skin.

"Then I guess they're all arseholes with exceptional taste."

God, I wanted Tom to put his mouth somewhere other than my ear so badly I thought my head might explode. I wanted him to pull an old-fashioned James Bond and kiss me even though I hadn't indicated that I consented to such a thing. I had to put some distance between us.

Fast.

"A-anyway," I stuttered, squeezing my thighs together as if the pressure could somehow stop the rush of chemicals flowing from my brain telling my body to wake the fuck up and prepare to get screwed, "it must be weird being the only one out of your friends who isn't married."

"I guess neither of us are doing very well on the whole long-term relationship thing, then," Tom said, sounding far too pleased about this. I risked turning my entire body towards him so I could actually talk to his face...and stop him whispering words into my ear until I lost all sense of reason entirely. It had been way too long since I'd had sex. It was going to be the proverbial death of me.

Hadn't that been the point of going on a date in the first place? To get rid of these depraved, traitorous desires aimed at Tom? I had failed miserably.

Tom had the sort-of decency to move away a few inches, though the way he leaned on his arm towards me, boxing us into the corner of the booth, suggested he had no intention of moving any further.

"...oh, come off it," I said, brain working overtime to process what he'd just said to me in order to formulate an appropriate response, "all you'd have to do is say *hello* to a woman in the right way and she'd be all over you." I made a pointed gesture towards...well, his entire frame. Tom *had* to know what he was doing right now. He was clearly doing it to fuck with me, given our current topic of conversation.

I couldn't let him win whatever challenge this was we'd entered into. I had to fight back.

The smallest smile curled Tom's lips. "It's gratifying you think so highly of my charm."

"Yeah, well, charm only gets you so far," I said, cocking my head to the side and daring to make a show of crossing my legs. When my foot clipped Tom's ankle I deliberately hit him a little too hard. He shivered at the unexpected touch. "Though I guess it's all you need when you look like, well, you."

Tom quizzed over this statement for a second. "Why do I feel like that's a back-handed compliment? What's the catch?"

"From my experience of guys who seem to have everything going for them, they tend to be somewhat...lacking...where it counts."

"Ah, yes, there's the catch." Tom's eyes glittered dangerously in the low light of the bar. When he leaned closer I mirrored his movement. "What makes you think I'm bad in bed?"

"What makes you think that's what I was referring to?"

"Is that what you were referring to?"

"Yes." No point in lying. I wanted to see what Tom would say back.

"Well I'm sorry to disappoint you, Elizabeth," Tom said, his voice taking on the critical tone he'd used in my PhD assessments to alarming effect, "but my arrogance in fact extends to being confident in the bedroom. Clearly you've just been rubbish at choosing men so far."

Well, fuck.

I wet my lips before I replied; Tom watched me do so with pupils so dilated I could hardly make out his irises. "How can I know if your arrogance is deserved? You could be lying though your teeth – or, even worse, you could genuinely believe you're any kind of good when in reality you're *all* kinds of terrible."

"Why don't you kiss me and find out?"

"...excuse me?"

"I'd suggest fucking on the table but something tells me the rest of the bar wouldn't appreciate that."

The slow grin that crept across Tom's face was wickedly perverted as he took in my appalled reaction. Except I wasn't appalled. Well, not nearly as much as I should have been, given what he'd just insinuated. Here Tom was, assuming the issue with us fucking on the table wasn't whether I wanted to do it or not but whether anyone else would have issue with such a public affair! He was so sure of himself I couldn't stand it.

He was so sure of himself because he was right.

It didn't matter if I was only entertaining the idea of sleeping with Tom because I'd been drinking – he'd been drinking, too. Who was to say he'd want to sleep with me sober, either? The two of us were being equally reckless fools, playing a game of horny chicken until only one of reigned victorious.

Well, I'd be damned if the victor was Tom.

"Okay, then," I said, heart thumping with anticipation of

Tom's reaction. Surely he'd be shocked. No way did he expect me to *actually* say yes.

But I didn't have time to gauge any kind of visual reaction from him. Before I knew it Tom's hand – the one that had been resting on the leather seat behind me – snaked into my hair and pushed my lips against his.

Just like that, he kissed me.

My first, numb impression was that Tom tasted of gin, floral and lemony. But then he tilted my head back and gently used his entire body to press me against the booth, and all such insignificant thoughts like gin were lost to the wind.

Tom's kiss was soft and slow, his mouth moulding to mine as he tested what worked and what didn't. He caught my lower lip between his teeth, sucking on it when I didn't pull away.

The action teased out a moan from the back of my throat I'd been holding onto for a shamefully long time.

At the sound Tom's entire frame stiffened, and his eyes fluttered open. It was then I realised that I hadn't closed mine at all, though for the life of me I couldn't recall being able to *see* anything over the course of the last few seconds.

"Close your eyes, Liz," Tom murmured, the words an order spoken directly into my mouth. My hands were trembling by my sides, begging to be used, so I slid my fingers up the front of Tom's maroon shirt. It confirmed my suspicions that the material was soft as sin.

I wanted it gone, gone, gone.

Tom resumed our kiss immediately. This time I closed my eyes, as ordered, and when Tom dipped his head lower to mine I opened my mouth and tugged at his collar until he ran his tongue over my teeth and deepened the kiss with an urgency I'd never experienced before.

What I *did* know, with a certainty that ached between my thighs, was that if Tom suggested we sleep together tonight I'd let him fuck me senseless until morning. Hell, screw waiting for him to suggest it. *I'd* suggest it.

I brushed my right hand up his neck and along his ear, tucking curls of his hair behind it as I did so. This time Tom was the one who moaned, a guttural sound which awakened something feral in me that had lain dormant for what felt like forever. Then—

"Last orders!" the bartender called out, ringing a tinny bell that brought me and Tom back to such startling reality that our eyes flew open and we stared at each other, half-possessed and unable to move, for several agonising seconds.

Tom's face was so flushed a stranger might have thought him feverish. His lips were swollen and wet; the Adam's apple of his throat heaved with every breath he took.

"Liz," he uttered, my name barely audible against the noise of the bar. But it was enough to send me tumbling back to reality.

This was *Thomas Henderson* I was kissing. Professor bloody Henderson. I was supposed to be fucking *with* him as revenge for my PhD assessments, not full-on fucking him.

"Home," I bit out. "Home. We should leave. Dad will be waiting up for me."

If Tom's eyes lit up at my first statement, the light was gone by the time I mentioned my dad. There was no quicker way for me to point out that what was currently happening...well, was not going to continue happening, than mentioning my dad.

"...home," Tom relented, moving out of my personal space – out of the bubble we'd created where only ourselves and our stupid wanton brains had existed – with obvious reluctance. "You're right. I never meant to stay out so late." He stood up, pulling on his jacket before handing me mine, all without looking me in the eye.

In the morning Tom would agree that stopping now was the right thing to do. He didn't really want this. I didn't really want this. We had simply needed a distraction for the evening. That plus gin was a dangerous combination, and we both knew it.

So why did Tom have the audacity to look so disappointed...
and why did I feel that way, too?

Chapter Twelve

TOM

Never had I experienced so much awkwardness during a taxi ride before, not even during bumbling one night stands back in my undergrad. Liz and I were looking out of opposite windows in the black city cab, her watching the rain begin to fall in earnest whilst I watched her in the reflection off the glass. Her face was impossibly blank and unreadable.

I wanted to break the silence between us. *Had* to break it. What happened in the bar felt too real to be a stupid drunken dare, though it had surely started out as one. But considering how much Liz purported to dislike me I'd never expected her to rise to my ridiculous challenge.

The way she'd kissed me back felt like nothing even close to hatred. It felt...well, it felt fucking incredible. I ran a hand over my mouth, willing my brain to commit to memory every minute detail of how Liz's lips had worked against mine. God, I was reeling from a damn kiss like a hormonal teenager, that's how good a kiss it had been.

The way Liz had touched my neck, my hair, my ear, willing me closer to her, told me all I needed to know about *her* thoughts on the kiss.

And yet she'd put a clear end to the night. A clear end to *us*...whatever we had been for the last few hours. Could I consider the evening a date? It certainly felt like one.

I doubted Liz would call it that. Already she had retreated from me as far as she physically could within the confines of the taxi, making it painfully apparent that trying to continue where we left off in the bar was firmly off the table.

Off the table, I mused, turning from the window to look at Liz in person. She resolutely continued staring through the window. *When I joked about screwing on the table she looked like she might have said yes.*

"Fuck..." I muttered under my breath before I could bite back the word. I was getting hard merely thinking about it. I twisted my legs away from Liz when she glanced in my direction.

"What was that?" she asked.

"Nothing. It's raining a lot, isn't it?"

"It's Glasgow. Of course it's raining."

"I suppose you're right."

Could I really think of nothing better to fall back on than the weather? Where had all my charm and wit from back at the bar gone to?

When Liz's phone buzzed and lit up with a notification she eagerly checked it out, pleased for an excuse not to have to talk to me. But as she read the screen a frown darkened her lovely face, and she heaved out a sigh. Without replying to the notification she slid her phone back into her bag.

"Something wrong?" I dared venture. I couldn't let the night end on such a silent, awkward note. If we reached the front door of my house without getting back on better ground I knew, without a shadow of a doubt, that Liz would go back to blithely ignoring me.

Liz caught my eye, immediately blushed, then fixed her attention on the window once more. "It was Alan."

"Alan?"

"My date. The one you sabotaged."

"I didn't—"

"What would *you* have called what you did?" Liz countered, her reflection staring at me with an intensity she clearly couldn't handle directly.

"I was...I don't know. Trying to help, I guess."

"You never told me why. You couldn't have possibly heard what we were saying over the music. So what made you interrupt the way you did?"

I could have lied, but at this point I didn't see why I should. "I overheard him calling a friend when I went down to the toilets," I admitted, scratching my nose self-consciously at the confession. "He was...not being kind about you. "

"Oh."

Going by the tension in Liz's shoulders and the set of her mouth she didn't need me to elaborate any further. Even though I could only see her reflection I could tell her eyes had become a little too bright.

I reached out a hand towards her before I could stop myself. "Liz—"

"I guess I should thank you for making me look a little less pathetic, then," Liz said, voice clipped. She deftly avoided my touch with a twist of her shoulder, though in return she finally looked me in the eye. "And it makes me feel a whole lot better about not replying to his shite apology. He actually invited me to his place so he could *apologise properly.*" Liz offered me a self-deprecating chuckle. "If you hadn't done anything I probably would have said yes to going back to his. How fucking stupid is that?"

Something dark and ugly festered inside me at the thought

of Liz going back to the bastard's flat even after everything he'd done. "...would I be out of line to say you should have more self-esteem?" I said, knowing I was risking Liz decking me in the face for saying as much. "And that you should raise your standards?"

"You know, after meeting another arsehole a few years ago I told myself the same thing," Liz said, a glint in her eye that told me I was very much supposed to take the jibe as being aimed directly at me.

I deserved it. Of course I deserved it. But I was desperate for another chance. The only problem was: how did I go about appealing to Liz that people could change and were deserving of a second chance without that including every other prick that wanted to get into her pants?

When the taxi crunched to a halt on the gravelled driveway our stilted conversation was put on pause. Liz thanked the taxi driver and got out of the car whilst I paid, though she politely waited for me to join her before heading over to the front door, despite the rain.

Sometimes progress was the little things.

Liz moved to the side so I could unlock the storm door and then the front door proper, brushing past me when I held both open for her. I wanted to grab her hand, to hug her, to do *anything* that would stop the night from being over. We'd had a dizzying couple of hours of gin-fuelled fun together, but if I did nothing then that was all it ever would be: the product of alcohol.

"Liz," I said, as she fumbled in the darkness for the light switch. I put my hand over the switch just as she reached it, angling my body against hers until her back was to the wall. She tilted her head up, eyes bright with confusion.

And excitement.

"What is it?" she asked in an undertone, not wishing to disturb the quiet of the house. Hadn't she said her dad would be waiting up for her? Clearly that had been a lie to fob me off.

Reject me before I could make my intentions clear. Which meant I only had this one shot.

"I like you. A lot. That isn't the gin talking, though I know you probably don't believe that."

Liz simply stared at me, though when I inched closer to her I felt the throbbing of her heart against her chest keeping imperfect time with mine. She didn't move away, not even when I raised my hand to graze my fingertips over the line of her jaw.

Then she swallowed, glancing down at my hand before tilting her chin up. A better angle for me to kiss her. A sign that this was okay.

I bent my head down.

"Lizzie, is that you?" Jim Maclean called out, voice booming down the stairs like a crack of thunder. I recoiled from Liz just in time for her dad to turn the light on using the switch at the top of the stairs.

Liz waved bashfully at Jim's grumpy exterior. "Hi, Dad."

"You promised you wouldn't be out late."

"I made no such promises."

It was then Jim noticed I was standing in the hallway, too. His frown deepened with obvious suspicion. "What are you both doing down there?"

"Nothing," Liz lied smoothly. Had she always been such a flawless liar? She wasn't flustered in the slightest. "We ran into each other in town. He paid for our taxi back."

Jim chewed over this information, in search of something he could complain about. Finding nothing, he finally smiled at his daughter. "Get to bed, then. We're going shopping in Edinburgh tomorrow, remember?"

"I never forgot in the first place. Night, Dad."

"Night, Lizzie." A pause. "Tom."

"Good night," I offered, and then the man disappeared into his bedroom. I turned to Liz. "I—"

"I'm going to bed," Liz cut in, scurrying up the stairs faster than my brain could comprehend what she was doing. But as I stood there, alone and stunned, I realised that at least I could be safe in the knowledge that I'd done it: I'd told Elizabeth Maclean how I felt about her.

And she hadn't immediately rejected me.

I could take that as a win, right? That was no small thing.

All I had to do was work out where we went from here.

Chapter Thirteen

LIZ

"Okay, I understand. Please let me know if anything else shows up."

I hung up my phone, banging my head against the back of the desk chair I was sitting on in the computer room of Daichi's lab. I was having the worst luck with my flat-hunt, made even worse by my already rotten mood.

"What's with the woe-is-me sighing today?" the very reason for my rotten mood asked. Tom popped his head around the door frame of Daichi's office, polite curiosity plastered across his stupid face. Complaining to Tom was better than huffing to myself, though, especially when Chloë and Peter were away getting their 'morning' (three in the afternoon) coffee.

I scowled. "Another flat I wanted to view has been taken. Already. How am I supposed to get a bloody place to live when all the flats I want are taken by undergrads who can go to viewings at like ten in the morning on a Tuesday? I can't compete."

"That must be frustrating," Tom said, as if we frequently talked to each other about our banal life problems. Over the last six days he hadn't once acknowledged that we, well, kissed each other's faces off. Never mind the fact *he said he liked me.*

What did that even mean, that Tom liked me? Since when? It had to have been pretty recently, right? I was sure he'd only said it because he was drunk even though he'd insisted, whilst intoxicated, that it wasn't.

But though he hadn't brought up our bizarre and impossible evening together even once, something about Tom's demeanour towards me had changed nonetheless. It was as if he'd stopped being careful about what he said to me and how he said it, which of course made me realise he'd been careful about what he said to me *before.*

I didn't know how to proceed with Tom going forward, with all of that in mind.

I sighed again, spinning on the desk chair like a five-year-old. "Looks like I'll be staying in your house for a while longer."

"How terrible for you." Tom moved from the door to lean against the desk I was in front of, then crossed his arms over his chest as he contemplated something. He held himself with the languid certainty of a rich white man who'd never had to worry about anything of significant importance his entire life. It was annoying that it suited him, but didn't make me hate him the way it should have.

"Just stay until the wedding," he said after a moment or two. "Saving three months of your salary will work wonders towards buying a place."

"...I know that," I said, frowning at him. Just what was his angle here? "But I have to live with *you.*"

I wasn't sure what kind of reaction I wanted my insult to have, but Tom merely rolled his eyes. "You know it's a good deal, living with me notwithstanding. Your dad'll be ecstatic. And I know you've been enjoying spending hours in my bloody bathroom."

That was true. On more than one occasion my excessive

usage of the steam room, enormous bubble jet bath and even bigger shower had resulted in Tom having to moodily stalk downstairs to use the first floor bathroom that his mum had appropriated as her own.

I risked a smile in Tom's direction. "There are perks to living in a Park Circus mansion, I admit. Fine. Until the wedding it is. At least I won't have to pay any energy bills over winter."

"And who said you're getting away with that?"

"You did, by being many times wealthier than I could ever aspire to be."

"You're a precocious brat sometimes," Tom chuckled, spinning my chair for me when it slowed to a halt. I grabbed at his arm when he put far too much force into the spin, threatening to topple me to the floor, but he deftly moved out of reach. I just barely managed to keep my balance by gripping the table on my fourth spin.

Tom guffawed whilst I tried and failed to regain my composure. "Who's acting like the brat now?!" I countered, blowing stray strands of hair out of my face. "...and besides, I can't be precocious at twenty-seven. Go look at a dictionary sometime."

"You wound me."

"Somehow I—"

"How are you getting on with those enhancer trap lines, Liz?" Daichi said as he swanned out of his office, stopping my stupid conversation with Tom in its tracks. I quickly righted myself in my chair and brought up the email I'd been about to read when the estate agent called and threatened to ruin my day. Funny, I wasn't in nearly as bad a mood now as I had been after hanging up.

"It says here they should be finished sequencing them by next Tuesday," I informed my boss, scanning the email for all appropriate information. "I'll get started on a third batch of flies tomorrow morning."

"Grand," Daichi said, then to Tom, "stop bothering my postdoc. Go do some work."

Tom snickered. "I have two gels running right now, and I'll have you know I got in before you this morning. I'm taking a break. And I thought you said I could commandeer Liz to help with *my* experiments for a while?"

"Excuse me?" I interrupted, spinning from the computer screen to face my boss. "I never heard about this."

The man had the good sense to look ashamed. "It may have been said in jest. Under no circumstances did I ever expect the two of you to work together, given..." He waved towards us in a way that made 'me and Tom' feel like far more of an official thing that it had any right to be. After all, there *was* no 'me and Tom'.

So why had he said he liked me?

As Daichi and Tom engaged in a friendly battle of insults with each other the door to the computer room opened. A red-faced Chloë and Peter came stumbling in.

Chloë waved at Daichi as she handed me a mocha. "Professor Ito," she said. "I hope you don't mind the imposition before I head off to do some, you know, actual work."

"Not at all. I'm fast becoming used to you as a regular fixture between my two postdocs."

Peter, Chloë and I grinned at each other. All thing considered, working in the Functional Genomics lab was shaping up to be exactly as fun and interesting as I'd hoped it would be *before* Thomas Henderson nosedived into my life once more. It was odd how quickly you got used to something unpleasant and inevitable.

The only problem was...how unpleasant *was* Tom to me, now? I could hardly deny what happened on Friday. Not just the kiss and the confession, but how Tom stood up for me against Alan so I could walk away from the encounter with a modicum of dignity intact, earned or otherwise.

But that didn't mean I suddenly liked the guy, or that I was completely over wanting to screw with him as revenge for my hellish PhD assessments. Tom was going to be part of my life for the foreseeable future thanks to our parents getting married, so yeah, I couldn't go *insane* with my revenge, but I didn't have to abandon it entirely.

After all, over the last few days Tom's confession of his so-called feelings had only added fodder to my vengeance ideas.

"Right, Saturday," Peter said, not all that subtly firing a glare at Tom until he moved away from the desk to allow Peter to sit on the chair next to me. He nudged my arm when I didn't respond. "Liz?"

"What about Saturday?" I asked. I tried a sip of my mocha but it was far too hot to drink. "We don't have plans, do we?"

"No," Chloë said, "but Peter and I thought it would be fun to go climbing in the southside. We've been meaning to try the centre down there for months now!"

"Ah, damn it. That sounds like fun."

"But...?"

I couldn't help but catch Tom's eye as I admitted, "I have a date."

His previously upbeat demeanour vanished in an instant, though Tom maintained a strained smile on his face. "Have you tried finding this one from somewhere other than Tinder?" he asked, much to the shock and scandal of our collective audience of best friends.

Well, if he was going to play the pointed jibe game, so was I. "Have you tried shutting the fuck up?"

"Not yet."

"Then add it to your list of things to do today," I said, before turning my attention to Chloë and Peter. Peter seemed far too sad about me not being able to make it to climbing but, then again, I hadn't been able to afford to go since summer. He probably thought this had been a wonderfully spontaneous idea.

"How about Sunday?" I proffered. "I can do Sunday. My Saturday date is an afternoon one; I doubt I'll be hungover or whatever the next day."

"I'm going to Ikea with Harriet, unfortunately," Chloë said. Of course they were going to Ikea. Bloody lovebirds. I wanted to go to Ikea and pick out cheap Lack tables and lime-scented candles and indoor plants with a significant other, too. I just needed to find said significant other first.

"I'm free," Peter said, much perkier than he had been a moment ago.

"Then let's go for Sunday."

When I looked back in Tom's direction I discovered he'd left for our shared lab bench. If I was being honest I was far more interested in his reaction to my hastily-arranged Tinder date than the date itself. If the best way to make Tom suffer was to twist his feelings for me against him then so be it.

He'd earned a healthy dose of suffering.

Chapter fourteen

TOM

I ONLY EVER WORKED AT THE weekends when I was in dire need of a distraction. After Dad died I spent a lot of time in the lab pouring over protein purifications or *in vivo* activity assays or marking student lab reports.

The Saturday afternoon of Liz's date was most definitely something I needed to distract myself from.

Having exhausted the actual experiments I could set up during the afternoon, my evening work of choice was Daichi's poster for the conference in November. Since I was going in his stead I needed to know it better than *he* knew it – no matter how much Daichi insisted I didn't need to know a thing about his damn flies and their ideal usage as a model of age-related neurodegenerative disease.

"Why this font, Dai?" I wondered, raking my hands through my hair as I scanned the legends for his cell assays. "And what's with the borders on your tables?" The poster needed a complete formatting do-over.

I glanced at the time. It was barely seven; if Liz's date was going well then she probably wouldn't return home for hours yet...if she returned at all.

In an entirely uncharacteristic outward loss of temper I bashed my fist on the desk in front of me. Daichi's poster was in no way distracting me from my thoughts. Ever since I confessed to Liz I'd been sure things had been going smoother between us, with far more easy conversations flowing and not nearly so many glares thrown my way. But I'd been careful to give Liz as much space as I could muster so she could process what I'd told her. After all, I could hardly expect her to go straight from hating me – obvious physical attraction when drunk notwithstanding – to reciprocating my feelings.

But for her to arrange a date with another stranger so soon after I'd told her I liked her? It rankled me to no end. And the way Liz had looked at me when she announced said date...what had that meant? Had she arranged the date simply to spite me?

Surely not. That was me being arrogant again and assuming the world revolved around me. Liz had admitted that she was looking for a long-term relationship. If she didn't want one with a man she already knew of course that meant she had to seek out fresh faces.

"Screw this," I muttered, slamming my laptop shut, throwing it in my bag and then grabbing my jacket. If I was going to toil away all night overthinking I was as well doing it in the comfort of my own home. I could throw on *Vampire Hunter D* or *Ninja Scroll* to drown out the noise in my head with copious quantities of animated murder.

When I got outside I was supremely grateful I'd brought my car. It had been a grey but dry afternoon when I'd left for the lab; now a torrent of rain battered the pavement, filling potholes to the brim with water and clogging the storm drains on the roads with muck and leaves. I wasted no time in bolting for my car, glad for the lack of fellow Saturday researchers which left the parking spaces next to the lab blessedly empty.

The sun had set, reminding me that we had truly entered October and, with it, the promise of a wet, dark and windy winter. There was no such thing as a golden-leaved autumn in Glasgow, fuelled by vanilla chai lattes, woollen coats and dog walks in the park. Not that I actually had a dog, but I liked watching them in Kelvingrove Park when I went jogging.

When I pulled onto Dumbarton Road a strangely familiar figure caught my eye through the rain-splattered windshield. Hunched against the weather – with no discernible jacket on – was Liz, making her way back to what I could only assume was my house going by the direction she was headed in.

And the fact she was alone.

I beeped my horn as I pulled up to the kerb and skidded to a halt. Liz yelped and frantically turned around, scared senseless as she tried to work out what was going on.

"Get in," I said, a cruel grin spreading across my face when she realised she recognised who had driven up beside her. She justifiably gave me the finger. "You look like you chucked yourself in the Clyde. Where's your jacket?"

"It wasn't raining when I left," Liz grumbled, forgoing swearing profusely at me in favour of climbing into the warmth and shelter my car promised. But when she closed the door she shook out her hair and showered me in icy droplets, which I took as a physical alternative to 'fuck you'.

"Just because it wasn't raining when you—"

"Ugh. Don't go all parental on me."

"Insinuate I'm a dad again and I swear to god I'm going to assume you have a kink you don't want me knowing about."

Given the weather I couldn't risk taking my eyes away from the road but I could nonetheless tell that Liz didn't know how to respond to my comment. Taking her silence as a personal victory, I said, "I assume your date didn't go very well."

"He got a call from his fuck buddy and decided to take her up on her offer of immediate sex," Liz scowled. "That's what I get for agreeing to a date with a hot, blonde blues musician. Named *Josh*. Ugh, I should have known."

When we hit a traffic light I watched Liz as she wiped her face of excess water then immediately pulled out her phone. I caught her password without meaning to, in that way that brains always retain information they aren't supposed to have.

"What are you doing?" I asked, noticing that Liz was scrolling through one of her dating apps.

"Updating my preferences. Hell if I'm wasting time on arseholes like him again."

"Why don't you try meeting someone from literally anywhere else but a dating app?" I'd suggested the same thing in the lab but Liz had shot my answer down with her usual delightful snark. Now, however, as the traffic light changed to green and I took the turn-off for Park Circus, she gave me an actual answer.

"What would you have me do, Tom?" she demanded. "Join a club? Pick up a new hobby? Mingle at a comic con?"

"...is there a reason none of those are viable options?"

"I *like* what I do with my spare time already!" Liz complained. "I like climbing with Peter and Chloë – when I can afford it. I like playing board games with my old undergrad friends. I like spending time with my dad. And I like watching stupid Japanese cartoons with absolutely no intention of ever setting foot in a comic con. The smell and sheer volume of bodies at conventions would cause me to pass out. Never mind the harassment women receive as cosplayers."

"Ah, so cosplay isn't out of the picture so long as it's in private?"

"*Tom!*"

"Sorry," I snorted, "but you walked into that one." Liz said nothing: another silent victory for me. A few moments later, when I pulled onto the driveway, yanked up the handbrake and turned off the ignition, I asked, "So what you're saying is that you want to meet someone who won't change the way you already happily live your life. Would that be accurate?"

"Exactly. Exactly that."

"Then have fun staying single."

"How can you just out and say that?" Liz threw at me, slamming the passenger door shut and huddling onto the porch step alongside me, away from the rain, whilst I fumbled with the key.

"I can say it because it's the truth, Liz," I said, deciding to answer her question seriously. "If you're not willing to step out of your comfort zone or compromise on the little things then you'll end up compromising on the *big things* just to make a relationship work. Which I know *you* know is the worst-case scenario, and should be avoided at all costs."

Liz desperately looked like she wanted to argue with me, but then she sagged as if all the fight had been punched out of her. "I'm going for a bath," she muttered, hanging up her sodden jacket and dumping her handbag by her shoes on the rack the moment I unlocked the door. When she stomped up the stairs my mum came out to say hello, but I mouthed *don't ask* at her and she retreated into the warmth of her lounge.

My eyes zeroed in on Liz's bag as I hung up my own jacket; inside it her phone had begun buzzing with new notifications. I knew I had to stop interfering in her life. Of course I did. Looking at her phone when she wasn't around was a line I should never cross.

I sold my soul and unlocked her phone, anyway.

Liz had several new matches on both Tinder and Bumble; three men had already initiated conversation with her. I blocked them immediately, then put her phone back in her bag and headed into the living room to get a fire going.

By the time I'd changed into comfier, drier clothes and the fire had begun heating the room up properly, Liz came sauntering in with damp hair and wearing a ridiculously oversized jumper that hung to her knees. Her legs and feet were bare.

"You'll catch your death of cold dressed like that," I said, chucking her a blanket when she sat down on the couch.

She scowled. "What did I say about you acting like a dad?"

"What did I say about that silly little kink of yours?"

Her face grew hotter than the damn fire. "...I don't have any kinks like that."

"Not a daddy one, at least, but I hardly have enough evidence to suggest you don't have *other* kinks. You're remarkably easy to wind up, you know that?" I added on, when a display of indignation from Liz became imminent. I held up three Blu-Rays as a peace offering. "*Vampire Hunter D, Ninja Scroll* or *Demon City Shinjuku?*"

At this Liz forgot her previous grumpiness in an instant. She leaned forward on the couch, flapping her hands towards me to take a closer look at the options. "I never had a TV in my old place, only my laptop," she murmured, checking out the special features on *Ninja Scroll* with a burning interest I knew all too well, "so I've never seen any of these on a big screen."

"Luckily for you I'm rich. So what'll it be?"

Liz considered her answer, glanced at the time, then offered me a small smile. "All three? It's only just turned eight."

"That's the answer I was hoping for. Takeaway?"

"Ramen or Indian."

"Indian it is."

I took a risk and sat beside Liz on the right-hand side of the couch, near the fire – though there was ample space on it elsewhere – and pulled out the recliner function. To my delight Liz put her feet up and settled in against me, throwing the blanket over both of us in the process. I could feel her bare legs rubbing against mine, filling me with regret that my legs were not similarly completely naked.

After we ordered food and began our anime marathon I noticed that Liz was watching me instead of the TV. "What?" I asked, hoping my face hadn't started flushing red like an idiot beneath her gaze. It was hard enough coping with the fact that Liz was most definitely not wearing a bra beneath her jumper; whenever she shifted position the softness of her ample chest brushed my arm, and I had to fight the knee-jerk reaction to pin her down onto the couch beneath me.

"Did you decide to do all of this just for me?"

It took me a moment to realise what Liz meant. "What, watch anime and eat karahi?" I said, waving towards the TV to emphasise my point. "Two of my favourite things to do on a Saturday night?"

"So you *just so happened* to decide that this was what your evening would look like completely independently of me saying this exact scenario was one of my favourite things?"

"Not entirely independently," I admitted. Then: "I had a shitty day."

Liz mulled this over, her bottom lip between her teeth an agonising distraction for me to bear witness to. "And that's...to do with me?" she concluded after a moment.

"You're clever enough to not need an answer for that."

But Liz didn't respond to my pointed comment, choosing to return her attention to the film, so I did the same. Her response made something clear to me, however: Liz knew what she was doing. She was aware of my feelings – she wasn't ignoring them.

Well if that were the case, and she was choosing to spend the evening curled up on the couch with me to watch TV until the early hours of the morning, I'd consider that progress.

Even if it came at the expense of balls so blue they were in danger of imploding.

Chapter fifteen

LIZ

SOMETHING WEIRD HAD BEEN GOING ON for the past two weeks with Tom. We'd spent several evenings watching all manner of anime and films and TV shows together, and aside from the first time we'd done so he hadn't once brought up the fact he liked me in any way, shape or form. Nor did he seem at all bothered by my sudden willingness to huddle close to him on the couch, sharing a blanket and wearing far too little considering it was October. I didn't know what his angle was, and it infuriated me.

What bothered me more was the fact I was having a really good time with him.

Okay, I guess it wasn't that weird that we'd been having a good time. Our tastes in films and TV, especially when it came to anime, were remarkably similar. It was so easy to forget who Tom was to me during my PhD in order to lie back on his stupidly ginormous couch, share a bottle of wine – whilst our parent did the same upstairs – and while away a couple of hours watching *Gundam* or *Hellraiser* or *Cyber City*.

But I *couldn't* forget who Tom was. I was in this for revenge, however petty it was. Once I was satisfied that I'd messed with him enough I'd back down and settle into my role as reluctant...ugh, step-sister. I was never going to get used to that. I shouldn't have to; it was wrong, plain and simple.

"Sister-in-law?" I tried aloud, wondering if I could get away with that instead. It certainly sounded more acceptable than step-sister. But acceptable to whom, exactly? Tom and me? That would involve me fully acknowledging I liked him far more than I was letting on...otherwise being adult step-siblings wouldn't bother me nearly as much as it did.

It was an unusually sunny morning in Glasgow, so I'd chosen to take my time getting to work by walking a longer route to the university in order to wind through Kelvingrove Park on my way there. Tom hadn't been around when I left which meant he'd probably been out jogging to the Clyde and back. God, I knew his schedule too well.

But now he was sitting at our lab bench, having somehow made it into work before me (even though he insisted he only used his car when it was raining), head in his hands in obvious despair. As I walked towards him it became obvious he couldn't hear my approach, so I made the incredibly mature decision to creep up on him and scare him shitless.

"*What are you doing?*" I breathed into Tom's ear, grabbing at his shoulders and squeezing with as much pressure as I could muster. They went rock hard beneath my hands in response. The sensation did plenty of wicked things to my own body, but since it was half past nine on a Wednesday morning and my dating app profiles had turned as sterile as a fucking desert I had no choice but to dungeon all my horny inclinations away for now.

"What's got you pulling out your perfect, pretty hair?" I asked, when Tom didn't immediately reply to my provocation.

Tom gave me a warning glare, signalling that he wasn't in the mood for joking around. He looked haggard and stressed.

I knew that look. Was achingly familiar with it.

Plonking down on my stool I grabbed his lab book, ignoring

his protests. "What isn't working, then? Spill."

"Liz, it's fine, so—"

"Stop lying and just tell me. Why are you crying over your lab book?"

For a moment it looked like Tom was going to complain again. But then he sighed, resigned, and said, "I need to purify one of my hybrid proteins but for the life of me I can't get it to overexpress. I've never had issues with it before, just to answer the question you're about to ask."

"Okay, smart Aleck, have you had to make more of it since moving over to this lab, or is this the first time?"

"First time. There's nothing wrong with my *E.coli* strains or the incubator, though, and the same batch of IPTG worked fine for Peter only last week. But I can't get the damn bacteria to grow enough to overexpress the protein."

From his bench Peter – who was at the tail end of a very long night of experiments, if the fact he could barely stand was anything to go by – nodded in agreement. He looked far too happy that something was fucking up Tom's lab work; I mouthed *behave* at him, though Peter ignored me on his way out of the lab.

Turning my attention to Tom's notes I searched for the likely culprit that was ruining his experiment, though I didn't expect to work it out off-the-bat given that Tom himself was flummoxed.

It was therefore to my surprise when I noticed what was wrong almost immediately. A small smile curled my lips, and I unsuccessfully muffled a laugh behind my hand.

Tom narrowed his eyes at me. "What's so funny?"

"This," I said, waving at his lab book. "Your mistake is funny. How can you not see it?"

"Are you going to help me or are you going to continue making fun of me?"

I was tempted to go with the latter, but the tired glaze of Tom's eyes was too familiar and pitiable for me to continue with my mocking. "Your chloramphenicol is ten times too concentrated," I said, pointing at Tom's calculation. "At that strength your poor *E.coli* won't even have a chance to grow unless you leave them overnight."

"You're fucking kidding me."

"Alas, I am not. Easy mistake to make."

"Not after fifteen bloody years of lab research..." Tom grumbled, checking the numbers to confirm that I was, in fact, correct.

Unlike his calculation.

"How did you clock this so fast?" Tom asked. "You barely read anything on the page."

I shrugged. "It happened to me during the second year of my PhD. You were the one who pointed out my mistake, actually, during my first assessment that year. You were very quick to criticise me for making such a – and I quote – *rookie error*."

For a moment neither of us moved. Then Tom turned his attention from his lab book to me, on the verge of apologising, before cracking a smile and shaking his head in disbelief. "Of course I did. Thanks for being more understanding than I ever was, Liz."

It was a gratifying *thank you* yet it left a bitter taste in my mouth nonetheless. Tom was still so dismissive of the way he'd treated me before, as if it truly didn't matter. So why did it matter so much to *me*? Why couldn't I just let it go?

"Anyway, are you planning on using that?" I asked, pointing at the Miniprep kit sitting on the bench in front of Tom. "Rodrigo has the other one and I have twelve samples to purify."

"Lucky for you I'm doing ten. If you don't mind sharing the kit and the centrifuge with me?"

By the look on Tom's face he expected me to say no. But this was work, and I needed my samples so I could move on with my work. "Deal. Don't expect me to label any of your tubes, though."

With a grin Tom pulled an Eppendorf tube rack out of his drawer, full of not just ten but thirty labelled tubes – one for each sample, for each of the three steps that required a new tube.

"All right, Professor Organised, no need to show off," I said, although to be fair I was pretty impressed by his forethought. Labelling tubes that were going to get thrown away ten minutes later was annoying as shit.

Tom shrugged his shoulders. "I'm always organised. That's the reason I can appear so laid-back all the time."

"Laid-back? Since when?" It was certainly not a phrase I would've ever used to describe the Tom who assessed my PhD reports. Although, now that I thought about it, he *was* pretty laid-back with everyone else, and he was so relaxed at home he was practically horizontal. When he wasn't outside furiously jogging like his life depended on it, of course, which he was doing rather frequently these days.

"Since forever," he said. "You're the one who's frazzled and grumpy all the time."

"Oh, I'm grumpy now? Since when did this turn into an 'insult Elizabeth' session?"

Tom snickered into his hand, then stood up. "If you insult me then expect it right back. You're almost thirty. Deal with it."

"Twenty-seven is not *almost* thirty."

"Twenty-eight in three months. Clock's ticking, Liz."

The fact Tom knew when my birthday was stopped my incoming rebuttal right on the tip of my tongue. Satisfied with my response – taking it as a win, no doubt – Tom headed for the cold room. "I'll grab your samples for you!" he called over his shoulder, which was a far more gentlemanly gesture than I deserved.

For the next hour the two of us worked through the motions of Miniprepping our collective twenty-two samples, the stages memorised by rote over the years until they were as automatic as breathing. Spin the sample, spin the sample, spin the sample. Buffer P1. Buffer P2. Mix the contents and leave for five minutes. Buffer N3. Invert the tube to mix. Centrifuge for ten minutes. Run the supernatant through a column. Buffer PE. Spin the column. Buffer EB to elute the DNA.

It was only when we reached elution – me labelling a final set of tubes whilst Tom blissfully sat back on his stool and waited for the centrifuge to do its thing, the arsehole – that I realised how, well, *nice* the morning had been so far. Working side-by-side with Tom had been surprisingly easy.

Why was he turning out to be a good guy? I couldn't reconstitute *this* Tom with the hellish man who'd literally brought me to tears (privately, of course) after my two third year PhD assessments. The Tom who flirted like his life depended on it when he had a drink in him but, really, far more enjoyed curling up on his couch watching anime, couldn't possibly be the same person who once tore apart my solid *in vitro* activity protocol for cutting non-existent corners.

Which version of Tom was real? It couldn't be both, could it? But if that were the case...which version of him liked me? And *why*?

Before I knew it I'd made it through the day's lab work with not a single argument to be had between me and Tom. He'd remade his chloramphenicol stocks, prepared a new protein purification timetable and booked the culture shakers, and I'd separated the afternoon's virgin flies so I could visualise male versus female brain activity on the fluorescent microscope on Friday. We were strangely aware of what the other person was doing, handing over the right pipette or a new pair of gloves whenever one of us needed them, in bizarre and unsettling harmony.

Why did we work so *well* together?

Eventually Peter came back into the lab just as Tom and I – and most everyone else – were beginning to wind down for the day.

"Liz," Peter said, his voice a heavy huff of air as if he'd been running.

"What's up? Why are you so out of breath?"

"Avoiding Claire. I think she's caught wind of Ray's party."

Claire was Ray's ex. I knew from experience that she was, well, a bit much. Far too much for Ray to handle, hence why he enlisted Peter to help him break up with her. I didn't personally like the cowardly, underhanded tactic of getting your friend to break up with your girlfriend whilst you ghosted her, but given that I'd recently gone on a date simply to fuck with Tom I suppose I didn't have a leg to stand on.

"I'll be sure to be on the look-out when I leave the building," I said, expecting Peter to then head to the computer room to dump his stuff.

Instead he said, "Harriet needs you to send your measurements again, by the way. For your Hallowe'en costume."

I slapped my head as I remembered that we'd all made plans. "For Ray's party. Right."

"It better not clash with lab karaoke!" exclaimed Daichi, materialising out of nowhere like he always did. I was beginning to believe my boss's shoes were lined with fucking clouds.

Peter and I frowned in confusion. "Lab karaoke?"

To our surprise it was Tom who answered. "Dai has booked out the mezzanine of a karaoke bar every Hallowe'en for almost as long as we've been friends. It's next Friday. Miss it if you dare."

"That's the same day as Ray's party..." Peter began, trailing off at the look of betrayal on Daichi's face. Clearly it was me to the rescue.

"Since when have we ever gone to a party on time, Pete? We can go to karaoke until, like, eleven, then show up fashionably late to the party." I turned to our boss. "Can we bring Chloë and her girlfriend? Our costumes kind of come as a set."

Harriet was a seamstress and a huge nerd. She'd been working on these costumes for weeks now. It made me feel bad that I'd forgotten all about Hallowe'en until now.

Daichi beamed at the request. "The more the merrier! I tried to make it an Institute thing a few years back but it never took off."

"Much to the relief of most everybody," Tom said, scandalising his friend.

"You act as if you don't hog the mic after you've knocked back three shots! Are we still doing our couple's costume?"

I choked on something. A laugh. A yell. My tonsils. "Are you still doing *what*?"

Tom let out a self-deprecating sigh. "It's a thing we do every year. His idea," he said, pointing at his best friend. "Not mine. And yes, of course we're still doing it. Your wife will flay me if I say no."

Daichi clapped his hands together, reminding me for a moment of Tom's mum. "Excellent. Right, I'm off for the day. The beautiful wife in question finishes in ten minutes so I'm picking her up."

"Must be nice to be in such a sickeningly lovey-dovey relationship," I mused, once Daichi had left and Peter headed to the computer room. "How long have they been together?"

"They met during their undergrad so...twenty years?" Tom offered, scratching his nose as he pondered the question. "Christ, that's a long time."

"Clearly they cracked the code to a lasting relationship. So what's this couple's costume, then?" I poked Tom in the bicep; all day I hadn't been able to get his damn arm and shoulder muscles out of my head. Punishment for scaring him, clearly.

The smirk Tom gave me could only be described as devilish. He leaned back on his stool as if it were a throne and he a king, tossing a pen in the air before deftly catching it. "What's yours?"

"It's a secret." It hadn't been before now.

"Then so is mine."

"No hiding behind a mask to get me to unknowingly fall for you, right?"

"I wasn't aware there was any need for me to go that far."

Tom maintained steady eye contact with me - daring me to suggest otherwise, or blush, or match his outrageous comment with one of my own. All three options cycled through my head on repeat.

"...I guess that's something we both need to find out," I ended up saying, which sounded far too much like the truth for my comfort.

But knowing what I was dressing up as, and how that would likely be received by Tom, soothed away my discomfort and replaced it with excitement. My plan to use his attraction towards me against him had been on the backburner the last two weeks. It had been too easy to fall into a routine with him.

Next Friday I'd shake things up and leave him wishing he'd never made the mistake of ever liking me.

Chapter Sixteen

TOM

"Lizzie, are you ready? Lizzie? Tom, can you go up and get her?"

Mum was in the doorway, Jim impatiently honking the horn behind the wheel of his rusting late-nineties Ford Fiesta. We were all headed to Balloch to look out local food and furnishings for the wedding, and Liz was nowhere to be seen.

"I'll get her," I told Mum, waving for her to head to the car before jogging up the stairs. "Liz, hurry it up! Everyone is ready to g—"

The door to her room was wide open. Liz was sliding out of a pair of ripped tights right before my eyes, dress hoisted around her waist and flashing the incredibly revealing, emerald lacy underwear she was wearing beneath it.

My brain completely flat-lined as I stood there, staring and staring and staring. I couldn't stop. It was like the white bra and orange juice situation all over again.

"Tights ripped," Liz said, her cheeks flushing faintly pink as she pulled them off, a little too slowly to be entirely innocent. Perhaps I was reading too much into things – turning this situation into something I wanted it to be. But Liz's underwear, to my eyes at least, looked far too sexy to be worn for a regular family trip to the country on a Sunday morning.

Was this some kind of unholy test of my self-restraint?

Liz continued to watch me watch her, hands inexorably slow as they pulled off the damaged article of clothing. When she straightened and let her dress fall back to her knees she raised an inquisitive eyebrow in my direction.

"Are you going to keep watching me get dressed or are you going to turn around, walk back down the stairs and wait in the car?"

"...is this a situation where I *have* to pick option two, or is option one actually on the table?" I asked, surprised by my own audacity. Not that anything I said really mattered; a careful flick of Liz's gaze to my crotch confirmed that the dark brown canvas of my trousers was doing very little to hide my raging hard-on.

I turned around and walked briskly down the stairs without waiting for Liz's answer. She already had too many cards in her hand against me. She knew I liked her, and clearly knew she could fuck about with me because of it. Had she been waiting upstairs for me to retrieve her, door ajar and ripped tights at the ready?

It should have pissed me off. Instead it excited me to no end.

Not the best situation to be in when I had to sit in a cramped car with Liz, my mum and her dad for an hour.

"I could have driven, Jim," I said, grateful to have been given the passenger seat so that I didn't have to sit in the back with Liz when she neatly folded herself in beside my mum, new tights ladder-free and flawless. She caught my eye in the mirror of the sun visor, the devilish hint of a smile playing across her lips.

Damn her. Damn her to hell.

If I'd ever doubted Liz was aware of what she was doing I

didn't now. How was I supposed to respond? Was she simply fucking with me for the sake of it or was this some kind of game she was inviting me to play?

I had to work out my next move...soon.

"It's nice to get out on a drive," Jim said, bringing me starkly back to reality. Family outing. Family outing. No thoughts of ripping Liz's new tights with my own two hands and using them to tie *her* hands to my bedpost and—

"You've driven enough for a lifetime already, Jim!" Mum protested. In the visor mirror I saw her turn to Liz, looking for her agreement. "Hasn't he? And he wants to return to work!"

"Only part-time," Jim huffed. "I'm not old yet."

"Nobody said you were. But you've earned a break. Let me take care of you."

Liz cackled at this, a wonderfully ugly sound that could only be the result of genuine glee. "Sounds like you're a kept man now, Dad. Soon you'll be hiring a maid to do your washing."

"Hush, you, don't encourage her," Jim said. When he turned to *me* for support it took me far too long to work out what to say. After all, Jim hadn't exactly cared for my opinion on anything thus far.

"You drive buses?" I asked. "Liz mentioned once that you've spent most of your life as a bus driver."

"Aye, until her mum was...well. Didn't imagine I'd ever be up for going back but now I feel like it might be good for me. Never thought I'd consider my old job as something I *want* to do, but I think I actually miss it. And like it."

"Then absolutely do it." I looked over my shoulder at Mum. "You should know better than to deny a man his hobbies."

Mum had the audacity to act innocently ignorant of what I meant. "What a cruel thing to say to your mother!"

"You know fine well Dad hated going to those book clubs you dragged him to just because you didn't want to go alone.

Give Jim his space."

"Is that why you don't want me to go back to work?" Jim asked, narrowing his eyes at the road. "So you aren't alone?"

"That's not – don't be daft!" Mum spluttered, flamingo-pink. She'd never been able to lie well.

Jim's face softened into a smile. "You should have said that from the start. I don't have to go back to work immediately. We can talk it over. It would only be a shift or two a week, anyway."

Jim and Mum continued their now disgustingly affectionate discussion for most of the journey to Balloch, Liz uncharacteristically quiet as she gazed out of the window. But every so often she caught my eye and held my gaze for too long for it to have been accidental. I wanted nothing more than to continue what our earlier interaction could have led to...well, the version of it my over-active imagination was currently playing out in my head, at least. Additional present company excluded.

When we arrived in Balloch I got out of the car and gulped down fresh air as if I'd been locked in a box. My entire body felt like a coil wound too tightly, ready to unravel at any given signal from Liz that such an unravelling was welcome.

"Thomas, dear, are you quite all right?" Mum asked, taking one look at my face and realising something was wrong.

"Just a little car sick."

"But you're never—"

"Do you want me and Liz to have a look at the florist's whilst you and Jim tackle the table placements, then we can regroup for the food tasting?" I cut in. Talk of her wedding immediately put Mum's concerns for my well-being to rest. She smiled warmly at me, excitement bubbling at the day's prospects.

"You've always had a much better eye for flowers than I do," she said, "so that sounds like a good idea. Purple and white, remember, Thomas!"

Liz for her part didn't disagree with this divvying up of tasks. She kissed her dad good-bye and obediently followed me away from the car, in the direction of the florist.

It was a gorgeous autumn day – the kind Scotland experienced perhaps only once or twice a year before the winter rain ruined it all. The River Leven, running into Loch Lomond, was a mirror-flat snake of sunshine gold from one angle and a perfect reflection of the red-leaved trees lining the bank from another. The sky was a pale but brilliant blue, unfettered but for two insubstantial, wispy clouds and a handful of seagulls hovering overhead.

I breathed in the crisp air, revelling in how it was helping to clear my head. Beside me Liz walked in companionable silence, a serene look on her face and relaxed set to her shoulders that suggested the gorgeous weather had elevated her mood, too.

This morning's antics notwithstanding the two of us had been getting on remarkably well. Work was pleasant enough, given the fact I was displaced from my own lab and office, and the evenings we'd spent watching TV so far had been too enjoyable for me to believe Liz was merely putting up with me for the sake of our parents. I knew it would be much easier for both of us if I could simply stop liking her the way I did.

The problem was that I didn't want to. If I could only work out whether Liz fucking with me was because she liked me back in some capacity – or was simply messing with me for the sake of it – then I could work out what to actually do with this stupid, self-inflicted situation we were both in.

When we reached the florist's I pushed the shockingly blue door open and let Liz walk in first. A bell tinkled above the door, alerting the owner of the shop that they had new customers. "You should be expecting us," I told the florist, a woman with dyed blonde hair pulled back into a perfect ponytail who looked to be around the same age as I was. "Henderson."

Her eyes lit up as she took in me and Liz. "Ah, so this must be the happy couple! Aren't you both *gorgeous*? Thank you so much for choosing—"

"A-actually, it's our parents who are getting married," Liz cut in, laughing awkwardly. She indicated towards me with a thumb. "His mum and my dad."

The florist took a second to process this. "So the two of you...you aren't together? You looked so lovey-dovey coming into the shop!"

"We get that all the time," I easily lied, taking advantage of Liz's silence to see if I could get some revenge on her. I slid an arm around her waist, pulling her to my side despite her protests. "We *do* look good together, don't we?"

"Get your moronic hands off me," Liz complained, a blush colouring her cheeks as she pushed against my chest – then paused, before promptly stepping away.

It was clear the florist didn't know what to do or say, so I saved her the trouble of having to respond. "We're looking for something Scottish and understated, if possible. Purple and white with green undertones. I was thinking white gypsophilas and common chickweed for the spray, heather and lavender to bulk it out, then white water-lilies and violet pansies as the main event. Or something along those lines."

I didn't know who looked more impressed – the florist or Liz. Though I had pulled my arm away from Liz her hand had found its way to my elbow, as if she was about to turn me around and demand an explanation for my ridiculously specific bouquet requests.

It was the florist who spoke first. "You certainly know your stuff!" she exclaimed. "I think I have some sample arrangements in the back that fit your vision...two minutes." With that she scurried into the back of the shop, leaving me and Liz to browse. I found myself honing in on a beautiful selection of vibrant red tulips, bundled together into a decorative wrought-iron watering can. I rubbed a velvety petal between my thumb and forefinger, a longing for spring to come around tugging at my heart. I hated the cold.

"Are you going to buy them?" Liz asked, indicating towards the tulips. "I didn't know you liked flowers so much."

"There's a lot you don't know about me."

"...care to let me in on it, then?"

I offered her a small smile. "My grandfather was into horticulture back when he could still walk. The country estate...the gardens are amazing, all thanks to him. Unfortunately the townhouse doesn't have much space for a proper garden. Damn Glasgow."

At the mention of the country estate Liz perked up. "Do I get to see this *actual* mansion today?"

"I doubt it. Mum wants it to be a surprise. Even *I'm* not allowed to visit."

"And you're actually listening to your mum's silly orders?"

"If it makes her happy. Did you never humour your mum just for her sake?"

The question caught Liz by surprise. She gulped, her throat bobbing, and I regretted turning the conversation in that direction. But then Liz pulled one of the tulips out of the watering can and spun it between her fingers. "Mum was the practical sort," she began. "Grew up in foster care, then went from bar job to bar job to make ends meet. She and Dad...well, they never really had the luxury of indulgences. For themselves, I mean. The moment they had a spare quid they threw it at anything they hoped would make me happy. So I guess...she never really gave me the opportunity to humour her. Maybe if she were still alive, and I had enough saved up so that she could finally take it easy, I'd have been able to."

I let that sink in for a long moment. I'd never once thought about how money could factor into one's grief, or how important it was in the amount of quality time you could spend with someone.

I was a rich, entitled arsehole, but I knew it would serve nobody but myself to say that now.

There was one question regarding Liz's mother that I'd been burning to ask for a while now, however, so I risked asking it. "She passed away early in the final year of your PhD," I murmured, entering what I knew full well to be forbidden conversation territory, "so why didn't you say anything? To me, to the Institute? You should have taken time off. We're obviously lenient about these things."

All at once, as I should have expected, Liz shut down right in front of me, reverting to the cagey, affronted version of herself I'd been reunited with in The Whisky Barrel last month. "Why would I have expected you to be lenient?"

"I would have never...Liz, a family death is a more than reasonable excuse to get a respite from assessments and academics."

"Oh, because you were *so* reasonable an assessor? You'd given me no reason to believe you'd be sympathetic."

There was only one acceptable, long overdue response. "Sorry. I'm sorry."

To my surprise, Liz stared me down long and hard, then replaced the tulip she'd been twirling into the watering can. "I guess I should have realised even *you* have a heart. In truth I wanted to keep busy, anyway. Not working would have driven me mental. Would I be wrong to hazard that's why you didn't take time off or tell anyone, either?"

"That's...exactly right, yes." It was an unnervingly observant remark for her to make, but it didn't make me uncomfortable. "Only Daichi knew. He helped me carry Dad's coffin, actually, though he was about five inches shorter than everyone else so was kind of useless."

Liz snorted despite herself. "Sorry, was I supposed to laugh at that? Comedy so dark it was birthed from the Shadow Realm itself is kind of hard to work out."

"*Yu-Gi-Oh!* reference. Nice one, nerd. And yes, we even laughed about it at the funeral. I think we all appreciated the humour of it."

The two of us shared a small smile, though we said nothing to each other. Something about our dynamic had changed for the better thanks to our frank conversation. I wasn't sure what, but it felt promising.

"So are you going to buy them?" Liz eventually pressed, nodding at me still touching one of the tulips. The petal between my fingers had creased to the point of tearing; guilty, I removed it and brought it with me to the counter.

"Just this one," I said. "They're out of season, so there won't be enough light in the house to keep them blooming long."

The florist reappeared then, and I either approved or disapproved of particular flowers until, together, we had chosen a bouquet I knew my mum was going to go absolutely nuts over.

"You're a good son," Liz observed. "Like, seriously, a total goody two-shoes. Even this morning you ran up to find me like she asked without a word of complaint."

"Oh, so we're talking about this morning, then?" I asked, raising an eyebrow as we exited the shop.

Liz gave me the most indecently serene smile I'd ever seen. "And whatever do you mean by that, Tom?"

"I know what you're doing."

"And what would that be, exactly?"

"I'm not giving you the satisfaction of letting you know out loud."

"Well then I have no idea what you're talking about." That innocent smile turned sly. "Green *is* your favourite colour though, right?"

"Are you sure the reason you can't keep a man around is because you make his life hell?"

"If you can't handle the fire, get out of the fucking pan."

"I don't mind a bit of fire."

"A bit?"

Ahh. I realised far too late that the entire conversation was a trap. Liz had been gauging my reaction to this morning's antics to work out where it likely was on the 'scale of things Thomas Henderson can handle'.

I had no doubt things were going to get a lot worse for me.

With a flourish I held out the solitary tulip I'd purchased for Liz to take. "Here's to the fire, then," I said, noting with calculated satisfaction how flustered this gesture made Liz.

She snatched the flower from me then, far more gently, stroked the crooked petal I'd half-destroyed back into place. All the while her skin turned a similar shade of red as the flower in her hands – from her neck right up to her temples.

"...thanks," she said, looking anywhere but at me.

And therein lay my strategy against her, clear and simple. Liz had been similarly flustered when I told her I liked her, and it had hardly escaped my notice up to now that she often physically reacted to my flirtations before she could stop herself. All I had to do was fight fire with fire – to give as good as I got – to stop Liz from playing around and start giving me an honest answer about whether she was considering me as a viable, dateable prospect.

Good thing Hallowe'en was just around the corner.

Chapter Seventeen

LIZ

THANKS TO DAICHI'S NOT-SO-SUBTLE pleas for help, Peter, Chloë, Harriet and I got ready for Hallowe'en much earlier than expected in order to show up at the karaoke bar at the same time as him ("Nobody ever arrives on time and I end up sitting there by myself for half an hour every year!" he'd complained).

So it followed, of course, that my boss had chosen this year to arrive late.

That left the four of us to sit on the private terrace which Daichi had booked out, enjoying a couple rounds of tequila shots as the bar filled out downstairs and the air became filled with the sounds of singers of incredibly variable quality. It set my adrenaline going.

I was a bat shit awful singer. Harriet was wonderful. Chloë was decent. Peter was tone-deaf. But none of that mattered; we all fucking loved karaoke once we'd had a few prerequisite shots.

The place was decked out for Hallowe'en – spiderwebs, skeletons, pumpkins, smoke machines, the works – as were all the people. It was a cacophony of colours, shapes and bizarre costume choices. There were the usual ones people always fell back on during Hallowe'en, of course. Half-assed mummies. Sexy bunny girls. American football players. An eighteen-year-old undergrad using the sheet from his bed as a shitty ghost costume. But there were many far better quality costumes on display, too. No doubt all comic book, film and anime nerds, going by who or what they'd chosen to go as.

There was Captain America, drinking shots of luminous green Apple Sourz with nineties-era Scarlet Witch. Singing along to a resplendent Gandalf on stage were a group of hobbits and a slender Legolas, all well on their way to pissed. I wondered where the inevitable rest of the Fellowship had gone off to. There were two girls both dressed as Sailor Moon taking a selfie – along with one comically broad, bearded man also dressed like the character – and a solo Tuxedo Mask, who gave all three of them a rose.

Thanks to the increased mainstreaming of anime and the skyrocketing popularity of super hero films, the karaoke bar had become a drunk cesspool of cosplayers. My friends and I lorded over it all from our private terrace, happy to people-watch, drink and wait for some familiar faces to show up before singing our lungs off. A few strangers tried their luck at coming up the stairs to join us but we told them to fuck off. They stalked away muttering far worse.

Two tequilas and a vodka orange later (I was measuring time in drinks, not minutes), an unfamiliar man dressed as an immaculate Aziraphale, along with a group of poorly costumed but familiar undergrads, came through the door and skipped up the stairs to join us. It was only once the man was in front of me that I realised it was my boss.

"I didn't recognise you at all!" I exclaimed, a sentiment echoed by my friends. Daichi had on the most perfect platinum blonde wig I'd ever seen – if I hadn't known better I'd have thought he dyed his hair. He was wearing green contacts over his deep brown irises, and his clothes were so perfectly tailored that, for a moment, I wondered if he'd commissioned Harriet to make them. Daichi usually wore comfy sweaters and jeans at work unless he had a meeting; dolled up in Aziraphale's classic waistcoat, bowtie and long, cream jacket he was an entirely different person. Only his bubbly energy remained the same…which was perfect for the cosplay.

"You…look…wonderful!" Daichi cried, bouncing on his heels as he took in me, Peter, Chloë and Harriet. He extended a hand to Harriet, who dutifully shook it. "You must be the *super talented seamstress girlfriend*," he said. "This is some exceptional work."

Harriet beamed at the praise. "I'd wanted to try my hand at some comic book stuff for a while. It's good for my commissions portfolio. So *no destroying the costumes*," she warned us, the glint in her eye putting the fear of god in me. She never made idle threats.

When three other researchers from the lab arrived and joined us on the terrace Chloë dashed downstairs to put the four of us in for a song on karaoke. Half the bar followed her do so, admiring the way she looked, before tracking Chloë back up to the terrace to take note of me, Harriet and Peter. Usually I didn't care for this kind of attention being directed at me but tonight was another matter entirely.

We made a fucking excellent Poison Ivy (Chloë), Harley Quinn (Harriet), Night Wing (Peter) and Catwoman (me). Classic nineties costumes, of course.

Michelle Pfeiffer Catwoman for me, to be specific.

I knew I looked great in the costume. Harriet had lovingly recreated it, though because I was a living, breathing person with a bladder she had incorporated a couple of invisible zips to ensure the costume was much easier to manoeuvre than I knew from a late-night Wikipedia search the original had been for Pfeiffer.

So I had the costume. I had the tequila buzz. I had weeks of pent-up sexual frustration buzzing inside me. All that was missing was Tom.

Just where the hell was he?

He was nowhere to be seen even when I sauntered downstairs with my friends to sing *Bat Out of Hell* (Peter's choice) on stage, which was saved from mine and Peter's scream-sung destruction only by the fact Chloë could harmonise with her girlfriend and Harriet could sing everything up the octave with a fucking belt, to boot. Damn theatre show-off. The bar was singing along, the atmosphere was great, and when we finished there were several folk wanting to buy us drinks.

Normally I'd be excited about getting free drinks but I'd just been paid for my postdoc for the very first time. I'd never seen so much money go into my account – especially not in tandem with absolutely zero outgoing rent or energy bills. "Drinks are on me, guys," I told my friends, even though Peter and Chloë both earned the same as I did and had been in their positions longer. But they were only too happy to oblige.

When I was at the bar I felt someone's hand crawl down my back. Thinking it was Tom I turned around, a quip about him being late firmly on my tongue, only to realise it was a complete stranger dressed as a poor imitation of the Joker.

"We match," he slurred, clearly already wasted. "Can I buy you a drink? I saw you singing. You were *soooo* good."

I absolutely wasn't.

"No thanks," I said, keeping a smile on my face. "I've ordered some for me and my friends already."

"A shot, then? You could do a shot. And then—"

"I said no," I cut in, firmer this time.

The guy's entire demeanour twisted into something unpleasant. "Fine then. Was just trying to be nice. Why do you have to be such a bitch about it? I bet under that mask you're not even *that* hot."

"Good thing for you, then, that you'll never find out. Fuck off."

I turned back to face the bar, ending the conversation, and the Joker skulked off to rejoin his friends. It didn't escape my notice that he kept looking at me, though, as if calculating if he could somehow successfully chat me up on a second attempt.

By the time I'd made it back to the terrace with the drinks – awkwardly held in both hands against my chest because my friends had disappeared upstairs already, damn them – I'd been accosted by no fewer than four men. Grabbing at my hips, attempting to unzip my costume, standing in front of me to force me to stop walking, the works. That feeling from before that I didn't mind having all eyes on me for one night very quickly evaporated. Fuck this; this was why I never went to conventions. Put a woman with boobs and an arse in a catsuit and she'll know no peace. There was only one man I wanted to see me looking like this, anyway, and he was nowhere to be seen.

Where the fuck was Thomas bloody Henderson? Given that Daichi was Aziraphale I knew Tom had to be coming as Crowley. His costume was literally just clothes. How could it possibly take him so long to get ready? Just what was holding him up?

"I wonder what's holding Tom up," Daichi called out the moment I sat down, annoyingly reading my mind like he was Professor X rather than an angel. On the table was a tray full of dubious-coloured shots bought for the entire lab, some of which had already been drunk. I downed one without asking what they were. "Dyeing his hair can't have taken him *that* long."

"Professor Henderson is *dyeing his hair* for a *costume?*" Chloë exclaimed, disbelief plain as day on her face. "But his hair's *blonde*. Does he know how long it'll take for him to get back to his natural colour? Does—"

Daichi's laugh cut through Chloë's protests. "Temporary hair dye. The wig he bought didn't look right and he's much too vain to do things by half-measures if it means he won't look good."

I took all of this in with as bland a smile on my face as I could. Going by the glances Daichi kept throwing me I had an inkling that he must, at least, know that his best friend liked me in some capacity, and now he had some booze in him he could no longer hide the fact he knew something was up.

I was determined not to add any fuel to lab gossip, but then again...if and when Tom actually arrived, what was it I intended to do? If I wanted to mess with him then other folk would see me do so. Like the people I worked with, and my friends, and my boss. Tom's best bloody friend. Clearly I hadn't been in my right mind when I thought this was going to be a great idea.

"I'm going to the toilet," I announced, heading downstairs along with two of the undergrads who also decided they needed to go.

"Do you need any help, you know, getting that off?" one of them – Maria – asked me when I locked myself in an empty cubicle.

I laughed lightly. "There's a hidden zip so no worries," I reassured her, fiddling with said zip between my thighs for a few seconds before unlocking the tiny catch that stopped it from unzipping whenever I moved. Harriet really was far too good at her job.

I stood in front of the full-length mirror by the row of sinks after I was done, turning this way and that to see how the light hit the shiny material of my costume as well as fixing my eye make-up. My mascara had smudged from the heat of the bar; knowing it was only going to get hotter, I decided to up the smoke factor of my eyeshadow to ingeniously hide any future smudges. Then, in a rebellious act that served literally zero purpose, I deliberately smeared my red lipstick so it looked like I'd been engaged in a hot-and-heavy kissing session with Michael Keaton's Bruce Wayne.

When I got back to the bar a swift gust of cold air blew in, signalling that the door had just been opened to let someone out – or someone in. A flash of red-orange hair was all I needed to see to know Tom had finally arrived.

My stomach lurched and I stood, frozen, to the spot, even when some arsehole standing behind me began whispering into my ear and crawling his fingers up my spine.

For Tom had somehow, impossibly, immediately spotted me, his sharp eyes zeroed in on mine, and as folk moved around between us we unashamedly took in the appearance of the other.

Holy fuck did he make a good Crowley.

His now fiery hair was perfectly blow-dried and pushed back to emulate David Tennant's longer-haired version of the character to alarming effect. Alongside Crowley's signature round sunglasses, skinny scarf, waistcoat and black jacket, he looked far more like he'd actually come off the set of *Good Omens* than he looked like a cosplayer.

How close did I have to be to see the little snake tattoo Crowley had by his sideburns? I was aching to see it.

When Tom removed his sunglasses to better take me in I cocked my hip to the side and tilted my chin upwards slightly as if I were looking down my nose at him. Haughty, that's what my stupid horny-ass brain was going for. Clearly it worked. Tom licked his lips, completely ignored the sound of Daichi calling for him from the terrace, and took a step towards me.

"Ah, I see Crowley has finally arrived!" cried out the karaoke presenter, stopping Tom in his tracks. "I have orders to drag you up on stage the moment you arrive as punishment for being late. Ladies, if you don't mind helping me out..."

Several women standing nearby were only too happy to oblige the request, nudging and pawing Tom towards the stage and away from me. A burning sensation that felt far too close to jealousy for my liking filled my core, but my pride kept me firmly stood where I was. But then the guy behind me took that as I sign I wanted him to keep touching me and spitting in my ear, so I pulled out of his reach to stand at the edge of the small gaggle of folk – mostly women – who had crowded around the karaoke stage to hear Tom sing.

And you know what? Fuck it. Even sober I could admit I was curious to hear him sing. Was he terrible? Was he amazing? Was he decidedly mediocre? I wanted to know.

And now I'd find out.

Tom held my gaze for a moment, his expression a plea for help if ever there was one, but then he was handed a mic and the music started. With a glare shot up at the terrace – I turned to see Daichi waving at Tom with a shit-eating, angelic grin on his face – Tom took a deep breath and listened to what song his best friend had picked for him.

It sounded oddly familiar. As in, that afternoon in the lab familiar.

"Oh, fuck off," I mumbled, just as Tom mouthed something similar. I'd been playing mid-2000s pop all day to get in the mood for a night of cheesy Hallowe'en fun. The classics, like Destiny's Child and Natasha Bedingfield and McFly.

It was McFly who were playing now. *Obviously* – my favourite of their big hits. I'd badly sung along to it before finishing work today. Why had Daichi chosen that for Tom?

But then Tom started singing and I stopped caring.

He wasn't just good; he was great. Like, ridiculously so. And he was getting *into* it, singing the words to the women fawning over him – and sometimes at his best friend, who pretended to swoon. I couldn't fucking believe it. Even the karaoke presenter was impressed.

When it hit the chorus Tom turned his attention to me. He sang every single word.

To.

Me.

I thought I'd die of embarrassment. I couldn't look away, even though I knew everyone from the lab must surely be watching Tom serenade me with pop-rock.

And yet, when the chorus ended and Tom continued the song, once more paying attention to the rest of his adoring crowd, a surge of disappointment left me feeling alternately hot and cold. Tom's unabashed, cheesy display of affection was absolutely not my cup of tea, but the fact he hadn't cared for the fact anyone was watching and did it anyway had felt kind of nice. Maybe. God, I didn't want him to do it again, did I?

I retreated to the bar and ordered two gin and tonics, lurking there until Tom's song was over. Not that the second drink was for him; both were for me. I wasn't acting right. I was supposed to tease and toy with *him*, not the other way around. But so far it felt like Tom was winning and I was losing – badly.

Out of the corner of my eye I spotted Tom get off the stage to rapturous applause. Immediately he was bombarded by women vying for his attention so I turned *my* attention back to my drink, mood thoroughly soured. How was it that I'd forgotten how big of a flirt Tom was, or how attractive he clearly was? Of course he'd be surrounded by hopeful dating (or one-night-stand) prospects, including all three Sailor Moons from earlier.

He didn't have to deal with me if he was horny and tired of my shit, even if I'd believed he was as excited by the prospect of drunk flirting again as I had been.

When a hand slid over my hip and a warm wave of breath fanned across my ear I prepared to kick whichever fucker wanted to chat me up this time right in the balls.

"Get your hands off me or I'll—"

"You got me a drink?" Tom said, the entire length of his body pressing against me as he leaned over my shoulder to pick up one of my gin and tonics. His grin was feral when he took in my expression. In all honesty I had no idea what that expression was. "You shouldn't have."

"...I didn't."

"Either way, I'll be taking this. I didn't have nearly enough to drink when I was getting ready. Come on, let's head to the terrace so I can punch Daichi in the face."

There was so much I could have said. *No*, for example. I didn't like how easy it was for Tom to pull me into his sphere of influence. I didn't like how much I'd genuinely enjoyed him singing to me, or how jealous I was of all the attention he was getting.

His hand still firmly gripping my hip overwrote all of that.

I gave Tom a smile. "After you, Crowley."

Chapter Eighteen

TOM

THERE WERE THREE THOUGHTS THAT RAN through my head within the first five minutes of my arrival at the karaoke bar, late as I was with last-minute costume mishaps.

First and foremost: Liz. Liz, Liz, Liz. She was Catwoman. Fucking Michelle Pfeiffer Catwoman, as if she'd read my mind and discovered what my childhood sexual awakening character had been. She looked down her nose at me as if she might step on me. Fuck, I wanted her to step on me, if it meant I could get within an inch of that amazing costume stuck to her curves like a second skin.

My second thought: where had all these leeches come from, attaching themselves to Liz regardless of the fact she was vocally and physically not interested? Even as we stared at each other there was some loser wriggling his tongue in her ear, hand touching her way below the hip.

Lastly: fuck Daichi and his stupid song.

I tried to make the most of the moment by embarrassing Liz to high hell, but after she slunk away to the bar all I wanted was for the song to end. It had been like fighting against the tide to reach her.

But now the torment was over, and Liz and I were sitting on the terrace of the karaoke bar with the rest of the lab. So why had she chosen not to sit *beside* me? Why was she sitting opposite me, out of reach and surrounded by her friends? Peter, dressed as an impeccable Nightwing, glared at me.

"Why aren't you Batman?" I asked before I could stop myself, having to raise my voice quite a bit to be heard over a screeching woman on karaoke.

"Because Nightwing is cooler. And Dick Grayson becomes Batman, anyway," Peter said, still glaring as he sized me up.

"You would be an *amazing* Batman!" Harley Quinn gushed. Since she was practically sitting in Liz's friend Chloë's lap, I assumed she was Harriet. The one who made everyone's costumes. The one who had transformed Liz into my wildest dreams.

God, I owed her big time.

"Had we known early enough we could have done Batman and Joker!" Daichi said, clearly delightfully drunk and enjoying himself supremely.

I could only laugh. "You, the Joker? Stick to your wheelhouse, Angel."

"But you *do* make a good Crowley," Harriet mused. "You have the snark and everything."

"Tell me you haven't ruined your hair with that dye!" Chloë exclaimed, surprising me with how genuine her concern sounded.

Peter rolled his eyes. "Because that would be the worst thing in the world – his hair staying orange."

Okay, his passive-aggressiveness was beginning to really piss me off. I glanced at Liz, who was watching me with an amused expression on her half-mask-obscured face. Her artfully smudged lipstick drove me insane when she quirked her lips into an almost smile.

I wanted to ruffle her perfect feathers. And I wanted to make some jibe at Peter that would shut up his insults for the night (and preferably forever).

Luckily for me, I had something I could say that would cover both those things *and* remain on-topic to the conversation at hand.

"I bought special shampoo to help strip out the dye," I explained, taking a casual sip of my gin. "Speaking of shampoo: Liz, you could have told me we were all out. I'll have to pick some up tomorrow."

Silence fell over the entire group. And then:

"Wait, are Doctor Maclean and Professor Henderson...?" one of the undergrads stage-whispered, pausing halfway towards downing a shot.

Rodrigo, Daichi's third year PhD student, couldn't decide whether to focus his attention on me or Liz. "Are you two going out?"

"*Absolutely not!*" Liz spluttered, outrage overcoming dumbstruck horror in an instant. I think if she had a knife on her she would have chucked it at my head, but honestly it was worth it. Peter was speechless, Chloë murmured something to Harriet to explain what was going on – confirming that she already knew – and Daichi shook his head at my immaturity.

Still worth it.

"You all know his mum and my dad are getting hitched," Liz said loudly, desperate to explain herself. "They were staying with Professor Henderson already when my landlord kicked me out of my flat, so I moved in with them for a bit. That's it. That's the gossip."

The undergrads looked disappointed. I'm sure they'd been looking forward to telling their peers all about what their current teacher was getting up to, now that I was teaching them the DNA block alongside Mike.

"That must be nice, all living together," Chloë said, sticking her tongue out at Liz when Liz gave her the finger. "Although I think I'd go mad if I had to live with my mum again."

"Ah, our parents tend to go off on romantic weekends away more often than not – it's mostly just me and Liz in the house together," I said, grinning like the doomed fool I knew I was. There was no way Liz was letting me get away with that.

Sure enough, Liz stood up abruptly. "I need to use the toilet."

"Again?" Chloë said, clearly shit-stirring. I liked her more and more with every passing second. "You only went half an hour ago."

"Must have broken the seal, then," Liz fired back, rushing down the stairs before anyone else could make a comment.

Everyone turned their attention to me.

"Are you...really not going out?" Rodrigo asked. "I'll be honest, we all kind of thought you were exes or something." He indicated towards the undergrads and Daichi's other two PhD students.

"We're something, all right," I said, choosing to be intriguingly – annoyingly – vague as I stood up and followed Liz downstairs.

"Get me a drink when you're down there!" Daichi called after me. I waved an acknowledgement of his request, then snaked through the ground floor in search of Liz. Had she really gone to the toilets?

How did she even *go* to the toilet in that outfit? Suddenly, knowing how to get into her catsuit became my highest priority.

When Liz came back up the stairs to the ground floor there were two men following her, one of them dressed in a pitiable excuse for a Joker costume. She looked just about ready to murder them. Immediately I swanned over and slid my arm around her waist, directing her away from her furious suitors and towards the dance floor hidden away at the back of the bar.

It was already full of drunk people dressed in all manner of costumes – from the amazing to the ridiculous to the terrible – so, using my height to my advantage, I pulled Liz through the crowd until we reached the very back corner.

She slapped my arm when we came to a stop, then did it again for good measure.

"Just what is wrong with you?" she demanded, leaning up on her tiptoes to my ear to make sure I could hear over the music. I'd never been so happy for out-of-tune karaoke blaring all around me in my entire life. "I thought we agreed that the lab shouldn't know!"

"I'm sorry, it must be the booze," I lied, daring to put a hand on Liz's hip to pull her a little closer.

She didn't pull away.

"Bull shit if you think you can blame it on being drunk. You did that deliberately."

"And if I did?" I stared Liz straight in the face. "If I did, what of it? It wasn't as if I lied about anything. And Peter was annoying me."

"What does *Peter* have to do with this?!"

"I'll wager you'll find out soon enough." Something told me he now saw me as a real and present threat to his slow-burn pining after Liz. Good.

Liz looked like she wanted to argue, then all at once the steam went out of her. With a cry of indignation she ripped her cat-ear mask from her head, then tugged out a dozen Kirby grips to shake her hair free. Ah, fuck. She looked even sexier without the mask.

"This is why I hate cosplaying at conventions," she complained, wiping her brow of sweat. "You can hardly breathe, there are so many people, and—"

"And every time you turn around another guy has grabbed your arse or tried to upzip your clothes," I finished for her, deftly taking the mask and Kirby grips out of her hands to tuck them away into the inner pocket of my jacket. Liz raised an eyebrow. "You think I didn't notice? How could I not? You're practically assaulted every three steps you take."

"And what about all the women falling over *you*?" she muttered, red-faced and indignant. "I've never seen anything like it."

"Oh, are you jealous?"

"Hardly!"

"Because I'm jealous of all the men who touched you without permission," I said, leaning down to breathe the words directly into Liz's ear. I wrapped my right arm around her waist again, holding her against my chest, then trailed my left hand down her spine. When she shivered it was all I could do to stop myself from kissing her.

Liz stood up on her tiptoes to reach *my* ear. "You're touching me without permission right now."

"Am I?" My hand drifted down to the base of her spine, and Liz gulped. "Should I stop?"

She splayed her hands over my chest and, for one horrible moment, I thought Liz was going to push away and insist that, yes, she wanted this to stop. Instead, she ran her fingertips down to the buttons of the black waistcoat I was wearing, and inexorably slowly began undoing them.

"If you're touching without permission then I'm going to do the same."

"That sounds awfully like consent to me. Are we actually making some progress tonight, Liz?"

When Liz's hand shot up behind my neck and pulled my lips within an inch of her own the hard-on I'd half been nursing for the last few minutes was no longer half-anything, pressing against Liz with all the subtlety of a sledgehammer.

"What are you looking for down my spine, Tom?" she

murmured, dark eyes glittering with mischief as her breath fanned over my lips. "A zip? It's on the side, under my arm."

"That must be hell for going to the toilet."

"There's another one here," she said, her hand sliding over mine to direct it between her thighs. If it wasn't for the low lighting of the dance floor and the crowd of people around us I'm fairly certain we would have been kicked out for indecent exposure. As it stood I didn't care, and clearly neither did Liz.

When I pressed my fingertips against her she bit her lip, and wriggled against my touch. My vision went hazy.

"Come home with me," I growled against her ear, barely able to contain myself. "Screw your party. Screw me, instead. You can't look at me with a straight face and tell me you don't want to."

Well, I couldn't have been more obvious in my proposition than that. If Liz rejected me now, after everything that had transpired this evening – let alone the last few weeks – then clearly I was in hell.

The music changed, then, as someone went up to sing some slow nineties ballad I vaguely recognised. Liz wrapped her arms around my neck and I, on instinct, wrapped both of mine around her waist, though the last thing I'd wanted to do was pull away from the secret zip that was pretty much the only physical barrier between the two of us fucking each other senseless on the spot.

"What are you doing?" I asked, curious about what Liz was up to.

Liz shrugged. "Practising for our parents' wedding."

"Are you going to ignore what I just asked you?"

"No."

"Then...?"

"I'm thinking."

"About what?"

"About you."

Liz locked her eyes on mine with the same intensity I'd seen when I confessed that I liked her. I realised, then, that I couldn't mess this up – whatever *this* was between us. Liz was taking a risk with me. She knew it and god if I didn't know it, too.

I turned my head to kiss her elbow where it lay on my shoulder, not once taking my eyes off hers. "I'm always thinking about you."

"Really? You don't show it. Every night when we watch—"

"Oh, trust me, I'm aware of what you're doing and I'm sure you'll be delighted to know that you're driving me out of my mind."

A delicious smile curled Liz's lips. It looked decidedly feline – though maybe that was because of her current attire. "Maybe I could be convinced to skip the party. Our parents aren't back until Sunday...right?"

Oh, fuck me.

This was actually happening.

I pulled out of our slow dance, grabbed Liz's hand and rushed to the door. Every second we spent inside this damn karaoke bar was a second wasted.

"There you are!" Peter called out the moment we set foot outside. I could have murdered him. At least a dozen inventively Crowley ways to do so crossed my mind. "Our taxi's here to take us back to mine."

Liz froze in the face of her friends, her hand dropping from mine as if I'd burned her.

Harriet frowned. "Liz, where's your mask?"

"Ah, it was too hot so—"

"Here," I said, numbly handing it to Liz without quite being in total control of my body. Of course we were going to get interrupted; it had been far too optimistic of me to believe that tonight was going to go flawlessly.

Liz looked at me without really seeing me, already retreating from my side to join her friends. "Thanks. I'll...see you later."

"I'll probably be in bed by the time you get home."

I wanted her to make some sort of innuendo at the notion of me in bed. A joke. An insult. Anything to prove that Liz had literally just agreed to come spend time in it.

It was quickly becoming apparent that she would only entertain such a notion so as long as nobody knew.

All Liz said in response was, "Okay," before retreating into the black cab without giving me the opportunity to appeal to her to stay with me, instead.

I could only hope that, in the morning, we weren't back at square one once more.

Chapter Nineteen

LIZ

I'D BARELY SPENT AN HOUR AT RAY'S party and was regretting, with every passing second, not taking Tom up on his proposition. It was partially the booze talking, I knew, but I wasn't so ignorant as to believe that was all there was to it.

I wanted to sleep with him. I'd been lusting after him for years, even when he'd been my ice-cold PhD assessor. Even though I hated the fact this was true. I'd been given an opportunity to indulge my stupid, reckless lust, in a situation that was *clearly* more than mutual, and I'd...walked away from it.

Sure, Tom was probably frustrated as hell. That meant the evening had been a success in terms of getting my petty revenge.

Only problem was...so was I.

Ray had decorated his and Peter's flat to extraordinary proportions. Everywhere there were spider webs, skeletons, faux-chandeliers and candlesticks dripping fake wax. He'd even wrangled Peter into stealing some dry ice from the lab so he could fill a gaping silver chalice with the stuff, causing twisting, curling steam to hover over the living room table like smoke. All around me people were having a great time but I kept disassociating from conversations to get lost in my head.

I filtered from the kitchen to the hallway to the living room, not sure what to do with myself, before eventually finding myself in Ray's empty bedroom. It was dark but for a curious light shining by his bedside. Curious, I crept forward to investigate. It was a strip light set on a stand over a glass jar full of moss and some tiny tropical plants.

"It's a terrarium," Ray said from behind me, startling the life out of me. "Do you want a closer look?"

Dimly I nodded, so the two of us went over to the terrarium together. "It grows fine under the light, then?" I asked, genuinely curious. "It doesn't need anything special added to it?"

"Nah, the light is enough along with regular misting every day. Well, in summer. In winter you water it less. Need to keep the light on more then, of course, because it's darker."

"Hmm." I ran my hand along the edge of the light, thinking of how Tom's eyes couldn't look away from those gorgeous red tulips in the florist's shop in Balloch. "Are these lights expensive?"

"Ah, it depends on – here, I'll link you to it," Ray said, pulling out his phone and searching until he found the right website. He smiled at me as if he'd found a new comrade. "I didn't know you were wanting to get into this stuff."

I lifted my hand to self-consciously tuck a curl of hair behind my ear but then remembered I'd put my mask back on, so there was no hair to tuck away. My scalp itched with the urge to remove the mask again and wash the accrued sweat from the night out of my hair. "It's a...recent...interest," I said, which was at least not a lie. "Thanks for the info, Ray. I should probably, you know, get back to the party instead of lingering in the dark on my own."

Ray laughed as we exited his bedroom. "That reminds me. Peter was looking for you. Think he's in his room, actually. Seems like he's in a bad mood. Did anything happen at karaoke?"

I thought of what Tom had said about Peter, then pushed it to the side. "No clue. Guess I'll find out. Thanks again, Ray!"

"Let me know when you build your first terrarium!"

Peter wasn't in his bedroom when I found him but instead sitting on the floor in the hallway beneath the coat rack. I eased myself down beside him, then bumped his shoulder with my own. "Ray said you were looking for me. What's up?"

Peter had removed his mask and clearly rubbed a hand over his eyes, for the black paint he'd so carefully applied hours earlier was smeared to shit. He took a swig of beer and tipped his head against the wall.

"Nothing much. Just haven't had a chance to talk to you all night."

"That isn't true!"

"Alone, I mean."

"Oh." I didn't really know what else to say. What did we have to specifically talk about alone?

"...how are your Tinder dates going?" Peter asked after an awkward beat of silence between us.

I could only laugh. "They dried up a couple weeks ago. Seems I've moved past anyone wanting to go out with me!"

"I don't see how that's true."

"But it is," I insisted. "Everyone I match with doesn't message me back at all. Maybe I'm cursed." It should have bothered me but because of everything going on with Tom I hadn't really had the opportunity to be sad about my lack of dating app popularity.

"...could go out," Peter said, speaking so quietly I missed the first half of his sentence to the din of the party.

I leaned in closer. "Say that again?"

"I said maybe we could go out sometime," Peter repeated,

turning to face me with an eager expression on his face I'd never seen before. "You know, on a date."

I...what?

When I laughed again Peter frowned, and I realised it was the wrong reaction entirely. "I'm sorry," I said, "but you're having me on, right? You're just taking pity on me."

But Peter shook his head. "I'm being serious, Liz. I've...well, I've liked you for a few months now. I waited to see if you'd catch on but you – well, you're just so oblivious, aren't you?"

"Way to insult someone you apparently like."

"Come on, don't joke around. I'm being serious here. I've been working on how to tell you for weeks, and I just...well, you know now. I like you. Will you go on a date with me?"

It took me a few seconds to process this. Not because I was considering Peter's proposal – I'd never seen him as more than a friend – but because, at the mention of going on a date, all I could think about was Tom.

Tom, Tom, Tom.

"I'm sorry, Peter," I said, hating how crestfallen he looked as I apologised. "I just don't see you that way. And I don't want to lose you as a friend, either."

"Okay..." Peter chewed over what to say next, then got to his feet. "Okay. I'd be lying if I said I hadn't thought you'd turn me down. I want to stay friends. Of course I do. But can you just...can you give me some space so I can get over you? Just for a while."

My smile felt far too tight. This night really was going to shit. "Of course. I understand. I'm tired now, anyway, so I'll head off."

I didn't even say good-bye to Chloë and Harriet – who were busy canoodling in the living room – before leaving. Peter's flat was only a twenty minute walk away through Kelvingrove Park to

Tom's house, and it wasn't raining, so though I knew fine well that walking in the dark at one in the morning at the weekend was a dangerous idea, I was too tipsy and overwhelmed to give a damn.

By the time I fumbled with the lock on the front door, kicked off my shoes and ripped away my mask (without damaging it, lest Harriet kill me) I was ready to chuck myself in the shower to sit under a steady stream of hot water until all the horrible feelings inside me melted away. My costume felt disgusting against my skin, so I unzipped it and pulled it off then and there, not bothering to turn on the hallway light. I was being far too loud but I didn't care - Dad and Jenny weren't in, and Tom was likely still at the karaoke bar. I could be as loud as I wanted.

I stomped up the stairs like a teenager throwing a strop, picking out kirby grips from my hair as I went until my scalp was finally free of them. I was just about to unlace the ridiculous black corset I'd been wearing under my catsuit to make my figure as comic-book-perfect as possible when the door to Tom's bedroom clicked open.

I froze in the beam of light the open door cast over me, helpless to do anything but stare as Tom - in the process of taking his own costume off - took in the sight of me stripped down to my underwear.

"You're killing me," he uttered, scanning me from my head to my toes with a pained expression that suggested I really was.

"Good," I fired back, too riled up to come up with any other response. My heart was beating wildly in my chest, the emotions of the night catching up with me and threatening to turn me into an impulsive mess. I all but ran for my bedroom and slammed the door behind me, before undressing entirely and chucking on the biggest towel I could find from the storage bench beneath the window.

When I reopened my door and headed for the bathroom Tom had retreated into his bedroom once more.

Peter admitting to liking me reminded me of why I *shouldn't* sleep with Tom; I had to focus on finding someone I actually wanted to be with in the long term. Given everything that had happened so far it was wrong and stupid of me to even *want* to shag the man. So as I turned on the shower and threw myself beneath the wonderful pressure of the steaming water, I weighed up how I currently felt in the frankest terms possible.

I was horny as fuck. That was all. Had any of my Tinder dates been successful (or if I had any new ones to begin with) then I probably wouldn't even be feeling like this.

Where was my vibrator again? My suitcase? I hadn't dared use it since moving into Tom's house in case he, you know, heard it or walked in on me using it or something. But desperate times called for desperate measures, and if I'd all too easily wanted to screw Tom that meant I was *beyond* desperate. He wouldn't be able to hear it in the shower, surely.

I reached for the shampoo only to realise there was none, and that Tom had even mentioned this earlier in the evening.

"Fuck's sake…" I mumbled, poking my head out of the shower to see if the special stuff he'd bought to strip out hair dye was lying around. But it was nowhere to be seen, and I didn't want to get out to try to find it or run down to Jenny's bathroom to steal some of hers.

I knew what I had to do. I had to shout for Tom to get it.

A slow grin spread across my face as a mad plan ran through my brain. This was an ideal situation for me to mess him around and prove to myself that I was entirely in control of the insane urges he elicited in me, especially since I knew he was awake and he'd just caught me in a corset and little else. And, if I played my cards right, I might also be able to do something about my off-the-charts horniness.

I pulled in a breath and opened up the shower a little more, glad that in my drunken state I hadn't completely closed the bathroom door on my way in.

"*Tom!*"

Chapter Twenty

TOM

I WAS SO SEXUALLY FRUSTRATED I WAS beginning to hear Liz's voice in my head. Great. I really was in hell.

"Tom!"

"Shut up," I told the air, shedding the rest of my costume before pulling on a pair of jogging pants. But before I could put a T-shirt on I heard Liz's voice again.

"Tom, I need that shampoo you bought!"

Shampoo? Why would the evil Liz in my head talk to me about shampoo?

I opened the door, frowning at the sliver of light coming through the gap in the bathroom door frame. "You want my what now? My shampoo?"

"Yes!" Liz replied, voice muffled. "There's none left, remember? Can you bring me that stuff you bought to clear out your hair dye?"

For a moment I considered saying no just so Liz would have to get out of the shower and inconvenience herself by getting it from me personally. But I was too tired with confrontations to do so, so I retrieved said shampoo from the bag of shopping I'd left at the base of my bed and wandered over to the bathroom.

I lingered by the door. Why had she left it ajar? "I'll just put it—"

"Bring it to me,"Liz cut in. "I forgot to lock the door, so you can come in."

Was this some kind of Herculean test of my resolve? How was I supposed to respond, especially after witnessing Liz a mere five minutes ago wearing nothing but a black corset and a scrap of lace that could hardly even be defined as underwear?

I entered the bathroom and stalked straight over to the steamed-up shower. Liz's head popped out between the two doors, her hair going curly around her face like it always did when it was wet.

"Here," I said, averting my eyes as I held out the shampoo. "You have some audacity, stealing the shower just when I was about to take one." This was true; like hell was I getting red hair dye all over my pillows.

But Liz didn't take the bottle out of my hand. "Come closer," she insisted. "I can't reach it."

"That's a bare-faced lie." I was standing three feet way – if Liz stretched out her arm of course she could reach the damn shampoo. But still she didn't move so, sighing, I closed the gap until there were mere inches between me and the steamy glass doors. I stared Liz straight in the face now for fear that looking anywhere else would result in me seeing far more than I had the resolve to ignore.

When Liz's hand crept out to cover mine her skin was soft and warm and wet. "Thanks," she purred, gaze flicking from my eyes, to my lips, then down across my naked chest. Fuck. What game was she playing now? "I feel bad about stealing your shower from you. If you want some help rinsing out that hair dye I'd be more than happy to offer myself as tribute." She opened the door, and I was rendered helpless.

Okay, *now* I couldn't tear my eyes away from Liz's naked body, steam curling hazily all around her. Was this a dream? A nightmare? Hadn't Liz only just said it was good that she was driving me crazy and then stormed off to her room? Hadn't she ultimately declined my invite to come home with me in favour of going to that party with her friends?

"You're letting all the hot air out," Liz complained, gently squeezing my hand as she urged me inside the shower. The temporary chill had perked up her nipples, somehow making Liz logarithmically sexier than she had been a mere three seconds prior. "Are you really going to say no to showering together? It'll save water. It's good for the environment. Do you really want to kill the environment, Tom?"

Her stupid comment elicited a laugh from me before I could stop it. "Certainly not," I said, letting Liz take the shampoo from me so I could slowly – self-consciously – remove my jogging pants. Liz watched me do so with ravenous eyes trained on my crotch, which caused my cock to stand firmly to attention. As if it hadn't been already.

Well, there was no getting out of this now. I stepped into the shower and closed the door behind me.

The shower had two heads – a large waterfall one attached directly to the ceiling, above us, and a manoeuvrable one that sat in a socket on the left-hand wall. Liz had both of them on for some ridiculous reason, so I edged past her to turn off the mobile one.

"I like it when they're both on," Liz huffed, moving out of the torrent of fat water drops coming from the remaining shower head so I could stand beneath it. The water quickly ran red as it soaked my hair.

"How are you supposed to save water if you have two showers on, pray tell?"

Liz rolled her eyes. "I'm poor; I'm allowed to enjoy it. You look like you just murdered someone and rolled around in their blood."

"And you look unbelievably sexy, even with mascara running down your face."

"You think I'm sexy?" Liz put the shampoo bottle in a holder on the wall in order to rub her fingers beneath her eyes until most of the mascara was gone. I could do nothing but watch her every movement like my eyes were a camera, committing every line and curve of her body to memory. Screw seeing her in a white bra soaked in orange juice, or in green underwear and ripped tights, or in a black corset and scrap of lace; this was the only version of Liz I wanted to possess. Naked, wet, and completely at ease in front of me. *Only* me.

I leaned my right arm against the wall and tilted my entire body towards her. "You know damn well I do. I haven't been this blue-balled since second year of my undergrad."

Liz wrinkled her nose. It was adorable. "What happened in second year of your undergrad?"

"I had the hots for my microbiology teacher."

"Oh? You didn't manage to seduce her?"

"Twenty-year-old Tom Henderson didn't have nearly as much game as he thought he had...especially not when the object of his lust was a thirty-six-year-old married woman."

At this Liz laughed – her ugly, barking laugh which I knew meant she was genuinely amused – then grabbed the shampoo bottle to pop the lid open.

"Turn around, Tom," she ordered, voice low and gravelly. "And bend down a little."

Though I absolutely didn't want to look away from the sight of Liz completely naked before me I still all-too-happily obliged, turning around and standing slightly bent beneath the shower head. When she pressed her entire body against my back and began massaging her fingers into my scalp I let out the most outrageous moan I had quite potentially uttered in my entire life.

Liz paused at the sound. I didn't need to look behind me to

know she was smiling at my reaction. When she slid her body against mine again I found myself leaning a hand on the wall for support. Was I allowed to jerk off in this situation? Or was I supposed to stand and obediently do nothing whilst Liz washed my hair?

"This stuff is actually coming out," Liz mused aloud, smoothing hair out of my face with one of her hands as the other one ran along the base of my neck. My cock was so hard it was fucking painful.

"I told you it was spray-in stuff," I replied, struggling to form a coherent sentence. "I really am too vain to ruin my hair."

Liz snickered against my ear, rising on her tiptoes to do so. I felt every inch of her move against me in the process. "You make a good red head but I must admit I'm partial to the blonde."

"Is that – is that so? You never pay me any compliments."

"To your face."

When I tried to turn around Liz placed a hand on either side of my head and forced me to stay where I was. "Conditioner next. We can't scrimp on haircare."

I surrendered and let Liz have her way with me. After my hair was thoroughly conditioned I was just about ready to explode; going by the look on Liz's face when she finally let me turn around I realised that was the point.

"...am I supposed to wash your hair now, too?" I asked, breathless and dizzy from the combination of hot water, residual alcohol and the off-the-charts horny situation I was currently in.

Liz's dark eyes twinkled in mischief. "Of course. It's only fair."

Since Liz was around eight inches shorter than me it was far easier for me to wash her hair than the other way around, though because hers was much longer I had to be careful not to get my fingers caught in tangles.

Despite the obvious tension and even more obvious hard-on I had pressed against the very bottom of her spine – which she wiggled against, lord help me – there was something unexpectedly intimate about washing her hair. Liz closed her eyes and tilted her head back, sighing happily when I kept my touch gentle on her scalp. We stayed quiet, enjoying the peace between us for the next couple of stolen minutes.

But when I was done with her hair I wasted no time in lathering my hands in body wash and daring to move down from her head. Along the line of her neck and shoulders, across her clavicle to her breasts, which were too large to fit in my hands. I groaned when my fingertips grazed her nipples.

Liz's eyes opened, though they were heavy-lidded with desire. "Where do you think you're touching?"

"I'm just making sure you're clean," I insisted, murmuring the words into her ear. I bit her earlobe; she shivered so violently it sent a shock wave through my dick. I rubbed it against her arse. This time it was Liz who moaned.

Fuck. Were we doing this? Were we really going to do this?

Slowly, deliberately, Liz dragged my left hand from her chest, across her stomach, her hip bone...and down between her thighs.

"You know, you're right," she said, her other hand running up my neck to curl into my hair. "I sweated so much in that cat suit...and even looking at you tonight made me feel filthy. You better clean me off."

My brain completely short-circuited. Good thing my fingers moved of their own accord. "Fuck, Liz..." I let out, the slickness of her against my fingertips threatening to tip me over the edge. "You're so wet already."

She tilted her head up to graze her teeth against my collarbone, dark-lashed eyes trained on my every reaction. "I have been all night."

I bucked my hips against her, and Liz fell against the wall. It made things much easier, pressing her into the tiles and gaining enough friction to rut the ever-loving hell out of my dick on the curve of her arse.

"Oh - like that, god - Tom—" Liz barely got out, when I changed the angle of my fingers on her clit and she began rubbing against me in earnest. She was close. We both knew it. Clearly I hadn't been the only one pent-up like a volcano overdue an eruption. Just how had she been hiding it so well?

Liz gasped when I slipped a finger inside her, then two. "Tom!" she gasped, tugging at my hair so hard it hurt. I revelled in it.

"Say my name again," I urged, breath hot and heavy against her ear.

"Tom," she obediently repeated. "*Tom*. I'm—"

Liz didn't get the rest of her sentence out. She shuddered, and her thighs clenched around my hand, and with a heave of her chest and a bite of her lower lip she came.

For a few seconds all we did was breathe together, neither of us daring to move. Then I squeezed one of her thighs, and turned Liz around to face me. Her expression was all hazy contentment and desire. I knew the only thing I wanted was to be inside her.

Inside her.

Fuck.

"Condoms," I bit out, feeling as if I could slap myself for somehow not thinking to have any in my shower, even though why on earth would I? "I have some in - in the cabinet over the sink. I'll—"

"I'll get them," Liz said, shaking her head as if to wake her brain back up. She slid free of my grasp, opened the shower doors and padded across the floor.

Towards her towel, which she wrapped around herself on her way to the bathroom door.

"Liz...?" I wondered aloud. Were we taking this to one of our bedrooms? I was only too happy with that.

She plastered the most evil smile to her face, her gaze casting down to my aching cock and back to my face. "Have fun being blue-balled. Clearly you can't seduce twenty-seven-year-old single women, either."

She slammed the door on her way out.

I couldn't believe it. This was not happening.

Liz had just played me for an absolute fucking fool and, like a fucking fool, I'd fallen for it.

I had no idea where to go from here.

Chapter Twenty-One

LIZ

I WAS NEVER ONE FOR WORKING ON a Saturday but, considering what I'd done with Tom the night before, the last place I wanted to be was his house.

What I'd done *to* Tom.

Part of me knew I'd gone too far.

Part of me revelled in the power I'd had over him.

A much, much bigger part of me was still reeling over how fucking great it felt when he made me come.

It took Tom all of sixty bloody seconds to do it. The entire lower half of my body coiled and twisted merely thinking about it.

How was I supposed to concentrate on fluorescent microscopy? The burgeoning migraine that was creeping up on me wasn't helping, either. I hadn't thought I was that drunk by the time I fell asleep – swiftly and blissfully, thanks in no small part to fucking around with Tom – so I hadn't expected much of a hangover today. Clearly the promise of a migraine, and more twists in my stomach that weren't entirely pleasant, were my punishment for leaving Tom high-and-dry.

I still couldn't believe my own resolve.

"Oh! I didn't expect you to be in, Liz," Daichi announced from the lab proper, scaring the living daylights out of me. My haggard-looking boss came over to the fluorescent microscopy room and leaned against the door. "How was your friend's party?"

I offered him a smile. "It was fine. Not as fun as karaoke, though. Did you have a good time last night?"

"Can you not tell? I look and feel like death."

"Maybe death warmed over."

Daichi chortled at the remark. "That feels accurate. Anyway, I'm glad I ran into you, as it happens."

"Oh?"

"You know the functional genomics conference happening in London in a couple of weeks?"

I nodded. "I was thinking of asking you if I could take a few days off to head down for it."

Daichi's eyes lit up. "Well then aren't I lucky?" he exclaimed, rocking back and forth on his feet. "I have a poster for the conference but I can't go anymore – last-minute holiday plans with the wife – so I was going to ask you if you wanted to go on my behalf."

"You don't want Peter to go?" I ignored the twinge of guilt I felt when mentioning him. "He's been here longer than I have."

"The research I'm presenting is more relevant to what you've begun researching so I thought it would be a good idea for you to go, instead. So what do you say?"

There was nothing to mull over, of course. This was a great opportunity, and I'd been planning on going in the first place. "I'd love to, Daichi," I said, grinning. "Thanks for thinking of me."

"Not at all! You're the one doing me a favour. Now, I best be off to find some coffee before I pass out. Damn essays needing marked before Monday..."

I watched my boss wander off with a sense of fuzzy contentment washing over my brain. I really did love working in this lab. Daichi actively *wanted* me to do things other lab leaders would insist on only ever doing themselves. It was great.

Another lurching from decidedly not my stomach spoiled my mood once more, though it at least finally explained why my head was beginning to ache.

My period was about to hit.

"Great..." I muttered, saving my microscopy images on the computer before clearing away my slides and shutting everything down. Ever since I went on the implant I hardly ever got my period - once every three or four months, tops - but when it *did* hit it hit fucking hard.

It was pointless to try and work through the oncoming assault on my uterus. Whether I could find it in me to face Tom or not - I suspected not - it was imperative I got back to his place, pronto, to huddle under a duvet with a hot water bottle and a giant bar of Dairy Milk.

And every rom-com the world of streaming services had to offer.

Chapter Twenty-Two

TOM

"WHAT DO YOU THINK OF CHICKEN with haggis bon bons for one of the mains, Thomas? I know back when we were looking at caterers you thought it was too simple, but - Thomas? *Thomas!*"

"Me what now?" I asked blearily, blinking at my mother as if that would someone allow me to parse what she'd said. We were in the kitchen, chatting about the wedding (of course) whilst Jim was making lasagne from scratch. Liz was holed up in her room and had been since yesterday morning, aside from heading into the lab for three hours which I heavily suspected had been her way of avoiding me.

Now it was Sunday night and I'd still not seen nor heard from her even once.

It was driving me insane. How could she have had the audacity to do what she did and then simply...disappear? I was dying to confront her. To ask her if what happened in the shower had truly just been her fucking with me or not.

I suspected not, but unless I put Liz on the spot and flustered her into revealing the truth I doubted she'd ever admit to anything that suggested she actually liked me. That she *wanted* me, as much as I wanted her.

I desperately wanted to knock on her door and talk things over with her, with a level head and absolutely no alcohol involved. We were both well beyond the point of being able to hide behind reckless, drunk behaviour, after all. But intruding on her personal space felt wrong. If I forced my presence on Liz in her bedroom that would only serve to remind her that this was *my* house, instead of it being somewhere she could feel safe and comfortable. I didn't want that.

Instead I over-thought my entire weekend away until I was tempted to tear my (no longer red) hair out and scream.

"Honestly, Thomas, what are you thinking about to put that expression on your face?" Mum sighed, stroking my cheek with a forefinger before pinching it. When I flinched away she laughed. "Tell me what's up."

I glanced at Jim who had chosen that exact moment to look at me, too. He turned his attention back to the meat sauce he was making with the same kind of flustered reaction his daughter would have made when caught watching someone. The family resemblance between them truly was startling.

"I'm just wondering why Liz has hidden in her room all weekend," I said, surprising myself by admitting to the truth.

"I thought she was nursing a two-day hangover," Jim offered. "She's in a right foul mood."

A frown of worry creased Mum's brow. "Oh dear! Should I see if she needs anything?"

"No, just let her be. Lizzie isn't one for letting folk see her in any kind of pain."

I pondered this for a moment. Was she in *pain* because of what happened between us? Some kind of guilt or anguish over fucking around with me? Considering how I'd treated Liz during her PhD, was I allowed to feel even a little bit happy about this?

Jim pointed his spatula at me. "Why are you asking, anyway?"

"It's just been quiet this weekend without her around. I'm not used to it."

Clearly the man hadn't expected this answer, which was honest if not the entire truth. Jim frowned, then lowered the spatula, then returned his attention to the hob. "You're really not what I expected," he muttered.

"Jim!" Mum exclaimed, scandalised. "Just what does that mean?"

Another wave of the spatula in my direction. "He knows."

I did indeed. The problem was that I didn't know what to say in response.

At that precise, very awkward moment, the sound of someone stomping down the stairs caught my attention. A few moments later Liz appeared in the kitchen, wrapped in a duvet and so pale in the face she looked like she'd just spent the last hour throwing her guts up. Wordlessly she shuffled over to the fridge and pulled out the filtered water jug, filling her empty bottle to the brim before scanning the fridge for...something. Whatever it was, I didn't have it. A quick search of the freezer followed by the cupboards confirmed that whatever Liz wanted was nowhere to be found.

"Lizzie," Jim said, brightening at the arrival of his daughter. "I'm making your favourite for dinner. It'll be ready in an hour."

To his surprise, Liz took one look at the pot of meat sauce and seemed about ready to vomit. "I'll pass," she mumbled, voice hoarse and husky from disuse. Without looking at my mum or me she scurried out of the kitchen and back up the stairs.

"That's not like her," Jim worried. "She loves lasagne. Must be a really bad hangover."

"I remember when I was pregnant with Thomas," Mum said,

putting me on immediate alert, "I could barely *touch* red meat! Made me gag to high heaven."

Jim's face darkened. "If she's pregnant—"

"She's most definitely not," I said before I could stop myself. Liz being so careless as to fall pregnant was ludicrous. She'd never allow it. But Mum's comment sent an epiphany coursing through my brain that was so fucking obvious I could have hit myself.

I pushed myself off the counter and fished beneath the kitchen sink for a couple of plastic bags. "Anyone need anything from the shops?"

Mum and Jim both raised their eyebrows in surprise. "No...?" Mum said. "We went earlier. What do you need?"

"It doesn't matter," I replied, leaving the kitchen to slide on some shoes and my jacket before running out through the rain towards my car.

The roads were thankfully clear of traffic, and since I wasn't sure what Liz would want I travelled further out to the massive Tesco on Maryhill Road. Once there I filled a trolley with everything I could think of that she could possibly have been looking for: cheese pizza, chocolate, ice cream, Haribo, heavily salted crisps, chips, Coke, wine, the works.

Painkillers. Lots of painkillers.

When I checked out the cashier looked at me like I'd gone mad. I merely shrugged. By the time I returned home Mum and Jim had already eaten ("There's lasagne on the hob for you!") and retired to the first floor lounge, so I put the oven on and set about getting a fire going in the living room. I knew there was a hot water bottle *somewhere*, but for the life of me I couldn't find it. But in the process I found an old electric blanket, so I set up an extension cord in the living room and plugged it in before dumping it on the end of the couch closest to the fire. Then I put a pizza on, laid out the various non-refrigerated snacks on the coffee table, and...

Willed myself the courage to go up and knock on Liz's door. For what was the point of all of this if Liz didn't actually know about it? Rubbing the stubble on my chin and wondering if I should have shaved before kicking myself for thinking such a stupid thing, I forced myself to stalk up the stairs.

I lingered outside Liz's door, a few seconds passing whilst I listened through the wood to try and work out what she was up to. Watching a film, by the sounds of things. My heart was hammering in my chest as I held my knuckles to the door. All I had to do was knock. I wasn't intruding; I was trying to help. If Liz wanted me to fuck off then she could tell me to do so.

I knocked on the door.

"Fuck off, Tom."

Oh.

"How'd you know it was me?" I asked, crestfallen at Liz's immediate rejection.

"Dad and Jenny came knocking, like, half an hour ago. I don't want lasagne. Or anything else."

"...will pizza, chocolate, ice cream and Pringles persuade you to come out?"

A pause. "You don't have any of those things," Liz said, slowly, as if she expected my words to be a trap.

"I do now," I told her through the door. "I have a fire going, too. And an electric blanket. So come out."

Another pause, longer this time. I heard Liz stop whatever she was watching on her laptop, scurry around her room, then finally open the door a few inches to peer at me through dark-circled eyes.

"What are you up to?" she asked, face too twisted in pain to even look suspicious.

I wanted to give her a hug or – I don't know. Something. Codeine, maybe.

"I'm just trying to help," I said. I waved towards her general haggard appearance. "It's your time of the month, isn't it?"

Liz looked like she was ready to punch me in the face. "Just say *period*, Tom. You're a grown man."

Well, she had me there.

"Okay. You're on your period, and it clearly fucking hurts. So will you let me look after you or do I have to somehow trick you into that?"

For a moment it looked like Liz was going to refuse. To be honest I wouldn't have blamed her; for all I knew the only thing she really wanted was to curl up in bed, alone and undisturbed.

But then her shoulders relaxed, and she opened the door wide enough to squeeze through it. "Did you say you had an electric blanket?"

"Ready and waiting to go on the best spot on the couch, by the fire."

"What kind of pizza did you get?"

"Only cheese. No meat whatsoever."

"Ice cream?"

"Mackies Original. No other flavour allowed in this house."

Liz emitted a noise that could only be described as a crow of happiness. She eagerly bounded towards the stairs, then bent over in pain before she reached the second step.

I slid an arm through hers and eased her downstairs without thinking. "I thought I told you to let me look after you?"

"I assumed you said that as part of some twisted game of revenge for what I did on Friday night," she admitted, not looking at me.

"Not all of us are as cruel as you, Liz."

"I don't know, Tom, you can be pretty fucking cruel."

"Do you actually want to argue or is that the hormones talking? Because I'm content to leave Friday behind us and wait on your every whim if you would only *let me do so.*"

Liz froze for a moment, on the verge of arguing, but then we entered the living room and a wave of heat hit us both. Liz made a beeline for the sofa and collapsed into the electric blanket, sighing in relief when she wrapped it around herself.

She offered me the smallest of smiles, which brightened up her pained, haggard face. "No arguing, and in return you wait on me hand and foot. Is that it?"

I could only laugh. "Will I regret this?"

"Absolutely. Can you put *Marley & Me* on?"

"Isn't that the one where the dog dies?"

"Yes. I need to cry and I've run out of videos on Youtube where guys reunite with their dogs after spending time in the military."

"I'm not even going to pretend like there's not a lot to unpack there." I made my way over to the kitchen door to retrieve the pizza. "Do you want wine?"

Liz shook her head, then snuggled into the electric blanket like a little bird. "No alcohol. Just junk food and you."

I wasn't sure if Liz was aware of what she'd just said – whether it was a slip of the tongue or spoken deliberately to get a rise out of me – but in that moment I didn't care. A flush of heat that had nothing to do with the roaring fire in the hearth, nor anything to do with the sexual tension from Friday night, spread through me.

Of all the things I could be doing on a Sunday night, watching sappy films with Liz whilst plying her with chocolate and pizza had become absolutely top of my list.

Chapter Twenty-Three

LIZ

"SO WHAT ARE YOUR THOUGHTS ON Doctor Levi? The new postdoc in the cell lab?"

"Eh, I could take him or leave him."

"But he's gorgeous!" Mia crooned, stealing one of Rachael's chips as she did so. "Those lovely brown eyes, ink-black hair, pale skin..."

"That's way too close to Liz's ex for her to like him," Chloë said. "What was his name? Elliot?"

"Eli," I said, nodding. Chloë had come in much earlier than she usually did in order to join me, Mia and Rachael for a midweek chippie delivered straight to the communal area of our research building. Mia and Rachael had run over from their lab specifically for it; like hell was Chloë missing a gossip session with our old undergrad-turned-PhD girl group for a few extra hours in bed.

Rachael scanned her eyes across the atrium. The stairs leading up to the floors above us were all visible, as were the glass walkways that joined different parts of the building together. All in all we were positioned perfectly to people-watch.

Currently we were playing Rachael and Mia's favourite game: spot the hot researchers. Back in our undergrad days it had specifically been 'spot the hot lecturers' until we ourselves became researchers and met a score of new faces within the Institute.

"How about him?" Rachael suggested, locking eyes on a target crossing the third floor walkway. "Works in the Human Molecular Genetics lab. Professor – Professor – ugh, what's his name again?"

"Lionel," I said, glancing at the man before returning my attention to my half-finished lunch. I'd ordered far too much food but I felt bad about throwing it out so it remained in front of me, steadily growing cold.

"Professor Lionel's wife is really hot," Chloë added. "Total blonde bombshell. My type if ever there was one."

"Don't let your brunette girlfriend hear you say that."

"Oh, she knows. I have a poster of Margot Robbie up in our bedroom. Turns out that's Harriet's type, too. Makes it fun to watch films together because we love the same people in them!"

"That's some flawless logic," Mia said. "What about you, Liz? Who in the Institute do *you* find hot?"

All three women stared at me with laser-focus. Like hell was I saying who they wanted me to say, even if it was clear they'd all been gossiping about me and Tom behind my back. I couldn't blame them, if I was honest. If the situation was reversed I'd absolutely be talking about it.

"Um, Evan Jackson, probably," I ended up saying, which at least wasn't a lie. I *did* find him hot.

It took Rachael, Mia and Chloë a few moments to chew this over. My best friend narrowed her eyes at me, deeply suspicious. "Wait, are you talking about Professor Evan Jackson, the head of undergrad molecular biology?"

"Yes, and?"

"He's fifty years old!"

I merely shrugged. "I like what I like."

Quick as a flash, from behind me, a hand darted for my phone – which was lying on the table by my right hand – and pulled it out of reach. "We better change the age range on Tinder for you," Tom said, when I turned around to face him in abject horror. Just how long had he been standing there? Had my friends known?

"Give that back," I demanded, jumping from my seat to try and pry the device from Tom's stupidly long-fingered hands. He cuffed me away with a shoulder as he *unlocked* my phone. "Clearly you won't find love looking amongst your peers..." he muttered, opening Tinder of all things right before my very eyes.

"How on earth do you know my password?!" I exclaimed, barely able to keep my voice from reaching screaming pitch. Behind me my friends were gently snickering.

Tom flashed an evil grin my way. "I thought only fools used their debit card PIN for their phone, Liz. Honestly."

"How did you know it was my PIN?"

"I guessed," Tom's grin turned into a laugh. "I saw your password when you typed it into your phone yesterday. Who knew it was actually your PIN? I thought millennials were supposed to be tech-savvy?"

"That doesn't mean much coming from you, Grand-dad."

"Does that put me in your datable range, then? Right next to Professor Silver Fox himse—"

A cough from Chloë reminded us both that we were not, in fact, alone. Tom straightened up, turned my phone screen off, then made to hand it back to me.

Thank god.

But then he childishly yanked it out of reach when my hand

was bare millimetres away. "Ask for it nicely," Tom said, clearly enjoying how uncomfortable he was making me.

I scowled. "Professor Henderson, *please* give me my phone back."

"Oh, that's nowhere near personal enough."

What the hell was that supposed to mean? I looked up at Tom, determined to stare him down, only for my face to start reddening. The last time I'd said *please* to him had been – had been—

In the shower.

The wicked glint in his eyes told me that was what Tom had intended I remember.

I took a step into his personal space, landed a hand on his bicep and squeezed it because, honestly, nobody was around but my friends and they were going to give me hell anyway. It was worth it for the way Tom stilled beneath my touch, cocking his head to the left as he wondered what I was doing.

"*Tom*," I purred, so low only he could hear me. "Tom, please...give me my fucking phone."

He handed it back to me without a word.

Then he turned from me to address Mia, as if the last fifteen seconds had never happened. "I was on my way over to check in on you. Do you mind jumping up to Professor Ito's office with me so we can go over your thesis?"

Mia seemed to be suffering whiplash from the drastic change in Tom's tone from teasing to professional. She blinked rather uselessly a few times, then stood up. "Of – of course!"

Before the two of them left I bundled up the rest of my chips and pushed them into Tom's arms. "I'm full. Don't let this go to waste."

"Look at you feeding me, Dr Maclean," Tom said, extricating a chip from the bag to chew on it. "It's like we're married already." With a sly smile he was off, leaving me torn between wanting to hit him or laugh at the ludicrous comment.

A beat of silence fell. Then: "Tell me the truth, Liz," Chloë said, "you're fucking Henderson, aren't you?"

"I'm not sleeping with him!"

"Yeah, and I'm straight."

Rachael spluttered out a laugh. "It's pretty obvious he has the hots for you, and there's no way you can deny you have the hots for him. Come on."

"Just because I find him attractive doesn't mean I'm sleeping with him," I muttered, slumping back down into my seat. I crossed my arms over my chest defensively. "It's not like you actually want to sleep with the dozen researchers you literally just admitted to finding hot, do you?"

"True, but I don't live with any of them or have any of them look after me hand-and-foot while I'm on my bloody period. Pun intended."

I fired a glare at Chloë. "That was meant for your ears only."

Chloë held up her hands. "Sue me. You really wanna tell me you'd *let* Tom look after you when you feel like shite, look like shite and—"

"Thanks."

"You know what I mean. You let him be around you when you were definitely at your worst and he still publicly all-but-professed his love? You don't joke about being married with just anyone, Liz."

I had no words to fire back at Chloë. Truth be told, she was right. When my period hit Tom had been nothing short of a fucking angel whilst all I did was groan in pain and cry at the dog dying in *Marley & Me.* He'd brought me every kind of food I could possibly have wanted. He got me an electric blanket, and refused to let me get up for anything, and let me put on whatever the hell I wanted on TV regardless of whether he agreed with it or not.

"...he didn't profess his fucking *love*," was all I could grumble. Since I knew neither Chloë nor Rachael would let it go at just that one comment, I added, "Okay, so what if we're both attracted to each other, and he treats me with the bare minimum decency required from a sympathetic human being?"

My friends glanced at one another. Then Rachael sighed. "There's no helping her, is there? Liz, you're so screwed. God help you this weekend."

"What do you mean? I'm away in London for the genomics conference this weekend."

Chloë chewed her lip. "Yeah, about that."

Oh fuck off.

"No. Do not tell me Tom is going."

"I'm afraid so," Rachael said. "I overheard him telling Michael about it on Monday, complaining that he had to go so Professor Ito could go on holiday. Didn't you know? I'm sure Peter knew."

"Peter and I...are not on speaking terms right now." That still stung, but I had to respect him and give him space. Even though I was dying to get back on equal ground with him again.

Chloë patted my arm sympathetically. "He will soon. He just needs some time. And regarding the conference – it isn't as if you and Tom will be sharing a room, is it? Going to the conference together will be easier than living together, I'm sure."

"Yeah, sure," I said, knowing I sounded unconvinced. Irritation and nerves were scratching up my insides. Tom had known he was going to the conference all this time and hadn't thought to mention it to me even once?

He was dead. He was so dead.

Chapter Twenty-four

TOM

"I swear I thought you already knew I was coming. I only found out *you* were going two days ago."

"Sure. That's why you mysteriously came down to London straight after work yesterday, thus escaping the need to see me whilst I packed for the conference – a perfect time for you to mention that you were going *for the first time ever.*"

"If you want to blame anyone for this, blame Daichi," I complained. I knew *I* did. If he'd been planning to ask Liz to stand by the poster and answer questions all along then he'd never needed me to do it in the first place. And yet here Liz and I both were, checking in for our rooms at the hotel. Not adjacent but on the same floor; I was quite certain Liz would have requested another floor if she could have.

She gave me some seriously suspicious side-eye. "So why did you go down to London early, then, if it wasn't to avoid telling me you were coming?"

"Believe it or not, Liz, I have friends. One of whom I decided to catch up with."

That finally seemed to mollify her. "Fine," she muttered,

when we reached the third floor and our rooms. She checked the time on her phone then turned to me. "I'm just going to chuck my stuff in then take ten minutes to clean myself up, if that's okay. I hate early morning flights."

"I can see that," I said without thinking, for it was true that Liz looked decidedly ruffled, and there were dark shadows beneath her eyes. Then, quickly, I added, "I'll get us some coffees."

"Thanks," Liz said, surprising me by ignoring my insensitivity and focusing on the promise of hot caffeine. "I need one."

Well, at least her anger at Daichi's poorly-executed meet-cute had evaporated quickly.

In truth I was very happy to have company for the conference. It wasn't my field of expertise, and though Daichi wanted me to spy on his 'competition' I had no interest whatsoever in networking. Having Liz with me made everything a hundred times more bearable.

Even better: I'd be able to see her actively talking about research with her peers. Presentations were very firmly in Liz's wheelhouse if the talks she gave throughout her PhD were anything to go by. Her final year presentation of her research had been outstanding.

By the time Liz and I met back up – Liz gratefully taking the latte I handed over to her and immediately drinking it – we barely had enough time to sign up at registration and pin our poster on its allotted board before the conference proper began.

Liz had worked her ten requested minutes supremely in her favour. Gone were the hoodie and leggings she'd worn to travel, replacing them with a royal blue pencil skirt paired with a sleeveless blush-coloured top that buttoned all the way down her spine. There were no longer dark circles under her eyes, the magic of make-up transforming Liz into a lively, exaggerated but still very natural version of herself. She kept her hair loose and wavy for once, framing her face and preventing the ensemble from looking *too* prim and proper.

Liz caught me staring at her. Obviously. "What?" she asked, smiling self-consciously as she sipped her coffee.

"You look nice."

"Don't I always?"

"Is that a trick question?"

The softest laugh escaped her lips; Liz held a hand to her mouth as if she could push it back in. "Nice save," she said, breaking eye contact to turn her attention to the poster behind us. "Do you want to wander around the convention whilst I field questions about Daichi's research? To be honest I still need to familiarise myself with the poster..."

"In which case you'll need me to stick around," I said, puffing my chest out in mock self-importance. "Since I'm the one who made the damn thing and all."

For a moment Liz scrutinised my face for any hint of a lie, then properly scanned the poster from top to bottom. I tried not to focus on the curve of her arse in her tight blue skirt as she did so and failed miserably. When Liz reached the fourth figure on the poster her eyes widened in clear surprise. "Those are the fluorescent microscopy pictures I took *four days ago.*"

"God, don't I know it. They were much better than the ones Dai had given me to work with initially, so I had to get the entire poster reprinted."

"I didn't know you were keeping such a close eye on my work."

"I can't help it. We work on the same bench."

Liz seemed unconvinced. "I don't really know what *you're* working on."

"That's because I'm repeating random experiments to get better results for my grant proposal; unless you read the entire thing I wouldn't expect you to know what the hell I'm doing."

"But you aren't working with integrases anymore. Are you changing the focus of your research?"

"Oh, so you've been *actively trying* to work out what I'm doing," I mused, unreasonably happy about this. I nudged Liz's shoulder with my own; her face flushed pink. "Are you missing the good old recombinase days from the Molecular Genetics lab?"

I expected Liz to get flustered and thoroughly deny my claim. Instead she shrugged, scratching her nose as she pondered my question. "I don't know," she admitted. "I mean, I much prefer the Ito lab. The atmosphere, how social it is, the people. But I kind of...I don't know. Miss protein work. Never thought I'd hear myself say that. And I've discovered I don't care much for dissecting flies."

The only response that was appropriate to that was laughter. I nudged her shoulder again. "A true comrade in arms. Once you become accustomed to how easy *E.coli* is to work with you can never work with more complex organisms again."

Liz pushed against my shoulder with deliberate force. "Don't hand your vendetta against Drosophila over to me, Tom."

"So you think you'd like to return to molecular microbiology after your postdoc is up?"

"I want to veer towards viral gene therapy," she said, resolute in a way that meant she'd thought about this long and hard on many an occasion. "That was always my goal. I thought Mike's lab was the right fit for that, but my PhD was far too much about biological computers. That's why working in a higher model organism on a functional level was a good direction for me to go – for a while, at least. I guess I don't know how to pivot after that."

Considering my grant proposal was all *about* pivoting to focus on viral gene therapy I felt the mad urge to laugh maniacally in Liz's face. But I resisted; if I was successful then she'd find out in due course.

We were interrupted, then, by our first curious bystander of the day, so Liz and I politely moved to the side of our poster to allow the woman to take a closer look at it. When she asked about the fly lines that were being used in question I indicated towards Liz.

"Take the floor, as it were," I said, enjoying the fact I needed to do precisely zero work.

Liz smoothed her hair back, gave me the tiniest of nods, cleared her throat and then answered the woman's question.

Three hours later she was still doing the same thing with the hundredth nosy researcher who'd come up, talking to the man with as much enthusiasm as she had at the beginning of the session. Liz was unrelenting, passionate and very, very careful about how she worded things. She hid any flaws in the work in such a way that one never knew there were any flaws in the first place, or pre-emptively addressed said faults with already-prepared solutions and troubleshooting protocols.

Of course I already knew she was great at this. She'd had to be, with me as her supervisor.

A knot of guilt twisted my stomach.

"I'll get us another coffee," I told Liz, gently touching her on the arm so as not to interrupt her fielding another question.

Thanks, she mouthed at me, then added, *and water, please.*

As I wandered through the conference I barely paid attention to my surroundings – something which Daichi would be thoroughly annoyed about when he returned from his holiday. But I had too much on my mind, and none of it was good.

I hadn't properly thought about what I'd done to Liz during her PhD in a while, truth be told. Nor had I thought about how I'd intercepted her Tinder dates or sabotaged her flat hunt. I'd been so wrapped up in the two of us getting to know one another, flirting with one another, fighting with one another. Playing whatever game it was that Liz was playing with me.

Now it was *all* I could think about. Was it something I should tell Liz about? The growing weight of my conscience suggested I should. But if I did I knew that whatever relationship was growing between the two of us – however fucking twisted it was – would be ruined. For how could it not be?

I had to keep all of my treachery to myself. All of my purely selfish, egotistical decisions made on Liz's behalf.

It was in this way that I returned to our poster, new lattes in hand, in a considerably worse mood than I had been when I left. When I spotted a dark-haired man notice Liz and make a beeline for her my mood only darkened further.

The man clearly had one thing on his mind, and it certainly wasn't the neurogenetics of *Drosophila melanogaster.*

"For you," I said, announcing my presence before handing Liz her coffee. She wrapped her hands around the cup with a look of bliss on her face.

"Fuck, thank you, Tom. I'm absolutely dead. And it's barely lunch!"

Lunch. A great excuse to scurry away before the man reached Liz. He was only two posters away, fighting against the crowd. So I placed a hand on Liz's back and turned her in the opposite direction from her desperate suitor. "There's a Japanese place down the street I planned to try when I was down here. What do you say to jumping off early for an extended lunch? Yuzu sake included."

Liz positively chirruped at the notion. "I'd love that. Do you think they'd mind if we came back half-cut?"

I smirked. "Wouldn't be the first time we'd gotten inappropriately tipsy at an official event, would it? So long as nobody spills orange juice all over us and you don't go stripping off your clothes in public I think we'll be okay."

"*Tom!*" Liz slapped my chest, scandalised, but then she laughed. "I didn't *strip my clothes off in public*, or even because I wanted to."

"Is that so? Didn't look like it from where I was standing."

"You perverted—"

"Liz! Elizabeth! Wait up, hey – excuse me, sorry – Liz!"

Liz paused, agonisingly close to the exit from the conference, a frown creasing her brow. "Is that...?" she wondered uncertainly, turning around to find out who had shouted after her. I wanted nothing more than to continue rushing Liz out, but when she made no move to do so I gave in to curiosity and also turned to see what the man with the black hair had to say to her.

What I hadn't expected was the look on Liz's face. Shock first, wide-eyed and pale-skinned. Her hands were shaking. *Shaking.* Then Liz blinked a few times, got herself together, and plastered on the same easy smile she'd worn the night we discovered our parents were getting married.

A smile that hid everything she was feeling.

"Eli?" she said, when the man finally caught up with us. "Eli, is that really you?"

One good look at this Eli was all I needed to put two and two together. He was of an age with Liz, after all, and the expression on *his* face was one of such pure, unadulterated joy that I knew he could only be one person.

Liz's ex.

Chapter Twenty-five

LIZ

"ELI? IS THAT REALLY YOU?"

The ghost of my past nodded eagerly. His cheeks were slightly flushed, as if he'd been running. He let out a long breath in one great big whoosh of air before exclaiming, "Hell yeah it's me. I can't believe it's *you*!"

Neither could I. What was Elliot Jones doing in London, at this conference, standing right in front of me?

My head was spinning. This didn't feel real.

Elliot looked older than when I saw him last. Well, of course he did. That was over four years ago. But because of the social media of mutual friends it hadn't really clicked that, if I were to see Elliot again, he would look any different than he had done before.

His previously foppish, indie-boy-band hair had been cut into a classic short-back-and-sides style, which suited him much better. Elliot was also dressed better than he used to – he was wearing a suit that actually fit him, for one – and his skin held the kind of glow one only attained after several years spent living in a sunny place.

He looked good, damn it.

Worse, he looked happy to see me.

"What—" I tried to say, before my throat caught on the word. I took a sip of coffee, though it was still scalding, swallowed, then tried again. "What are you doing here?"

Elliot chuckled at the question as if it highly amused him. "What am I doing at a functional genomics conference when my research is in functional genomics? I should ask what *you're* doing here! Don't you work in synthetic biology?"

"Um, I—"

"Doctor Maclean began a postdoc in the Ito laboratory at the University of Glasgow in September," Tom said, voice slow and steady and full of polite pleasantry. He held out a hand to Elliot. "You must be an old acquaintance of hers. I'm Professor Henderson."

"Nice to meet you," Eli said, frowning as he tried to work out why he recognised the name. I could practically see the light bulb go off when he worked out why Tom's name seemed familiar. "As in...Doctor Henderson, who taught some of the DNA block in undergrad genetics?"

"I see my reputation precedes me."

"She never went to your lectures," Eli said, indicating towards stupid, still tongue-tied me. "Said it was because you never replied to her request for a third year summer project, so she decided to pass the DNA block without learning anything from you."

"*Eli!*" I cried, beyond mortified. Out of the corner of my eye I saw Tom staring at me, his lips quirked into the most infuriating smile I'd ever seen. This was definitely not something I'd ever wanted him to know.

"I thought you missed them because you slept in," Tom teased, nudging my arm. He'd been nudging me playfully all morning, damn it, ensuring I never once forgot about how fucking rigid his muscles were beneath the pale yellow cotton of his shirt.

Eli wrinkled his nose. "Seems I got you in trouble. Sorry, Liz. How're your parents doing?"

"Mum died two years ago," I bit out unthinkingly. All my filters were off, my brain was running on emergency power and I had no charm or guile or social grace left. It was therefore to absolutely nobody's surprise when Eli reacted with a horrible mix of shock, sadness and pity.

Beside me Tom touched my elbow, gently, tracing vague circles against my skin.

It was enough to reboot my senses.

"It was ovarian cancer," I elaborated after three very awkward seconds. "But that's not exactly an appropriate catch-up topic, is it?"

Eli's expression crumpled, and he took a step towards me. I almost took a step back, but Tom's tiny touch on my elbow kept me grounded. "I'm so sorry for your loss, Liz. I wish you would have told me."

"We haven't exactly spoken much over the last few years," I pointed out. "Or at all."

"Um, I actually tried to reach out a few times this year. Didn't you get any of my messages?"

"I may have muted you on all social media and blocked your number."

I didn't know what to expect from Eli in response to that; I certainly didn't expect him to look so sad. "I deserved that. I—"

"Liz," Tom gently interrupted, bending down to murmur into my ear. His voice sent shivers down my spine, but by now I was so used to Tom eliciting that exact reaction from me it was easy to brush it aside...for now. "Let's turn lunch into dinner, instead. I can see a couple of researchers Daichi definitely wanted me to spy on."

"Oh." A wave of disappointment washed over me; I'd been

so excited barely five minutes ago about lunch together. Why was Tom running off? I was fairly certain there were no researchers he wanted to chase after but I wasn't pathetic enough to beg him to stay, either. Was I? "Okay, then. See you later?"

He offered me his most blindingly charming smile, though something about the set of his eyes looked a little tight. "Of course."

After Tom left Eli waved towards the exit. "I was about to get lunch. Why don't we go together?"

"I'm not actually hungry, to be honest," I lied. I was fucking starving. "I might just go sit in the atrium and drink my coffee."

Eli seemed crestfallen. "Well, let me walk you there, at least."

I couldn't find a reason to refuse, so I let him.

"To be honest, Liz," he said, when we reached an empty couch. I didn't sit down. "If I hadn't just run into you now I was going to find a way of contacting you over the next few days, anyway."

I took a sip of coffee. It was finally a drinkable temperature, though for some reason it tasted like ash. I glanced at Eli over the brim of my cup. "Why on earth would you do that? Last time I checked you broke my heart."

There. I said it. Straight to the point and, above all, honest. Then I sat down on the couch because why the hell was I letting what Eli wanted stop me from sitting down? I wasn't some timid, wilting flower. If I didn't want him to sit beside me for longer than thirty seconds I could just tell him to fuck off.

Luckily, Eli *didn't* sit down. He simply fixed me with a pining, doe-eyed stare and fiddled with his hands, which was a sure-fire sign he was nervous as hell.

"A-actually," he stammered, shifting on the spot, "I moved back last month. To Scotland. I just began a postdoc in Edinburgh."

Oh.

"So you...what? Wanted to catch up?"

He shook his head. "That doesn't cover even the least of it. Liz. I know I fucked up when I broke it off with you. I know I fucked up well before that, too, when I didn't tell you I'd applied to study in the US. But more than that, I fucked up when I heard you say you didn't want kids and immediately rejected you based on that and that alone."

I went to swallow a gulp of coffee and realised I'd somehow inhaled the whole thing. Funny, I didn't remember drinking it. But Eli was looking at me expectantly, waiting for me to react, so I tried to remember how to speak.

"Thanks for the sort-of apology, I guess," I managed. "Bit late but I appreciate the sentiment."

To my surprise Eli laughed, his posture finally relaxing in the process. "God, I missed you. I missed how grumpy and sarcastic your sense of humour is. Every day in California I wished I was with you, instead."

Wait, what?

What was happening?

"Eli..." How did I say this? Bluntly? Yeah, that would have to do. "All you had to do was message me or call me or reach out through a friend and you could have told me any of that when it *actually mattered.*"

"Yeah, but that's so selfish, isn't it? We were both focusing on our careers, and I liked my research too much to quit it. To tell you that I missed you – that would have only made us both feel worse."

"Careful," I said, taking great risks by attempting to smile, "that almost sounds like personal growth talking."

When Eli saw my smile he broke out into the biggest, most boyish grin I'd ever seen. I'd forgotten how beautiful he was when he smiled at me that way. "I did a lot of growing up on my own the last four years. And I discovered a lot about myself."

"Such as?"

"Such as the fact I know I don't want kids. Or to get married. I love science and travelling and my hobbies and my goddamn free time too much to commit to any of that. Do you still feel that way?"

Numbly I nodded. "Never planned to change my mind. I told you that four years ago."

Relief washed over him. "And I knew it. You always know what you want, Liz. It's what I love about you. So I was thinking – hoping, really – that we might be able to start fresh. Is that something that could ever be possible between us? Starting from the beginning?"

The coffee cup in my hands had long-since crumpled in my fist. "That isn't something I can give you an answer to right now, Eli," I said, quietly, feeling very small for some reason.

But Eli seemed to have anticipated my answer. "That's totally fair. But now I'm back in Scotland, and I'm less than an hour away on the train. I'd settle for baby steps."

"And what would the first baby step be?"

"Unblock my number?"

I giggled before I could stop myself. Regardless of the shock I still felt it was clear Eli was being genuine, and he *was* the only guy I'd ever loved. Of course his earnestness appealed to me.

"I guess I can consider that," I relented. "Now be off with you before I change my mind."

Eli flashed me his boyish grin again, cheeks flushed with excitement, before waving and running off. I swear I saw him whoop the air.

But why did his happiness make me feel so hollow?

By the time I returned to the poster I had a text from Tom, and my mood worsened. He wanted me to man the poster whilst he continued wandering around on Daichi's behalf. I couldn't blame him, of course – I'd been the one who suggested he do so – but still. The disappointment I felt was bitter.

Thinking of his fingertips tracing circles on my elbow made me feel something far more intense that disappointment.

"Stupid horny brain," I muttered under my breath, when the conference finally ended for the day and I stalked back up to my hotel room. Tom hadn't reappeared once, which only intensified my pent-up feelings. Part of me wanted him to fuck my bloody brains out for some kind of physical relief; another part of me wanted him to simply *touch* me – to hug me, or stroke my hair, or lie on a bed with me. To graze his fingers along my arm to make sure I knew I wasn't alone. That I could handle things.

Since when had I begun relying on Tom so much?

When I ran my key card through the scanner on my door the light remained resolutely red. I tried a second time. Three times. No luck.

Thinking Tom and I must have mixed up our room keys that morning – we'd sat them both down on the same table with our bags – I headed down to reception to have them make me a new one. By the time I finally made it into my room I was about ready to explode.

Yes, I needed a fucking release, and I didn't care where it came from. I yanked out my suitcase from below the bed, chucking stuff out until I reached the bottom.

Then paused.

Tom's green flannel shirt was in there. I'd completely forgotten I'd hidden it in my suitcase to stop me from wearing it in his house.

"Well he isn't around now," I reasoned, chucking off my clothes and sliding into the sinfully soft material for the first time in forever. After spending almost two months living with the guy it was easy to imagine Tom's scent still remained on the fabric – not least because I used the same shampoo as him. Coconut and lime, then his sandalwood, pine and neroli aftershave beneath that.

Now that I had fully committed to whatever sin against my better instincts this was, I riffled through the zipped compartment of my suitcase for what I'd *actually* been looking for. My long-neglected vibrator.

Nobody was around. I was in a hotel room, and dinner wouldn't be for at least another hour – if Tom still wanted to go for dinner with me in the first place.

That left me plenty of time to use filthy thoughts of Tom and the power of a rechargeable sex toy to forget about everything Eli had said to me.

Considering that Tom was my source material, it was disconcertingly easy to do so.

Chapter Twenty-Six

TOM

MY KEY CARD WASN'T WORKING. It felt like a suitably inconvenient end to a day that had started out promising but had thereafter devolved into me acting like a jealous toddler by running away from Liz and her ex instead of standing my ground. She had clearly been uncomfortable with the reunion. I shouldn't have left her alone.

But how could I look on whilst Elliot was gazing at her with the biggest heart eyes I'd ever witnessed outside of a damn anime?

At least Daichi would be happy. I'd spied on his competitors for him, as asked, and I'd even taken detailed notes and recorded some of the conversations I'd been part of. If that wasn't dedication to my best friend I didn't know what was.

I knew he'd still criticise me for shying away from an awkward situation simply to save myself, though. But what would Daichi have had me do? Pull Liz away from her ex as if I owned her? Force my feelings on her to make her feel bad about reconnecting with him? Deny Elliot – who did seem like a good guy, from what I'd seen (never mind that Liz had gone out with him for two years) – the chance to make things right with her? It was clear he was happy to see her. More than happy. Of course Liz had been taken aback by it, but that was pure shock. I was sure, after I left them alone, that she'd recovered just fine.

What had they talked about? Had they gone for lunch together? Was Liz interested in rekindling her relationship with Elliot?

God, I needed a distraction. An outlet for all of this furious, jealous energy inside me. I knew it was only a matter of time before I well and truly exploded.

But my key card wasn't fucking working.

Reasoning that the reception desk could give me a new key I thundered down the corridor, past the door to Liz's room...then paused. I looked down at the card in my hand. Had we swapped keys during the conference by mistake? Not that it mattered; she was probably still busy catching up with Elliot now the conference was over for the day. It was better for me to head down to the ground floor and—

I slid the key card through the sensor on Liz's door. The light went green when the lock clicked open.

Knowing that what I was doing was a huge invasion of her privacy – just what was I hoping to find, anyway? Liz lazing on her bed instead of out with Eli? – I opened the door and walked into the room.

The first thing I noticed before I rounded the corner past the en suite was that I could hear the very faint sound of buzzing. The second thing I noticed was that the duvet on the bed was shifting, as if someone was beneath it, though that movement froze upon my approach. The third was that Liz was definitely not out with her ex, because she was in bed, cheeks flushed, hair a flyaway mess around her head.

Her heavy-lidded eyes flew wide open when they spotted me.

"Our key cards were mixed up," I said, holding up the offending item to explain my intrusion. "I didn't actually expect you to be in here."

Liz hiked the duvet up to her chin. "Get out, Tom!"

"I..." That buzzing sound grew louder as I approached the bed, doing the exact opposite of leaving the room. I cocked my head to the side, regarding a very flustered Liz with increasing curiosity. "What are you doing, Elizabeth?"

I had an idea. I wasn't stupid; I knew how to observe the situation before me and the conclusion it was only natural to reach when presented with it. It was just that I couldn't *believe* it.

Liz grabbed a pillow and threw it at me. I deftly avoided it. "*Get out!*" she cried again. "Get ou—*ah!*"

"Okay, that was definitely a moan," I teased, creeping towards the bed before kneeling upon it. I loomed over Liz, who responded by pulling the duvet all the way up to her nose. "What on earth are you doing?"

"I'm – nothing – just go away and leave me—"

"Did you think you were going to get away with what happened on Hallowe'en so easily, Liz?" I cut in, tracing my hand along the line of her thigh through the duvet until I reached the source of the buzzing. Fuck, she really *was* getting herself off. She was masturbating, and I'd swanned in and interrupted it. No wonder Liz was mortified. If she'd caught me jacking off I'd just as equally want to die.

Except all I could think of was the fact that, going by the way Elliot had looked at her, Liz could have easily been reconnecting with him in a very physical way once the conference was over. Instead she was in bed, alone, relieving herself with the help of some AA batteries.

I yanked back the duvet like a human possessed. I wasn't in control of what I was doing anymore, except that I very bloody well was, and I was in the mood to see how far I could push Liz.

And that wasn't the only mood I was rapidly finding myself in.

"No!" Liz complained, grabbing at the duvet with her free hand – the other one was still decidedly between her thighs, clinging to the source of the buzzing – in her attempts to stop me pulling it away completely. "Tom, this isn't funny. Just leave me..."

Liz's voice trailed off when I stopped pulling at the duvet. For something had caught my attention that had entirely nothing to do with the incessant noise of her vibrator. The shirt she was wearing.

"Did you raid my wardrobe or something?" I asked, but then realisation dawned on me as subtly as a hangover the day after drinking a full bottle of gin. It *was* my shirt. More specifically: it was my shirt from four years ago. Green flannel. Linen for summer, flannel for winter. The one I'd let Liz borrow after the orange juice fiasco.

"I lent you that," I murmured, tracing my fingertips along the collar. Liz tilted her chin to avoid touching my hand; her face had gone so red and flustered the colour was creeping down her neck. I could see her artery pulsing, pulsing, pulsing, in time with the sinfully distracting vibrations that were coming from between her thighs.

Liz bit her lip and thoroughly avoided looking at me. "I don't know what you're talking about."

"Yes you do. You got orange juice all over your white clothes and I gave you this exact shirt to change into. I never got it back."

"So I kept your shirt. Get the fuck out." Finally Liz looked me in the eye. I could tell she was embarrassed beyond belief – by the fact I'd caught her with my shirt rather than the far more obvious reason. She reached up to push my chest, but I caught her hand in mine and promptly pinned it above her head.

"Why do you still have my shirt?" I asked, breathless with excitement. "Why are you wearing it *now*?"

"Stop reading into it!"

"How am I supposed to 'read into it', given the circumstances?"

Liz wriggled her wrist beneath my grip too weakly to actually be her putting up a fight. "You're the one who kept touching me all day! What was I supposed to do?"

If Liz had possessed a third hand it would have covered her mouth in horror. It took me a second or two to process her words. Liz had reunited with her ex – a man she hadn't wanted to break things off with in the first place – but all she was thinking about was how I had been innocently touching her at the conference? And now she was decidedly *indecently* touching herself, whilst wearing my shirt, whilst thinking such things?

I let go of Liz's wrist, undid my belt and unbuttoned my trousers. My cock fucking ached with longing, which only grew in intensity when Liz's eyes caught sight of it and she arched her spine against me, seemingly against her own control.

It was Liz who grabbed *my* wrist this time. "Tom—"

"You're not ready for whatever 'we' are, or might be," I said, bending low until I was breathing the words into Liz's ear, "but that doesn't mean I can't join in on your secret horny pining session. So let go of my wrist, Elizabeth."

"Don't – don't call me Elizabeth," Liz protested, though she let go of me nonetheless. My left hand wasted no time in moving to my dick, whilst I leaned on my right arm for balance. Why the hell was there still a duvet tangled between us? Why was I still fully clothed?

It didn't matter.

I dared to kiss Liz's neck once, twice, three times, down the line of her artery to her collarbone, just barely visible above the edge of my shirt. "You get off on me calling you Elizabeth, though, don't you?" I growled against her skin as I stroked myself into a frenzy. Beneath me, Liz writhed and shifted until the duvet finally fell to the floor. When she hooked an ankle around my back I almost lost control entirely.

"S-stop that," she gasped, eyes barely focusing on me.

"Stop what – calling you Elizabeth? Telling you off? But you seem to like it. This dataset is sloppy, Elizabeth. Where are your repeats? Did you even *try* a cell-free extraction–"

Liz smacked the back of my head, then threaded her hand through my hair and pulled, hard.

I could only laugh. "I like it rougher than that, Liz. Just a little – *aghh*, that's it."

She was pulling so hard my eyes were watering. It was worth it. Liz's legs were wrapped around me now; there was barely enough space between us to continue getting ourselves off.

"You're a – bastard," she gasped.

"And you're the one touching yourself, thinking of me, so what does that make you?"

There were no more words to be had then. In all honesty I'd lost the ability to *form* words. It was all I could do to keep my cock in my hand instead of spreading Liz's thighs further apart, holding her down and—

"*Ffffuck,*" I hissed through gritted teeth as I came all over Liz. Well, over my shirt. The sight of me losing control – spilling out all over her – was enough to send Liz over the edge, too, and with a shudder an orgasm spasmed through her. Her legs were still wrapped around my waist. They squeezed reflexively, pulling me even closer to her.

Before I knew it my forehead was leaning against hers, the two of us breathless, red, and covered in sweat.

When Liz focused her gaze on me I knew that, if I kissed her now, there would be nothing on hell or earth that would get between us for the night.

I also knew, instinctively, that if I slept with Liz in this situation then she'd find a way to pass it off as a stupid mistake, rather than something that was a long time coming.

I couldn't sleep with her hours after she'd met with her ex for the first time in well over four years. The man who'd broken her heart. This entire situation was wrong.

A frown shadowed Liz's beautiful brown eyes. "Tom...?" she wondered aloud, squeezing my waist again. All of her previous protestations had melted away to leave only brazen, wanton lust. How long had I waited for this moment? Longed for it? Dreamed of it?

Slowly, agonisingly, I hauled myself upright, tucked myself back into my underwear and redid my belt. Liz watched me do so with a look of such confusion and betrayal on her face it felt like torture.

"Next time you're getting off to the thought of me," I barely managed to spit out, "consider asking the real me if I want in on it. I swear it will be beneficial for the both of us."

I didn't dare hang around to see how Liz would react to such a depraved statement. It was only when I left her hotel room that I remembered, blithely, that I had to get a replacement for my own door. Such a banal mix-up, but it had resulted in...well, what just happened.

I wanted to hit myself for walking away, but I knew it was the right thing to do. Because I knew one thing for sure: if I was what Liz really wanted – not her ex, nor some faceless Tinder date she hadn't yet met, nor Peter or another hapless male friend – then the ball was now well and truly in her court.

All I could do was wait and see if the reality of me was more appealing to Liz than the *thought* of me.

Chapter Twenty-Seven

LIZ

"That colour looks so good on you, Lizzie!"

I could do nothing but nod as Imogen Henderson cooed over my bridesmaid dress fitting. It felt as if I'd been running on the barest autopilot ever since the conference. A week had now passed without me knowing how I'd managed to speak a single word or walk a single step or breathe a single breath.

Just how had I ended up in a bridal shop again?

I forced myself to pay attention to my reflection in the full-length mirror inside the shop. Jenny had picked out a dusty, pale green dress for me which worked perfectly with the winter colour scheme of her entire wedding. It was an off-the-shoulder number, with a sweetheart neckline, cinched-in waist and floaty skirt that fell all the way down to my feet. Admittedly Jenny's choice looked great on me, and as I regarded my reflection I could see how I was going to do my hair, apply my make-up and what jewellery I'd wear.

A slow smile spread across my face. "It's perfect. Dad will love it."

Jenny clapped her hands in excitement. "I can't believe he

was as strict about not seeing what you were wearing as he was with me! What an old-fashioned man."

"He must have caught the wedding bug," I joked. And then, before I could stop myself, and because it was true: "He and Mum signed their wedding registry when I was five. It wasn't exactly a lavish affair; I imagine he wants to make the most of this. To make a memory you have to live it first and all that."

The way Jenny looked at me told me she already knew about how and when Dad got married the first time around, though she still asked, "Do you remember much of it?"

"Not really. I think I was wearing jeans though, because Mum had saved up to buy them from Gap for me and I was obsessed with them. They had stars sewn into the ankles." I laughed at the memory. "I grew out of them in about six months."

When the older woman put a hand on my shoulder and squeezed I realised I was perhaps an inch too close to crying. But so was Jenny, which made it okay. Sort of. She beamed at me. "You look so beautiful. She would be so proud of you walking your old Dad down the aisle. She'd be so proud of you, full stop."

I reached up a hand to cover Jenny's. The sudden lump in my throat made it altogether too difficult for me to form a response, but I swallowed it down. "Mum knew I didn't want to get married," I said. My voice sounded very small, absorbed as it was by the long curtains and lush carpet of the bridal shop, so I shook my head and tried again. "She'd joked that she'd have to go to all of my friends' weddings just so she could see me dressed up as a bridesmaid every time. Honestly I don't think she was joking even a little bit."

Jenny's laugh was so honest and sad a tear *did* fall down my face. "Then we'll have to take a hundred photos of you, just for her. Won't we?"

"I guess we will."

A look passed between us – understanding, perhaps – and

then the sadness that had clouded the last few minutes lifted. Jenny let go of my shoulder and walked around me, inspecting the flow of my dress from every angle. "I think it needs to go in at the waist another inch."

"Do you want me to be able to eat solid food at this wedding?!"

"Och, it'll be fine. It'll really show off your figure."

"To whom, exactly?" I countered. "My Dad's friends? Yours?"

"Thomas, of course!"

I made a face. I knew it, because I was in front of a mirror, but I also knew it because Jenny rolled her eyes at me.

"Don't give me that. Do you think I can't see or hear?"

"But you spend half your time teasing us about the fact we act like" – I internally vomited – "brother and sister."

"Oh, that's just to rile Thomas up," Jenny laughed, as I got off the viewing pedestal to get changed. She waved over the shop assistant to settle the bill. "But why would it bother *you*, Lizzie, if you have no romantic feelings for him?"

"Because it's weird to suddenly be Professor Henderson's step-sister?" I offered, as the assistant lifted up my arms so she could double-check the waist adjustment Jenny wanted for my dress. Yup, I definitely wouldn't be eating anything at the wedding.

Jenny's usual gentle and easy-going face sharpened, and in that moment I saw a hell of a lot of Tom in her looks. They had the same curl to their hair, the same cheekbones, the same nose, and with that intelligent, cut-the-crap glint in her eye it left me under no uncertainty about which parent Tom had clearly taken after most.

"We both know that isn't why, Lizzie," she said. "Or perhaps it used to be true, but it isn't anymore. I certainly hope it isn't, for Thomas' sake."

I flinched. Could this woman see right through me? Did she somehow know how much I'd been fucking Tom over for my petty, ill-advised revenge?

She motioned for me to turn around so she could unbutton the back of my dress, her fingers nimble and careful so as not to damage a single one of them. "He was a difficult birth," Jenny said, when I didn't respond. "Truly, it was awful. Even as a midwife myself I couldn't possibly have prepared for how badly labour went. Afterwards there was so much damage I was told it would be next to impossible for me to safely conceive another child."

"...Jesus Christ, Jenny, I'm so sorry," I said, for what else *could* I say?

But she merely turned me back around, a firm smile on her face that I knew painfully well: it was armour. This was a hurt Jenny had learned to protect.

"It's all in the past now, and besides, the only thing that mattered was the fact Thomas was a safe and healthy boy. You must know he means the world to me, just as you mean the world to your father." She stroked my cheek with the back of her index finger, a tender look on her face. "Which means I know my son well. He holds you in such high regard, Lizzie. He's never introduced me to a single woman he likes before, so I was beginning to believe he truly *did* want to remain alone and unattached. But when I see the two of you together...I know that isn't true. So be careful with him for me. Please? And if you truly don't feel anything for him, be kind when you turn him down. But turn him down nonetheless. He deserves a straight answer."

Jenny left me to get changed into my clothes, and all I could think of was this: had I truly been that transparent? Here I'd thought that whatever was going on between me and Tom had been, well, between me and Tom. But if his mother had caught on to it – if, lord save me, my *dad* had caught onto it – then that meant we had to stop. It wouldn't just be Tom I hurt now if I kept going.

And I was discovering pretty fucking quickly that I didn't want to hurt Tom, either.

As I laced up my boots I spied Jenny reapplying her lipstick in the mirror of the bridal shop and thought again of how Tom had inherited much of his looks from her. It occurred to me, then, that I had no idea what his dad looked like, aside from what I'd seen from the sparse, fuzzy family photos that adorned the living room wall in his house. Given that Jenny and I were preparing things for her wedding to *my* dad it didn't exactly feel like the right time to ask her how handsome her late husband had been, or how he acted, or how similar his son was to him.

Could I ask Tom about it? Did even *wanting* to ask him about it mean I finally had to buck the fuck up and admit to the fact I not only wanted to get to know him better, but that I was having to physically stop myself from doing so simply to feign disinterest in him?

Was I really so immature? Could I really not see that I liked Tom, or that however he might have acted during my PhD he evidently didn't want to act like that with me now? Couldn't I just...let the past go, and enjoy what the two of us were ever more rapidly building with each other?

Was that not something I was allowed to have? After all, who stood in my way other than myself?

God, I had to stop asking myself questions I knew the answers to. It was exhausting.

When we got back to the house Tom's car was gone.

"Oh, I asked Thomas and Jim to do the food shopping whilst we were out," Jenny explained, before pausing outside the porch door to look down at an unmarked box left by the stairs. There was a delivery note on top if it so she bent down to pick it up. "It's for you, Lizzie. Odd that they left it out here instead of redelivering it to—"

"That's okay!" I bit out, realisation dawning on me about what exactly the box contained. I picked it up as quickly as I dared, kicking off my shoes the moment we got through the front door and running up the stairs.

The light I'd drunkenly bought on Hallowe'en had shipped from China, so it had only arrived a couple of days ago. In an effort to stop myself thinking about what had happened at the conference over and over (and over) again I'd browsed through countless tulip varieties, trying to work out which ones Tom would like best, before finally settling on vibrant red ones like the florist in Balloch had.

And now they'd arrived.

I couldn't bear the thought of simply handing Tom the flowers and the grow light. That was just...wrong. But so was going into his bedroom when he wasn't around in order to set them up. I still hadn't been in his bedroom, after all, and since he'd been gracious and respectful of my privacy whilst staying in his house the least I could do was return the favour. Which left...

"His office?" I said aloud, grabbing the grow light from my room before wandering over. The door was closed but it wasn't locked, so I let myself in. I'd been in the office a couple times before to take advantage of the printer, so it wasn't weird to be in the room without Tom.

Setting up a grow light over a clay pot full of flowering tulip bulbs certainly was, though.

The light wasn't actually tall enough to sit over the flowers. Cursing the fact I should have followed Ray's advice and bought the taller one, I fished out a couple of outdated chemistry textbooks from Tom's bookshelf and sat the light on it.

There. Perfect. Well, not quite perfect, because of the books, but it would work. Now Tom could grow tulips in his house even in the dead of Glasgow winter. A thrill of excitement ran through me at the prospect of him discovering the flowers for the first time.

Ah, fuck.

I really liked him. I genuinely liked Thomas Henderson in

an unironic, I-want-to-be-with-you-and-not-just-as-a-hate-screw kind of way. Having the guts to continue where we'd left off at the conference wasn't going to be enough anymore; I wanted the damn snuggling and pillow talk *after* sex just as much as I wanted to rip the expensive clothes off the man and let Tom rail me until the sun came up.

"Lizzie!" Jenny called up the stairs, startling me out of my horrible, equal-parts-horny-equal-parts-sentimental epiphany. "Could you help me clean the kitchen before the boys get back?"

"A-anything you need!" I stammered back, feeling as if I needed to shove my heart back into my chest or smash it to pieces or something as I tripped my way down the stairs.

This was terrible. I really did like him.

Tom was going to laugh his fucking face off when he found out.

If I ever swallowed my pride enough to tell him.

Chapter Twenty-Eight

TOM

"I SWEAR SHE DOESN'T LIKE BEN and Jerry's," I told Jim for the fourth time, as we took the shopping out of the back of my car and made our way inside the house. "She only likes Mackie's."

"Well she always ate it before."

"Doesn't mean she actually likes it. Liz—"

"Shh," Jim said, putting a hand on my chest to stop me moving further down the hallway towards the kitchen. Slowly the man put down the bags he was carrying, so I did the same. There was music playing from the kitchen. Music that was familiar, plus the sound of two very off-pitch voices singing on top of it that were also familiar.

Were Mum and Liz...singing together?

"I know that song," I murmured, creeping closer to the kitchen to try and get a closer look without being spotted. A flutter of nerves blossomed inside me. Just why did I know that song?

Jim put a hand on my shoulder to stop me moving any closer. "It's a Texas song. Christina – Liz's mum – adored them.

At some point that rubbed off on Liz."

When the chorus rang in I realised I knew the words, and it struck me that I wasn't so much feeling nervous as I was feeling...out of place. Or, rather, out of *time*.

"Mum and Dad must have seen Texas about ten times when I was younger," I told Jim, keeping my voice hushed. "Funny, I don't think Mum's listened to them since he died."

"I don't think Liz has, either."

The two of us stood by the door to the kitchen, the volume of the radio ensuring Liz and my mum remained cheerfully ignorant of the fact we were spying on them cleaning the surfaces and singing along to the song.

God, they were terrible.

I wanted to cry.

Glancing at Jim I could only conclude by the too-bright sheen of his eyes that he did, too.

I watched Mum knock her hip against Liz's. "Can you go down to the basement for me, Lizzie? I think we have spare bleach down there for the sink."

Liz twirled around, happy to oblige, and immediately froze when she saw me and her dad not-at-all-creepily watching her. Her eyes widened, cheeks going pink, before tapping Mum on the shoulder. "We have an audience," she called over the radio.

Mum lowered the volume before turning around, surprise turning to happiness when she saw us. "You took your time at the shops."

Jim indicated towards me with a thumb. "He kept arguing with me over ice cream."

"You got Mackies, right?" Liz asked, catching my eye for the first time since the conference to confirm this. She frantically dropped her gaze a moment later.

"Ha!" I fired at Jim. "I told you. Right, I'm going for a

shower. Unless you had plans to hog the bathroom for two hours, Liz?"

Meekly she shook her head.

As I left the kitchen and went up to my bedroom to strip off a wave of shame washed over me. What I'd done to Liz at the conference was nothing short of full-on sexual harassment. Sure, she'd fucked with me in the shower, but we'd both been drinking and, at the end of the day, it had been entirely consensual. But in her hotel room Liz had repeatedly demanded I leave, and I ignored that. So what if she'd ended up clinging to me and wanting me to kiss her – to take things further? It had been out of line for me to be in her hotel room in the first place.

I was compromising all my morals because of my feelings for her. I had to stop, I really did. If Liz wanted to pursue anything with me that was more serious than whatever the fuck we had going on now then she'd tell me.

Wouldn't she?

Or was that hoping for too much? Liz was clearly loathe to admit any kind of feelings for me, obvious lust and alcohol-induced lowered inhibitions aside. But watching her sing with my mum...I knew I wanted more than what we currently had. I wanted it all.

Minus marriage, kids and that holiday in Tenerife, of course. Mine and Liz's version of it all. I wanted to get a dog and go for Sunday walks in Kelvingrove Park together. I wanted to learn to cook proper ramen together and go to anime film festivals together and fall asleep in the same bed together.

I wanted more than Liz would likely ever want to give me.

By the time I'd showered, shaved and headed back downstairs Mum and Jim were busy making a curry, according to them, would take three hours to cook, and Liz was curled up on the couch. When I sat down a respectable distance away she frowned in confusion.

"What is it?" I asked.

"...nothing," she mumbled, looking away. "You never sit that far away."

"Is that an invitation to come closer?"

"It's not *not* an invitation to come closer."

I was achingly aware that this was the longest interaction we'd had since the conference – I'd been so busy with Mia's thesis edits and grant writing that I hadn't been in the lab all week. Not wishing to look a gift horse in the mouth, I sidled closer.

Then I realised what Liz was watching.

"You are *not* watching *High School Musical Three* on my hundred-inch OLED television."

"But the blacks!" she cried, waving towards the TV. "They're so vibrant! And the depth of vision, and the colours—"

"Change to something else or so help me—"

"So help you what, Thomas?"

"I'll rip the remote from your hands and change it myself."

A rebellious glint shone in her eye as Liz clutched the remote control to her chest. "Oh, I'd like to see you try."

So, of course, I launched myself at her.

Liz hadn't expected me to move at all, let alone move as quickly as I did, and before she knew it she was pinned beneath me on the couch. "Give me the remote," I growled, attempting to pry it from her fingers. But Liz was quick to recover from her shock, kicking me in the stomach before dangling the remote behind her head, out of reach.

"Nice try," she laughed, wriggling beneath me to try and free herself as I winced from the force of her kick.

"I can't believe you assaulted me!"

"And what do you call *this*?" Liz countered, indicating towards me lying on top of her.

"This is called me rightfully taking back possession of what belongs to me." I lunged for the remote, but Liz responded by chucking it over my back to the far side of the couch. Then she tickled my ribs.

Tickled. My damn. Ribs.

I pinned her wrists above her head, my sides hurting from laughing because Liz was laughing, too, then said, "You have no leverage now. Do you surrender or are we fighting to the death?"

The eyebrow Liz rose could only be described as filthy. "I like the sound of—"

"Oh my," my mother gasped, looking suitably scandalised as she popped her head through the kitchen door. "This rather looks like something you should be doing in private."

"This is *my house*," I reminded her.

Just as Liz exclaimed, "Nothing *private* is going on!"

Jim tutted when he came to see what was going on, clearly disgruntled by the whole situation. "Fighting over the remote like bloody children. Tom, just let her have her way. You'll never see a moment of peace otherwise."

"Speaking from experience?"

"Almost twenty-eight years of it."

And so Liz got her way. Triumphantly she returned her attention to her stupid film, and uttered a delighted thank-you when Mum got her a glass of prosecco.

Teenage musicals *and* alcohol? In my opinion you were allowed one or the other. Clearly Liz was one of those special people who was allowed to indulge in her childhood interests without anyone telling her to grow up.

I ended up banished to my grandfather's winged armchair for 'scowling too much at the TV' – according to my mum whenever she came through from the kitchen – leaving me to sulk in the corner over the fact I had apparently become a million years old.

When Liz caught my eye her lips slowly curled into the most evil of smirks to have ever been smirked.

"I'll get you for this," I stage-whispered to her. "And your little dog, too." See? She wasn't the only one who could enjoy musicals. They just had to be good ones.

Liz merely sipped on her prosecco and huddled into a blanket, content in her victory.

Eventually I couldn't deal with sitting in the corner with only my thoughts for company and Liz out of reach. Needing a distraction I headed up to my office, deciding that looking over my grant proposal was much better for me than pining and complaining about what was on TV.

But when I opened the door I was met with an unexpected sight: a vase of vibrant crimson tulips sitting on my desk. A thin, bright light propped up on a couple of textbooks illuminated the flowers.

Approaching the vase as if it were full of piranhas instead of tulips, I wondered who on earth had put them there. Mum? She couldn't tell a tulip from a primrose. And these were such a deep, beautiful red. They reminded me of the tulips I'd seen in Balloch – like the one I'd given Liz.

Ah.

Just as I realised she must have gotten them for me I spotted a scrawled note propped up beside the clay vase. It was definitely Liz's handwriting.

It said:

Through the power of science you can now grow plants in the middle of winter. Eejit.

I held a hand to my mouth, unable to stop the foolish laugh that left my lips. It was such a ludicrously thoughtful gift given to me with as little attention to the act as possible. If I brought it up I had no doubt Liz would deny any such knowledge of having done something so kind on my behalf.

It was so perfectly Elizabeth Maclean that I couldn't stand it.

How was I supposed to give up on this woman? Twisted, confusing sexual games aside, she was making it fucking impossible.

Chapter Twenty-Nine

LIZ

Every moment spent working in the lab beside Tom was torture. My should-have-been-obvious-but-wasn't-because-I'm-stupid epiphany that I, in fact, liked him, was making me act more awkward than ever. How had we *fought over the remote control* last weekend? I couldn't fathom it. Such physical contact felt forbidden.

I knew Tom had to have found the tulips in his office but he hadn't said anything about them yet. Yeah, he was super busy with his grant proposal – this was the first day he'd been in the lab in two weeks and there were dark shadows under his eyes that suggested many a late night spent working – but still. I thought he'd have said *something* by now.

He caught me staring at him. Of course he caught me staring; he always did. I hadn't even known I *was* staring.

"Am I supposed to telepathically know what you want or...?" Tom ventured, a small smile curling his lips that immediately sent my heart racing.

"The P200. A-are you finished using it?" It was the best excuse I could come up with, though since I was setting up a double digest I didn't need anything bigger than a P20 pipette. But if Tom knew this he didn't call me out, instead handing me the pipette handle-first like a pair of scissors or a knife.

"Knock yourself out. In a couple of weeks you'll no longer have to share pipettes with me – or a bench. I'm sure you'll be thrilled."

"I...what?" This was the first I was hearing of it. "Have they finished the renovations to your lab?"

He nodded, pen scratching over the page of his lab book as he did so. When I glanced at what Tom was writing I saw that he wasn't actually writing but was in fact drawing a tiny steam train.

I couldn't contain my disappointment, though I didn't want to admit to it. Not now. Not ever. But I found it impossible to stop myself from asking, "Why didn't you tell me? When did you find out?"

Tom continued drawing his little steam train, adding shading to the funnels at a measured, glacial pace. He didn't look at me. Above us, the sound of fat raindrops banging on the ceiling was the only thing that broke the silence. After a solid minute he said, "Nobody was expecting the builders to finish up over a month early. I only found out on Monday."

"It's Friday."

"And I've been busy."

"I know, but—"

"Is this your way of saying you want me to keep you in the loop when it comes to any life updates I might have?" Tom cut in, abruptly stopping his drawing to snap his lab book shut. But he didn't give me a chance to reply. "Don't answer that."

"Tom—"

"I have a meeting with Gill over lunch. I better go now if I don't want to be late."

Tom left in a hurry, leaving me wondering just what the hell was going on. Was he angry with me? Had he...given up on me? Was I no longer worth bothering with?

Had I ruined things between us before I'd even had a chance to tell Tom how I felt?

I counted on my fingers how much time had passed since he'd been thrust back into my life. It was the seventh of December now. Daichi had gone mad with deliberately garish Christmas decorations in the lab so it was impossible to hide from the fact the festive season was upon us (though the horrible rainy weather didn't exactly lend itself to an appropriately festive mood). That meant three weeks since the conference, and five weeks since Hallowe'en. Ten weeks since we'd kissed. Almost three months since Tom came to The Whisky Barrel for that stag do.

Could so little time really have passed? It felt like a second, but it also felt like a lifetime. Whatever was going on between us was over four years in the making, after all.

But had I ruined it? Even after three years of Tom being the worst PhD assessor on earth, was I the one responsible for fucking things up just when they were beginning to look...well, good?

That wasn't fair in the slightest.

"He has been distant lately," I grumbled, setting up my digest before reluctantly making my way to the foyer of the building for lunch with Chloë. She was once more coming in early to keep me company even though my lunch time was barely morning for her, but with Peter still not talking to me I had a sneaking suspicion this was the only way Chloë could see the both of us separately without losing her damn mind.

Peter. That was another relationship I'd fucked up. Could I even fix it, since I'd been so blind that I hadn't seen what was wrong in the first place?

"Why the long face?" Chloë asked the moment I sat down on the table surface; I couldn't even be bothered to collapse onto a seat. Looking at my best friend I noted that she'd clearly managed to find a lucky ten minute break in the rain to walk into work, because not an inch of Chloë's clothes were wet. She was always lucky that way.

I huffed out a breath, causing a curl of hair that had been annoying me for a few minutes to finally dislodge from my eyelash. "Just the usual."

"Does that mean Tom?"

"That means everything. Peter. The wedding. Elliot texting me to meet up again." That last one was confusing me more than ever. Was I supposed to be friends with Eli now? Were we really starting over fresh?

"And Tom?"

I frowned at my best friend, though she stared me down easily. "Why do you keep circling back to him?"

"Because you aren't even bothering to deny you're thinking about him," Chloë explained. "You used to be so quick to do so."

"Don't start psychoanalysing me," I groaned. "I'm so not in the mood."

"Well are you in the mood for a Calippo?" Chloë thrust a box of the push-pop ice lollies at me. Orange flavour. "They were on sale. And everyone knows winter is the best time for ice lollies. They don't melt in five minutes."

"They do when the building you're having lunch in has every radiator on full blast," I pointed out, because the foyer was roasting. It meant a Calippo was welcome, though, despite the fact I'd have to eat it before I ate the rest of my actual lunch to prevent it from melting. When I ripped off the lid I licked the top of the obnoxiously orange ice, savouring its sweetness, then rolled the paper tube between my hands until the outside of the ice had melted enough for the lolly to push up. Chloë followed suit, garnering us several curious looks from other researchers at our out-of-season lunch choice.

"They're just jealous," Chloë joked, making me wince when

she bit the top off her Calippo with no regard for her teeth. She pushed me a little on the table top. "Anyway, tell me what's wrong. What has Professor Hen—"

"Go on. Finish that sentence," I dared Chloë, when she paused halfway through Tom's surname. I pushed my ice lolly up several inches to suck on it. I realised this was a terrible mistake about half a second too late.

Tom had walked into the foyer and was staring straight at me.

All at once I realised how ridiculously sexual the act of sucking on a fucking Calippo was, and that the fact I was draped over a table like I owned the place probably didn't help things. Now I had two choices: let melted orange juice dribble down my chin, or commit to licking the damn ice to make sure the juice went into my mouth. Even though, now I was making eye contact with Tom, it would look very much like I was being deliberately suggestive.

Tom's gaze burned through my eyes, his entire frame stiff and tense as he watched me. It sent a thrill down my spine; surely he wouldn't react in such a way if he was over me, right? Right?

I chose the latter, sexier option of licking the Calippo from the bottom all the way to the top, refusing to look away from Tom as I did so. As if I could indeed telepathically communicate with him and I was screaming: I want to do this to *you* and get absolutely railed in return. But, like, in a romantic way where Tom also knew I genuinely liked him.

I'd spent ages in the bathroom this morning, shaving the lower half of my body to within an inch of its life and washing my hair with expensive shampoo and lathering cocoa butter into my skin. It was a Friday, and I had it in my head that I had to be prepared in case I managed to tell Tom how I felt and he immediately whisked me up to his bedroom. Or mine.

Tom didn't know this, of course, but surely witnessing me going down on a damn ice lolly would give him an idea of what

I hoped our weekend might involve, especially after him demanding at the hotel that I should actually tell him the next time I was lusting after him.

This counted as telling him, right?

Tom let out a low sigh and headed in the direction of Daichi's lab, dashing my strictly-eighteen-and-over dreams before they'd ever had a hope of coming true.

"I'm so *stupid*," I groaned, wishing I could put my face in my hands and dematerialise into atoms. How could I have just done that – in public, no less – and Tom basically responded with the physical version of the phrase 'grow up'?

I'd fucked it all up. I'd wasted so much time hating him that I'd destroyed everything we had.

"Okay, *now* will you tell me what's wrong?" Chloë asked, voice pulling me out of my rapidly descending inner spiral. "Because what I just witnessed was...well. I'm not really sure what I just witnessed. Care to explain?"

"...I like him," I mumbled, because what was the point in lying about it now?

"Well it's nice you finally have the balls to admit it but that's not really something that's gone *wrong*, is it?"

I gave her the finger. It was dripping with stupid melted orange juice, reminding me of the equally stupid orange juice that had set off my entire story with Tom in the first place. "It means that *everything's* gone wrong, actually. I wasn't supposed to like Professor Thomas Henderson. Remember?"

"The way I remember it you *always* liked him but were too stubborn to admit it."

"What does that say about me that I continued to like someone who was a total dick to me for three years?"

I expected Chloë to bow down to this point. She always had done before, after all. It was therefore to my surprise when she said, "He was doing his job, and if he was doing his job poorly you should have reported him. I told you to report him so many times but you refused. What if Professor Henderson doesn't actually know he's being too difficult in PhD assessments?"

"Oh, he knows. When I called him out on the way he treated me he admitted to it."

"And did you ask for a reason? Or any kind of elaboration on why he found it appropriate to act that way?"

"...no."

"Liz!" Chloë cried, exasperated. She looked close to pulling her hair out. I understood that feeling only too well. "You can't keep over-thinking things without actually doing something about the problems you have. It seems like literally everything would be resolved – one way or the other – if you fucking *talked* to this man. Without a PhD assessment between you, or booze, or the most ridiculous unresolved sexual tension I've ever witnessed. I swear to god, you could cut it with the back end of a bloody spoon if—"

"You're right." I jumped off the table, feeling like an idiot that I'd wasted so much time inside my own head. Because Chloë really was right: all I had to do was the one thing I'd been avoiding doing thus far.

Talk to Tom honestly.

Lay my feelings out in front of him about everything.

Then see how he felt in return.

"I know I'm right," Chloë said, a smarmy grin on her face when I chucked my half-eaten Calippo in the bin and hugged her with sticky fingers. "Let me know how it goes."

"Naturally. When have I ever not given you regular life updates?"

"You can wait until *after* you've screwed him to update me this time. You have my permission."

I didn't even bother to correct her. I didn't have time. I

needed to talk to Tom *now*, then for better or worse let the chips fall where they may.

He wasn't in the lab.

"Oh, didn't he tell you?" Daichi said, when I sheepishly popped my head into his office to see if Tom was hanging out with him. "Your dad's car broke down halfway to Balloch, so Tom left to pick him and Jenny up then take them the rest of the way."

"Is that so?" I said, forcing a smile to my face. "Thanks for letting me know."

It looked as if my boss had more to say but something told me I wasn't in the right state of mind to hear it, so I rushed back to my lab bench and pulled out my phone to text my dad. Sure enough, Tom was indeed on his way to help him out.

So why hadn't Tom told me? I'd only seen him fifteen minutes ago. I could have gone with him.

Unless he hadn't wanted to be alone with me. Unless he was sick of me.

Unless I'd left things too late.

Chapter Thirty

TOM

"Oh, it was lucky we had enough signal to send an *SOS* out to you, Thomas. With the way the weather's going it looks like we'll all be stuck in Balloch for the night!"

I tried to smile but it was more of a grimace. The last thing I'd expected midway through my meeting with Gill was a frantic call from my mum, begging me to come and pick her and Jim up because Jim's car had given out a couple of miles shy of Dumbarton. I'd been able to collect them and organise a tow truck to pick up Jim's car, but because of the ensuing storm his car likely wouldn't get fixed until Monday.

All things considered, I didn't want to stay in the almost-completely-renovated Henderson country estate with Mum and Jim. Even though it was best if I avoided Liz for now. *Definitely* for the best.

All I wanted to do was race home and see her.

"Might be best to stay in a hotel in Balloch so you're close to public transport," I said. "It isn't good to stay out in such an isolated place when the weather is like this." I waved out of the window of the restaurant we'd stopped in for an early dinner to emphasise my point. Torrential rain was slamming against the glass, practically horizontal, whilst the wind was so violent the restaurant manager had to get a waitress to stand in front of the door to stop it from slamming open. Every now and then a flash of lightning, followed a few seconds later by a crack like a whip, permeated the air.

It hadn't been nearly this bad this morning. I hoped Liz got home okay.

The Christmas music cheerily blaring through the restaurant was fighting a losing battle with the screaming wind; every time Slade yelled out about Christmas Day I winced. The waitress by the door was equally as unimpressed as I was, if not more. I couldn't blame her. After all, she'd probably heard the song six times this afternoon already, and was sick of tripping over red and green tinsel whenever it fell from its poorly taped position on the wall.

Jim followed my gaze to the gale outside and nodded. "That would be smart. I know you wanted to check out the estate, Jenny, but it'll be best to wait until the morning."

Mum looked as if she wanted to protest – she hated being behind schedule – but another howl of wind made her decision for her. "I guess you're right. We shouldn't have bothered trying to come through today, should we? We even inconvenienced you, Thomas! Didn't you have a meeting about your lab today? I shouldn't have interrupted it. I'm so sorry!"

This was true but I knew better than to say so. "It's fine. Honestly. Gill was understanding, so we're going to meet first thing on Monday. The important thing is that the two of you aren't stuck on the side of a road tearing up a ditch."

Mum beamed at me as she always did when I acted like the golden son. "I knew I raised a good boy. I think I might ask the manager for a decent hotel recommendation, if the two of you don't mind keeping each other company?"

Jim and I both nodded.

When Mum sauntered off to talk to the manager – an older

man dressed in an ugly Christmas jumper with thinning hair, whose eyes lit up when they caught sight of her – Jim took out his phone and responded to a few messages now we had access to the restaurant's Wi-Fi.

"Is that Liz?" I asked, unable to stop myself. All I could think about was her...not least because of how I'd found her in the foyer a few hours ago, sucking on a damn ice lolly with her eyes trained solely on me. It was funny how quickly my need to stay professional evaporated in the face of Liz draped over the table, daring me to try something. But since I'd decided that I had to at least *try* and take a step back from her – to let her decide where we went next, not me – I'd forced myself to walk away without making a single comment.

It took Jim a few seconds to reply, choosing instead to finish typing out the message he was writing before addressing me. "One was from Liz," he said. "The other was from Tiny Jim from work."

"Tiny Jim? So you're...Big Jim?"

"No, I'm Jim Senior. Big Jim is taller than you, and three times as fat as me."

I chuckled. "Must be confusing working with so many folk bearing the same name."

"Not really." Jim shrugged. "Isn't like we're all working on the same bus at the same time."

"I suppose that's true."

"Why were you asking if I was messaging my daughter?"

The question was shot out like an arrow, sharp and pinpoint accurate. Jim locked eyes on me with such a steely expression I knew it was pointless to lie to him.

"I'm worried about her getting back from the lab in this weather," I said, which was true. I'd expected to be around to give her a lift home. "She'll never get a taxi."

Jim huffed in agreement. "She's always been one for

walking. Why didn't you ask her to come with you to pick us up, then?"

"That would have interfered with her work."

"She could have made that decision for herself if you gave her the option."

I couldn't help but flinch. How was I supposed to tell Elizabeth Maclean's father that I couldn't stand being in such close proximity to his daughter because all I could think about when I looked at her was pressing her against a wall and kissing her until we were both seeing stars?

But clearly I *didn't* need to say anything, because Jim rolled his eyes and tutted loudly. "You're both absolutely useless, do you know that? I thought Lizzie was bad, but you...you're on a whole other level."

"Excuse me?"

"Don't let her spend the night alone in your damn house if you're so worried about her," Jim said, just before Mum rejoined us with a delighted expression on her face.

"Good news! The manager here knows a *wonderful* B'n'B right on the water's edge. The only problem is that there's only one suite vacant, but he said his friend Sam's B'n'B down the road is—"

"I won't be staying," I cut in. "Once I know your car is sorted, Jim, I'll be heading back to Glasgow."

Mum looked from me to Jim then back again. "Am I missing something here?"

"Nothing. I just have a lot of work to catch up on."

Jim huffed in a way that almost sounded like he was laughing at me, though Mum didn't notice. She glanced outside. "Are you sure? It looks awfully dangerous outside..."

"You know I'm a good driver, Mum."

"But even so..."

"Just let the man do what he needs to do," Jim said, coming to my defence for the first time in, well, ever. "We'll have a much nicer time just the two of us, Jenny."

Mum considered this for a moment, torn between concern for me and knowing that what Jim said was true. Eventually she relented. "Okay, but make sure you call me when you get home! I need to know you're safe."

"I'm thirty-eight, not eighteen."

"And yet you're still my only son. Don't be an eejit on the road."

I kissed her on the cheek. "I won't be, I promise. I'll check you into that B'n'B, stop by the garage to ask about Jim's car, then be on my way before it gets too late. Is that acceptable, Mum?"

"I guess it will have to be."

I had no idea what I'd be going home to, all things considered. Liz and I had been avoiding each other all week. But that look she'd given me today, paired with how we'd left things at the conference, made me believe that something might still happen between us.

The only problem was, given everything I'd done so far to sabotage Liz's life for my benefit, did I *deserve* for something to happen? That thought had been why I'd been avoiding her, after all. Why I'd been short with her in the lab that morning, even though she didn't deserve it.

Regardless, I was genuinely worried about leaving Liz in the house alone during the storm. Did she know how to work the central heating, or how to start a fire? I'd never shown her how to. For all I knew she was freezing her arse off.

For better or worse I had to get back, and fast.

Chapter Thirty-One

LIZ

By THE TIME I GOT BACK to the townhouse I was cold, shivering and very, very wet. The weather had been horrendous the last few months but at least it hadn't devolved into a full-on storm.

Until today. The day Tom bolted off to help our parents.

Along with his car.

Jenny had messaged me around three to say they were all planning to stay in Balloch for the night, which meant there had been no point in me sticking around the lab as the weather got worse and worse in the hopes that Tom would, miraculously, return and give me a lift home. Of course that meant it had also been impossible to book or flag down a taxi; everyone had clearly been as desperate as I was to get home. I'd even left the lab at four to try my luck at getting a taxi instead of braving the rain on foot (my usual solution to all weather conditions), but of course there had been no luck to be found.

So now I was cold, miserable, wet and all alone in a giant house. Which was also cold. It felt even colder because the house wasn't full of sparkly fairy lights and tinsel and Christmas trees like the university currently was; Tom was one of those people who only decorated his house on the eve of the twenty-fourth. If we'd been talking properly then I'd have made fun of him for it, but as it was it was a jibe left undelivered.

So by god was it freezing. *Where do you turn the heating on from?* I wondered, shivering off my sodden coat to hang it on the coat rack. It dripped onto the hallway rug, as did my boots when I finally managed to peel them off my feet, but I was in too foul a mood to care.

Heading into the kitchen I searched through every cupboard for the central heating controls, then braced myself against the bitter air that came from the basement when I swung open the door to see if the controls were down there. But they weren't, so I shoved the door shut, thundered down the hallway and up the stairs. When I finally found the central heating box on the first floor landing I sighed in relief, but that relief was short-lived.

"Is this...*password protected*?!" I cried, outraged at the unfairness of it all. For the system was, indeed, password protected; I'd have to contact Tom so I could unlock it. Even though I didn't want to have any kind of communication with him right now I fired off a text asking him for the password, but when five minutes passed and he hadn't responded I resigned myself to keeping busy until he did. I couldn't stand around soaking wet and developing pneumonia just because I was by my fucking self, after all.

Thank god the shower was electric, though in all honestly I craved a bath. Standing up felt like too much effort. But at least the steaming water set hot enough to melt the flesh off my bones finally chased the chill of an encroaching cold away, and I let out a long sigh as my fingers and toes finally regained sensation.

Then I looked down and remembered how much effort I'd put into shaving and moisturising this morning, all because I'd become convinced by the notion that if I only told Tom how I felt then everything would be perfect between us. I couldn't wait for it to finally be acceptable for me to give into my sinful desire to be fucked senseless by the guy I was foolishly crazy about.

A heat that had nothing to do with the scalding shower and had everything to do with shame intermingled with lust bloomed inside me. I covered my face in my hands, wishing I hadn't been so stupid. So childish. I was twenty-eight next month, damn it. Why had I been playing around with Tom's feelings whilst avoiding having an honest-to-goodness conversation about how conflicted I felt because of the way he'd treated me as my PhD assessor? Chloë was right; I should have spoken up a long time ago.

Going by the way Tom was avoiding me, it was clearly too late now.

Eventually I grew too dizzy to stay in the safe, warm embrace of the shower, so I wrapped myself in a towel and ran for my room as quickly as possible. I threw on Tom's green flannel shirt – since he wasn't coming home to bear witness to me doing so – then grabbed my duvet off the bed, hauled it down to the living room and threw it on the couch. I'd received no response to my plea for the central heating password, and I had no idea where Tom put away the electric blanket he'd let me use when my period hit, but at least the living room had a gigantic fireplace.

Lighting a fire couldn't be that hard, right?

Twenty minutes later and I discovered that it was, in fact, pretty fucking hard to light a fire, when you couldn't find any timber or coal to start one. Now I was shivering uncontrollably as if the shower had never heated me up. Resigning myself to my fate – I was so frustrated and tired I couldn't even fathom going into the kitchen to make dinner, though I was hungry – I curled up under the duvet and tried to get warm, cursing the fact I hadn't actually put on more clothes than Tom's shirt in my haste to get a fire going.

Well, I was under the cover now. I wasn't going back upstairs.

Turning on the TV I decided only *Gundam* would work with my mood the way it was. I didn't want to watch anything new. I needed something comforting; something I'd watched over and over again to lull me to sleep through my freezing bones. I'd gotten a few episodes into *Zeta*, so Amuro and Char were set to reunite soon. That would be a small consolation if the Baltic evening prevented me from sleeping.

I turned the lights off, the volume up, and settled into a very lonely Friday evening.

When I blinked awake it took me a long time to get to grips with how and when and where I was. The first thing I noticed was that, against the odds, I had actually fallen asleep. This wasn't surprising once I took in how wondrously warm the living room was. The merry crackling of a fire cut through the noise from the TV – which was much quieter than the volume I had originally set it to – and flickered in the corner of my vision as I pulled myself back into consciousness.

And I was very much no longer alone.

"...Tom?" I croaked, voice still thick with sleep. He was sitting right by the fire, recliner out and a blanket over his legs. I realised, then, that I was fully sprawled across basically the entirety of the right arm of the corner sofa – save for where Tom was sitting. I huddled under my duvet as if that somehow made up for the fact I was taking up so much space.

For a moment Tom didn't react. He continued watching *Gundam* – two episodes away from Char and Amuro's reunion, which meant I'd been asleep for over an hour – without acknowledging me. His hair was a little damp as if he'd recently showered, and he had his tortoiseshell glasses on. They made it difficult for me to see Tom's eyes until, eventually, he turned his head in my direction. He looked as if he hadn't slept in days.

"Sorry I didn't reply with the central heating password," Tom murmured, voice barely audible over the crackling of the fire. "I had no signal on the road; I only got your message when I was back in Glasgow already."

"But why – why are you here?" Surely he hadn't returned simply to make sure I wasn't cold. "Your mum told me you were staying in Balloch for the night." Tom didn't reply, choosing instead to return his attention to the TV. But I didn't want an awkward silence to fall between us – even though everything was horrendously awkward already – so I said, "Thanks for lighting a fire."

"You're welcome."

Polite and distant. God, I hated it. Where had all our previously easy conversations gone to? Even when I was fighting with him the words had flowed like water.

I tried to focus on the TV, too, but for the life of me I couldn't concentrate knowing Tom was there. Did he plan to ignore me? But then why had he come back through the terrible weather, lit a fire, and made sure I was okay? Was I allowed to believe he'd come back for the sole *purpose* of making sure I was all right? Because if that were the case then I couldn't let Tom get further away from me than he already was. I mean, I was physically close enough that if I merely stretched out my hand I'd be able to touch his elbow, but I felt like if I did that Tom would flinch away when he never had done before.

"So...some storm outside," I said, before promptly hating myself. The weather? Really?

Tom nodded. "Haven't seen it this bad in years."

Well at least he replied. I gazed up at him through my eyelashes, still wrapped up like a caterpillar in a duvet cocoon and not daring to move closer, even though I wanted to. "Did Jenny and my dad manage to do everything they wanted to do?"

"They got nothing done. They shouldn't have gone with the forecast so bad." A pause. "Still, Mum seemed pretty happy about the B'n'B they're staying in, and once your dad's car is repaired it'll miraculously still function for another year or two, so it wasn't all a complete failure."

I risked a smile. "That's good. I'm glad they're both okay." It was my turn to pause. I'd managed to wrangle the semblance of a conversation out of Tom, which was the most progress we'd made since we fought over the remote control last week. "So how are *you*?" I ventured. "How is the grant proposal going?" It was the least offensive topic of conversation I could think of.

To my surprise Tom grimaced, a frown shadowing his features that made him seem angry at me. "Can we not talk about work?"

"Why, because you don't want to waste your time talking to me about something important?"

The words flew out of my mouth before I could stop them; an age-old grudge against the way Tom had dismissed the topic of research way back when we first met. But it was the wrong thing to say, going by the look on Tom's face.

Very, very wrong.

"Where – *why on earth* would you think that?" he asked, his entire frame gone tense in an instant. Though I had learned over the last three months that Tom was a very easy-going guy who rarely allowed anything to annoy him, I could tell his dormant temper was bubbling beneath the very surface of his skin.

I knew that lying would make things worse; tackling the subject honestly was the only thing I could do. After all, hadn't that been what I'd promised myself I'd do with Tom – have an honest conversation? "When we met," I mumbled, wanting to look away from the searing heat of Tom's gaze but forcing myself to maintain eye contact, "you brushed past the topic of what you were researching. And didn't seem to care about what I was doing at all. I figured you didn't..."

"Didn't what?"

"It doesn't matter." What a way to chicken out.

But Tom was having none of it. "No, Liz, I think it really does. What exactly does the image of me in your head look like?" He wrenched his glasses off to slide a hand down his face, a resigned sigh escaping his lips before continuing, "Am I some pig-headed man who doesn't want to overload the pretty little head of the woman he's talking to? Or am I a man who doesn't think it's worth bothering discussing work with women full stop? Is that what you think?"

"I – no. Not as bad as that. Just—"

"Just *what*?"

"I believed you didn't think it was worth discussing work with someone you were flirting with. That it was a waste of time."

"I *did* think it was a waste of time!" Tom exploded, anger well and truly ignited. His hand clenched as if he wanted to grab me from where I lay hidden in the duvet and shake some sense into me. I almost wished he would. "There would have been so many occasions to talk about our research after that! At the time all I wanted to do was get to know *you*, not your work. I'd thought you felt the same!"

"But then what about *right now*?" I countered. God, why couldn't I stop needling him? He'd already perfectly reasonably explained away a complex I'd had against him for four years with one sentence. "Why not talk about it now?"

"Because I'm fucking tired." Another slide of his hand across his face. Then Tom put his glasses back on, tilted his head up, and visibly swallowed down his anger. It was only when the vein in his temple stopped throbbing that Tom spoke again, though his nostrils were still flaring. "I'm sorry. I don't want to lose my temper; it isn't like me. But I really am just so, *so* tired."

I knew fine well he didn't mean physical exhaustion, and

also that it was all my fault. Once upon a time I'd have revelled in causing the man this much grief, but now? Now I just felt awful. To what end had it been worth messing Tom around like this? I'd been such a child.

"I'll go upstairs so you can...have your space," I mumbled, making to get up. But Tom held out a hand to stop me.

"No," he said, the word coming out harsh and ragged. A moment of painful silence. Then: "No," he repeated, more softly this time. "You don't have to do that. Don't do that. Please."

Slowly I settled back onto the couch, pleased that Tom didn't want me to go but unsure of what was supposed to happen next. So I gave Tom the only suggestion my stupid brain could think of. "...then do you want to watch *Gundam* together?"

To my relief the suggestion elicited the smallest of smiles from Tom. "Yes. Yes, that sounds great."

Chapter Thirty-Two

TOM

When I returned home I hadn't expected to find the entire house dark and freezing, though because the TV was blaring from the living room I knew to check in there for Liz before venturing upstairs. She was asleep on the couch with a duvet pulled tightly around her; when I risked brushing my fingers across her forehead she was bitterly cold to the touch. Her hair was soaking wet.

It was my fault she was this cold. I hadn't once thought to give her the password for the central heating system throughout the entirety of our three months of living together, nor made sure she knew where the supplies for the fireplace were stored. And I'd had no signal the whole journey home, so I hadn't been able to call or message to rectify that mistake.

A roll of thunder almost seemed to shake the house, emphasising my stupidity. I deserved to have Liz hate me for putting her in this position when there was a storm raging on outside. So why, now that the room was warm and Liz was awake, was *I* the one acting out, not her? Clearly all Liz had wanted to do was talk but I couldn't trust myself to do that. I kept saying the wrong fucking thing, even though I didn't want to.

I was therefore only too happy to agree when she asked if I wanted to watch *Gundam* with her. Sitting together, watching TV together – those were things I could do. I wouldn't have to risk running off my big mouth and saying something I'd most likely later regret.

I was still the one who broke the silence between us, anyway.

"I can't believe you watched so much of *Zeta* without me this week," I mumbled, unable to help myself as the beginning credits began rolling for the next episode. "Where were you watching it – on your tiny laptop up in your room?"

"...I might have been."

"You're such a traitor."

I glanced at Liz out of the corner of my eye to find her watching me from her duvet cocoon, the firelight flickering across her face as she determined whether I was genuinely starting up a conversation or not. It was a terrible idea, to be sure – I didn't trust myself around Liz at all right now – but even so, I discovered I neither wanted to leave her side nor remain silent.

"I wasn't sure if you still wanted to watch it with me," Liz finally admitted, "and I sure as hell wasn't going to wait around when this" – she pointed at the screen, where Amuro and Char were mere minutes away from finally reuniting after eight years – "was imminent."

I could only laugh. "That's fair. *Zeta* goes downhill in its back half so may as well enjoy it at its peak."

"Exactly!" Liz replied emphatically, happy that someone agreed with me, and I smothered a grin.

It wasn't as if I'd never found another woman who was into anime – or, indeed, a woman who was into the same anime as me – but Liz was definitely the one I *wanted* to be watching cartoons with. The one I wanted to be laughing with, and sharing food with, and living under the same roof with, and—

And Liz was staring at me staring at her.

"What?" she asked, self-consciously tucking a curl of damp hair behind her ear. Even in the dim glow of the fire I could tell she was blushing.

"Your hair's still wet," I said. "Why didn't you dry it?"

She shrugged; the entire duvet moved with her. "I came down to light a fire, thinking I could get it going and *then* dry my hair. Turns out I was entirely useless at such a task."

I had the sense to look ashamed. "That's my fault. I should have told you everything was in the shed outside."

"I doubt I would have stepped foot outside even if I knew, to be honest. What with, you know, the storm and all."

"So you were content to lie on the couch, cold and wet?"

Liz wrinkled her nose. "Obviously not. But I wasn't about to call Chloë to ask if I could crash with her and Harriet just so I had access to central heating and wasn't alone."

"Ah, so you can't handle being alone?"

I deftly avoided a cushion when Liz chucked one at my face, catching it before it landed in the fireplace.

"I'll have you know I was perfectly fine being on my own before," she complained.

"Before?"

"Before none of your business."

I could only chuckle. Then I checked the time; it was after eight, and though I'd eaten with Mum and Jim at five I was beginning to get hungry again. Reasoning that Liz was probably starving I threw the cushion back at her and said, before she could protest my assault, "I was thinking of making nachos."

As expected, her eyes lit up like fireworks. "Is there any chorizo in the fridge?"

"No, but there's some spicy salami from that deli you like on Dumbarton Road."

That settled it for Liz. "Will you make it without me moving from the couch as an apology for not giving me the central heating password?"

"Ah, I knew that was going to bite me in the arse." I got up from the couch and bowed like a gracious gentleman. "But your wish is my command, m'lady."

Liz positively chirruped as I left to put the grill on, though she had the good sense to pause the TV whilst I went about preparing everything we needed for our incredibly unhealthy dinner. Salami, red onion, salsa, tortilla chips, and three kinds of cheese: mozzarella, sharp cheddar and pecorino sardo. Liz's favourites.

It didn't take long for the grill to heat up, and within fifteen minutes we were both digging into over-spilling bowls of nachos. Liz had finally sat up to do so but still she had the duvet wrapped around her like a protective shield. I hoped it wasn't against me...even though I knew that was probably for the best. Yet her father's words were ringing in my ears.

Could I really leave things off the way they were? Could I be content being sort-of-friends with Liz and nothing else? Was the current distance between us something I could tolerate forever?

Before I knew it we'd finished scarfing down our food and the pivotal Char and Amuro reunion episode of *Gundam* had come to an end, with another one just beginning. "Oh, I love this episode so much," Liz remarked, snuggling against me in her duvet as if she was completely unperturbed by the distance I'd so far maintained between us. She tugged on my sleeve. "Kamille is such a little bitch to Beltorchika. Wish Amuro had told her to fuck off, too."

I gulped back a flurry of nerves. Liz was much too close. "Is he your favourite?"

"Favourite what?"

"Character. Kamille, I mean."

Liz pondered this for a few moments. "Maybe not my favourite character but my favourite protagonist? Char is hard to beat, and then there's Amuro and Hathaway and Sayla..."

I was listening but also entirely not. This woman was too much for me to bear. If I actively paid attention to Liz's nerdy and relatable opinions then I was in very real danger of pinning her to the couch and professing my love for her. Since I knew that was very wrong and entirely inappropriate, I resisted.

"Should we watch something else after this episode?" I asked, thinking that if we watched something we hadn't both seen a million times then I'd be able to focus on the TV instead of Liz.

"Ooh, we could watch *Gundam Thunderbolt* parts one and two. We have time for both. Although..." Liz scrunched up her face as if immediately regretting her suggestion. "You said you're tired. You probably don't wanna stay up until one in the morning with me."

"There are few things I'd rather do than stay up until one in the morning watching anime with you, Liz," I said, because it was true.

I put on the first of the films and eased back onto the couch, far too happy when Liz resettled as close to me as she dared. I wished it were closer – stomach full of nerves notwithstanding. Her hair had finally dried in the heat from the fire into a complete flyaway bird's nest if ever there was one. But Liz seemed blissfully ignorant of the matter or perhaps simply didn't care, though when she caught me looking at her out of the corner of her eye for the third time in as many minutes she rounded on me.

"What are you staring at?"

"Your hair," I answered honestly.

"*Again*?"

"To say that it's a mess would be an understatement."

"I can't help the way my hair dries."

"Have you ever heard of a brush or, pray tell, a hair dryer?"

"Because you're so perfect?"

I pointed at my own hair. "I managed to shower and come downstairs *without* my hair looking like I dragged it backwards through a bramble bush."

"That's because you're vain as fuck. I simply do not care."

I kicked at her leg hidden somewhere in the duvet; she kicked me right back. "I don't believe that for a moment."

"Well, okay," Liz relented, "I didn't care when I thought I was going to be on my own tonight."

"So my opinion is taken into account when you decide whether to brush your hair or not? Noted."

Liz scowled, though it was good-natured. "Whatever rise you're trying to get of me, it won't work." And yet despite saying that, for the next few minutes all she could do was flatten down her hair and try to tame it into something more presentable. I almost felt bad for making Liz so self-conscious but, in all honesty, it was too entertaining watching her squirm because of me.

Unbidden I thought once more about what Jim had said. To just go home and be with Liz if that's what I wanted. And being here with her, teasing her, watching mindless television and eating nachos together, truly *was* exactly what I wanted to do.

Except it wasn't what I wanted to do with her *tonight*. I couldn't deny the burning, twisting coil that was building in my groin, driving me to distraction every time Liz bit her lip or wiped a stray eyelash from her cheekbone or tilted her head to the side to drag her fingers through her hair, exposing the length of her neck to me. I could see her artery throb beneath the skin.

God, what was I, a vampire?

After a few minutes of companionable silence – I didn't take in a moment of *Thunderbolt* part one – Liz huffed out a breath and sloughed off the duvet. Her cheeks were flaming hot so I was surprised she hadn't let go of it earlier. But then I saw she was wearing my flannel shirt and realised exactly why she hadn't wanted to let go of her feather-down armour. I knew I shouldn't comment on it.

I knew it. I knew it.

"Yes, I'm wearing the damn shirt," Liz said, cutting through my thoughts as if she could read them. To be fair, it probably wasn't difficult to work them out. She undid the top four buttons to fan the material away from her chest. "God, it got hot in here so quickly. You'd never think a room this large would heat up so well, would you?"

I nodded, though my body was burning because of another reason entirely. The shirt was now unbuttoned well past Liz's cleavage, showing me a tantalising view of her skin and her curves. Not knowing how else to stop myself from looking I took off my glasses and, in doing so, accidentally whacked my head against the couch.

"Tom, what are you – didn't that hurt?" Liz asked, a worried frown creasing her brow as she propped herself up her knees to inspect my head when I cursed aloud.

"I'm fine," I said, waving her off, "I didn't actually – *why aren't you wearing any trousers, Liz*?!" For her legs were entirely bereft of clothing. Going by the continuous, uninterrupted skin of her thigh up to her hipbone where my shirt pulled up I strongly suspected she had no underwear on, either.

Liz yelped and collapsed back into the duvet, covering her face with her hands in extreme embarrassment. "I totally forgot! I didn't...well, nobody was *supposed* to be coming home, so I didn't bother!"

"Do I dare ask if you make it a habit of yours to go parading around in my shirt and nothing else?"

"It's *my* shirt, not yours. You surrendered it four years ago. And so what if I *did* do that back when I lived alone?" Liz shrugged, trying her best to appear unbothered. The fact her cheeks were still scarlet did little to hide how mortified she was.

I turned from her. How was I supposed to sit through an innocent evening of watching anime knowing full well Liz was barely fucking dressed right beside me? "...you don't live alone now, though," I mumbled, cleaning my glasses on the edge of my sleeve in an effort to keep my attention anywhere but on Liz.

"Yeah, you're right. And it's – well – I like it much better that way. Not living alone, I mean." A beat of silence passed between us; I didn't need to be looking at Liz to know she was likely self-consciously scratching her nose. "And I really *was* lonely earlier, when I realised nobody was going to be in tonight. Honestly it made me more upset than I thought it would. So thank you for coming back, even if...even if you didn't do it for me."

"Of course I did it for you."

I kept my out-of-focus gaze on my glasses sitting uselessly in my hands, so I didn't notice Liz moving until her hand was on my chin and she tilted my face towards hers.

Her lips touched mine.

It was barely a kiss. A blink-and-you'll-miss-it affair. I hadn't expected it, so of course I stilled to stone beneath Liz's touch. My brain hadn't even *registered* what was going on when she jerked away as if I'd slapped her.

"I'm – fuck, Tom – I'm sorry," Liz stammered, wide-eyed with horror as she took in whatever expression I had on my face. Shock, maybe. Disbelief, certainly. "You've obviously been avoiding me and I was *so* inappropriate at lunch with the *fucking Calippo* and—"

"Liz."

"And now all you've done is be a little nice to me and I warped that to mean—"

"*Liz.*"

"And I go and *kiss* you—"

My mouth swallowed the rest of her damnably ridiculous words, smothering them with my lips and teeth and tongue. Liz froze for a fraction of a second in delicious surprise. Then she softened beneath me and eagerly reciprocated the kiss, turning her body towards mine so I could wrap an arm around her waist and hold her close.

I couldn't believe what was happening. Something was bound to go wrong; so far it always had.

I had to make certain it went right.

I pulled away from Liz's mouth, just a little, just enough to breathe a word or two between us. "You really have no idea how much I like you, do you?"

Liz's gaze met mine beneath her lashes. Her eyes were dark and heady with a longing I realised, with the perfect clarity of hindsight, had been there all night. I simply hadn't let myself see it.

When her hand gently clasped over mine and directed it to the open strip of skin her unbuttoned shirt revealed my breath stuttered to a stop. I could feel Liz's heart hammering in her chest, just as rapid as my own.

"...then why don't you show me?"

Chapter Thirty-Three

LIZ

For a second it looked like Tom had, to my horror, taken my invitation as a joke, or that he thought it was just another one of my games. It would have fit our current fucked-up pattern, after all. In that moment I was sure that finally daring to make a genuine move on him had been a fool's errand.

But I meant what I said. With every fibre of my being I desperately wanted to know just how much Tom liked me in a way where words couldn't get twisted or misconstrued. Where we could be well and truly honest with each other.

Then Tom's mouth was on mine again and my worries were blasted away. From where I'd dared to press his hand against my bare skin Tom crawled his fingers beneath the fabric of my shirt, rubbing the pad of his thumb against my nipple when he reached it. It sent a shudder straight down my spine; Tom responded by squeezing so hard it probably hurt me.

But all I felt was longing – the same visceral longing Tom was clearly making no attempt to mask anymore – so I leaned into the touch and allowed my own fingers to trail beneath the hem of his long-sleeved T-shirt.

We were far too clothed. I wanted them gone.

Tom groaned when I dragged my fingernails along his stomach. Reflexively he breathed in. "Do you know how long I've wanted to do this, Liz?" he murmured, the words fanning across my lips. His eyes glinted in the firelight, locked on mine, as pale as glass but somehow dark with longing. With the shadows beneath them he looked half-feral. I wanted him to let go entirely.

It would give me permission to do the same.

"I might have had an idea," I replied, voice as shaky as my hands when I withdrew them in order to undo the rest of the buttons of my shirt. I was in such a rush to do so that I became clumsy.

Tom wrapped his hands around mine and undid them for me.

"Am I allowed to indulge the belief that you feel the same way, then?" he asked, dragging his lips along my jawline to my ear. When he bit it I let out perhaps the most pathetic whimper to have ever been whimpered.

"W-would I be acting like this if—"

A blinding flash of light immediately chased by a rumble of thunder cut through the rest of my long overdue confession. The noise startled me and Tom both, who directed his attention to the TV when another flash of lightning and inevitable crash of thunder followed the first. The screen had gone dark.

"Power cut," Tom announced after a few seconds. Without the sound of robots fighting in space the silence in the room was startling, punctuated only by the howling wind and battering rain outside. We still had the fire to see by, but all at once the living room seemed empty and cavernous and *wrong* for what we were doing.

The two of us stared at each other, hands paused in the act of removing my shirt. Our breathing was heavy and flustered.

Then:

"Fuck it," Tom said, decisive, "my back'll give out if we do this on the couch, anyway." With a strength I had so far only been able to imagine in my filthiest daydreams he bodily picked me up, kicked closed the recliner and carried me out of the living room.

It was dark in the hallway – pitch black, even – but Tom didn't hesitate for a moment, his footsteps sure and practised as he bounded up the stairs. I kept my legs wrapped too tightly around his waist, anyway; the last thing I wanted was for us to fall and break our necks. That would have been just our luck, going by the way our relationship had progressed so far.

Tom chuckled when I squeezed my thighs against him. "Are you scared of the dark...or something else?"

"If you're going to make some kind of innuendo about being scared of your di—"

"Way to ruin the mood."

"If this is enough to ruin the mood then perhaps I'll just head to bed on my own and go to sleep?"

"Not a chance, Dr Maclean," Tom cut in. He trailed kisses down my neck to my collarbone with increasing urgency. "You're mine tonight."

I'd never been one for the dark, possessive love interest in books and films and TV shows, but the way Tom was acting as his lean arms easily carried me upstairs against the backdrop of the storm was very quickly changing my mind.

When we reached his bedroom door he paused. "Would you rather your room?" he asked, inclining his head towards my door.

"I've never been in your lordly chambers before," I replied, my lashes brushing against Tom's cheekbone when I kissed the corner of his mouth. Beneath my lips I felt him smile at the stupid comment. "I think I'd like to find out how the wealthy Thomas Henderson spends his nights."

"You won't see much. The power's out."

"Do I need a light to see how you're going to spend *this* specific night?"

The grin that spread across Tom's face did something to my insides I couldn't quite describe. "Now *that's* the kind of innuendo that sets the mood."

Tom all but kicked open the door and slammed it behind us. He crossed the vast, shadowy expanse of his bedroom floor in several broad strides before very unceremoniously tossing me on his bed.

I could do nothing but stare, wide-eyed, as Tom wasted no time in stripping off his clothes. He pulled off his T-shirt and chucked it carelessly on the floor, my gaze following down, down, down when he slid out of his jogging pants and boxers in one fluid motion. He was rock fucking hard as he loomed over me.

"Take that damn shirt off, Elizabeth," Tom ordered, making no move towards me but instead choosing to watch me squirm beneath his undivided attention. But my brain wasn't working, not at all.

I couldn't stop looking at him.

How many times had I watched this man, fully clothed, and fantasised about how he'd look exactly as he was now, naked and very obviously turned on? Sure, I'd seen Tom naked in the shower, but I'd been drunk and, really, we'd been too physically close for me to take him in properly.

The dimmest glimmer of moonlight through the huge, uncurtained window which Tom's bed rested against only served to further emphasise every angle of him. He was like a damn Greek god carved from stone, only granted a much bigger dick than the sculptors ever graced the statues with.

Tom's expression grew uncertain when I continued to do nothing but stare at him. "...Liz?" he wondered aloud, making the barest motion towards the bed.

"Why do you have a body *this good*?" I exclaimed, unable to stop myself. I climbed onto my knees and crawled to the edge of the bed, allowing myself to run my hands down Tom's chest to his stomach. His erection pressed insistently against my navel, fighting for my attention, but I forced it out of my mind.

For now.

Tom laced his fingers through my hair, curled them into a fist and tilted my head up. "Are you really asking me *right now* why I'm in good shape?"

"...it's crossed my mind more times than I care to admit. You work in a lab all day. Is it really just pure vanity?"

"I don't insist on running in the rain every god damn day for vanity," he replied, tracing the line of my jaw before kneeling down on the bed to join me. "I've had something – someone – driving me to distraction recently. Exercise was just about my only healthy outlet."

A flush spread across my face when I realised what he meant. "It's not fair that you're so beautiful," I muttered. "I never stood a chance."

"Funny, I was about to say the same thing about you."

Slowly, never taking his eyes off mine, Tom removed my shirt – his shirt – and threw it to the floor to join the rest of his discarded clothes. His fingers traced down my shoulders, my waist, my hips. I didn't move as he did so. I didn't *want* to. I wanted nothing more than for this moment to stretch on forever.

Except we both needed more, and we knew it.

Though I was aware that Tom was perfectly capable of pushing me down with next to no effort, he was incredibly gentle when he leaned against me until we both fell onto the bed. The duvet beneath my bare skin was cold to the touch, though clearly the radiators were on because the air was warm. There would be no hiding beneath the covers tonight; everything would be out in the open.

Tom ran his fingers down my leg then all the way back up between my thighs...and paused. Dangerously close to where I was dying for him to touch me.

"Your skin is so smooth," he said, gliding a curious hand over my leg again.

"Um...thanks?"

"Did you shave today? As in—"

"If you're insinuating that I shaved in the hopes of being seen and touched like this by a certain someone, then yes. I did." It was such a fucking embarrassing thing to admit. But what was the point in not admitting to it now? I really liked Tom and I was done pretending that I didn't. All that burying my head in the sand had achieved so far was grief, frustration and a ridiculous amount of unresolved sexual tension.

Tom huffed out a laugh and buried his head against my stomach. "You're so...god, you're impossible, Liz."

"Is that a bad thing?"

"Absolutely not. But next time consider not doing things backwards."

"What, you'd rather I jumped your bones and *then* got the razor o—*ahh*!"

Tom slid his fingers inside me, so easily that my shock quickly turned to a moan. Fuck, he felt good. I hadn't realised quite how wet I already was, though I was unashamedly aware of it now.

"I wish you'd *jumped my bones* months ago," Tom said, eyes trained on my reaction as he began experimentally moving his fingers. I felt so close to coming undone entirely and he'd barely bloody touched me; going by the look on his face it was clear Tom knew it.

God, we were really doing this, weren't we? There was nothing and nobody getting in our way this time, not even me.

"Get out of your head, Liz," Tom said, loud enough that it

starkly brought me back to the present. There was a shrewd look in his eye I knew all too well. When I pushed a knee against him Tom took the hint and climbed up to kiss my lips, though I missed the sensation of his fingers inside me immediately. "Are you nervous?"

"Very," I admitted, because I was. I twisted a finger through a curl of Tom's hair to keep my voice from shaking. "I don't – what if we mess this up?"

I didn't expect Tom to laugh in my face but that's exactly what he did. "How could we possibly mess up having sex?" he asked, chuckling into my neck before gently biting down on my shoulder. I made no attempt to withhold the shiver that ran down my spine. He gave me a reassuring smile. "Even if it's bad it's still sex. And trust me...it won't be bad."

"How can you be so sure?"

"Because I've liked you for so long I have your entire damn body memorised. So let me take the lead, if that will ease your nerves."

I didn't think I'd ever heard a single hotter thing said to me in my entire life. The barely-constrained tension in Tom's entire frame as he continued handling me so gently only lent credence to what he was saying. He *would* take the lead if I wanted him to.

I wanted him to.

"Do your worst, as it were," I said, twisting my hand through Tom's hair to pull his lips to mine. "Or your best."

In one deft motion Tom reached over me towards a bedside table and wrenched open a drawer. His eyes glittered dangerously when he pulled out a condom and ripped the packet open. "Then you'll forgive me for jumping straight to screwing you first. We have all night, after all...and I've wanted this for so long."

I gulped, helpless to do nothing but watch him slip the condom on. It felt like he took his time doing so just so he could watch me watch him. "...I'm definitely wet enough for that already."

"Damn fucking right you are."

Oh god. I thought I'd witnessed Tom at his most flirtatious, his most charming, his most seductive, but I'd never seen him like *this* before. Moody shadows cast across his face, the storm crackling around him, his entire body tense and rigid like a piano wire dying to be cut loose. I wasn't sure how I was supposed to keep my wits about me.

Then I remembered I *wasn't*.

The moonlight limned Tom's shoulders as he lowered himself onto me, a breath kept trapped behind his teeth as he paused right when I thought he was going to break the final barrier between us.

"Tom?" I whispered, sliding my arms around his neck to land a kiss below his ear. He glanced at me out of the corner of his eye, slowly letting out the breath he was holding in a slow whistle.

"Last chance to tell me this is all some big joke to mess with me, Liz."

I thought my heart might stop. He still didn't trust that my behaviour so far this evening had been genuine? "Is that – is that what you want?" I asked, panic bubbling inside me. "For me to not be serious about...whatever we are?"

Tom shook his head against my shoulder. "The *only* thing I want is for you to be serious about whatever we are."

"Then you'll have to trust me when I say I want this." I tightened my arms around his neck, pulling Tom as close to me as I could get. "That I want you. That I've wanted this for longer than I'll ever admit to out loud. And that I may well explode if you don't get inside me, right now."

It was all the reassurance Tom needed – and me, as well. Actually hearing myself tell him these things only solidified how true they were, and how I was okay with that. I didn't really need to know why Tom had been such a bastard to me during my PhD; all I needed to know was that his feelings *now* were genuine.

It was painfully obvious they were.

Tom placed a hand behind my neck and kissed me, hard, swallowing my cry of surprise when his entire length slid inside me.

Fuck.

Fuck.

I already knew his cock was big – I'd only just been admiring it, after all, and I'd spent many a guilty night imagining what it would feel like inside me. But now it was *actually* inside me. For real.

Whoever said fantasies were better? Nothing could beat how this reality felt.

"Are you okay?" Tom murmured, barely breaking from my mouth to voice his concern. I responded by hitching a leg over his back and driving him deeper inside me; when he groaned it was all I could do not to come from the sound alone. Tom sounded desperate. Barely restrained.

It was hot as hell.

"Faster," I urged, sliding my tongue back into Tom's mouth and kissing him with reckless abandon. He was only too eager to respond.

As our breathing accelerated I found myself gripping onto Tom's shoulder blades; they were slick with sweat. When I dared to dig my nails in Tom bucked against me.

"Fuck, do that harder," he growled into my mouth. It reminded me of what he'd said back in the hotel room at the conference – how he'd wanted me to pull his hair.

"Are you a masochist, Tom?" I asked, a small smile curling my lips at the revelation.

He responded by biting my lip so hard it almost bled. "I just prefer things a little rough. If you don't then—"

"I do. I do. I just want to know what you like."

At this Tom pulled away an inch or two. His eyes found mine, soft and intense all at once. "I like *you,* Liz. I like you so much I can't stand it. The last couple of months have been torture. In fact..."

The look in Tom's eyes at once turned wicked. Without warning he pulled out of me.

"I thought you said you couldn't wait any longer?" I complained. I keenly missed the sensation of him filling me up. But Tom's lips merely pulled into a smile that was more of a snarl than anything else.

"I changed my mind," he said, crawling down my body until his head was between my thighs. When his tongue found my clit I cried in surprise and delight in equal measure.

"Oh, god – that's – right *there*," I gasped, barely audible against Tom's slow but assured onslaught. When I cast my gaze down I saw that he was observing my every reaction, his left hand gripping into the fat of my thigh as if his life depended on it.

This was the kind of torment I could get behind.

"Do you know how sexy you are?" Tom asked when he paused to take a breath. A flash of lightning crossed us, then, illuminating his face as he watched me. His lips were slick; when he licked them I instinctively gulped.

How could *I* be the sexy one when he was acting like this?

"H-how many girls has that line worked on?" I stammered, no longer able to maintain eye contact. I threw my head against the pillow, my fingers threading into Tom's hair as I writhed beneath his touch. I couldn't stand how good he felt.

I expected Tom to laugh at my remark but, instead, he kissed the inside of my thigh with the most feather-light of kisses. "You're the only one who's ever mattered. Nobody is sexy in my eyes when compared to you."

And I believed him. How could I not, when his fingers were lazily circling my clit and he was kissing my skin and the grip he had on my thigh was rigid and shaking, like he was still holding himself back?

I thought he'd return his mouth to where it had been but Tom insisted on slowly tormenting me with his fingers, instead. I'd believed I could wait out his punishment – because it *was* punishment against what I'd done on Hallowe'en, pure and simple – but I was an impatient woman.

"Tom," I moaned, tugging on his hair to grab his attention, "I can't take this. You're driving me crazy!"

I glanced down to find an unhinged grin plastered on his face. Tom's entire body was strained and tense; clearly it wasn't only me who was suffering right now. "Then you know what you need to do."

"I don't—"

"Beg me to let you come."

"...what?" I could barely comprehend what Tom was saying; his fingertips insistently stroking me were threatening to push me over into insanity.

"Say 'please', and I'll do it. I'll do it so many times you'll end up begging me to *stop*."

There was no amount of pride I had left that was going to stop me from doing or saying anything that he wanted. At this point I would have confessed to bloody murder just to find a release by Tom's hands.

"Then *please*, Tom," I begged, making hazy eye contact with him. My grip tightened on his hair, my nails raking against his scalp. It was Tom who moaned this time. "Please. Let me come."

Tom was only too eager to comply. With a few deft strokes of his tongue and his fingers combined I came undone entirely, bucking my hips against him even as Tom pinned me down to enjoy the intense pulses of my orgasm.

But he didn't let me ride it out in peace.

Wasting no time, Tom slid his cock back inside me to alarming effect, rubbing me in just the right position to rip a cry of pleasure from my mouth. When he knelt up, slinging one of my knees over his shoulder as he mercilessly slammed into me, the new angle left me helpless to do nothing but obey his every whim.

"Liz," Tom said, my name barely audible through his gritted teeth.

I hardly had the brain power to respond. "What is it?"

"I really like you."

The actual words weren't nearly strong enough to match the way in which Tom said them, the way he was touching me, the way his eyes went absolutely wild whenever I clenched around him, but I'd already told myself tonight was not the night for words.

Words were for later.

When I reached up to grab Tom he eagerly leaned down to let me wrap my arms around him once more. Every inch of his skin was blazing hot and soaked in sweat; his heart felt like it was seconds away from bursting through his chest. Tom's mouth urgently found mine.

A few seconds later, his grip on my leg turned to steel and he gasped into my mouth. Tom bucked once, twice, three times. His kiss turned shallower, then with a final slide of his lips on mine Tom rolled off me onto his back.

His chest was heaving. I had no doubt mine was, too.

It was only when he turned his head to face me I discovered I was already staring at him.

"That was…" I began, not really knowing what to say.

Tom could only laugh, though he was so breathless it was

barely audible. With his sweat-drenched hair curling across his forehead and intermittent shadows and moonlight playing over his face, I became starkly aware of a much younger version of Tom that I'd never know.

Then I remembered that Tom himself had once told me I'd have hated his younger self, and I decided against chasing ghosts.

"That was...not bad?" Tom finally offered, when I didn't finish my sentence.

It was my turn to laugh. With a shaking hand I reached out to cup his face, revelling in the feeling of Tom nuzzling his cheek against it. The stubble I had so blindly ignored in my urgency to be screwed senseless scratched against the palm of my hand, simultaneously itchy and comforting.

"That was the opposite of bad."

"So you had nothing to worry about?"

"I had nothing to worry about."

"Good. Then you won't be offended if I take a minute or thirty to sleep before we pick things up again?"

Fuck, I was helpless to Tom's ridiculous pillow talk. I rolled against his side, kissed his shoulder and shivered when he slid his fingertips down the side of my body to pull the duvet over us. "I think some sleep might be a great idea."

As we dozed off with the sounds of the storm raging on outside, knowing we were merely resting until we regained the energy to start everything all over again, I was struck by how *right* it felt to be lying in Tom's arms. It didn't feel weird or awkward or wrong. It didn't feel like everything leading up to this – our not-quite-first-date, Hallowe'en, the conference, and everything in-between – had been a mistake.

It felt like I was always meant to be here, with Tom, like this. The only difference between *now* and *before* was that I was finally ready to embrace that wholeheartedly.

Chapter Thirty-four

TOM

When I woke up the first thing I noticed was how quiet it was. The wind, the rain and the thunder had at some point in the small hours of the morning tired themselves out, leaving nothing but perfect tranquillity in their wake.

The second thing I noticed was a dull, satisfying ache in my body, because I hadn't slept more than perhaps an hour or two all night and I'd been using every muscle I possessed to facilitate the very reason I hadn't slept.

The third thing I noticed was Liz, gracelessly sprawled on her front across half the bed. Her right hand was grazing my hip; when I shifted experimentally away she followed the movement so we didn't break skin contact.

The fourth thing I noticed was that I desperately needed to pee.

"Sorry," I whispered to Liz as I slid out of bed, though she was out cold and didn't hear me. The house was freezing because the heating was set to turn off at midnight but I was yet to program it to turn *on* in the morning – something which I had procrastinated about since September but only really regretted right now. I jumped down to the landing to rectify my mistake.

Once I'd relieved myself I couldn't resist the allure of a scalding hot shower. Deciding that Liz would in all likelihood not enjoy being woken up just to ask if she wanted to join me, I turned on the hot water and resolved to be as quick as possible. Like hell was I spending any more time away from her than was required – not when what had occurred between us still felt altogether like I'd imagined it.

The flashbacks flooding my brain as I washed my hair ensured I knew that the events of last night were decidedly *not* the product of my imagination.

Considering how our evening had started out I was rather impressed Liz and I had actually managed to have sex. Our track record would have suggested that one or both of us would fuck things up, whether intentionally or otherwise.

When I got out of the shower I remembered, suddenly, that I'd abandoned my glasses in the living room, so I made the effort to put in a pair of contacts before towel drying my hair and padding back to my bed.

Liz was awake when I walked through the door, sitting up in bed with the duvet help up to her chin. I couldn't blame her; it really was freezing. Walking around with a towel slung around my hips, skin still dripping wet, was a terrible idea.

It seemed altogether less terrible when I caught the way Liz was eyeing me up.

"I was wondering where you went," she croaked, holding a hand to her throat in surprise at her own voice. Then Liz picked up a glass of water from the bedside table – I'd brought a jug and two glasses up at some small hour of the morning – drank down several thirsty gulps, and tried speaking again. "Why didn't you wake me up?"

"Would you have appreciated being woken up just to shower with me?"

"Is that a trick question?"

"That depends. What's your answer?"

"Hot water and shower sex sounds pretty great to me."

"Now you're making me regret my chivalrous decision to let you sleep."

"You? Chivalrous? After last night I would hardly use that to describe you."

I could only laugh. Part of me had been concerned that Liz would close off to me once she woke up, full of regret about what had occurred between the two of us. Clearly I'd had no reason to be worried. "How are you feeling?" I asked, finishing drying myself off before slipping back into bed beside Liz. I kissed the top of her riotously wavy hair. "Are you hungry?"

She nodded. "Starving, but I'm too exhausted to move."

"How would you have managed hot and steamy shower sex, then?"

"Oh, there's always energy for that if you're horny enough."

"I'm beginning to think you're far filthier than I am, Liz," I murmured against her lips, rolling her on top of me to kiss her properly. The weight of her pressed against my body in tandem with our topic of conversation was rapidly springing my cock back into action, as if it didn't care that we'd been at it all night.

When Liz felt my erection growing against her she squirmed. "Seems like somebody operates rather well on two hours of sleep," she said, tracing the line of my collarbone with the tip of her index finger as she did so. "You have a hickey, by the way. How unprofessional."

"Says the woman who gave me it."

"I couldn't help it," she giggled, cheeks turning rosy as if the thought of giving me a love bite was something to be shy about. "How could I resist sinking my teeth into such a handsome man?"

"Now I can see why you've never paid me any compliments

to my face before. They're going straight to my head."

"I'd rather say they're going straight to somewhere else, Tom."

Well, she had me there.

"Can you see me properly now?" Liz asked.

"Huh?"

"Contacts," she said, poking the bridge of my nose. "You have them in."

"Oh. Yes, I can see now. My eyes aren't that bad, though."

"I caught you squinting whenever I wasn't right next to you during the night, though," Liz pointed out. I bit her finger when she made to poke my face again.

"What kind of a fool *doesn't* want to commit to memory every second spent with someone they've been longing for in actual focus?" I countered.

The blush that crossed Liz's face, then, was dangerously close to *actually* being shy. "...that's very romantic, Tom," she murmured, avoiding my gaze as she did so.

"I didn't realise you enjoyed romantic gestures," I teased, knowing full well that she didn't know how to handle them. She'd barely been able to take being gifted a single tulip, after all. "You certainly didn't like being sung to at karaoke."

Liz made a face. "That's because that was *embarrassing*. And besides, you sang to everyone else, too."

"Ahh, so you were jealous? Noted."

"I wasn't—" Liz bit out, but then she scowled. "You're making fun of me."

"Only a little. Were you, though?"

"Was I what?"

"Jealous."

I expected Liz to dramatically deny any and all such feelings.

To my surprise, however, she kissed my chest, then looked up at me through her eyelashes. "I was. What are you going to do about it?"

"Celebrate that you liked me enough to feel threatened by random drunk women the very same night you blue-balled me to fu—*ahh*," I bit out, because Liz had begun grinding against my dick.

"Did you finish yourself off after I left the shower that night?"

"I quite possibly stayed up *all* night physically channelling my frustrations, yes."

"How terrible for you."

"If you feel bad then how about you make it up to me?" I suggested, making my tone as indecent as possible. "I'd quite like to see those skills you have with a Calippo in broad daylight."

Liz ugly laughed, her face now bright red. "God, don't remind me about that. I can't *believe* I did that."

"You have no idea how much self-restraint I needed not to do something about that."

"So...why didn't you?"

"Because I didn't want to keep pushing my feelings onto you. Until you explicitly said you wanted to actually make 'us' a thing I didn't want to force anything. I was worried I'd push you away."

It wasn't the whole truth – it didn't cover my guilt over our past and how I'd manipulated things to keep Liz living in my house – but it was, at its core, still *true.*

Liz scratched her nose self-consciously, not quite managing to conceal the smile that was spreading across her face with her hand. "So where does that leave us now? Are we an 'us', as you put it?"

"Do you want that?"

"...yes."

"Good."

"And what about you?"

"I thought that was bloody obvious by now. I've wanted that to be true for y—months now."

If Liz noticed my slip of the tongue, she didn't show it. "Then I guess we're...a guess we're kind of a thing now, then?"

"You couldn't have sounded more unsure about that if you tried," I laughed. "We can take it as slow as you want to. You don't even need to tell your friends, if that makes being with me in some capacity any more bearable."

"And what makes you think I want to hide things from my friends?"

"Well, you weren't exactly...forthcoming...about even hinting at the fact we were attracted to each other when we left the karaoke bar."

"That's not fair," Liz huffed. "I was in blatant denial back then."

"You were *blatantly* still ready to come back with me and—"

"Look, do you want a blow job or not?" Liz cut in, emphatically rubbing against my dick.

"You make an excellent point. No more making fun of you it is."

With that Liz dragged her hair away from her face, satisfied with having (unfairly) won against me, and proceeded to crawl down to my groin and—

The dull thump of the front door opening carried up the stairs.

"Shite," Liz and I said in unison. She leapt from the bed, swinging her head around wildly for something to wear before eventually finding my flannel shirt where it had been discarded on the floor.

"Definitely not the time to inform our parents about us," Liz said hastily, fumbling with her buttons as she did so.

"God, absolutely not." I checked the time; it was barely ten. "I never thought they'd be back so early. I feel like we're teenagers."

"Cosplaying as teenagers, maybe."

"I thought you didn't cosplay."

"Not in public, remember?" Liz winked at me.

"That's hardly a fair thing to say just as you're leaving the room," I complained, keenly feeling the absence of Liz's body heat already. "I'd ask when I'll see you again but..."

Liz laughed softly, then quickly exited my bedroom just as the sound of footsteps could be heard on the stairs.

I couldn't believe Liz had left me blue-balled again. But more than that: I couldn't believe I was *happy* about it. There was always tomorrow.

Or tonight, when our parents were in bed.

Chapter Thirty-five

LIZ

"RIGHT, SO...ARE YOU READY?"

"Ready to deal with everyone being insufferably curious that something has changed between us? No. But it'll only get worse if we deny anything has happened so...I guess I'm as ready as I'll ever be."

Tom nodded his head as he parked his car in front of the research building. The moment he turned the engine off his hand slid from the gear stick to my knee. When he squeezed it a thrill ran down my spine; I had to turn away so that he couldn't see me blushing.

"I can see your reflection in the window," he chuckled. "Are you embarrassed?"

"Of you? Always."

"Of literally any kind of physical display of affection."

"I thought we already established that yesterday."

Tom responded in exactly the way I should have known he would, except I reacted too late so didn't manage to avoid the kiss he landed on my cheek.

"If you don't want anyone to know, Liz, then say so with your words," Tom said, laughing even harder when I pushed him away and rubbed at my cheek as if his kiss had been poisonous.

"I'm tempted to," I threw at him. "Going by how much you're enjoying yourself."

"You wound me."

"You have no heart to wound."

Another laugh. God, everything rolled off Tom's back like water off a damn duck. It used to annoy me. *Used to.* Now I could see why he did it: it was much easier to laugh things off than let people know you were bothered about something.

Ah.

Feeling ridiculous, I gingerly reached for Tom's hand and laced his fingers between mine. He stared down in obvious surprise. "Am I having a stroke, Liz, or am I witnessing you willingly holding my hand in a public space?"

"It's only the car," I muttered, looking anywhere but at Tom. To be fair it wasn't as if anyone outside was watching us; after all, why would they? And even if they knew us, Tom had been giving me lifts to work for three months now. Had seen us bickering and making fun of each other and, if I was being honest with myself, flirting. We probably looked no different than we had done last week.

Except that everything *was* different.

Tom let out a low sigh, shook out his shoulders, then offered me a smile. "Last chance to tell me you want me to act like *this* isn't happening," he said, indicating down towards our hands.

"Nah, I'm done being in denial. Let's just...get the day over with."

Pleased with my answer, Tom let go of my hand with obvious reluctance and then got out of the car. Immediately he cursed. "Damn rain," he spat, holding a hand uselessly over his head to protect his hair from the rain. It had been dry mere seconds ago.

"Feels like it might snow soon," I said, rubbing my arms for warmth as the two of us rushed inside to the glorious central heating and weather protection the building afforded us. "Although, knowing Glasgow's luck, it'll just be more rain. Will you put up a Christmas tree early if it *does* snow? For me?"

Tom raised a teasing eyebrow. "Bold of you to assume I care enough about you to change the way I live my life, Liz."

"Bold of you to think you can lie to my face."

Was it just me or did Tom flinch at my jibe? But I figured it was either my imagination or he had shivered from the previously cold air outside.

When we reached the lab only Trevor the technician and Daichi were in. "Undergrads are at a lecture," Daichi explained when we took off our coats and said hello. "Rodrigo's off sick and everyone else is in the common room getting coffee. Some representative from a new café brought along some of the good stuff to get everyone hooked."

Going by his dilated pupils and even bouncier than usual attitude, I could only come to the conclusion that Daichi had already consumed some of the 'good stuff'.

"Is it okay for me to use the culture shaker today?" Tom asked when we all walked into the lab.

Daichi nodded his assent but I frowned. "I thought you were done with lab work for your application? And aren't you moving back into *your* lab next week?"

"True, but I'm impatient and I think I worked out a way to maximise my protein yields that I hadn't thought of before."

"Okay, well," I said, "I'm doing a purification on Wednesday so you can't steal the machine from me then."

Tom held a hand to his chest in mock dismay. "As if I didn't know your schedule by heart, Dr Maclean! I booked the machine upstairs already."

"You know that's creepy as hell, right? Knowing my schedule by heart?"

"Not if I—"

"Right, what's going on?" Daichi interrupted, casting his curious gaze over the both of us. "And don't lie."

I cringed at how easily he'd worked things out; in all honesty I hadn't thought we were acting any different than usual, and literally only five minutes had passed.

"This idiot keeps reaching out to touch you but then stops himself at the last second."

"Very observant," Tom said, seeming surprised that he'd been doing exactly what his best friend had witnessed. I hadn't noticed, either.

"And *you're* smiling even when you're insulting him, Liz," Daichi continued, rounding on me. "Since when have you ever publicly smiled at my dear best friend?"

Christ, he had me there.

"Maybe something happened," I admitted, moving to my bench and busying myself checking my stock of Eppendorf tubes simply to hide the embarrassed grin that crossed my face. When my boss clapped his hands in excitement my grin only grew wider.

"Thank goodness for that, and not a moment too soon," Daichi said. "Nobody else will say it to your faces but you were doing everybody's heads in."

"Thanks for that, Dai. Don't you have an exam to invigilate in five minutes?"

Daichi stared at Tom, confused, then checked the time and all but yelped. "That I do! I'll see you at lunch!"

And with that the chaotic energy that was Daichi Ito on too much caffeine disappeared. The lab was eerily silent in his absence. Tom caught my eye as he put on his lab coat, brow rising in amusement when I made no move to do anything other than stare at him.

"What?" he asked.

"Nothing. I just...I don't know. Didn't realise we were both so transparent. Daichi worked us out in all of about thirty seconds."

Tom shrugged. "The entire lab has assumed we were in some stage of getting it on for weeks now. The only one who was in denial about that was you."

"*Tom!*"

"And Peter, too. Major denial from him."

I turned away from him to skim through my lab book, the topic of conversation having quickly caused me to forget what I was actually supposed to be doing. "...how long did you know?" I muttered after a moment.

I heard Tom settle down beside me. "Know what?"

"That Peter...liked me."

"Oh, I worked it out on day two of working in here."

"That fast?" That made me feel even worse about being so oblivious to Peter's feelings.

Tom must have picked up on the drop in my mood, for he slid his hand across the bench to graze his fingers against mine. "There's nothing you can do about him right now. Just give Peter time."

At that moment the door to the lab flew open, and all the missing PhD students and postgrads flew in. Tom's hand lingered by my own, clearly reluctant to move away. But then he sighed, pulled his hand away and ran it through his hair. It was much curlier than it usually was.

"You didn't wash your hair this morning?" I asked, curious. I didn't comment on him removing his hand, because I knew he'd done it for my sake, but in all honesty I hadn't minded it.

But it was far too embarrassing to admit that out loud – not least because I was sure Tom would take complete and utter advantage of my saying so to shower me with the worst public displays of affection the world had ever seen.

Tom kept his gaze on his lab book, though his cheeks started flushing the faintest shade of pink.

"What is it?" I pressed, entirely unused to seeing Tom flustered. "Why didn't you wash your hair this morning?"

"It's stupid."

"And? Tell me."

Tom glanced at me, clearly considering whether to ignore my question, then finally said, "I was hoping you'd come over to my room this morning, so I stayed in bed much longer than usual."

"Is *that* why you didn't go jogging, either?"

He nodded.

His confession was equal parts heart-warming and hilarious. "Why didn't you just text me to come through?"

"That's hardly very romantic. Especially since our parents went to bed so late last night that you'd already fallen asleep before it was safe for you to join me in bed."

"You could have crept into my room, instead."

"That feels like an invasion of your privacy."

I burst out laughing. "Now you're just being ridiculous. After everything that's happened you're worried about *invading my space*? Trust me, I definitely wouldn't have minded being woken up by you crawling into be—"

A loud cough interrupted me, and I turned to see that most of the lab had, in fact, been standing behind me and Tom in order to not-so-subtly eavesdrop on our conversation. God, I should have been humiliated.

I wasn't.

"Rodrigo will be so mad he missed this," Laura – Daichi's second PhD student – told the undergrads, who had just appeared in the lab, their lecture clearly finished. "So have the two of you been lying to us all along or—"

"Go do your work, Laura," Tom said, the blush oh his face growing ever more scarlet as the students began laughing. A slow smile crept up my face; for all Tom had teased me about romantic gestures and public displays of affection it was clear that being caught having an obviously private conversation by students, no less, was enough to illicit some shame even in him.

The students, to their credit, took this as a genuine cue to go about their usual business, though all morning they exchanged glances and lingered a little too long by mine and Tom's bench as if hoping to bear witness to more concrete evidence that the two of us were together.

By the time I went over to the foyer for lunch – Tom had his rescheduled meeting with Gill, so I went alone – Chloë was already waiting for me.

"So how was he?" she asked the moment I sat down.

"Hello, Liz. How was your weekend, Liz?"

"Don't give me that," she said, rolling her eyes. "You've fobbed me off with radio silence since Friday, and I have to hear from *Rachael* who heard from *Rodrigo* who heard from *Laura* that you and Tom were totally all over each other this morning!"

"We weren't *all over each other*. We were simply having a...discussion."

"About which bed you screw in, going by what Rach said." When I didn't reply Chloë guffawed in laughter. "Jesus, Liz, talk about unprofessional. Keep that kind of talk for the bedroom."

I threw a crisp at her. "Says you. Don't forget what you and Harriet were like literally everywhere on campus when you got together. Ugh, I still can't get the bathroom incident at the

QMU out of my head."

"Touché. But you didn't answer me. How was he?"

"He – hang on a second, Chloë."

"That was the worst deflection ever."

"Sorry, I just—" I took my phone out of my pocket where it had been buzzing insistently. A missed call from my dad, followed by a text from him saying that he'd pick me up after work to take me out for dinner. But there were a couple of notifications below his text that caught my eye: private message requests from Instagram.

"Still waiting..." Chloë said, clucking her tongue impatiently.

The messages were from guys who looked oddly familiar. Curious, I opened the first and then the second, both of which read roughly the same way. I'd matched with them on Tinder and they'd apparently messaged me, only I totally ignored them, so they searched around to find me on Instagram. Never mind the fact that I found that creepy as hell, it did nevertheless ring not quite *true*. For I hadn't ignored either guy; they'd never contacted me on Tinder.

Had they?

"Liz, for god's sake, don't keep me in suspense!"

"Sorry," I mumbled, putting my phone away to focus on my best friend. "What were you saying?"

"*Tom!* What the ever loving fuck happened?"

"Oh." It took my brain a moment or two to spin back into action. "We...yeah. Let's just say it was a dark and stormy night well spent."

"Don't fob me off with the PG version, you bitch!"

I waved around emphatically. "You can have the X-Rated cut when we're not at work."

Mollified – at least for now – Chloë and I whiled away our lunchtime talking about Dad and Jenny's wedding, and whether the shite weather would turn the Henderson estate into one giant, frozen pond by the time the twenty-third of December rolled around.

When we bid each other good-bye I pulled my phone out again to frown at the Instagram messages.

I'd been sure these two guys had ignored me – just like every other man I'd matched with before I gave up on Tinder. Even though from experience it was odd that *all* of them would do so after matching with me.

Perhaps both of them thought they'd messaged me but had actually forgotten to, or they'd mistaken me for another hapless woman on Tinder whom they'd been trying to find.

That seemed more likely. Surely it was nothing more than that.

Reassured by my logical reasoning I laid the matter to rest. Then, for good measure, I deleted Tinder and Bumble.

With the way things were going I'd never need to use a dating app again.

Chapter Thirty-Six

TOM

I woke to the feeling of cold air across my skin, stark and unwelcome. Blindly I grabbed for the duvet to pull it around myself but only met air. An evil cackle filled my ears.

"Someone's alarm didn't go off this morning," Liz said, sounding far too happy about it. It took me a few seconds to find my glasses and sit up to face her, standing at the base of my bed with the duvet in her arms.

"What time is it?" I asked, shivering as I glanced out of the window. It was still dark, because it was December, so it gave me no further insight into how late I might be.

"Almost nine."

"And you're only waking me up *now?*"

A smirk crossed Liz's face as she took in my naked indignation. "Totally worth it to catch you out like this."

I let that sink in for a moment. "...did my alarm magically not go off or, pray tell, did someone happen to turn it off when we were watching TV last night?"

Gleefully Liz held up my phone. "You left it in the living

room. I was *going* to give it back to you before you went to bed but that would have been too kind of me."

I couldn't stand how cold I was, so I put all my strength behind yanking on the duvet to pull it back over me. Liz wasn't prepared for my assault and came falling down with it, too. She shrieked, though I was quick to grab her and cover her mouth with my hand to quell the sound. "Careful, you absolute monster," I murmured into her ear, "you wouldn't want to wake up your dad, would you?"

Liz responded by licking my hand until I let go. "Dad and Jenny left half an hour ago to visit the estate. Something about dealing with the flooding all this stormy weather has caused."

"Okay, so why are *you* still here? You're going to be just as late as me at this rate."

Liz didn't respond at first, choosing instead to clamber over me until she was sitting right over my groin. It was then I realised she was wearing neither tights nor underwear beneath her floaty, knee-length skirt. I stiffened immediately beneath her.

"Daichi might think I have a dentist's appointment," she purred, rubbing against my rapidly-growing erection, "and he might think you so graciously offered to drive me there. What with all the rotten weather recently."

"That's very nice of me."

"So what do you think? Do you mind being late for work today?"

Deftly I rolled Liz beneath me, much to her delight. "I think we could take the entire fucking day off if we wanted."

"I have experiments I have to do this afternoon that can't wait."

"The morning, then?"

The look she gave me was wicked. "I can do a morning."

It was close to two in the afternoon when Liz and I finally made it in. Daichi tapped his feet impatiently when I waltzed into his office. "So much for our lunch plans, huh?"

"Sorry, Dai," I said, having the sense to look ashamed even though I wasn't sorry in the slightest. "I thought Liz told you I was giving her a lift to the dentist?"

"What was she getting, four root canals?" I rolled my eyes then folded into the chair opposite his desk. Daichi sighed good-naturedly. "You're happy."

"Why wouldn't I be?"

"Have you told Liz about why you were an arsehole to her during her PhD?"

I cringed. "God, you don't pull your punches, do you?"

"Not when we're having a serious conversation and someone else's feelings are on the line, no."

Of course Daichi had a point. If he knew even half of the shite I'd pulled over the last few months to keep Liz living in my house – and single – then he probably *would* punch me.

But things with me and Liz were good now. Great. Inability to actually sleep in a bed together because our parents had suddenly decided to become night owls notwithstanding, I couldn't remember the last time I'd felt this content.

At the look on my face Daichi shook his head. "It'll come back to bite you if you don't tell her, Tom."

"If she asks me about it then I'll tell her. That's pretty reasonable, right?"

"Pretty cowardly," Daichi countered, "but better, I suppose. May is excited to meet Liz at the wedding."

"And what, pray tell, have you been telling that wonderful

wife of yours?"

"Only that you've been living with the love of your life for three months but said love of your life hates you," he said, sniggering when I chucked a pen at his head. "I'm not wrong."

"She might have hated me before but she certainly doesn't now."

"No objection to me calling her the love of your life?"

"I – you bastard," I muttered, feeling stupid at how easily Daichi had trapped me into confessing the true extent of my feelings.

Daichi's snigger became a full-on cackle. "You had to grow up at some point, Tom. Better late than never. Hence why you should be honest with Liz rather than keeping secrets."

God, if only he knew.

"Noted," I said, before taking my leave to head to my bench. Since Liz hadn't taken me up on the offer of ditching the entire day I was as well doing some actual work, too.

"Professor Henderson!" Maria, one of the undergrads, called out, jogging down the lab with a sunny grin on her face to stand by the bench. Liz was sitting down already; she regarded Maria with a curious expression on her face.

"Can I help you?" I asked politely. I'd helped her with a few experiments over the last three months but nothing major enough to warrant such a positive reaction.

"That house you recommended – Jake and I got it! Thanks for giving me the heads up. I'd never thought to keep the flat filter on so that upper and lower cottage houses stayed in the search. I can't believe we'll finally have a garden!"

"He recommended you a flat?" Liz piped in, leaning on her elbow to join the conversation. She flicked her gaze towards me. "That's very kind of him."

"Isn't it just?" Maria said, beaming. "Oh, and Lydia said—"

"It's no problem," I cut in, panic overriding all else as Liz grew more and more interested in what Maria was saying. Fuck, literally after just acknowledging that I was never, ever going to tell Liz about anything I did behind her back, here was a student intent on destroying me with one well-timed 'thank you'.

When I turned from Maria to give my false attention to checking if I needed to make more TAE buffer, the undergrad got the message and retreated to her own bench.

Liz coughed softly beside me. "You helped her find a flat?"

"Ah, yes, well – not really," I said, awkward as hell in the face of trying to come up with a believable lie.

"What does that mean?"

"It means I remembered a couple of the tricks you were using to filter your flat searches back in September and passed them on." I hoped that sounded enough like the truth to placate Liz. It *had* to be. Otherwise I knew fine well I was in for a world of trouble; our fledgling relationship wasn't remotely strong enough for Liz to tolerate any of my shitty behaviour if she found out about it.

"Oh." A pause. "Well, that was really nice of you all the same."

Her response was genuine enough. When I risked looking at her I saw that Liz was smiling at me. But there was a flinty, suspicious edge to Liz's expression that suggested she didn't entirely believe my lie. My stomach squirmed, though I fought to keep my own expression innocently neutral. There was absolutely no reason Liz had to find out about how I'd sabotaged her flat hunt. Everything had worked out in the end, after all.

If she wanted to start looking at places again I'd even help her. Somewhere in a nice neighbourhood, with a spare bedroom, maybe a balcony or a garden. Somewhere the right size for two people.

I just had to make sure Liz never, ever found out about all

of my terrible past lapses in judgement.

Chapter Thirty-Seven

LIZ

"If you sit any closer to the fire you'll burn yourself alive, Lizzie."

"And how delicious that would be, to be so warm."

Dad snorted out a laugh before returning his attention to the TV. "Why are the contestants on here always such tossers?" he exclaimed, waving a forkful of pasta at the rerun of *Who Wants to Be a Millionaire* that we'd put on for background noise. "How can you not know *Bohemian Rhapsody* was the UK Christmas number one at the end of 1991? Freddie died, for Christ's sake!"

"Clearly the guy doesn't have nearly so discerning a music taste as you," I said, just as the man in question incorrectly guessed *And I Will Always Love You* (number one in 1992, as Dad was bound to tell me imminently) and in-so-doing lost £32000.

"That was 1992, you jam pot!" Dad roared at the TV, incandescent with a rage he only held for silly shows such as this.

"You should have gone on back when it was airing. I bet

you'd have done well."

"Aye, well, I applied half a dozen times. Never heard back though, did I?"

"Did you really? I never knew that."

He tapped his nose conspiratorially. "There's lots you still don't know about your Dad. Man of mystery, I am."

I ugly laughed in response – the kind of laugh only my dad and, more recently, Tom, could pull from me. But then thinking of Tom began to make me feel nervous, and not in a pleasant way. When Dad returned his attention to the TV after calling through to Jenny in the kitchen to hurry up before *Eight out of Ten Cats* aired, I pulled out my phone and brought up the conversation I'd been having with Maria, the undergrad from Daichi's lab.

The one who thanked Tom for helping her find a flat.

Her most recent message to me after I reached out was:

> Tom was super helpful! He helped a couple of my friends in Professor Sorrel's lab back in September, actually. Does he help the Student Rep Council house students or something? Anyway, this is the place he showed me (I hope the link works now the property has been taken down!). I got really lucky – the estate agent told me they called someone else about it but they said they didn't want it anymore.

The link she'd given me took me to an upper cottage flat I'd inquired about the week after the conference. The estate agent never got back to me.

Or did they?

A sick fluttering of nerves bloomed in my stomach when I brought up my call history. I was being paranoid; of course I'd find nothing.

Except there *was* a call from the estate agent. Apparently I'd answered it.

"Dad," I said, not quite hearing my own voice, "did you

happen to take a call on my phone early last week? From an estate agent?"

"Not that I can remember," he replied, shrugging. Then he called over to the open kitchen door, "Jenny, did I take a call with an estate agent last week?"

The older woman appeared a moment later, a frown on her face. "You didn't, but Tom did. I had no idea he was thinking of investing in real estate! Never seemed interested in it before. Lizzie, are you quite all right?"

"Um, headache," I muttered, rising from the couch and rushing upstairs before more questions could be asked. So Tom answered my phone and said I was no longer interested in the flat, then helped an undergrad get it, instead? At a time when we were avoiding each other and I'd been convinced he was no longer interested in me?

Except he *had*, in fact, still been interested in me; it was all in my head that I'd messed things up. Which meant what, exactly?

When I reached the top floor I hesitated outside Tom's bedroom. He was out having drinks with Henry, his friend whose stag do had thrown him back into my life. If I was going to do some snooping then now was my best chance to do it.

I opened the door and flicked on the light.

Even though I was now used to the layout of Tom's room the sheer size of it still took me starkly aback. As large as the grand dining room beneath it, the room had both a bay window with a reading nook built into it and a floor-to-ceiling flat pane of glass against which Tom's king-size bed lay.

The bed itself wasn't elaborate – it didn't even have a headboard – but, against the view through the window and the most ridiculously comfortable mattress I'd ever had the privilege of sleeping on, it was an impressive centrepiece to the room.

The floor was all hardwood with a couple of rugs tossed over it which matched the ones in the living room, then against one wall were built-in wardrobes much the same as the ones in my room. There was also an expansive, mahogany chest of drawers which took up the lower half of the remaining wall; above them was a series of framed Japanese woodblock prints.

It was a large, pretty room, but it told me almost nothing about Tom himself. If I wanted to find anything out I knew I had to riffle through the wardrobes and drawers.

"Wardrobes first," I murmured, glancing back at the door to ensure Tom hadn't magically appeared behind me to catch me in the act. But nobody was there so, even though my stomach was twisting horribly, I opened the latch on the first of the wardrobes.

It was full of suits and formal wear – including a suspiciously high quality clothes bag that I assumed held his kilt for the wedding. Ignoring my curiosity over that I moved to the next wardrobe.

This time the clothes inside were more casual, but since this was Tom's wardrobe everything was clearly expensive as hell. Day-to-day shirts, linen trousers, wool jumpers and soft cashmere cardigans. Collectively I imagined that the clothes were likely worth what I'd earned during the entirety of my PhD. But aside from a shoe rack at the bottom of the wardrobe there was nothing of interest, so I moved to the final door.

This time I wasn't met with clothes. Instead, the space was separated into shelves. One held ties and cuff links; another a bottle of cologne and a very old bottle of whisky which looked, as yet, unopened. The bottom two shelves contained boxes, both without locks.

I opened them. Of course I did. But all that greeted me were photos. Hundreds of them, some of which were black and white or sepia-toned. When I spied a gangly teenager who was clearly Tom's father – going by the age of the photo and the striking resemblance to his son – a smile spread across my face before I could stop it.

Except this wasn't what I'd come in here to look for. Perhaps, once my increasingly neurotic curiosity was satisfied and I was reassured that everything I'd discovered over the past couple of days had reasonable excuses to explain them away, I could return and look at the photos. Or, you know, I could ask Tom to show me them. That would definitely make more sense than spying.

Having found nothing of interest in the wardrobes – and, really, what had I expected to find? – I meandered over to the chest of drawers and stared at the polished wood for a minute.

If I found nothing then I'd taken advantage of Tom's trust in me to go snooping through his stuff. But if I *did* find something my snooping would be justified, at the expense of...

Well, everything between us.

I couldn't simply ignore the weird coincidences that were stacking up, though. There were too many of them for them to be scientifically unrelated. There was a correlation here that was beginning to look like Tom was the causation.

I'd come too far now to not look through a damn chest of drawers.

At first all I found was underwear and properly casual clothes, like T-shirts, jogging pants and exercise gear, and then I found a drawer that contained what looked to be the spare parts for the model trains Tom had told me his grandfather adored. Then there were towels, all perfectly folded and colour-coded like the ones in my room (confirming it was Tom himself who had been responsible for their orderliness).

Which left the bottom drawer. I sucked in a breath, expecting something important to be found inside.

Only to be met with more towels.

"Oh," I muttered, feeling deflated somehow. I'd searched through Tom's entire bedroom and found nothing but very adult tidiness. I ran my hands over the towels, not really paying attention to what I was doing, and paused right at the back of the drawer when my hands moved from brushed Egyptian cotton to something which felt decidedly cheaper.

I pulled the drawer out all the way and spied a few inches of brown fabric poking out. When I moved aside the towels in front of it to wrench the fabric free two white pieces of clothing fell out of what transpired to be a cardigan.

A white T-shirt, a white bra and a brown cardigan.

"These are mine," I realised, though the epiphany was slow to come to me, like I was walking through mud. They were the clothes I'd worn when Tom and I had first spoken. First flirted. When we'd both been covered in orange juice and he graciously let me borrow his green flannel shirt, only for me to drunkenly run off and forget to collect my clothes from his lab. Since I'd been too mortified to ask for them back, and he'd never sought me out after that night, I had reasonably assumed he'd thrown my clothes out.

But here they were, clean and unstained and perfectly folded in a drawer.

"The fuck is this, Tom?" I demanded of nobody. Numbly I refolded the clothes and put them back where I'd found them, though in reality I was unsure why I did so. They were mine; they weren't supposed to be there. But they *were* there, and I knew for a fact I had no idea how to confront Tom about them right now.

What was I supposed to ask him, after all? If he kept hold of my clothes all this time...did that mean he *had* liked me four years ago? Why would he have bothered keeping them otherwise?

Was he some kind of raging pervert who had done a great job at keeping that part of himself a secret the entire way through my PhD, when he was assessing me to literal tears?

Add onto this the fact he was clearly sabotaging my flat hunt and...

Just what the hell was going on?

Chapter Thirty-Eight

TOM

TEN DAYS HAD PASSED SINCE THE stormy night Liz and I finally got together. During those ten days the weather had alternated between drizzle and Scottish hurricane. With a week left to the wedding both Mum and Jim were growing nervous in the face of the perpetual clouds, torrential rain and gale-force winds.

"It's a bad omen, Jim, I swear it," Mum said for the fourth time that afternoon. We were sitting in the kitchen making dinner although Liz was markedly absent, having gone over to Chloë's flat to spend the evening there. She'd been incredibly busy the last three days. I'd barely seen her, and I felt her absence keenly. I wasn't ashamed to admit that the house was lonely without her.

That I was lonely without her.

When she got back tonight I was going to ask her to spend the weekend with me down in London. See the Hyde Park Christmas Market. Go ice skating. Eat award-winning ramen at my friend Simon's Soho restaurant. The works. It would be the ideal breather to take before the madness of our parents' wedding. All I had to do was *ask* Liz if she wanted to go.

"You're too old to believe in bad omens!" Jim bit back testily, clearly in a bad mood if the violent way he was chopping carrots was anything to go by.

Mum gasped, scandalised. "Did you just call me old?"

"No, I called you too old to believe in silly fairy tales. There's a difference."

"Now see here, Jim—"

"Ah, that must be Liz," I cut in when I heard the sound of the storm door and, then, the front door proper being slammed closed. I wasted no time in vacating the kitchen to say hello to her. Liz was covered in large flecks of snow as she kicked off her boots and peeled her jacket off.

"I didn't realise it had started snowing," I said, announcing my presence in the process. "Maybe you'll get your wish after all and I'll buy a tree early this year." Liz flinched. Unsmiling she took off her scarf and made her way upstairs without a word. "Are you all right?" I asked, immediately concerned as I followed her upstairs. "How was Chloë's?"

"It was fine."

"You didn't answer my first question."

A pause. "I'm tired."

I breathed out a sigh of relief. I could work with tired. "The fire's lit in the living room. Do you want to sit by it and I'll run you a bath?"

Liz glanced over her shoulder at me when we reached her bedroom door, a flash of gratitude brightening her eyes. But then it was gone. "Actually, I lied," she said. "I'm not fine. We need to talk."

Oh, lord. That was never good. Not once in the history of humanity had 'we need to talk' ever led to something good.

"Of course," I said, because the only thing worse than partaking in this talk would be to fob Liz off, instead.

I expected her to go into her room but she barged into

mine. For a moment I was tempted to sit on the bed and ask Liz to do the same, but something about the look on her face told me this was a 'standing up' conversation.

She closed the door behind us, which meant Liz didn't want our parents to overhear. I couldn't work out if that was a good or a bad thing.

"So what did you want to talk about?" I ventured. Liz shivered against the damp that had set into her clothes. "Let me get you a towel. You're soaking—"

"No, I know where they are, it's fine," Liz cut in, moving to not the third but the fourth drawer to pull out a towel, which was where I kept the spares. I just barely avoided flinching at how close she'd been to discovering her old clothes hiding behind the towels.

But then it hit me: how had she known the towels were in there? I'd never shown her.

"...what's this about, Liz?" I pressed, anxiety causing my stomach to flip. I could feel myself walking into some kind of trap, but there was clearly no escape, either.

Her eyes were sharp on mine as she towel-dried her hair. "Do you know why I've been round at Chloë's so much the last few days?"

"...would I be wrong to hazard a guess that I might be the reason?"

I'd hoped my glib response might elicit a laugh or a smile from Liz. All it did was make her turn from me towards the bay window. With a sigh she peeked through the curtain towards the snow, which was falling in earnest. "You took a call on my phone last week. From an estate agent."

Oh, fuck. Fuck, fuck, fuck. I rushed towards her. "Liz—"

"You lied when you said why you'd helped Maria. Don't try to deny it; she told me how you'd helped the undergrads in Professor Sorrel's lab back in September."

I had to word my next few sentences very, very carefully. The time to have told the truth was weeks ago. *Months* ago. Well, in reality I shouldn't have sabotaged Liz's life in the first place. I knew that but still I'd done it, again and again and again.

"I didn't want you to leave my house," I ended up admitting. "I wanted a chance to – I don't know. Get to know you properly. Have you get to know me properly."

"Because you're a creep or just a full on fucking psycho?"

"...excuse me?"

Liz bowled past me towards my chest of drawers once more and I knew the jig was up. I didn't want her to pull out the clothes I'd held onto for so long, but she did. She threw them at my feet, shoulders shaking as she did so.

"Why did you never tell me you had these?" she bit out, terse and tense. "Why did you keep them? Why are they washed and perfectly folded away in your room, like some bloody trophy or – or something?"

When I reached out for Liz it broke my heart that she wrenched away from my touch. "Liz, it wasn't anything like that, I swear it."

"So what *was* it like? Why did you never give me my clothes back? Why did you keep them and then proceed to be a complete and utter bastard to me all the way through my PhD?"

"Because I liked you, and I couldn't!"

Liz pursed her lips for a moment, frowning as she took this in. My confession felt hollow and worthless, even to my own ears. "Why couldn't you?"

"Because I was assigned to be your assessor the day after I met you," I explained, desperate for Liz to understand even though I knew, in my heart, that I was screwed. "I couldn't risk anything unprofessional, and I couldn't refuse being your assessor, so—"

"So you acted like a dick so I, what, wouldn't like you

anymore? So I wouldn't fuck things up for you by flirting with you or something?" Liz took a step towards me as if she might slap me. I'd have deserved it. I *wanted* her to do it. I risked taking a step towards her, too, trying to narrow the distance between us even though it was quickly becoming a ravine.

"It wasn't like that...well, it was, but I know it was stupid. Trust me, I know." The words were spilling from me before I could string them together in a way that was properly coherent, but I couldn't stop them. "Every day since I regretted my decision. But by then it was too late. Or at least I thought it was, until my lab burned down and our parents got together and, well, your landlord kicked you out. Then—"

"Wait."

"That didn't sound good."

"Wait, wait, wait," Liz said again, biting her fist as she pulled out her phone and opened Instagram. "Tom, you wouldn't happen to have anything to do with the fact that I didn't seem to match with *anyone* online who ever messaged me to meet up? Please tell me you didn't. Oh, god. You did, didn't you? I can see it on your face!"

"Liz, just let me explain—"

"How many explanations do you need, Tom?!" she spat. She thrust my phone in her face, showing me that one of the men I'd blocked on her Tinder app had contacted her through Instagram. There was no walking out of this one. "Just what the hell is all this? You've been manipulating my life for months – fuck, years – now! What explanation could *possibly* justify that?"

I didn't know what to say. Didn't know what to *do*. How was I supposed to fix this? So I did the exact opposite of fixing it.

I went on the defensive.

"Wake up, Liz," I said, swiping her phone out of the way to grab her shoulders. She froze beneath my touch, though her eyes on mine were fiery. "You're completely oblivious to any man who likes you who might – and this may come as a complete shock to you – actually want the *same things as you.* You had Peter fawning all over you for god knows how—"

"What does *Peter* have to do with any of this?"

"You completely ignored his painfully obvious feelings even though it hurt him."

"At least he told me with his words that he liked me!"

"*So did I!*"

"That doesn't count when you manipulated *my entire fucking life* for your own benefit!" Liz screamed at me, pulling my hands away to grab her phone where I'd knocked it to the floor, shoving it into her pocket and heading for the door. "God, do you even *know* what genuinely liking someone feels like? You don't do all the crazy shite you did just to get them to like you back!"

I followed her to the door and slammed my hand against it, keeping it shut. Liz glared at me with all the venom of a viper. "Well what about you?" I demanded, even though I knew I shouldn't be on the attack right now. But I couldn't help it; everything that had been bubbling under the surface was well and truly past boiling point now. "What do you call everything *you've* been doing to me the last three months?"

Liz's murderous expression faltered. She crossed her arms over her chest as if to protect herself from what I was about to say. "...the hell does that mean?"

"You know exactly what you've been doing. Leading me on. Toying with my feelings when I made it clear how I felt about you. Making me go absolutely *insane*. Fuck, Liz, what happened on Hallowe'en. What kind of person does that? And for what – to get me back for being an arse during your PhD?"

"You *do not* get to lecture me about appropriate behaviour after everything you've done!"

"I'm not trying to lecture you! I'm not trying to justify what I did, either! But you aren't exactly a guiltless party in all of this."

Liz shoved me away from the door. "But I should be! You didn't give me a choice about being part of your life when you took it upon yourself to pull all the strings." She laughed humorlessly, an ugly sound that shattered my heart to pieces. "Fuck, how am I supposed to know if I actually like you? How am I supposed to know that *you* do? That this wasn't all one big narcissistic conquest for you?"

"Is that how you really see me, Liz?"

"I don't know *how* to see you! I don't know you at all!"

"You do, Liz, I swear. The last three months were all genuine."

"Bull shit. The last three months were a lie."

Liz shoved open the door before running into her own room. I followed close on her heels, desperate to fix this mess of my own doing, even as she threw some clothes into a bag and pulled on a dry pair of shoes.

"Liz, don't go, please," I begged, taking hold of her elbow to try and get her to turn around. "I haven't explained anything well at all. I'm just – this is all fucked up, and I know it's my fault, but if I could—"

"How many chances am I supposed to give you, Tom?" Liz fired back, twirling round to face me so quickly that my hands wound through her hair and tilted her head towards mine before I could think better of it. For one wild moment I considered trying to kiss her, as if that would magically solve everything and the last fifteen minutes could be eliminated from our collective existence.

She didn't remove my hands. That made her next words worse, because I could feel her shaking beneath my touch. "Do you know how much I liked you back when we first met? How excited I was when I went home that night?"

"Liz—"

"And then," she continued, eyes far too bright on mine, "how humiliated I felt when I had my first PhD assessment and you acted as if we'd never spoken?"

"I didn't mean to, I—"

"And you were so cruel, Tom, each and every time. Do you know how much it took for me to swallow my damn pride, let go of what I now realise was *justified* rather than petty revenge, and let myself like you again? To let myself lo—no." She shook her head, as if that might be enough to erase the word she'd almost uttered. "Fuck this. I'm not doing this."

Liz ripped my hands away and bolted down the stairs. I'd never seen her move so fast; she had the storm door open and was out in the snow by the time I had the sense to rush outside after her.

"Don't go, Liz," I called out after her. The snow bit at my bare feet but I couldn't care less. "*Liz!* Just – just come back inside. Please."

For a long moment Liz stood in the middle of the rapidly worsening blizzard, her figure partially obscured by the snow until she felt almost unreal. Like she was a mirage and she'd disappear entirely if I blinked.

Then Liz looked over her shoulder at me, her face wet with tears. I'd never seen her cry before.

"What we have is completely unbalanced, Tom," she said, making no move to wipe her eyes even though they were streaming. "You literally held all the cards and still cheated at the damn game. How am I supposed to feel like your equal given all of that? The answer is that I'm not. You never gave me the chance to be. And that's your fucking loss."

I didn't know what to say, because Liz was right. She was right.

Through the flurry of snow a taxi slowly rolled up – one which, I realised dully, Liz must have booked when she pulled out her phone upstairs. Or, even worse, had organised in advance.

Liz wrenched open the door of the car and locked it the

moment she sat down, refusing to look at me even when I came to my senses, ran over to her and banged on the window. Two seconds later and the taxi revved its engine and drove off, leaving me standing, bare foot, in the snow.

Rightfully and wretchedly alone.

Chapter Thirty-Nine

LIZ

I'D BEEN SITTING IN CHLOË'S LIVING room for three hours now and hadn't taken in a single thing from the film she'd put on to distract me from crying. Not that it had stopped me crying, anyway, but at least it obscured the *sound* of me crying from her and Harriet.

Perhaps that was the point; Chloë knew how much I hated crying in person, even to her. The only time my best friend had ever seen me cry was the day my mother died. Not at her funeral. Not when Tom's horrific eviscerations of my third year assessment, the week *after* the funeral, had me sobbing in the bathroom right by her lab.

But she could see me now, even if she couldn't hear me.

What was even worse was that *Tom* had seen me cry.

"Do you want to talk about it?" Chloë asked, during a quiet moment in the film. It might have been a stupid superhero movie.

I shrugged. "What's there to talk about? He played me for a fool. Clearly Tom thought it was hilarious to mess around with me on a scale far larger than anything I could have imagined."

"...I don't think it was like that, Liz. Ignoring how fucked up this all—"

"Ignore it?" I raised a sharp eyebrow.

"My point is," Chloë said, tone soothing, "that I *do* genuinely believe Tom cares for you. A lot. He just went about things the wrong way."

"Nah, fuck that," Harriet chimed in, tossing popcorn into her mouth as she did so. "Liz, be furious. Cry angry tears. If the man really cared about you then he would have told you what he'd been doing *before* you found out and begged for your forgiveness. Or, you know, he wouldn't have done any of his weird shit in the first place."

Chloë kicked her girlfriend's leg beneath the blanket they had sprawled over the two of them. They were sitting on the floor so that I could take the couch, which was much too nice of them. "Having now actually talked to Tom on numerous occasions," she said, each word practised and careful, "I'm inclined to believe that who he actually is as a person is someone *you* really like." I scowled when she pointed at me.

"You do know that makes it worse, right? That he didn't have to go to all these fucking creepy lengths to get me to like him?"

"Aye, but would you have given him the time of day if he hadn't pushed you to spend time with him?"

"You're such a bad lesbian. I thought all men were trash."

Harriet cackled. "She has you there, babe. Disagree if you dare."

Chloë huffed, leaned against the sofa and gently patted my knee. "All I'm saying is that I've legit never seen you as happy as you are with him, which is saying something. And it isn't like you weren't fucking with him, too. Because you were." As if I needed reminding of that fact. "But if you need tonight or the weekend or whatever to sort through this," she continued, smiling at my obviously tear-stained face, "then absolutely have your 'men are trash' moment...just remember that you still have to interact with this guy at your dad's wedding, and I don't think anyone would appreciate you murdering someone."

I didn't respond. I knew Chloë was being fairly reasonable but it was easy for her to do that when she wasn't the one who had directly been fucked. And, besides, what I'd done to Tom had been allowed. He knew about it. Let it happen. He'd been fine with it, right?

Right?

Well, if he'd been fine with it then he wouldn't have thrown it back in my face the way he had done earlier. Maybe he'd been accepting it as some kind of punishment for the way he'd been acting behind my back for the last few months.

The way he *continued* to act, time and time again even when he had every opportunity to simply...stop. Right up until we slept together.

Tears welled up in my eyes again. However reasonable Chloë was being she was wrong about one crucial thing: Tom couldn't possibly care about me the way he said he did. To me it looked like he fucked around simply because he could.

I was reminded, then, about how all his friends had thought he was a total womaniser. About how I'd been convinced he was a Grade A flirt and nothing more, talking to me because he was bored.

I must have been right all along, even though I sincerely hoped that I'd been wrong. That was what hurt the most.

I'd thought he was genuine.

A knock on the door took me out of my miserable, self-absorbed spiral. "Did you order food?" I asked Chloë, when she jumped up to answer.

"Yeah, but only five minutes ago. That'll be Peter."

"Peter?!" I stiffened on the couch. "He won't want me to – should I leave?"

"Calm your tits, bitch. He's coming because he *knows* you're here."

But I could not calm my proverbial tits, so I sat straight as a board and tried desperately to smear tears away from my face whilst Chloë answered the door. But when Peter entered the living room and grinned at me – only a little awkwardly – I felt all the tension leave my body.

"You look like you tried to drown yourself," he said, easily taking the seat beside me.

"...suicide humour. Nice."

"Would lighten the mood in here for sure."

"Double nice."

"Do you want to talk about it?"

"Absolutely not."

Peter nodded, then stole the TV remote from Harriet. "Good. Then let's watch something unspeakably gory."

Chloë groaned in dismay just as Harriet whooped in delight, which meant the casting vote fell to me.

I waved at the TV. "Blood and guts it is. Make sure the soundtrack's as obnoxiously loud as possible."

As we settled in to choose a film I felt my phone buzz. It had been going off every ten minutes for the last three hours, though since one glance at my phone told me it was Tom trying to reach me, and then my dad (clearly wanting to know what was going on) I'd resolutely ignored the rest of the vibrations. But something told me to pay attention to this notification, so I slid my phone from my pocket to check the screen.

It was Elliot.

He'd messaged:

> Hey, I know this is short notice but I'll be through in Glasgow on Monday for a few meetings. I thought I might stay overnight so we could go out for dinner, if you're free?

I stared at the message for a long time, too engrossed in it to do anything but nod along to Peter's suggestion to watch *From Beyond* – even though I'd watched it with Tom barely three weeks ago.

I had to stop thinking about Tom.

Would it be right for me to accept Eli's invitation, given my current state of mind? I didn't even know how I felt about my ex coming back into my life.

But Tom – of all fucking people – had told me, once, that I either had to expand my horizons to meet a new partner or I had to make things work with someone I already knew. Well, I couldn't possibly know a guy more than I knew Elliot. We were compatible. We'd loved each other once; we could easily love each other again.

Tom didn't have to be the right person for me. He'd never been the right person from the very start, anyway. I'd do just fine without him.

I messaged Eli saying I'd see him at half past seven.

Chapter forty

TOM

"That's the caterer pulled out of the wedding, too! So that's the flowers, the musicians, the serving staff and now the *food* that's cancelled because of the storm. What are we supposed to do? Jim? Jim?"

Jim was either not listening or was choosing not to respond. He had his eyes trained on me sitting in my grandfather's reading chair, watching me stare into space whilst desperately trying not to think about Liz.

I'd made her cry. I'd made Liz cry. A woman I'd always assumed had too much pride to cry in front of anyone had shamelessly done so, all because of me.

It was only natural she wasn't answering my calls or messages. There were two days left of the academic term before everyone stopped for Christmas but both of us had taken them off as holiday to help with the wedding, so going into the university to try and find her in person was pointless.

Considering Liz hadn't been taking her father's calls, either, I knew he couldn't possibly have all the details about what happened between us. But he'd heard the shouting as Liz left, and me pleading with her not to go, and he was a smart man. It was obvious I'd royally fucked things up.

"*Jim!*" Mum cried out again, at the end of her tether. Finally he paid attention to her, though it was clear something had snapped inside him. Which wasn't surprising – the two of them had been arguing back and forth ever since Liz ran out.

Another thing that was my fault.

"Why don't we postpone, then, if everything is in ruins?" Jim suggested, crossing his arms protectively against his chest and saying, with every fibre of his body language, that he was done with the conversation.

Mum, of course, was horrified. "How could you say that? It's not – everything isn't *ruined*, Jim, it's—"

"It sounds ruined to me. Why does the wedding have to be now anyway? Why not in January, or April, or even *next* December?"

Mum's upper lip trembled. "Do you not...I thought we were on the same page. I thought this was important to both of us. But if you're talking like that then I—"

"Come on, Jenny, be practical! Look out the damn window! Can the bloody wedding be more important to you than us both being comfortable enough to *get* married?"

I'd taken their conversation to be ridiculous – but usual – pre-wedding jitters right up until that point. Because at that point I saw Jim's face set to steel the same way his daughter's face had done when she told me she needed to talk, because she already knew everything was over no matter what I had to say.

Except my mum didn't deserve that.

"Don't say that to her," I growled, rising from my chair to tower over Jim. "She just wants things to be the way you both planned them to be."

"Don't you *dare* speak to me about this," Jim spat out, also getting to his feet. Out of the corner of my eye I saw Mum fussing and worrying about what must surely look like an inevitable clash between us, but I was too riled up to act like a mature adult and back down.

"You're upsetting her," I said, jabbing a finger at Jim's chest, "and for what? Some cancelled flowers and canapés? Get a grip and be a grown up."

Jim's expression darkened. He barked out a laugh. "That's rich, coming from the man who's upset my daughter so badly she won't even answer my calls."

I fought the urge to wince. "This has nothing to do with Liz and me."

"But it has *everything* to do with it! What did you do to her? How *could* you do that to her?" Jim squared up against me; the fact he was several inches shorter than me didn't seem to perturb him in the slightest. "When I discovered you were Jenny's son I thought – well, that's the end of this, how could I do that to poor Lizzie? – but your mother convinced me that whatever I thought about you was wrong. So I gave this a chance. Only to discover that you seem to be *exactly* who Lizzie thought you were."

I wanted to refute what Jim had said. Truly, I did. But what could I say? He was right. Going by his face he knew it.

"Lizzie had it right," Jim muttered, not looking at Mum's agonisingly heartbroken face as he spun from me, marched out of the living room and pulled on his boots and jacket. "I should have trusted her opinion of you from the beginning and not gotten involved with your mother. I should have stayed the hell away."

He paused by the door, anger momentarily replaced by what looked like sadness or maybe regret. Jim's shoulders slumped. "None of this is worth it. It's too soon after Christina's passing. You can't replace that kind of love with someone new...and especially not when they come with baggage in the shape of *you*, Thomas fucking Henderson."

Then he was gone.

Behind me Mum burst into tears. Jim, for all his raised hackles and gruff demeanour, had turned out over the last three months to be one of the gentlest, easy-going men I'd ever met. But in that outburst I saw his daughter, and realised how much of a defence mechanism lashing out must be for both of them.

My response to Liz lashing out had been to turn the situation around to be about her behaviour, rather than accepting what I'd done. I knew it had been the wrong thing to do back when I spoke every accursed word but, now, seeing the blast radius of my own actions, I understood more than ever before how much damage I was capable of causing. How much damage I *had* caused.

"I'll...I'll get him back, Mum, don't worry," I said, barely able to look at her as I squuezed her hand.

Mum was almost incoherent through her tears as she said, "W-what if he's right, Thomas? What if this was too soon? What if – what if—"

"Jim's just acting out. He doesn't mean it." Well, I knew he meant the stuff about me, but that wasn't important to the point I was making. "Mum, if I've learned anything over the last three months it's that the two of you love each other. He's just angry at me."

Even upset Mum fixed me with the shrewd stare that she used to use on me during my teenage years, when she knew I'd been out drinking with my friends. The one that meant she could see right through me. "What did you *do* to that poor girl, Thomas?"

"...I didn't respect her the way I should have." It was a summarised version of the truth but the truth nonetheless.

"Well how are you going to fix it?!" Mum exclaimed, beside herself. "You love her! What are you doing sitting around here moping when you should be out there proving to Lizzie that you're more than your worst mistakes?"

"I—"

"And on that note, you *idiot*," she cut in, fired up enough to stand up to face me directly, "do you know the lengths I had to go to in the first place to convince Jim and Lizzie that you deserved a second chance? I know you all think I'm blind to your faults but trust me, Thomas, I most certainly am not. So often I've wondered if you would ever grow up. Not to get married or have children – even I can accept that isn't for everyone – but to just grow. Up. And I finally thought you had!" Mum threw her hands in the air. "So why did that wonderful young woman run from you crying? Why didn't you run after her?"

"Because I don't deserve her." It stung, but it was true.

"Saying that is the easy way out. Honestly, the two of you have got to be the worst at actually *talking* to one another that I've ever seen. Did you use your words to tell Lizzie how you felt – and all the stupid stuff you might have done because of it – properly?"

"...no."

"God, you truly are your father's son. Just...get out of my sight, Thomas," Mum muttered, thoroughly resigned. She collapsed back into her chair. "I can't see you right now. And I don't want you seeing me like this."

"Mum—"

"*Go.*"

I retreated from the living room and closed the door to leave my mum alone; the moment we were separated she began crying in earnest. My own eyes stung, because what was happening was because of me. Perhaps not all of it directly, but certainly enough of it.

Even when shouting at me Mum was a hopeless romantic. Believing that mere honest words alone would fix things between me and Liz when it had been my actions, not my words, that had hurt her, was pure naiveté.

I had to accept that I'd ruined things and let her go.

But that didn't mean I had the right to ruin my mother's relationship.

I had no time to waste. Knowing that Liz was likely staying with Chloë, and that Chloë worked late most week nights, I got into my car and drove through the blinding snow to the university. To my relief Liz's best friend was dutifully finishing up her work for Christmas. When she saw me through the glass door of the lab she sighed enormously.

"She isn't here," Chloë said, coming over to open the door a few inches to address me.

"I know, but I need to see her. It's urgent."

She stared at me for a few seconds in silence, then finally relented to say, "Look, Tom...she's on a date. With Elliot. I don't think you should interfere with that. It isn't fair on Liz."

My breath caught in my throat. "She's on – with her ex?"

Already?

Chloë nodded. "Honestly I don't know what else you could expect her to do. Do you understand how much Liz put on the line to give you a proper chance? But then all you did was sledgehammer her heart to pieces. I don't see how she'll ever trust another guy again."

I didn't give a damn if Liz never trusted another guy again; all I needed was for her to trust *me*. Especially now, when more than just our relationship was on the line.

"Mum and Jim had a huge argument," I told Chloë, opting for the truth. I should have told it from the very beginning. "If I can't get Liz's help then the wedding may very well be off."

Chloë's face paled. She opened the door all the way so she could lean against it. "Oh my...oh my god. And she's been avoiding all her dad's calls because she thought he wanted to talk to her about *you*."

That stung. Another thing I'd potentially ruined forever. If I didn't get on some semblance of neutral ground with Liz then, even if our parents got married, her relationship with her father might be irrevocably damaged.

All because of me.

"Please, Chloë," I begged, "tell me where their date is. I need her help. No, her *dad* needs her help. And my mum, too. Please."

For a horrible second it looked as if Liz's best friend was going to refuse. But then she clucked her tongue, tucked her auburn hair behind her ears and pulled out her phone to check her messages. "Café Andaluz. The one in the city centre, not the west end. In half an hour."

Which meant I had no time to lose.

"Thank you!" I called to Chloë, already halfway down the corridor.

"Don't fuck this up!"

I risked a smile over my shoulder at her. "I won't."

I couldn't. I'd royally screwed up everything else; this was the one thing I had to make right, because it wasn't about me. Jim Maclean and my mother loved each other. There wasn't a doubt in my mind about it. I couldn't let them ruin what they had.

So even if it broke my heart that Liz was on a date with her ex, and even if I wanted to punch the guy for swanning back into her life, I had to let Liz make her own decisions about who she wanted to be with.

Even if that person wasn't me.

Chapter Forty-One

LIZ

Elliot was already waiting for me at the table when I arrived ten minutes early. He'd never once been late in all the time we'd been together; clearly that aspect of him hadn't changed.

"Hi," I said, giving Eli a little wave as I removed my coat and sat down opposite him. He'd gotten a little corner booth hidden away from the bustle of the rest of the restaurant. Unbidden it reminded me of the night I'd spent in Blue Dog with Tom, drinking and flirting and acting like a stupid fool.

God, I had to stop thinking about Tom.

Elliot broke into a grin as he took in my appearance. "You – Christ, Liz, you look amazing."

"So do you. You've levelled up your wardrobe."

It was true. Eli looked lovely in a soft grey shirt with a Nordic oversized cardigan left unbuttoned over it, along with navy trousers and brown lace-up boots.

I knew I looked good, too, and that Eli's comment hadn't been purely lip service. This was in no small part due to the fact Harriet had insisted I raid her wardrobe for my date, and she possessed an amazing seventies boho-style mini dress with long, floaty sleeves and a plunging neckline that looked perfect on me. Paired with black tights, thigh-high black boots, oversized hoop earrings and hair left long and wavy around my head and I knew I looked a million times better than I actually felt.

"Do you want a drink?" Eli asked, face flushing pink in the face of my compliment. "I was going to order wine if you're up for it."

I'd almost on default asked for gin but that only reminded me of bloody Tom again. "Rosé?" I offered. Eli nodded in agreement. Then I turned my attention to the menu set in front of me, wondering what to order. Usually I checked a menu in advance so that I didn't *really* need to look at it once I got to the restaurant, but I'd been all over the place all weekend. The last thing I'd thought to do was check out the food for my date.

When I saw what was being offered I frowned. "Are they only doing a Christmas menu?" I asked, taking note of the tasteful decorations strung up around the restaurant, "or is the main menu still on?"

"Both I think. Why, does the sound of a Spanish Christmas dinner not appeal to you?"

"Let's just say I'm done with Christmas." The bombardment of Christmas music and deliberately garish decorations in the Ito lab, along with the excessive amount of cheer and excitement at a potentially white Christmas in Glasgow from what felt like every citizen in the city, had severely grated on my nerves. I knew that, if Tom hadn't fucked with my life, I'd also be enjoying it, but I didn't have it in my heart to.

Blithely I thought of his stupid 'no tree until the twenty-fourth' stance. How he'd considered changing it just for me. My eyes began to sting like the traitors they were.

"Liz...?" Eli wondered aloud, reaching out for my hand before thinking better of it. "Are you okay?"

"I'm – yeah, I'm fine. Why?"

"You seem distracted, is all. Wait..." Eli straightened in his seat and peered to the right of my head. "Is that...Professor Henderson?"

I knocked my knee off the bottom of the table, cursing loudly as I turned to see if Eli was correct. And he was: struggling through the packed restaurant was none other than Tom himself, making a beeline for me with grim determination on his face.

"Looks like he's coming our way," Elliot said, politely curious. "Do you think something's wrong at uni?"

"Something's wrong, all right," I muttered into my hand. It was taking all my willpower not to scream. Hadn't I made it clear I didn't want to talk to Tom? I hadn't answered my *dad's* phone calls to avoid talking about the guy, for god's sake. How did he even know I was here? The only one who knew was Chloë.

Ah.

Just what was she up to, telling Tom where I was?

When he finally made it to our table I could scarcely look at him. "Liz," Tom huffed, clearly out of breath. "I need to talk to you."

"And I need you not to be here."

Elliot's curiosity took on a far more personal edge now that he realised this was clearly not a work thing. "Can we help you?" he asked Tom, far more nicely than he deserved.

But Tom shook his head. "Only Liz can help me. Please, can I have five minutes?"

"I don't even want to give you five seco—"

"It's about our parents."

That gave me pause. So the clearly concerned expression on Tom's gaunt face had nothing to do with me? He was here for another reason? Or was this another ploy of his to manipulate me?

Even if it was, I couldn't risk not hearing him out if it involved my dad.

I gave Elliot a smile that was more of a wince. "I'm really sorry, can you give us five minutes?"

"I meant to call my mum and let her know how today went, anyway," Eli replied, which was clearly an excuse he made up on the spot but I appreciated it anyway. When he stood up he inclined his head at Tom. "Professor Henderson."

"Thanks," Tom said quickly, before stealing Eli's seat and taking a long, shaky breath. I could do nothing but glare at him.

"Spit it out then, if you were telling the truth this time."

A pause. I found myself taking in Tom's appearance properly; he really did look like shit. Concern washed over me for the briefest of moments but I forced the stupid feeling away.

"Mum and Jim had a huge argument," Tom finally spilled out. "This afternoon. Your dad walked out the house and basically called the whole wedding off."

Oh, shit.

"...you're not kidding, are you?"

"Contrary to your personal experience of me, Liz, I'm not actually inclined to lying."

I bit back a scathing response. We had a more important issue on our hands. "How did this happen? There must have been some sort of catalyst."

"It was the weather, at first," Tom explained. "It's caused the caterers, the florist, the staff, the musicians – basically everyone – to drop out. They just can't risk getting to the venue through all this ice and snow."

"Okay, I can see how that might be a problem. But you said 'at first'. What happened next?"

Tom cringed. "I may have been indirectly responsible."

"*Tom!*"

"I said indirectly!" he protested, though he looked wretched about it. "Our falling out has your dad spooked, to put it in the lightest terms possible. And I deserve his ire. I know I do. But Mum doesn't deserve it. You know fine well they love each other, Liz. We can't let things end this way for them."

He was right; of course he was right. About this, at least.

"So what do you propose we do?" I asked, knowing Tom must surely not have come here without formulating a solution first.

"We fix it. Me and you. They won't listen to me on my own."

"That's because they have common fucking sense."

The hint of a smile caused Tom's lips to twitch; I resisted mirroring his reaction. "That may be the case," he said, slowly, "but my point still stands. Are we really going to let their relationship fall apart because of some snow and *me*?"

"I guess that would be inordinately stupid." I pretended to think things over, when in reality I knew fine well what my answer was. Already my date with Eli felt vapid and unnecessary; I'd never really wanted to go on it, anyway, and now I had something far more important to do than replace Tom with my ex.

I got up from the table and slid into my jacket. "Fine," I said, hating that I loved the way Tom's entire being lit up the moment I said it. "Let's save this damn wedding."

Tom leapt up to follow me to the door. "Thank you, Liz. Really. It means a lot that you'll help me, given...well. You know."

I eyed him carefully. "Did you really track me down with the sole purpose of asking for my help, or did you have anything else you wanted to say?"

"There are a thousand things I want to say, but it isn't right for me to force you to listen to them."

"Why couldn't you have been as considerate as that from the beginning, then?"

"Because I was an overgrown, possessive child who was in full denial that he needed to grow the fuck up for far too long." Tom admitted it so easily that at first I didn't believe that he'd actually said what he said.

"...just because you can admit it doesn't mean I forgive you," I muttered a few awkward moments later. Then, when we exited onto the bitterly cold street and I saw Elliot: "I'm so sorry, Eli, but I have a family emergency. Can we catch up in the new year?"

Eli looked first at me and then at Tom standing behind me, and he caught onto far more than I probably wanted him to know. Disappointment coloured his expression. I could have corrected him. *Should* have, but I didn't.

"Yeah, go ahead," he said, forcing a smile to his face. "I hope you sort out your family emergency."

"Me too. And thanks. For everything."

With that Tom and I ran off, Tom careening me towards the closest car park through the snow. "The hell are you doing driving in this, you idiot?" I complained, shivering heavily when we finally reached his car and Tom cranked up the heating. The headlights filled up the gloom of the car park; it was almost empty. It reminded me of about a thousand generic thriller films where someone is about to be shot in the head or exploded via car bomb.

Well, at least being with Tom was preferable to that. Barely.

"I was in a rush to reach you," Tom said, after checking it was safe to reverse out of his space and exit the car park, "and the subway was off because of the snow. And you know how impossible it is to get a taxi in this kind of weather."

He had a point. A weird silence fell between us as Tom drove through the city centre at a snail's pace, because the traffic was horrendous. Of course it was; Christmas was in five days and the roads were a mess of slush and black ice.

Tom kept looking at me, clearly expecting me to say or do something. Eventually I snapped. "What is it?"

"...do you know where your dad will be?"

"Oh." Obviously that was something he needed to know. My proverbial hackles lowered. "Normally I'd say Balloch having some drinks with his local friends, but in this weather..." I thought about it for a moment, then came upon the answer with a satisfied smile. "Big Jim. He'll be at Big Jim's. He lives in Dennistoun."

"East side," Tom murmured, indicating to change lanes so he could turn around. "Got it. How did you know that?"

"Dad would never stay in a hotel and he only has work friends in Glasgow. I'll double-check to be safe."

"You have your dad's work friend's number?"

"Naturally," I said as a typed out a text message to Big Jim. "I spent half my childhood travelling on buses with them all during the holidays."

"That's certainly an interesting way to while away your free time."

"Not all of us had the money to go to the Maldives and ski resorts, Tom."

"I didn't holiday in either of those places." A pause. "I spent my summers in France."

"What a basic bitch."

I knew Tom was smiling without seeing him. Fuck, why was it so easy to fall back into step with him? I hated it. I hated that I wanted it. I hated the distance between us. I hated—

"I'm sorry."

I let Tom's words hang in the air for a while. They sounded, for all the world, sincere, and in that moment I wished they were enough.

But I needed to understand. Properly, deeply understand why he'd made the decisions he'd made.

"Start from the beginning," I sighed, feeling like I would regret giving him permission to confess in full but nevertheless knowing I badly needed to hear what Tom had to say.

He tore his eyes from the steering wheel for the briefest of seconds. "Are you sure?"

"No, but go ahead."

When Tom didn't immediately respond I knew whatever he was about to say would be...interesting, to say the least. "Um, god, no, this is humiliating and may cause me to spontaneously combust," Tom eventually mumbled, his face growing unexpectedly scarlet even though he kept his gaze trained on the snowy road and away from me. But we were stuck in traffic and going nowhere, so he was clearly avoiding having to make eye contact.

I leaned slightly closer to him. "What? What did you do?"

"I don't think you want to know."

"I think I really fucking do. How are you struggling so hard at the first hurdle?"

Tom's hands flexed on the steering wheel. Beneath it he was tapping his leg self-consciously. "After we met – after you ran off –"

"I didn't *deliberately* run off."

"But even so. You never came back. I waited almost twenty minutes for you in the lab before going downstairs to look for you. I had your clothes in an autoclave bag. An *autoclave bag*. Ha, that's quite funny now. I should have searched the–"

"Stay on topic."

Tom grew even redder. "Fine. I couldn't find you, so I decided to go home and look for you the following day. When I got home I chucked all our clothes in the washing machine – I was hardly going to give you them back stained to high hell –

and thought I'd have an early night. Except I couldn't get to sleep."

"...I'm not following."

Tom rolled his eyes. "I was horny as shit. And I'd seen you undress in front of me. I fucking jerked off to you half the night."

Oh.

Oh.

It was my turn to flush red; heat crept all the way down my body. Of all the things Tom could have admitted to I hadn't ever imagined adding *that* to the list. "...so you meant to find me the next day, but you didn't. Why?" I asked, deciding that we could circle back to Tom's embarrassing confession after I'd heard the rest of his story.

"Because Gill cornered me first thing in the morning to be your PhD assessor. Given the number of staff members who'd retired that summer I didn't have a choice in the matter. I could hardly tell her that I'd—"

"Masturbated to the thought of me all night?"

Tom risked a chuckle. "Exactly."

"You could have said something else. Like we were seeing each other or something."

"But we weren't. I didn't even know if you were actually interested in me."

"I thought it was obvious that I was."

A thrill ran through me at the way Tom's entire body seemed to lift in response to what I'd said. "But even so," he coughed softly, only just making it through a traffic light before it turned red again, "I told Gill I'd do it, and I stupidly decided I had to be a dick to you to stop myself from flirting with you or letting you flirt with me. I *know* it was ridiculous, so don't give me that look. Daichi's chewed me out for it a hundred times already."

"Ah, so Daichi knew the whole time?"

Tom grimaced. "Not the whole time, and not everything, but yes. He knew."

"Is that why he hir—"

"Absolutely not," Tom cut in, quick to correct my sudden fear that even my *job* had been a set-up. "Daichi hired you without knowing you were, um, *my* Liz. If you'll pardon the expression."

His Liz. Why did that make me so fucking happy, even now.

After a moment I said, "You could have just, you know, told me that we had to keep things professional."

"I know. But I didn't."

I turned this over in my head. Everything he'd said was incredibly stupid, but it tracked. It made sense. I could follow Tom's twisted logic and understand why he'd done what he'd done. "So then...fast-forward to September," I said, twisting against my seatbelt to face Tom. "You've successfully but stupidly been a Grade A arsehole to me throughout my PhD, and I hate your guts. Why then go to such lengths to mess with my life to keep me near you?"

"Isn't that obvious?" Tom's laugh was incredulous. "I never *stopped* liking you, Liz. The moment I walked into that bar you worked in I knew I was screwed. When Daichi put me to work on your bench I thought I was going to die."

"Don't be so dramatic."

"How else was I supposed to feel when the woman I was crazy about was *right there*, in front of me, but wanted nothing to do with me? Even after we found out about our parents it was clear you wanted to keep as wide a berth as possible. If you'd had your way we'd never speak even when working beside each other."

It was true, of course, but it still didn't seem very fair. "I might have changed my mind, given time."

"Yes, but now I'm back in my own lab and, assuming our parents do indeed get married in three days, could you honestly say that three months of simply working beside me would have been enough for you to get to know me in a capacity that meant you wanted to *keep* getting to know me?"

"Well I guess we'll never know because you never gave me that chance, did you?"

I had him there and Tom knew it. He shook his head, then dragged a hand through his curly hair to push it out of his face. It had grown too long; when was the last time he'd had it cut?

"No," Tom said, dragging my attention away from his hair and his hand and the curve of his lip when I caught him staring at my mouth. "I had no right to mess with your flat hunt. Or your dates, even though you clearly have simultaneously impossible standards and *terrible* taste in men—"

"*Tom—*"

"Fine, a discussion for another day." Finally the traffic let up and Tom managed to pull out of the city centre and into the east end. The roads were a little clearer out here; in a few minutes we'd reach Big Jim's house. Was that enough time for us to finish clearing the air?

"I told myself I was helping you out," Tom continued a moment later, voice quiet. "Well, with the flat hunting, at least. You'd be saving money and you'd get to spend some time with your dad. Mum really was so thrilled, too. I'm not justifying what I did. I'm just giving you context for how I justified it to *myself.*" A pause. He watched me watch him through the windshield. "The dating apps I interfered with out of complete and utter jealousy. I didn't want you to meet an actual decent guy when I was trying to...trick you into thinking I was one."

I was at a loss for what to say. If I was to believe Tom – which at this point I saw no reason not to – then he really, properly, completely liked me, and had done the entire time he'd made me hate him. "Why didn't you just *tell* me how you felt?" I finally asked.

"But I did. The night we kissed. I couldn't have made it anymore obvious."

"But I thought – I didn't have any of the context you just gave me. I didn't think you could have liked me longer than a few days. That it was shallow and...I don't know. Fleeting."

"Is that why you decided to toy with me in return? Would providing *context* for my feelings have stopped you doing that?"

"I honestly don't know," I admitted, because it was true. Self-consciously I tucked a lock of hair behind my ear, knowing Tom was watching my every move out of the corner of his eye. "Originally I accepted living with you so I could make your life hell. The sexual fuckery came later."

"Ah, so you had ulterior motives from the get-go?" He sounded far too happy about that.

"Obviously. Why the fuck would I willingly live with a guy I hated, parents getting married notwithstanding?"

"Touché. It *does* mean you were being disingenuous from the beginning, though."

"Not from four fucking years ago."

"That's true."

"I can't believe you jerked off to me for half the night."

"I can. Do you know how sexy you are, Liz?"

"Stop trying to get into my good books."

"Oh, is that on the table now?" The way Tom said 'on the table' was shockingly indecent.

I withheld a traitorous laugh and forced down a retort I knew would keep the banter flowing. I couldn't let him make me laugh right now, even if I now knew the full extent of his ridiculous reasons for manipulating my life. Even if I knew I was no longer angry, not really.

But I *was* frustrated – with myself just as much as with Tom. How could the two of us be this dysfunctional? We were like children.

Hopefully, by helping our parents find their way back to each other and saving their impending marriage, we could finally grow up.

"Let's fix this mess and we'll see where we stand," I said, just as Tom pulled up in from of Big Jim's flat.

When Tom smiled at me it was achingly fond. I was torn between wanting to slap him and kiss him; clearly my body had no intention of getting over him despite everything.

"I like the sound of that."

Chapter Forty-Two

TOM

I COULDN'T STOP LOOKING AT LIZ as we walked up to the door of Big Jim's flat, the man from work her father had once told me about. Jim was crashing in his friend's spare room, though if Liz and I had anything to say about it he'd be coming back to the town house with us.

Liz. I couldn't believe she was beside me right now. That she was *talking* to me, and willingly making eye contact. In stark contrast to me she looked absolutely beautiful; a goddess stepped straight out of the seventies. It felt wrong for me to see her in such a temptingly low-cut dress – especially because Liz had worn it for someone else.

A shard of ugly jealousy stabbed my heart. I wasn't sure if Liz going on a date and dressing up for it meant our falling out hadn't hit her as hard as it was hitting me, though given how upset she'd been a few days ago I knew better than to base everything on appearances alone.

What I *did* know was that I had to be one hundred percent honest with Liz going forward. Like I should have been from the very beginning.

"Can you guarantee that your dad won't murder me on sight?" I asked Liz in an undertone, when we heard the heavy footfalls of someone coming to get the door.

She gave me perhaps the most evil smirk I'd ever witnessed. "I can make no such promises."

My stomach lurched.

When the door was flung open I was faced with perhaps the most enormous, ginger-bearded, balding man I'd ever met in my life. His face lit up when he saw Liz. "Lizzie! Your dad's through here, come on in, come on in. And who's this? Your boyfriend?"

"Something like that," Liz said before I could refute the man, hugging Big Jim and then following him inside. But she gave me a look over her shoulder as she did so that suggested she said such an outrageous thing simply to get a rise out of me.

Well, it bloody worked. I thought my heart was going to burst out of my chest with the strength of a bullet train.

When we reached Big Jim's living room – a reasonably-sized, classic tenement space with a nice bay window that was nevertheless still single glazed, so the central heating was on full blast – I was met with the sight of Liz's dad lowering the volume on the TV to see who had been brought in.

He leapt to his feet when he saw Liz, but grew absolutely thunderous when he saw me. "The hell are you doing here?" he demanded, thrusting a pointed finger against my chest.

"Fixing things," I said simply.

"There's nothing to fix."

"Don't be daft, Dad," Liz interjected, gently pulling him away from me to sit back down on the couch. She indicated towards Big Jim. "I don't suppose I could trouble you for some tea?"

"Of course!" he said, understanding immediately that this was a private discussion. When the giant of a man left the room it felt decidedly empty. There was a vacant armchair upholstered in a completely different fabric to the couch, and it looked to be about a million years old and uncomfortable as hell. Still, it was the only available chair so I opted to sink into it nonetheless.

"What's this I hear about you running out on poor Jenny?" Liz asked her dad the moment we were all sitting down.

"Why should I tell you?" he muttered, gruff and grumpy. "You ran off and ignored all my calls!"

Liz cringed. "I'm sorry. I was overreacting to something."

"Hell you were overreacting. *He* did something awful," Jim said, glaring at me. "You just won't tell me what it was."

"We've sorted it out."

"I don't believe you."

"Dad, I'm a big girl. I can handle myself. And -" Liz glanced at me "- Tom apologised. I know where he was coming from now. Even if...well, even if he was a shockingly stupid bastard who should really act his fucking age."

I almost laughed at the brutal comment. Instead I stayed obediently quiet.

"My point is, Dad," Liz continued, "is that you shouldn't use what's been going on with me and Tom as an excuse to run from Jenny. So what if every caterer and florist and musician and serving staff has pulled out? We can work things out!"

Jim held out his hand for his daughter's and squeezed, hard. "But it's too fast, Lizzie. Clearly this is a sign—"

"Since when have you believed in signs?"

"And it's not been *that* long since your mum—"

"She would whack you over the head if she heard you using her as an excuse," Liz scolded, clearly used to dealing with her father's nonsense. "You love Jenny, don't you?"

"'Course I do!" Jim fired back. "Wouldn't have asked her to

marry me in the first place if I didn't."

"Then what the hell is the problem? And don't you dare say Tom, because you can't judge a woman by her son. Even if he's a complete reprobate."

"You're painting me in such a good light, Liz," I said, once again struggling not to laugh at her candour.

"Shut up," both she and her dad said in unison, the same frown creasing their brows as they did so.

I could only nod and sink further into the incredibly uncomfortable armchair. "Noted."

"Come on, Dad," Liz urged, leaning towards him encouragingly, "don't choose *now* to be a stubborn coward. All your life you and Mum worked so hard, but you played it safe and never took risks. And I know why you did it, and I'm grateful for everything you did in raising me. But I'm an adult, and you don't have to live your life for me. You don't have to be worried about me."

All at once Jim's hard exterior melted away before my very eyes. "I'll always worry about you, Lizzie. It's my job."

Liz looked like she was about to cry. I felt altogether like this was a conversation I shouldn't be privy to but I didn't want to risk interrupting them to leave the room.

"E-even so," she stammered after a moment or two, "I can look after myself. I can deal with *him* just fine." Liz threw me a look that was *almost* a smile before turning her attention back to her father. "So you need to look after yourself, apologise to Jenny, and for the love of god let us help you save this wedding."

From the doorway I realised Big Jim was listening with no tea in sight; clearly he had anticipated how this entire conversation was going to go. "Your little girl is right," he boomed. "As usual. Go apologise to the poor woman before she realises she's made a horrible mistake in agreeing to marrying you."

At this Jim finally laughed. He fidgeted with his hands in his lap, slapped his knees, then got to his feet. "Of course Lizzie's right. She always knows what's best for me. Give us a lift back to the house, Tom."

I blinked in surprise at being directly addressed. "Is that an order or a request?"

"Don't push it."

"An order. Got it."

Liz sat in the back of the car with her dad as I drove, the two of them murmuring too quietly for me to hear. But as we approached the townhouse I noticed Jim growing increasingly nervous in my rear-view mirror, and he finally spoke to me again.

"Was she in a bad way when I left?" he asked, looking suitably ashamed of himself.

"Yes," I admitted, not bothering to sugarcoat it. "You really hurt her. She didn't deserve to be spoken to the way you spoke to her."

It spoke volumes that Jim didn't get angry for me criticising him, nor Liz. Instead the man took what I said to heart, gulped down his nerves, and jumped out of the car the moment I parked in the driveway.

But he needn't have worried. No sooner had we crunched over the snow than Mum threw open the front door and launched herself at Jim.

"I'm sorry for worrying over every little thing!" she sobbed, shivering in her dressing gown against the cold. Jim was quick to wrap his arms around her and stroke her hair.

"You have nothing to apologise for, silly woman," he soothed. "I was in the wrong. I'm sorry for everything I said. Of course I still want to marry you, Jenny."

"W-we don't have to get married r-right now if it's too soon. We can—"

"I want to. Trust me." He kissed her once, twice, three times for good measure. When they pulled away from each other Jim wiped my mum's tears away with gentle fingers.

Then:

"We have no time to lose!" Mum cried, back to her usual exuberant self once more. She broke from Jim's embrace to pull him indoors. "We have food, flowers, musicians and staff to sort out!"

At this Jim indicated towards me and Liz, who was leaning against the car and watching the entire interaction between our parents with a carefully-constructed neutral expression on her face. "They said they're going to sort it all out."

I held up a hand in protest. "We didn't say *all* of—"

"All of it," Jim interrupted, giving me the kind of threatening grin that was daring me to contradict him, "so we can just relax tonight, Jenny. God knows you've worried yourself too much already."

The two of them headed inside, then, leaving Liz and I alone. I offered her a bemused smile in response to the whirlwind that was our parents; she miraculously returned it. "How do you feel about finally seeing the illustrious Henderson estate, Dr Maclean?" I asked, opening the passenger seat of my car for her with hopeful optimism.

Liz slid onto the seat without a second thought, her smile growing wider. "I think I'd like that very much."

Chapter Forty-Three

LIZ

As if finally granting us a break the snow stopped five minutes into our journey to Balloch. This meant that the drive was surprisingly easy, even in the dark at nine in the evening. Honestly we should have waited until morning – it was the sensible decision to make – but the sheer excitement and frantic energy emanating off both myself and Tom in the face of organising a wedding in two days was hard to avoid.

So here we were, pulling onto a ridiculously grand driveway, its smooth-paned surface covered in snow. Light filtered through perhaps five or six windows upon the façade of a truly gigantic building. In the darkness I couldn't even perceive its edges.

I let out a low whistle. "This is a full-on manor, Tom. What is this, Pride and Prejudice?"

"I think it was built a little later than the Regency era," he quipped, giving me a wry smile as he parked the car, "but, yes, I get your point. It's a listed building so all the windows are single glazed; be prepared for it to be cold in most of the rooms. What with energy bills being so expensive and all."

I ignored his joke – just as I had done when Tom first showed me around the townhouse and said the same thing. "Who's in there already?" I asked, pointing at the lit windows. "Your *servants*?"

"May I remind you that this is my mum's house, not mine? She has a skeleton crew of staff that run the place, though they're off for the holidays from tomorrow. I think Josef the butler is coming to the wedding as a guest, though. He left the lights on before he finished work this evening at my request."

"I feel like you must be making fun of me," I said, when we got out of the car and Tom swept me towards the huge oak double doors that led into the manor. "This all sounds far too wealthy."

"You're the one who's always making fun of me for being rich, Liz."

"Aye, but I was taking the piss. About how rich you were, I mean. God...it never really hit that you were *rich* rich."

"My grandfather was the rich one. This is merely generational wealth."

I rolled my eyes at the distinction, a shiver wracking my spine when Tom closed the doors behind us and led me down a freezing, barely lit entrance hall. It was cavernous – as large as a bloody church – the floor made of broad slabs of pale, veined marble. It reflected the light from a dozen massive, twinkling Christmas trees like a mirror.

The Christmas trees were adorned in broad, fluffy tinsel in red and green and gold. Ostentatious baubles and other decorations reminiscent of the maximalist style of the nineties hung from their branches. In a normal-sized house the trees would have looked excessive; in the massive space of the Henderson entrance hall they were magical.

"Clearly your mum disagrees with your 'no Christmas trees until the twenty-fourth' rule," I said, too stunned to make any other comment than a joke.

Tom was also taking in the sight of the trees with a look of unmistakeable awe on his face. It was somewhat reassuring that even he was not immune to the splendour of such things. "She's always been one for flashy events," he eventually said, before walking across the hall. His footsteps echoed off the walls, as loud as a giant. When we came upon two staircases, one of which curved to the left and one to the right, Tom choose the left. "Come on, let's find the kitchen. You must be hungry, right? Since I gatecrashed your dinner and all."

I'd already forgotten about my date with Eli, though as soon as Tom mentioned food my stomach rumbled. The sound was magnified ten times over by the stone floor.

Tom laughed heartily at the sound. "I'll take that as a yes. We can bullet point what needs organised over pasta."

"Are you making it or is your family's private chef catering to our every whim?"

"Hilarious. Mum messaged me to say the kitchen was restocked today, since she and Jim were meant to be coming up. So you'll have to make do with me making it."

"Just so long as the kitchen is warmer than in here," I said, shivering once more as I followed Tom down a dark hallway. "It's bloody Baltic."

"There's a big fireplace in the kitchen, don't worry. Josef lit it for us before he left for the night so, yes, it'll be warm."

Thankfully Tom wasn't wrong. Heat rolled out of the kitchen when we came into the room, though it was much smaller than I had expected.

"Oh, this is just the personal kitchen," Tom explained as he rummaged through glass-fronted cupboards for the ingredients he needed to make dinner. "There's a catering kitchen downstairs, attached to the dining room."

"But of course there is."

"I'll show you around properly in the morning when we have some light. Do you want some wine while I cook?" he asked, first checking a chrome fridge and then a wooden rack beside it to inspect its contents. "We have red and white at our disposal."

Wine sounded dangerous. But wine also sounded great.

"White, please," I replied, settling onto a sumptuously upholstered tall stool situated by a kitchen island that took up much of the floor space. I eagerly took a – sizeable – glass of wine when Tom uncorked a bottle and handed one over to me.

He clinked his own glass against mine. "To being wedding planners."

I risked the smallest of smiles; my heart leapt of its own accord when Tom returned it. "To being wedding planners."

"Never thought I'd be adding that to my C.V. but there's a first time for everything," Tom joked, when he turned from me to fill up the kettle and set it to boil.

"What exactly do we have to sort out?" I asked, while Tom set about chopping onions, red pepper and a handful of basil he ripped from a plant pot by the window above the sink.

He thought for a moment. "Catering, bar and serving staff, flowers and musicians. I have a band in mind for the music, so that should be okay, and I have a friend in London who can help with the catering."

"Is that the one you went down to meet before the conference?"

"Yes, actually," Tom replied, surprise plain as day on his face. "I assumed you thought I lied about that."

"You're the one who told me you don't *actually* lie about everything. Is this a fancy rich friend, then?"

"Simon?" Tom scratched his nose. "I guess so. He runs a huge catering business. He doesn't cook himself, though. He's all the business side. But he owes me a favour, so I think I can wrangle his help with this."

"Must be a pretty big favour."

"A story for another time."

"Well leave the bar and serving staff to me," I said. My mouth was salivating to high hell when Tom began frying off garlic in a generous quantity of olive oil. Truly, that smell was the way to my heart. "Providing you can give me a bottomless bank account to tempt all my old work buddies into helping out on such short notice."

Tom looked over his shoulder at me and hitched a bemused eyebrow. "How much money are we talking here?"

It was then I realised he'd put on an apron to cook; it cinched in at his waist, rumpling his shirt in a way that made me think of entirely non-food-related things I'd like to do with him whilst he had said apron on.

And here was me thinking the forbidden gutter had been washed clean out.

"Liz?"

"A-as much as it takes," I babbled, hoping the heat of the room would explain away my flaming hot cheeks.

Tom considered this for a moment, then pulled out his wallet from the back pocket of his jeans – another drop into the gutter – and tossed it at me. "Have at it. Spend as much as you want. I trust you know good folk."

I flashed him a wicked grin before I could stop myself. "You're honestly giving me control of your finances?"

"Will I regret it?"

"Since Jenny and Dad's wedding is on the line, *regrettably* I'll have to say no."

Tom took a swig of wine before serving up our pasta and sliding a plate across to me. He sat opposite me, a polite distance away, though in all honesty I wished he were beside me. The distance felt forced – as if, now we'd cleared the air and I understood why Tom had acted the way he did, I *wanted* things to go back to the way things had ever so briefly been between us.

Was that what I wanted?

"You're spacing out, Liz."

I blinked at Tom, who was watching me like a hawk even as he impossibly gracefully slurped up a ribbon of tagliatelle. I couldn't tell what he was thinking at all. "The flowers," I said, grasping for something to talk about to avoid the obvious issue currently sizzling between us. "How are we handling them?"

"I'll do that, don't worry. If you can coordinate the staff and get to grips with the layout of the bar and kitchen downstairs to take them through it all that would be incredibly helpful."

"...I guess I'll have to familiarise myself with – did you say there's a bar downstairs?!"

"And a library, ballroom and billiards room."

"What is this, Cluedo?"

Tom snickered. "I used to think that. Upstairs is all bedrooms, living rooms and bathrooms."

"...how many in total?"

"Twelve bedrooms?" Tom assessed his answer, then nodded. "Yup, twelve. Your friends are getting two of them for the wedding, you'll be very pleased to hear. And then there are three living rooms and nine bathrooms."

"Nobody needs *that* many bathrooms."

"Clearly someone needed them in the past. And that's saying nothing about the cottage at the edge of the estate. I say cottage but it's at least half the size of the townhouse in Glasgow."

"I..." I shook my head, then swallowed a mouthful of pasta before saying, "Tom, have you ever considered doing something, I don't know, *useful* with all this wealth you inherited?"

He shrugged in the way only a very rich man ever could.

"Not really, if I'm honest. I don't even spend it; I earn enough on my own to live comfortably."

"We'll be changing that if I have anything to do about it..." I muttered, thinking about how much good all his money could do if he actually put it to use.

"What was that now?"

I realised my mistake too late. Why would I have anything to do with how Tom spent his money? "Um, never mind," I said, wolfing down the rest of my pasta and then my wine. "I think I might go to bed, then, if we're waiting until the morning to look around. Is there Wi-Fi here? I'll need to send off some pleas for help tonight before I go to sleep."

"Obviously. We're not living in the stone age." Tom was still looking at me curiously, trying to work out what I had meant with my stupid comment about his money. But then he sighed, finished his own food, and took our dishes over to the sink. "Josef won't have the heating on in most of the bedrooms but hopefully there will be two that are warm. With any luck one of those rooms will be *mine.*"

It transpired that Josef, who was clearly very good at his job, had indeed ensured two bedrooms were heated, one of which was Tom's. The room I was led to was ridiculous in size and scope – I could have housed my bedroom in Tom's house within it two times over – and contained a four-poster bed and floor-to-ceiling curtains made of the thickest, plushest red velvet. The curtains, along with the high pile carpet, were sure to swallow up the noise of every footstep once I set foot within it.

Yet I was disappointed that it hadn't been *only* Tom's room that was ready and waiting to be used. For if that had been the case then I wouldn't have to say good night to Tom right this second, and I could use the guise of forced proximity to remain beside him.

"Well...see you in the morning," I murmured, after Tom dutifully gave me the Wi-Fi password and we stood, awkwardly, by the doorway to my room. But when I made to go inside Tom grabbed my arm.

"Wait," he said, before hastily letting go when he realised what he'd done. I missed the feeling of his touch immediately; when he settled on leaning against the wall, unintentionally looming over me, it took all the impulse control I had in me not to reach up and – I don't know. Wipe the shadows under his eyes and tell him to get some sleep.

The hallway was dark but my vision had adjusted to it; I could make out Tom's expression clearly as he hesitated over what it was he wanted to say.

"Yes?" I pressed, though my voice was very small in the corridor. "What is it?"

What did I want him to say? What did I want him to *do*?

"It's – I – thank you, Liz," Tom eventually settled on. "For listening to me tonight. For helping me fix the mess I made. For...well, for everything. And hey, at least after the wedding you can fulfil your original intention of never seeing or talking to me again if you can help it."

He said it jokingly but I could see how much it stung Tom to even vocalise such a prospect. It stung me, too, stabbing at my heart even though I wished it wouldn't.

"I guess we'll have to wait and see what I can *help* doing." Then, when Tom didn't reply, "And thanks for reaching out to me. I'd never forgive myself if Dad and Jenny's wedding fell apart when I could have done something about it."

"That's because, unlike me, you're actually a good person."

"Doing a handful of absurdly stupid things doesn't make you a bad person, Tom."

"It does when you do those things to someone you care about more than anything."

The air between us seemed to grow thin. I couldn't breathe, couldn't speak. All I could do was hold Tom's gaze through the glim light of the hallway and wait for...what?

For him to make a move? For *me* to make a move? That was a confession if ever there was one. My insides turned to butterflies in the wake of his words.

"...night, Tom," I mumbled, escaping into my bedroom without daring to look him in the eye lest I see any kind of disappointment painted across his face. I had no doubt I'd over-think his last sentence to death.

Could I really say I wanted this to be how we ended things? That we'd move on and simply be two grown adults whose parents were married? I wouldn't be living with Tom, and he wouldn't be working in the same lab let alone the same bench as me. Aside from family birthdays and other non-negotiable events our parents forced us to attend, I had no reason to see Tom any more or less than I explicitly wanted, just as he'd said.

So the question was...how much did I want to see him? How much did I still want *Tom*?

All I had to do was feel my heart aching in my chest to know my answer.

I knew it. It was so easy.

Still, I was worried. Tom had fucked up and so had I. Would we be bad for each other? It was clear we were capable of acting like our absolute worst selves because of each other.

But then...what about our best selves? For the barest handful of days when we'd given into our feelings for each other I was the happiest I'd been in potentially ever.

Was I allowed to want that with him for real? Was all the potential for future pain and heartbreak worth it?

Having learned from my past mistakes, I knew there was only one way to find out.

Chapter forty-four

TOM

O N THE DAY OF THE WEDDING the sun was shining.

Regardless of whether Liz or Jim or Mum or I believed in fate, or karma, or cosmic signs, we all took it to be a good omen. There had been no rain in the two days leading up to the wedding, only snow, so every inch of the grounds was sparkling and white.

The air was abuzz with excitement all morning as we prepared for the early afternoon ceremony. Liz welcomed my mum's best friends and brought them upstairs for mimosas whilst they got ready; a barber friend of mine I'd harangued into helping out cut Jim's hair, then mine, and we shared a solitary morning beer before his friends arrived and helped him get prepared as slowly and as loudly as possible.

I didn't have a chance to speak to or even *look* at Liz all day. We were both too busy with our respective duties, and the house was so big it was easy to miss each other. But I was sick with nerves – by the time the clock struck midnight and today became tomorrow, where would that leave us?

What would we be?

Before I knew it the estate was full of people and the ceremony proper was about to begin. Having wrangled a gigantic gazebo, fairy lights, fifty chairs and several giant outdoor heaters from Simon, who responded to me requiring a favour with typical Simon gusto – we decided at the last minute to hold the actual wedding outside so that the snow-covered gardens could be the backdrop for the ceremony.

Now that I was getting ready to walk Mum down the aisle I was beyond pleased with that decision. The mix of fresh winter air, warm, creeping heat from the gazebo, and the dazzling afternoon sunlight on the sweeping expanses of snow all around us was wonderful. The evergreen trees surrounding the estate completed the landscape, deep and dark and peaked in white.

It was picturesque. It was perfect. No ceremony indoors could have compared to this.

But my mother was more beautiful than any of our surroundings.

"Are you sure you're old enough to be my mum?" I asked her in an undertone, as we prepared to take our first steps into the gazebo.

Her face flushed with an equal mix of pleasure, embarrassment and nerves. "You stop that, Thomas."

"You look sensational."

"Leave the compliments for Lizzie. She looks much better than I do."

I knew that if I disagreed with her Mum would continue refuting my statements even as we walked down the aisle, so I kept my mouth shut. But she *did* look amazing. Her platinum blonde hair was elegantly but loosely tied back in a French twist, and the make-up artist she'd hired had taken years off her face. Mum's gown was a high-necked, figure-skimming dress which flowed out into perhaps the largest fishtail train I'd ever witnessed in all my years of attending my friends' weddings. It was sure to drag snow into the gazebo with every step.

Mum was stark and dramatic and lovely. I couldn't wait to see what Jim thought of her entire look.

Selfishly, more than anything, I couldn't wait to see Liz.

"Ready?" I murmured into Mum's ear, when the music that was our cue to go began playing.

She laughed nervously into her hand. "Make sure I don't trip up, Thomas."

"Of course."

Then the entrance to the gazebo was pulled open, and we were off down the aisle.

At first I didn't see Liz; it took me a few moments to get used to the sunlight filtering into the gazebo at eye level, and the looks of awe sent Mum's way ensured I played the part of the perfect son to keep her walking in time and – as requested – safe from falling over. But when we reached the pedestal upon which Mum and Jim would be wed, and I exchanged a quick nod with him in the briefest of moments when he tore his astounded eyes away from his future wife, I finally turned my attention to the woman standing beside him.

Elizabeth Maclean was a complete and utter knock-out.

She was wearing an off-shoulder, floor-length dress that cinched in incredibly tightly at her waist – how was she breathing? – in the softest shade of green I'd ever seen. Even softer curls of hair framed her face, though most of it was pulled back in a similar style to my mum's to show off the delicate, dangling jade earrings she had on. The faintest peach-toned blush was spread across her cheekbones, and her lips were painted my favourite shade of apricot.

The colour that had made me desperate to kiss her all those years ago.

When Liz directed an appraising smile my way my heart dropped to my stomach. I returned the smile. At least, I think I did. Perhaps all I did was stare.

Liz kissed her father on the cheek, dangly earrings tinkling gently as she did so, before focusing on the celebrant when they began speaking.

By the time Mum and Jim said 'I do' I realised I had barely paid attention to a single word of the entire ceremony. All I'd done was watch Liz gently wring her hands together, or touch her hair to check for non-existent flyaways, or – and this may have been my imagination – licking her upper lip whenever she caught my eye.

I thought about what I'd chickened out of telling her two nights ago. I'd felt like I didn't have the right to properly confess the extent of my feelings to her, even though I was going to burst if I didn't. But the way Liz was looking at me, the way we'd worked so well together over the last two days to pull this wedding off, the way it had become clear she no longer wished to avoid me...

Would she allow me to fix things?

Liz had told me she hated public gestures of affection, though I knew from experience that she, in fact, enjoyed them. Which is why I knew what I had to do to confess to her, once and forever.

After the ceremony there was a drinks reception in the gazebo. I knew Liz was using this as a cover to coordinate the staff removing the chairs to fill up the entrance hall, turning it into a space for dancing and drinking and talking around small round tables. The two gigantic fireplaces in the hall had been roaring since five that morning, so the space would be warm and inviting, and the bar and dining room adjacent were ready to fill the wedding guests with copious amounts of food and alcohol.

I was too busy greeting this person and that person, and laughing off comments about how my mum had managed to get married again before me, to speak to Liz. In truth aside from a brief hello to Daichi and May and the briefest of acknowledgements that I existed from Chloë, Harriet and Peter (though Chloë gave me an encouraging smile, which I took as a good sign) I had absolutely no time to myself at all.

For the next hour I barely caught sight of Liz; she was bustling in all directions ensuring the staff knew what they were doing. Shamefully I thought back to when I'd all but vocally demeaned her for working in a bar instead of a lab. Seeing how efficiently she worked with the dozen or so folk she'd (handsomely) paid to service the wedding, I realised just how stupid I'd been.

There wasn't a single part of Liz that I didn't respect and care for, deeply. Trying to pretend for four years that she was merely a crush and that I'd get over her was perhaps the worst decision I'd made in my entire adult life.

Then we were seated at the top table for dinner, and it was time for the speeches.

Which meant I was up.

The top table was small – me, then Mum, then Jim, then Liz – but to me Liz felt a million miles away. When I stood up, however, and clinked a knife against my wine glass to signal for folk to be quiet so I could to speak, I was painfully aware of Liz's sharp and attentive eyes watching me. I had absolutely no doubt she'd listen to every word I said.

I couldn't mess this up. For the love of all that was good and holy I couldn't mess this up like I'd messed everything else up.

"Ah, ladies and gents and...everyone in-between," I began, feeling more awkward than I ever had before when public speaking. I taught rowdy undergrads, for god's sake, and I'd been the best man at three weddings. I could handle a 'son of the bride speech'...even if it also acted as a confession of my feelings for the woman who sat three seats away from me. "I'm sure you're all gathered here today to celebrate the marriage of my mum and this random man she found one day." Laughs. "And if you aren't you can fuck off."

"*Language!*" Mum chastised, though she thoroughly enjoyed the even bigger laugh the comment garnered. Out of the corner of my eye I saw that Jim seemed to appreciate the beginning of my speech, too.

"I have a confession to make," I continued, addressing the crowd at large. If I looked at Liz directly I knew, instinctively, that I'd make a mistake. "My darling mother didn't tell me she was seeing someone, let alone considering marriage, until *after* she was engaged." Faux scandalised gasps rippled through the wedding guests. I grinned. "Shocking, I know. In fact Liz – you've all met Liz, she's ensuring none of you are sober right now – and I found out at the same time, at the same dinner. To say we were shocked was an understatement." A pause for effect; I was nothing if not a showman.

"The thing was, though, that we both saw what was before us incredibly clearly: our parents were in love. For those of you who don't know, Imogen Henderson and James Maclean met at a grief support group. Both had lost the loves of their lives to cancer. My father. Liz's mother. I can't imagine how difficult things were for them. But they found each other. In the darkness they met, and they helped each other out into the light. That was cheesy. I know. But honestly, who cares? There's a reason there are a million clichés about love."

I knew I had the crowd in the palm of my hand. This wasn't my first rodeo, after all, and it was easy to give an emotional speech when you *were* emotional. But all I cared about was whether Liz was listening, and if she cared.

I still couldn't look at her.

Gulping down my nerves, and hoping it wasn't obvious my hands were shaking, I said, "Here's something I know for a fact most of you *don't* know. Three years before Jim and Mum first met, I had the most unexpected opportunity to meet Jim's daughter. Liz was beginning her PhD in the lab opposite mine. To say I was smitten would be an understatement."

A murmur went through the crowd at such impropriety. I zeroed in on Daichi and May, who were shamelessly gossiping under their breath about what I'd just said. Behind them Harriet was rolling her eyes, though Chloë was hanging on my every word. Peter was resolutely looking anywhere but at me. But it wasn't them I needed to see; it was Liz.

I turned to the left to address her. Liz's face was scarlet from neck to hairline, but behind the hand she held over her mouth I could tell that she was grinning. I took that as the sign I needed to continue.

"As it transpired, a large quantity of mimosas and a university mixer are a killer combination. Finding out you're going to be the PhD assessor for the woman you now have a massive crush on is less so. Which meant I decided that I had to give up on her – that I had to convince myself that my feelings really *were* a crush. Some things happened afterwards that I'm not proud of but, when Mum and Jim announced their engagement, Liz and I were thrown back into each others' sphere of influence. Now, for all my talk of fate, I am neither a religious man nor someone who believes in karma. But hell if this didn't feel like a sign from...something. But it would have meant nothing if not for Mum and Jim."

I took a few moments to inhale some oxygen back into my lungs. Never had every word I spoke meant so much.

I swept my hand towards the newly-weds. Mum was practically in tears already, and even Jim's eyes seemed to be (reluctantly) too bright. "They demonstrated day in and day out that you can fall in love in the most unexpected of places," I said. "You might not be looking for it – might be in complete denial, in fact, because it would inconvenience your life to be in love – but it happens all the same. Honestly, the two of them were disgusting. You'd think they were eighteen and experiencing love for the first time."

Another laugh, but I couldn't hear it. "I guess what I want to say, or what I want you all to know, is that it's pointless fighting against the way you feel. If you try to push things away or rationalise them as something else then you won't just hurt yourself...you'll hurt the person you love more than anything. Luckily, Imogen Henderson and James Maclean are two of the most forthright, honest people I've ever known, so I highly doubt we have to worry about that with them. So raise a glass for Jim, for making the wise decision to fall for the right woman. And raise a glass for my mother, who fell for the right man and who raised *me* right – in the end. I hope one day to do her proud."

There was a round of applause, and Mum got up to embrace me in a bone-breaking hug. "I'm already proud of you, Thomas," she murmured, voice thick with tears. "Although perhaps you might have to follow up on your wonderful confession by talking to Lizzie in *private*?"

"If she'll let me, yes," I could only laugh as we both sat down and clinked our glasses together. Jim nodded his head my way. "You're not half-bad at the speech thing," he said, which was perhaps the best compliment I was likely to ever receive from him.

I inclined my head towards Liz, though I didn't dare read into her expression for fear of being wrong about what I saw there. "She's better at public speaking than I am, though."

At this Liz smirked, and I realised I'd fallen into some kind of classic Liz trap. "He's right, Dad, I am," she said, squeezing his hand before standing up to address the room.

There weren't *supposed* to be any speeches from Jim's side – his friends weren't big talkers – but everyone grew silent once more when they saw Liz had stood up.

"So, I wasn't supposed to be doing a speech but I may have prepared one last night," she began, "and since I was five the *last* time Dad got hitched I figured this was my last chance to mortify him on his wedding day."

Damn it, that was hilarious. Liz flashed a toothy grin at her dad, who happily returned the gesture.

"To be honest I was of two minds about whether to say any of this, but since Thomas insisted on making his entire speech about him I figured it would harm precisely nobody for me to speak." Daichi let out a bark of laughter. He didn't even bother smothering it with his hand. Though he couldn't see it I gave him the finger beneath the table, but I quickly returned my undivided attention to Liz when I realised she – and everyone else – was looking at me.

"Annoyingly, though," she said, softly, "Tom was right."

Oh.

"When my dad met Jenny I was in shock," Liz continued. "He was marrying the mother of the man I hated more than anyone else in the world, after all. I mean, *really*? He could have dipped down to hell itself and chosen better."

It was me who laughed this time. Out of the corner of my eye I saw Jim was laughing, too. Liz had turned her gaze back to the crowd yet I was helpless to do anything but stare at her.

"But Jenny was wonderful," Liz said. "I'd never seen Dad so happy. Which meant, regrettably, that I had to give *Professor Thomas Henderson* another shot. Maybe I just love pain." Another laugh from the room. Fuck, Liz really was far funnier than I could ever aspire to be. "Either way, despite some... questionable circumstances...I discovered that letting go of the past was the only way to allow myself to move on. Even though it was scary. Even though it hurt. Even though I couldn't possibly know if what I felt was enough to get over any future hurdles that might be thrown my way. But if I ran from that then what would that make me?"

How Liz had moved so easily from the funny to the serious and sentimental I had no idea, but I was hanging on her every word. Was I really hearing what I thought I was hearing? Could I dare believe it?

Liz reached out for her dad's hand again. He was quick to crush her fingers with his – and were those tears running down his face? I was pretty damn sure those were tears. Beside Jim my mum was positively bawling her eyes out.

Liz gave them both her most genuine, dazzling smile. It lit up her face like the damn sun. "All I had to do was look at Jenny and Dad, completely and *embarrassingly* in love, to know that I had to proverbially man up...and grow up. I hadn't meant to fall in love when I did, just as I'm sure they didn't. But when you know, you know. And if *they* know...well."

Liz winked at me. *Winked.* It was the corniest, most mortifying thing she'd possibly ever done in her entire life, which meant what she'd just said could only be the truth.

The truth.

Liz raised a glass of prosecco. "To Jenny and Jim."

"Jenny and Jim!" everyone called back, just as Liz sat down and the starters were brought out for everyone to enjoy. Through the hustle and bustle I found myself gawking at Liz behind our parents' heads, at a complete loss for words.

"Did I surprise you?" she asked, self-conscious in a way she hadn't been when she'd given her speech.

"I quite honestly don't think I could have predicted a single word out of your mouth."

A satisfied smile. "Good. I'd hate for the two of us to be boring and predictable already."

"Does that mean—"

"Tom, get your arse over here and explain yourself!" Daichi called out, demanding my attention just as Chloë did the same to Liz. But though I badly wanted to continue my conversation with Liz – in private – I also knew I could wait a little longer.

Just a little.

We had finally both explained how we felt, publicly and with actual words, and neither of us had messed things up.

I took that the only way I could: a very, very good sign of things to come.

Chapter forty-five

LIZ

"Might I have this dance?"

I turned to face my dad, a goofy grin on his face which mirrored my own. He looked amazing dressed up in his kilt, his hair newly cut and styled by an acquaintance of Tom's whom he'd brought in that very morning to help out. Even the ruddy colour of Dad's cheeks - signalling the fact he was most certainly on the verge of tipsy - couldn't detract from how wonderful he looked. If anything it made him look even better.

Happy. Unselfconscious. Open and free.

It was the way I'd always known him growing up. The man my mum had fallen for. The man he'd been just for her, right up until she was gone.

She would be thrilled he could be that man again for someone else.

I took hold of Dad's outstretched hand. "Of course. What kind of daughter would I be if I refused to dance with her father? On his wedding day, no less!"

"A shite one, that's what. Have you spoken to Tom yet?"

The comment was so unexpected it gave me whiplash. A heat that had nothing to do with alcohol crept up my neck as Dad and I started dancing. The string quartet – also friends of Tom (where had they all come from?) – were playing a ridiculously classy version of what I was fairly certain was the *Thong Song* to remarkable effect; the wedding party was going mad for it even though most of the people in attendance were over fifty.

"Um, no," I admitted, tucking an errant strand of hair behind my ear. "I had to sort something out with the bar right after the speeches and he's been busy mingling with all his mum's friends, so...yeah. No talking yet."

Dad rolled his eyes with obvious impatience. "Even after those grand speeches the two of you are useless. *Useless,* I tell you!"

"I think it's sweet that he's pulled out all the stops to make today go as flawlessly as possible...including flirting with all of Jenny's friends." I was reminded of the fact Tom had once told me they were the *reason* he'd learned to flirt, back when he was a teenager, and my smile turned bashful.

"Well if that look on your face isn't a true proclamation of love I don't know what is." Dad considered something for a moment, then let out a long sigh. "He is a good son, though. I can see why Jenny was so adamant that he deserved a second chance."

"And a third."

A chuckle. "Yes, and a third. Any more and I'm chopping his balls off, you hear me?"

"*Dad!*"

"What?! It isn't as if either of you want kids, anyway."

"Mind if I cut in *before* you do that, Jim?"

I jumped in surprise when Tom's hand touched my shoulder. Curtly Dad nodded, though his expression softened a moment later. "My threat is serious."

"I don't doubt it."

Dad kissed my cheek. "I'm off to get a beer with Big Jim. He swears he's the reason the wedding went ahead; he's been going mad telling everyone from work that he's a damn hero."

"Just let him have his moment. Love you, Dad."

"And you, Lizzie."

Tom waited until my dad threaded his way out of sight before gently turning me to face him. God, he looked good. Too good. He'd had his hair trimmed and expertly styled away from his face that morning – though a couple of curls were beginning to come loose across his forehead – and his suit jacket and waistcoat fit him like a damn glove. His kilt, made of the deep, deep green of the Henderson tartan, brought out the jade in his eyes, which were trained solely on me.

"Did you really prepare your speech last night?" he asked, slipping a hand around to the small of my back before interlacing his other hand with mine. "Or did you decide to one-up me in the moment?"

"God, you really are so arrogant, aren't you?"

"I'd rather say I was competitive in this case."

My lips twisted into a smile. "I'd been thinking about what I wanted to say the entire time we've been staying here. I just wasn't sure what those words *were* until today."

Tom's eyebrows rose in satisfying surprise. Deftly he spun me around and pulled me back in, a little tighter than before. His breath fanned over my lips as he said, "Does that mean I'm forgiven?"

"Forgiven, maybe, but it hasn't been forgotten. If you even dare manipulate one—"

"Trust me, I'm never interfering with *anyone's* life again, least of all yours." A pause. "Can we start again, as it were?"

I considered responding with something suitably pithy. It would have been on-brand for me. And maybe it was because of the wedding, or maybe it was because of the forbidden mimosas I'd been drinking on-and-off all day, or maybe it was because it felt so damn right to be in Tom's arms like this, but I didn't feel like being sarcastic.

"Let's start again, then," I said, heart beating wildly when Tom let me go to drop into a gracious bow. Then he took my hand in his and just barely grazed my knuckles with his lips.

His eyes never left mine.

"Hi, I'm Thomas Henderson," he began, "though everyone but my mum calls me Tom. I'm thirty-eight, the Professor of Molecular Genetics at the University of Glasgow, a total anime nerd, and hopelessly in love with you."

To my left I clocked my friends not-so-subtly eavesdropping on our entire interaction, but I didn't care. "I'm Elizabeth Maclean," I replied, when Tom straightened out of his bow, "though my friends call me Liz and my dad calls me Lizzie. I'm twenty-eight in three weeks, a Doctor of genetics, and also a total anime nerd. Unfortunately I've fallen in love with this complete bastard at work, so romantically speaking I'm currently unavailable."

"Well that doesn't seem very fair. I think you need better taste in men if he's as awful as you say."

"But then you wouldn't be in with a chance, either."

"Oh, in which case by all means continue to have awful taste in men."

I let out a burst of ugly laughter; Tom's face went as bright as the sun at the sound. Gently he took me back into his arms and we began dancing again, slowly even though the music was upbeat and manic.

"I love you," Tom said simply. "With every fibre of my being I love you, Liz. I hope you know that."

"I...god, why are you so smooth?" I bit out, feeling the rumblings of nervous laughter beginning in my throat as my cheeks were set on fire. "I love you, too."

With a push against the small of my back Tom closed the distance between us entirely, my chest pressed against his. "Good," he breathed, resting his forehead on mine when I stood on my tiptoes to meet him halfway, "because I never knew how much I was waiting for you until I met you. How pathetic is it that I didn't realise how lonely I was?"

"So what am I now, disposable?"

We both turned; Daichi stood there with his wife, May, whom I had met briefly an hour earlier. Her dark hair was set in perfect, bouncing curls, and she looked absolutely bloody luminous.

"Fuck off, Dai," Tom cursed good-naturedly. "Can't you see we're in the middle of something rather important?"

"And yet what I have to say trumps that, so you'll forgive me for cutting in before we head off."

I frowned. "You're heading off? It's not even six yet."

"We want to get on the road before it gets too late," May explained. "I'm working tomorrow so we want to make the most of our evening."

Given how much I was dying to run off and be alone with Tom - properly alone - I could only nod my head in agreement.

"Telling me you're heading off isn't important enough to interrupt us," Tom said, continuing with his false irritation. "Give me something tangible, you arsehole."

"Something as tangible as hearing that your grant proposal has been approved?"

Tom's arms stilled around me, though I could feel his heart beating wildly against me. I'd never really thought about how nervous he was about his grant proposal being approved or not, which in hindsight was fucking stupid of me. Of course he was nervous about it; his career was on the line.

"How do you know that?" Tom asked, as his hand began

tracing circles against the small of my back. I resisted squirming against his touch for more.

"I know someone who works in gene therapy at King's College who was asked to cross-examine your application," Daichi explained. "He said you're pretty much golden."

"Wait, *gene therapy*?" I slapped Tom's elbow in indignation. "You never told me you were moving into gene therapy!"

"I was going to surprise you if I got the money!"

"This is *so not* something you surprise me with, you—"

"Are we witnessing your first argument as a proper couple?" Daichi interrupted, eyes twinkling with obvious mischief. Beside him May giggled against his arm. When he kissed the top of her head and she snuggled against him I could only come to the conclusion that twenty years was not enough to dampen how disgustingly in love they were.

"Not an argument," I countered, catching Tom's eye, "merely a heated discussion."

"Exactly," he agreed. "Debate is healthy."

"Well with that as the basis for the two of you going forward, I have some *actual* important news." Daichi bounced on the balls of his feet, clearly no longer able to contain whatever secret he'd been keeping all night. "May's pregnant. Baby's due in...well, May, actually. Which is hilarious, I know. Anyway, Tom, we want you to be their godfather."

The look on Tom's face was priceless.

"You better not die, then," he finally managed to say after a long moment of awkward silence, "because I sure as hell am not raising a child in your stead."

Daichi laughed assuredly. "I'll take that as a yes, then. And with that we're off. See you both in the new year!"

I waved goodbye to my boss and his wife alongside Tom. When he gave me a good-natured but long-suffering grin I let out a giggle. "He deliberately planned to interfere the moment we were finally alone, didn't he?"

"Down to the second."

"Are you really moving into gene therapy?"

Tom nodded. "Providing I do actually get the funding for it. I don't suppose—"

"Don't you dare steal Liz from us so early in the night!" Chloë cried, bombarding our conversation and yanking me away from Tom's grasp with the help of Harriet. "As lovely as your speeches to each other were and all but, you know, best friends trump new boyfriend."

"Every time," Peter grumbled, though he didn't look at Tom with the same animosity as before. I took that as a good sign that he wouldn't hate Tom forever.

Harriet pointed a finger at Tom. "You don't get any further chances to prove that you're not a complete and utter piece of trash, you hear me? No more making Liz cry."

"*Harry!*" I gasped, holding a hand over my mouth to smother the smirk I knew was creeping up my face. But when Tom caught my eye I said, "She does have a point, though. No more making me cry."

"Not unless it's from pure, unbridled plea—"

"That's our cue to leave!" Peter cut in, which was just as well because the look on Tom's face as he watched me walk away was absolutely filthy. If my friends hadn't shown up when they did I had absolutely no doubt in my mind I would have followed Tom upstairs and would not be seen nor heard from for the rest of the night.

Regretfully, that part of our reconciliation would have to wait until later.

It didn't help that, as I danced the evening away, I caught Tom stripping out of his jacket and waistcoat to leave him in a billowy shirt, which he untied down to his chest the moment he saw me all but salivating over him. But then I was struck by a sudden thought.

That man was mine. Tom was mine.

If this was the way I got to live my adult life: with a man I loved, who loved me in return, and who wanted the same things I did, then I could only conclude that I was on the right path. That I'd found the right *person* to walk that path with me.

No compromises required.

Chapter Forty-Six

TOM

I<small>T WAS AFTER ELEVEN BY THE</small> time I finally managed to tear myself away from Jim's work friends, who had insisted on necking back tequila shots at the bar until Little Jim vomited rather impressively into an ice bucket. I'd dutifully cleaned said bucket to save the wedding staff the hell of doing so.

Although I found Mum and Jim, rosy-faced and blissfully happy, polishing off a bottle of wine and a bowl of sticky toffee pudding by a Christmas tree, and Liz's friends still dancing as if the night was going to last forever, Liz herself was nowhere to be found.

It was the evening we met all over again.

"If I were Liz where would I be?" I murmured, just as horny and tipsy as I'd been after those fateful mimosas four years ago. We had been kept apart for far too much of the evening; I was determined not to waste any more time.

She wasn't in the library – although I did find one of Mum's book club friends engaged in a tryst with a woman who was decidedly *not* her husband – nor was she scarfing down leftovers in the service kitchen. Liz wasn't playing billiards or standing outside for some fresh but Baltic air. She wasn't in the dining room, either, and after milling about outside both of the bathrooms on the ground floor I concluded that she must have gone upstairs.

To her room?

It was the first place I checked when I went up the stairs, knocking first but then risking opening the door when I received no answer. But the room was empty; I even double-checked the bed to make sure I hadn't somehow missed Liz lying beneath the heavy duvet.

I wasn't sure if she knew which bedroom was mine but it was the natural next place to check. I was saved the trouble, however, when I caught the sound of footsteps and a long but familiar shadow cast across the hallway just in front of me, where it turned to the left to join another corridor.

I crept as silently as possible to the end of the hallway until I could see Liz with my own eyes, though I wasn't really sure why I was stalking her instead of announcing my presence. She was investigating the paintings hanging along the wall with a keen interest I'd never seen her take in art before. In truth I didn't know the significance of any of the paintings myself.

Liz's hair was in disarray, the sweat from dancing curling it around her face the way I loved it most. The bottom of her dress was dusty, and it looked like someone might have spilled red wine on the edge of the hem. When Liz shifted to the next painting I saw that she was barefoot.

She looked content. A little tired, perhaps, and in need of a shower, but completely at ease.

When the floorboards creaked beneath my feet Liz didn't even flinch. It was then that I lost the patience to stalk her from the shadows and made myself obvious. "You knew I was there, didn't you?"

Liz turned at the sound of my voice, a smirk twisting her expression into one of obvious amusement. "Maybe," she drawled, making no move to close the distance between us.

"Where am I? I think I'm lost."

"Were you looking for anything in particular?"

"Just somewhere to be alone." Her smirk turned wicked. "Preferably somewhere comfortable, with a lock on the door, and no possibility of my friends interrupting us."

I crept down the plush carpet towards her, more than pleased with the way Liz's gaze cast over my entire body with both approval and lust. "Us?"

"Well, if you want to go back to downing tequila shots in the bar then be my guest."

"I'd quite happily never have another one in my life." When I reached Liz I stroked a curl of hair away from her face, then brushed her cheek as gently as I dared. Her apricot lipstick alone remained unsmudged and perfect against the toils of the day; I was dying to be the one to ruin it.

Liz closed her eyes and sighed. I wanted to kiss her so badly my body ached with it. "You know..." I said, slowly backing Liz against the wall, "it's plenty private right here."

A raised eyebrow. "And what's that supposed to mean?"

"Well, I'd suggest fucking in the bar but—"

"Everyone else might not appreciate that. Nice callback."

"Glad to know you remember."

"How could I forget?" With one deft movement Liz grabbed the front of my shirt and pulled me against her. On her tiptoes her lips were millimetres from mine. "Especially when you were right."

My cock – every part of me, really – was just about ready to explode. "So you...you would have slept with me, even back then?"

"Against my better judgement, maybe, but yes. If I'm being honest the moment you stepped in to protect my pride in front of my date I knew I was doomed."

"But then the last orders bell rang."

"Then the bell rang."

"Good thing that doesn't matter anymore," I growled, before spinning Liz around so she was pressed against the wall.

"*Tom!*" she cried, surprised but delighted. "What are you—"

"How do you even breathe in this?" I asked, making quick work of the delicate buttons that ran down Liz's spine. When my fingers touched bare skin she squirmed. "It's pulled in so tight. Even without a bra on I can't believe you fit your boobs in it."

Liz chuckled over her shoulder, gaze heavy-lidded as she took in the sight of me stroking her skin. "Let's just say it took a while to get on and leave it at that. You have no idea how good it feels to have you unbutto—*ah*!"

I slid a hand around Liz's waist, beneath the fabric, and wasted no time in crawling my fingers down to stroke her clit. She was drenched beneath the silk of her underwear; I groaned against her shoulder when my fingers entered her with absolutely no resistance.

"How could you be like *this* and not actively seek me out earlier?" I complained, when Liz bucked against my groin and gasped when I hit her G-spot.

"I didn't – it wasn't deliberate – I lost track of time—"

"Bullshit."

"O-okay, maybe I wanted you to be so desper—*ah*—desperate you couldn't wait any longer," Liz admitted. She leaned her head against her arms on the wall, legs shaking with the effort of staying upright. It was just about the sexiest thing I'd ever witnessed with my own two eyes.

I rubbed her a little faster just to hear Liz whimper. "See? It wasn't so hard to be honest, was it?" I murmured into her ear, before biting down on it. "Does that mean you aren't done playing games with me? Or do you really want to be pun—"

"Are you sure your room is up here?"

Liz tensed against me, and the lecherous comment that had been about to spill from my tongue was stopped in its tracks.

"I'm sure, I'm sure. I recognise this painting."

Slowly, silently, Liz turned around to face me. She indicated for me to bring my ear to her mouth. "That sounds like Peter," she whispered.

"What about the woman he's with?" It was definitely a feminine voice I'd heard speak first.

"Probably one of the bar staff. Unless your mum has some especially spritely friends?"

"Thanks for that mental image. In any case" – I grabbed Liz's hand and pulled her along to the nearest door, opening and closing it with as little noise as possible – "we were right beside my bedroom, anyway."

Liz whacked my chest, appalled. "Your bedroom was *right there* but you thought it was a good idea to screw in the hallway?"

"I see no flaw in my plan."

"Well how would you like it," Liz began, her hands finding their way to my kilt and making quick work of its fastenings. It fell to the floor in a heavy thump. "If I undressed *you* in a public space and...oh. *Oh.*" Her face flushed deliciously. "You went full Scotsman."

I could only laugh, shameless, before bending down to unlace my shoes and kick them off along with my kilt hose. "Not for the ceremony, to be sure. I thought you'd appreciate it so I took off my underwear two hours ago."

"I now retract my previous statement. I should absolutely have sought you out earlier."

"What, so you could give me a hard-on in public that I could do very little to obscure from everyone?"

Liz's nose wrinkled. "Maybe," she said, sliding out of her

dress and letting it tumble to the floor. I already knew she had no bra on but the thong she was wearing was barely-there lace in a paler green than her dress. The silk was soaked through where I'd been touching her.

"Leave that on," I ordered, flicking my gaze towards the offending garment.

"If you keep the shirt on," Liz countered, laughing in delight when I picked her up and tumbled onto the ridiculous four-poster bed that was the centrepiece of the room. I even unravelled the curtains so we were completely enclosed in our own little world.

"Why do you like the shirt?" I asked, my fingers dancing down Liz's stomach to between her thighs once more.

"It makes you look like some kind of Regency hero. I dig it."

"Funny, I've been thinking the same thing about your hair whenever it curls around your face." I twisted one of those curls around the fingers of my left hand to emphasise my point. Liz's cheek was searing hot against my skin.

She bit her lip, dragging my attention to her mouth, where it had been for most of the day. "Just kiss me already, Tom," she said, so I did.

Even though it had been an excruciatingly long time since I'd last kissed Liz I took my time doing so. I began at the column of her throat, revelling in the sensation of her fingers gripping into my hips and rolling me against her for some kind of friction to counter my deliberately glacial onslaught.

I grazed Liz's jaw, her chin, and then her lower lip was caught between my teeth. When I sucked on it Liz hooked her legs around my waist and all but rutted against my erection, and all such thoughts as going slowly evaporated.

The moment she parted her lips my tongue found its way into Liz's mouth and we crashed together, my hand threading through her hair at the back of her neck to urge her closer.

Every one of my muscles was tense, barely able to keep me stable above her.

Then, between one moment and the next, Liz manoeuvred her grip on my waist to topple me over.

"It's nice to see you under me for a change," Liz breathed, breaking from my mouth to arch her back and squeeze her thighs against me. I didn't think I could possibly witness anything sexier than Liz straddling me, but when she slid down my body and deftly took my cock in her mouth I changed my mind.

Okay, *this* was the sexiest thing I'd ever seen.

"Is this you finally showing off your Calippo skills?" I asked, not caring that my voice was shaky. My hands found Liz's hair, dragging out the last of the Kirby grips that kept it in place; it fanned across my skin, soft and ticklish.

She met my gaze. "This is me finally showing off my Calippo skills."

Her tongue rolled around me as she took my full length into her mouth. "*Fuck*," I bit out, bucking against Liz, "you didn't go this far down the icy lolly."

Liz didn't reply. She was otherwise occupied and I, for once, was only too happy to be met with silence rather than a typically glib Liz response. As she worked away with her tongue and lips and throat I could do little else but dig into her scalp, steal breaths through my teeth, and allow the dangerous heat filling up my groin to overwhelm me.

Except I didn't want it to overwhelm me right this very second. Not when I wanted to be inside more than just Liz's mouth.

Even though it went against every instinct in my body I wrenched Liz away from my cock – more turned on than I thought possible by the disappointed look on her face that I dared pulled her off me – and reversed our positions.

"Tom, what are y—" Liz gasped, when I flipped her onto her

hands and knees and pressed the full weight of my body against her. A moan escaped her lips, almost a hiss, long and low and music to my ears.

"You didn't think you were going to finish me off that easily, did you?" I growled, my fingers slipping beneath her thong and wondering, in the process, why I'd bothered even demanding she keep it on. With a violent tug I ripped it away, then yanked off my shirt; Liz didn't even protest.

The heat of her back against my chest was bliss. "There should never be clothes between us," I said, sliding the pad of my thumb against her clit and basking in the sensation of Liz trembling beneath me.

"T-Tom," she stuttered, "don't you dare repeat what you did during the blackout."

"What, where I make you beg me to let you come?"

"*Yes.*"

I reached over Liz's head, pulling back the curtain of the four-poster bed to wrench open the top drawer of the bedside cabinet.

She turned around a fraction to stare at me suspiciously. "Do you have condoms, like, everywhere?" she asked, when I pulled one out and ripped open the packet.

I let out a shaky laugh as I eased it on. "Everywhere but my own shower, it seems."

"That was an oversight on your part."

"An oversight that was rectified the very next day."

"I noticed. You didn't hide them very well."

"I didn't intend for them to be hidden."

My hands found Liz's hips, then, and I dug my fingertips into her thighs. After one shallow breath, two, three, I slid into her like it was the easiest thing in the world.

Liz gripped onto the pillow beneath her head for dear life

when I began moving. "*Tom,*" she bit out, though her voice was muffled by the pillow, "slow down, I'm gonna—"

"No," I said simply, lowering myself until our bodies were pressed together and my hand crawled back around to stroke her clit. Liz cried out; she unclenched her right hand to trail it behind her, along my side, until she found my hip.

"Then go faster," she urged, "and harder."

I'd never complied with something so eagerly in all my life. Liz was slick and easy against my fingertips. It didn't take long before she tensed against me – *around* me – and stuttered out a cry.

I wasn't far behind, especially not when Liz, newly sensitive, writhed against me whilst repeating my name, over and over and over again.

"Tom," she gasped, "Tom, Tom—"

"Liz," I bit out, against her ear, before the heat that had been building in me all night spilled out in one fell swoop. I kissed her ear, the back of her neck, her shoulders, any inch of her that I could reach whilst I rode out my orgasm, before finally rolling onto my side and pulling Liz against my chest to kiss her properly.

We lay together like that for a while, silent aside from our panting breath slowly returning to normal and the vague thumps from downstairs that told us the dancing was still very much in full swing. My brain was pleasantly hazy; not a single bone in my body wanted to move.

Eventually, however, a thought occurred to me, and I broke from Liz's mouth even though she whimpered in protest when I did so.

"I never thanked you, by the way."

I just barely discerned her frowning in the darkness. "... thanked me? For what?"

"For the tulips," I said. "Nobody's ever bought me flowers

before."

"Oh my G—please do not remind me of that!" Liz cried, holding her hands over her face. "It's so mortifying!"

"Buying someone a gift is mortifying now?"

"Buying a man flowers that you saw him appreciate literally *once* and realising in the process that you actually like him is what's mortifying."

That was certainly new information. "Wait, you only worked out you liked me *then*? That was barely three weeks ago!"

"Well...I bought the grow light when I was drunk at Ray's party on Hallowe'en. It took a while to arrive."

Gently I pulled Liz's hands away from her face. When I kissed her, her entire body softened against mine, so I wrapped an arm around her waist and pulled her in close. "You're ridiculous. You know that, right?"

"I might now be aware of that, yes."

"I hope you always buy me flowers, Liz."

She nuzzled against my shoulder. "Then I hope you always like them, Tom."

"Completely unrelated but I was actually thinking of getting a dog."

At this Liz jumped up into a sitting position, as I had expected. I grinned at the look on her face. She was excited. Curious.

Happy.

"What kind of dog?" she demanded.

"Like a massive one. A bear of a dog."

"I hope you know *you'll* be walking said bear of a dog."

"Does that mean we'll be in a situation where we're sharing the rest of the responsibilities?"

"Such as?"

"I don't know...the same roof? Same kitchen, same living room, same bed..."

"Well it would be a shame to put the last three months to waste, wouldn't it?" Liz said, as nonchalantly as she could manage. But I could tell, even in the darkness, that her face was fire engine red. "What's a trial run if you don't follow through on it?"

"Oh, so you admit that you enjoyed living with me?"

"Maybe a little. I liked the giant TV."

"Is that all you liked?"

"Is this you fishing for me to pay compliments to your giant di—"

"Why must you always ruin the mood?" I sighed, rolling onto my back to stretch out a crack in my spine. But then Liz's hand crept beneath the duvet, her fingers pressing against the very telling hard-on I was fostering out of sight.

"I wouldn't call it ruining the mood when *this* is the mood," she all but purred.

"You have a point." I knew we were mere moments away from tossing aside all conversation entirely, but I had one final thing I wanted confirmation of. "So is that a yes, Doctor Maclean? To living with me?"

Liz pretended to consider her answer. But then she placed a kiss against my lips and wriggled into her rightful place in my arms.

"That would be a yes, Professor Henderson. No marriage, kids or holiday in Tenerife required."

Epilogue

TWO YEARS LATER

TOM

"Okay, and with that the website's live!" Liz closed my laptop with a satisfied slam, then spun around on my office chair to face me. "How does it feel being a philanthropist?"

"Maybe ask me *after* folk start applying for the grant. Now get off my chair." There was something very nice about finally doing something with my grandfather's money, though of course it had been Liz's idea to set up a fund for students in the life sciences to progress into postgraduate study who otherwise couldn't afford to do so. But it was something I could very much get behind.

Liz pouted. "Hey, as of today I work here too, remember!"

"Not in my *office,* Liz."

"What's mine is yours and all that," Liz said, laughing as she nonetheless got up from my chair and allowed me to sit down. She yelped in surprise when I pulled her down to sit on my lap. "How unprofessional, Professor Henderson!"

"It's after eight; nobody's in to see our sordid work affair."

"I'd hardly call being publicly together for two years a 'sordid affair'."

"True, but it's more fun this way."

"You have a point." Liz snuggled closer, brushing her lips against my stubble before asking, "I still can't believe Jenny is turning the estate into a foster home. She must be mental."

"Yes, well, being retired and wealthy is rather boring, it seems. And she probably thought it was a nice homage to your mum. In any case Jim is on board with the whole thing, so I guess she can't be *that* mad."

"Still, if they expect us to help with the kids more than once in a blue moon they have another thing coming."

"Oh, don't worry," I reassured Liz, wrapping my arms a little tighter around her waist. I wished we were at home and not dressed in thick sweaters to combat the bitter January weather so that it was acceptable to crawl my fingers up her skin. "We shall be otherwise occupied whenever they ask us to help more than we want to."

"Good." Liz wriggled free from my grasp to check the time. "Right, we have half an hour before we need to pick up Ludo from dog day care. Thank god Courtney could take him out of hours; this took so much longer than I thought."

"Actually, she's keeping him a little longer and bringing him back to ours for us," I said, easing both of us out of the chair to grab our jackets. "We have somewhere to go before then."

Liz turned and raised a quizzical eyebrow. "I was beginning to think we weren't actually going to do anything special today."

"What, getting to work in the same lab as yours truly once again isn't a good enough thirtieth birthday present for you?"

"That better not be my actual present, Tom, or I swear to God—"

"Of course not. I've bought you a kitten. We're picking him

---

up this evening."

Liz's eyes lit up as if I'd just told her I was taking her to Japan (although that was her other present; it simply wasn't happening until April). "Are you serious?!"

"I felt bad that Ludo obviously prefers me. If only you were less grumpy—"

"That has absolutely nothing to do with it. Of course a fucking *Tibetan Mastiff* prefers the person who takes him out jogging for miles every day to the person who can barely run for five minutes without wanting to throw up."

"You could always—"

"Don't say join you—"

"Join me." I grinned when Liz gave me the finger.

"What kind of cat is he, this animal that will evidently be replacing you as the love of my life?" she asked.

"Just your basic farm cat. Pure black, though, like your soul. Apparently he's a complete and utter nuisance."

"God, he sounds perfect." Liz reached up on her tiptoes to kiss me; I dutifully lowered my head to meet her halfway, then pulled her closer to deepen the kiss.

"Happy birthday," I murmured against her lips. "Welcome to your thirties. I'd argue that they're the best years of your life but, given that I'm now forty—"

"Positively ancient."

"Where have I heard that before?"

"Let's just say that things will continue to go up from here and leave it at that," Liz said, tracing her fingers down my arm and making small circles on my elbow when she reached it. She flashed me a devilish grin. "After all, despite my best efforts to find a guy better than you over the last two years he is yet to appear. Guess I better settle for you and accept my fate."

"You are so cruel, do you know that?"

"And you love it."

"Unfortunately."

"Can we get take-out ramen, then, since we're clearly not going out for dinner tonight?"

"Actually," I said, running a hand self-consciously through my hair. Liz was going to either love or loathe what I said next. "I thought I'd do something embarrassingly upper class, instead. We have a private chef preparing ramen back at the house as we speak."

Liz stared at me in disbelief. "Tell me you didn't. That's so – so – *excessive!*"

"Not for the woman I love it isn't." I kissed the top of her head. "And besides, he's Simon's new head chef for the restaurant he's opening in Glasgow at the end of spring. He wanted to test the menu on a willing audience."

"Oh, so we're guinea pigs, then? I think I can accept that."

"Splendid. Right, shall we go get this black ball of terror that you've determined will replace me?"

"Way ahead of you," Liz said, jingling my car keys in front of me to demonstrate that she'd pilfered them from my pocket. "And I'm calling him Jerry."

"*Jerry?*"

"As in *Tom and Jerry.*"

"But Tom is the cat."

"It's called *irony,* Thomas. Maybe you've heard of it."

I could only roll my eyes. "I'm going to say you named him after Jerry Seinfeld whenever anyone asks."

"But that's so weird," Liz protested.

"So is naming a cat after a mouse."

"If he was gonna be named after anyone from *Seinfeld* it would be Cramer."

"Ah, you have me there."

It was a universal certainty – for me – that talking to the young scientist who liked anime all those years ago was my rather circuitous route towards happiness. And as the two of us walked through the dark, crisp winter quiet towards my car, Liz's hand slipping into mine even though it was barely a two minute walk, I was struck by the fact that, even after everything that had happened to get us to where we were, the destination we'd arrived at was pretty bloody perfect.

All things considered, I wouldn't change anything for the world.

COMING SOON

COURTNEY CAN'T DECIDE

Courtney Miller is notoriously bad at making decisions.

She can't pick between jobs – she works both.

She can't pick what to eat – she eats nothing.

She can't pick which film to watch – she gets wasted with her friends instead.

Struggling with her mental health, jumping between jobs and constantly postponing the appointment that would confirm her ADHD diagnosis, the last thing Courtney needs is the attention of a wealthy Londoner currently staying at the hotel she works reception for every evening.

Right?

The only problem is...Courtney can't make the decision to stay away from Simon Saint any more than she can decide *not* to order takeaway three days in a row. Add in dog day care centre owner – and Courtney's best friend – Richard Blake professing his feelings for her, and Courtney is stuck in the middle of a dilemma no amount of booze, insomnia or procrastination can solve.

She can't date them both...right?

Acknowledgements

I needed a break from writing fantasy and this is what I ended up with.

It took me a long time to plan and outline *The Unbalanced Equation* (perhaps *too* long), but I'm happy with the end result. And I had tonnes of fun writing it, which is why I'm going to follow it up with another two rom-coms set in Glasgow. Liz and Tom will be sure to make an appearance again!

The Unbalanced Equation is set in a world where the pandemic never happened because, frankly, I didn't want to write about it. I wanted the book to be pure and simple escapism like all good rom-coms should be! So I hope I managed to do that. It's also based in a world where every lecturer, professor and researcher I know at the Univeristy of Glasgow has conveniently retired or doesn't work there anymore, for obvious reasons.

For those of you who don't know, I have an undergraduate degree in genetics and a PhD in molecular genetics, both received from The University of Glasgow. I've written past protagonists with science backgrounds before (Claire from *Careless Assassin* has an undergrad degree in genetics, Poppy and Fred from *Invisible Monsters* both have Masters degrees in ecology, and Grace and Lir from *The Boy from the Sea* are working towards a PhD in molecular biology and an undergraduate degree in marine & freshwater biology, respectively) so *The Unbalanced Equation* isn't anything new for me! However, since *The Love Hypothesis* exists I imagine some folk probably think Liz and Tom are biologists because

I'm trying to emulate Ali Hazelwood. Imagine if more than one woman in STEM could write a rom-com! *laughs*

During the second year of my PhD I went through some tough times with my biannual assessors. Yes, I cried. A lot. It was awful. I highly doubt either of my assessors had a crush on me, though; they were just being super strict and a little unfair. But that happens quite a lot in academia. That doesn't excuse Tom's behaviour, of course, and if *The Unbalanced Equation* were real life then there would definitely be more repercussions for his actions than there were in the book. Alas, it *isn't* real life. It's a rom-com! And rom-coms have their own magical rules. Someone should kick Tom in the balls though.

Tom was based (in appearance and partially in personality) on Joe from *Halt and Catch Fire* i.e. the god that is Lee Pace. Liz is based on a mix of Jennifer Connelly and Hayley Atwell. After all, what's the point of writing a rom-com if I can't make my characters stupidly pretty? Tom really is an arrogant arsehole but I love that for him. Liz's personality is an amalgamation of so many of my wonderful female friends, and a bit of me as well!

When I was trying to come up with Tom and Liz's careers and interests I basically phoned it in and went, "Fuck it, they're geneticists because that's what I studied, and they love anime because so do I." Lazy? Maybe. Did it work well? I think it did. It was certainly fun to write them nerding out together. Nerding out is my true love language with both my friends and my partner.

It was tough to write this over the last year because of the pandemic going on, so I can say with absolute certainty that *The Unbalanced Equation* would not have been completed if not for the support and encouragement (and silly drinking sessions) of my friends and family. I also went to a couple of weddings this year which really helped me with writing the wedding chapters in this book! So thanks to my big sister and one of my best friends for getting hitched – it was much appreciated.

Of course I have to thank Jake, my partner, for always being there for me. We recently got a kitten whom we named Kamille (after Kamille Bidan from *Zeta Gundam*!). This made editing and rereading *The Unbalanced Equation* especially hilarious, given Tom and Liz's discussion during the blackout chapter. Kamille (the kitten) is a Maine Coon x Norwegian Forest Cat cross, and we love him very much. One of my bunnies seems to have accepted him but the other bunny still gets spooked by him. They'll all be best friends eventually... hopefully by the time I'm writing my next acknowledgements section!

Lastly I'd like to thanks everyone who picked up this book, read it and loved it. I do it all for you! So if you feel like giving me a review it would mean the world to me.

Until the next one,

Hayley

About the Author

Hayley Louise Macfarlane hails from the very tiny hamlet of Balmaha on the shores of Loch Lomond in Scotland. After graduating with a PhD in molecular genetics she did a complete 180 and moved into writing fiction. Though she loves writing multiple genres (fantasy, romance, sci-fi, psychological fiction and horror so far!) she is most widely known for her Gothic, Scottish fairy tale, Prince of Foxes – book one of the Bright Spear trilogy.

You can follow her on Twitter at @HLMacfarlane.

Also by H. L. Macfarlane

FAIRY TALE SHARED UNIVERSE:
BRIGHT SPEAR TRILOGY
PRINCE OF FOXES
LORD OF HORSES
KING OF FOREVER

DARK SPEAR DUOLOGY
SON OF SILVER (COMING 2023)
HEIR OF GOLD (COMING 2023)

ALL I WANT FOR CHRISTMAS IS A FAERIE ASSASSIN?!

CHRONICLES OF CURSES
BIG, BAD MISTER WOLFE
SNOWSTORM KING
THE TOWER WITHOUT A DOOR

OTHER BOOKS:
GOLD AND SILVER DUOLOGY
INTENDED
REVIVAL (RELEASE DATE TBC)

MONSTERS TRILOGY
INVISIBLE MONSTERS
INSATIABLE MONSTERS (COMING OCTOBER 2022)
INVINCIBLE MONSTERS (COMING 2023)

THRILLERS
THE BOY FROM THE SEA

ROM-COMS
THE UNBALANCED EQUATION
COURTNEY CAN'T DECIDE (RELEASE DATE TBC)

SHORT STORIES
THE SNOWDROP (PART OF ONCE UPON A WINTER: A FOLK AND
FAIRY TALE ANTHOLOGY)
THE GOAT
THE BOY WHO DID NOT FIT